DEFIANT HEARTS

THE CLASSIC SHORT STORIES

Praise for Lee Lynch

"Lee Lynch has been writing lesbian fiction since the 1960s, and is an important influence in modern lesbian literature."—*RVA Magazine*

Sweet Creek

"Like Chaucer's pilgrims, Lynch's characters tell stories throughout the novel. The novel wanders through stories of the characters' past lives and present events at a leisurely pace. Chick, Donny, Jeep, and the women who comprise their closest circle of friends are compelling characters, and readers will want to know more about their motivations, fears, and dreams. Lynch has to be commended for tackling a novel of such grand scope. From characters who lived their early years deeply closeted to characters who have benefited from the pioneering work of those women who were brave enough to break away and blaze the trail to places like Waterfall Falls. These women—warts and all—show the reader that this pilgrimage is still underway."—*Story Circle Book Review*

Beggar of Love

"Lynch is the master of creating the 'everydyke,' championing the underdog and providing a protagonist with whom garden variety lesbians can relate."—*Lambda Literary Review*

"The highest recommendation I can give Lee Lynch's writing is that you will not mistake it for anyone else's. Her voice and imagination are uniquely her own. Lynch has been out and proudly writing about it for longer than many of us have been alive. In her new novel, *Beggar of Love*, she creates a protagonist, Jefferson (known by her surname), so fully realised that the story seems to distill the last several decades of lesbian life. Lee Lynch finds the words."
—*Lesbians of North London Reviews*

Lambda Literary Award Finalist
An American Queer: The Amazon Trail

"Thirty years ago, Lynch moved from the East Coast to the West Coast and started her amazing journey depicted throughout almost 400 'Amazon Trail' columns. Editor Ruth Sternglantz has distilled these through the selection of 73 Trails, providing the author's half-century perspective of lesbian life as lesbians have moved from invisibility to public life and even marriage—for most LGBT people in the United States...*An American Queer* follows the tradition of 'the personal is political' in an accessible quick read, both heartfelt and gentle, that stays in the reader's thoughts. It is recommended for all public and academic libraries."—*GLBT Reviews: ALA's Gay Lesbian Bisexual Transgender Round Table*

"This very fine collection of columns by Lee Lynch, spanning the period from the 1980s to 2010, is required reading for those who want to remember and for those who are hazy or inadequately informed about LGBT history. *An American Queer: The Amazon Trail* is not a stiff academic text. Lynch is a passionate advocate with a quiet humor, and her columns are an entertaining yet informative read."—*Carol Rosenfeld*

"Lynch, whose novels, such as *Old Dyke Tales* and *Sweet Creek*, have won numerous awards, deserves to be in the pantheon of legendary lesbian journalists since her columns straddle the literary and the journalistic, always contemporary in their look at queer women's culture and beyond."—*The Advocate*

"Some stories crawl under your skin, diving deeper until you can't separate yourself from them. Reading that kind of book is like throwing down a time marker, because who you were before is not who you are when you've finished it. And even when you try to explain to someone why it's so important to you, you may not be able to access the right words because you're trying to describe an experience, which is so much more than a plot or set of characters. And yet, try you must because all you want is for someone else to love the book as much as you do."—*Curve Magazine*

Rainbow Gap

"Sometimes it is hard to write a review because you can't find the words, in this case it's hard to find words big enough to describe such an epic tale…This is both a coming out and growing up story, but also a timeless work of literary fiction, with classic writing that draws you into its world. *Rainbow Gap* will win awards across the board, and deservedly so. It is simple in plot, but complex in emotion. It is a genuine classic telling of nothing more or less than real life. More than anything it's a story of the birth of our community and the fight to be openly who we are."—*Windy City Times*

"*Rainbow Gap* by Lee Lynch is a book so exquisite that I just want everyone to go read it. Like, seriously, stop reading this review, buy it and read it right now…*Rainbow Gap* is not only a wonderful, moving book, it's also an important book that should be required reading…it reminds us that we've been here before and we can do this again. I cannot recommend it highly enough."—*The Lesbian Review*

"[T]his book covers a broad period of lesbian history, seen through the eyes of two relatively ordinary women…A real feel-good novel: I can see I need to catch up with this author's back catalogue."—*The Good, the Bad, and the Unread*

Previous Books by the Author

Bold Strokes Books

Rainbow Gap: Book 1 of the Rainbow Gap Lesbian Family Saga

Accidental Desperados: Book 2 of the Rainbow Gap Lesbian Family Saga

An American Queer: The Amazon Trail

The Raid

Beggar of Love

Sweet Creek

Naiad Press

Cactus Love

Morton River Valley

That Old Studebaker

Sue Slate, Private Eye

The Amazon Trail

Dusty's Queen of Hearts Diner

Home in Your Hands

The Swashbuckler

Old Dyke Tales

Toothpick House

Flashpoint Publications

Our Happy Hours, LGBT Voices from the Gay Bars,
Curated With S. Renee Bess

TRB Books

The Butch Cook Book, Edited with Sue Hardesty and Nel Ward

New Victoria Publishers

Rafferty Street

Off the Rag: Women Write About Menopause,
Edited with Akia Woods

Visit us at www.boldstrokesbooks.com

DEFIANT HEARTS

THE CLASSIC SHORT STORIES

by

Lee Lynch

2022

DEFIANT HEARTS: THE CLASSIC SHORT STORIES
© 2022 BY LEE LYNCH. ALL RIGHTS RESERVED.

ISBN 13: 978-1-63679-237-8

THIS TRADE PAPERBACK ORIGINAL IS PUBLISHED BY
BOLD STROKES BOOKS, INC.
P.O. BOX 249
VALLEY FALLS, NY 12185

FIRST EDITION: SEPTEMBER 2022

CREDITS
EDITOR: RUTH STERNGLANTZ
PRODUCTION DESIGN: STACIA SEAMAN
COVER DESIGN BY ANN MCMAN

Acknowledgments

Thank you Radclyffe, President, and Sandy Lowe, Senior Editor, of Bold Strokes Books, for publishing my early stories in this volume. I am still amazed you said yes.

Editor Ruth Sternglantz has my deep respect for her insights and for finding order in disorder.

My gratitude extends to my wife, Lainie Lynch, for her many hours researching, scanning, and formatting the older stories. For always being on hand to untangle knots I tied in the work and in me. I simply could not have tackled this without you.

To my sister lesbian storyteller and Fairy Goddaughter, Lori Lake, I am indebted to you for consistently encouraging me to create *Defiant Hearts*. Connie Ward, my Sister Butch, thank you for your enthusiastic advocacy of this vision.

Thank you to the pioneers of lesbian publishing who put their beliefs and hearts into the early periodicals, the anthologies, and the presses that made it possible for our tales to be told.

To the best of my ability, I have credited publications where these stories appeared. I extend my sincere apologies for any errors or omissions. The majority of stories can also be found in *Old Dyke Tales*, *Home in Your Hands*, and *Cactus Love*, published by Naiad Press in 1984, 1986, and 1994, respectively. Individual credits have been placed at the end of the relevant stories.

For Lainie Lynch
With unending wonder that these stories brought us together.

DEFIANT HEARTS

THE NIGHT QUEEN

"Let's forget breakfast and go straight home to bandage you up," I say. I was too hot and tired for any more trouble that night.

"Nah. This is nothing," Merle tells me, sucking on the knuckles of her right hand, one by one. She cleans the blood from the broken skin on every finger, and by the time she's through, the first one's red again.

"You need some iodine," Callie says. "Right, Flo?"

Flo has dimples as big as her eyes. She towers over the rest of us. "What she needed was to let her buddy in on the action, baby," she announces in her foghorn voice. "If Callie and me hadn't been making out in the can, we would've creamed the SOB, Merle."

"Merle did enough damage," I say, trying not to nag. I squiggle around next to Merle to look over my black-and-white checked suit. Small checks. I usually wear it to work at the elementary school office, but it goes good with the sheer blouse Merle likes because it kind of shows that mole right over my bra. Lord, it was hot that night. Even with the diner door open and the floor fans going, I could feel a puddle of sweat inside the bra.

Merle's sleeves are rolled up to her forearms, jean jacket on a hook. Her hair's sand brown and brushed straight back from her forehead. Her eyebrows slant up over her nose so she always looks a bit put out, like nobody wants to answer some hard question she asked. "That loser was after my woman, what do you want?"

I love when she calls me her woman, how she doesn't have any question about how it is between us. Too quick for anyone in the diner to see, I dart an arm through hers and squeeze close, then scoot away and tease up my hair, like Miss Innocence. "I hate you getting hurt is all, Merle."

Slouched down in the booth, Merle's no bigger than me, but never tell her that. She's watching her knuckles bleed, sneering like Elvis. "I hated her making a play for you, Tiny. Friggin' Upton bulldaggers."

"They're the worst," Flo agrees.

Callie's hair is beauty-parlor straightened. They gave it a reddish tint this time. She uses the menu she's been fanning herself with to slap at Flo. "Don't be silly—you don't like my ex from Upton is all."

"Got that right."

I laugh, but not hard, so my eyes don't turn into slits. It takes a good makeup job to make them look bigger as it is. "What's a girl to do? Morton River's not exactly Provincetown. You and me grabbed the most eligible butches in the valley, Cal."

"Merle's forehead is bleeding again."

"Ooh," I can't help saying. I grab napkins from the shiny metal holder and dip them in my water glass, pushing the paper compress at Merle.

"Thanks, Doc," she says. She pushes back the hair she's always combing into a sideburn and presses the wet wad of paper to her cheekbone where it's going dark. "I think she wore brass knuckles."

I wince. It's almost like I can feel the cold napkins on that sensitive bruise.

"She knew she needed something, coming up against you," Flo tells her. Those dimples make Flo look good-natured even when she tries to be as tough as Merle. Which she always tries.

Merle rolls her jaw back and forth. I'm hoping she didn't chip any teeth. We finally paid off the dentist bill last month.

This is at the Night Queen Diner on our way home from the River's Edge Tavern. Stopping at the Queen, drinking at the Edge, walking home in the early a.m. are rituals on the weekends when Merle and Flo don't have overtime. They both run machines at the spring factory, do setup, maintenance, and whatever else the bosses can make them do without paying them extra.

Merle sets the napkins down and leans back, folding her arms across her chest, eyebrows up again, but this time her eyes are laughing at us. When she looks straight at someone, her eyes are amber, I swear, like light's coming through from behind. One glimpse and I always feel like it's the first night all over again.

"What the hell," Merle says, holding out her scarred hands for us to see. "These mitts are always a mess from those damn wild coils anyway."

"Tell me about it," Flo agrees, showing the calloused ruts along her fingertips. I always wonder how that feels to Callie. "Wire at those speeds," Flo says, sad eyed, "is nobody's friend."

"It's a job," says Merle. She takes out her comb and fixes the back sweep of her hair. "Right, buddy?" She winces as the comb nudges her forehead.

"Puts beans on the table," Flo agrees, poking an elbow at Callie. They laugh. Flo aims and swats a mosquito on Callie's arm.

"What's the joke?" I reach over to Merle with my stocking feet and rub her ankle. "They remind me of us, our first year."

Merle taps the ring on my third finger. "When are you two going to tie the knot?"

"Leave them alone, Merle. They've been together, what, three months?"

"Is that all?" asks Callie. Her wide eyes are like a kid's at a birthday party. I didn't see much of Callie after she dropped out of high school to get married and didn't realize I missed her, but looking back, I can see that I was always trying to find another best friend like her. Once she chucked out her husband, I helped find her a job at the school cafeteria.

Foghorn Flo says, "It feels like we're about to have our golden wedding anniversary."

"Shh," I whisper quick. They're forgetting that we're not at the Edge.

"To hell with the squares." Merle's sulky again, hiding underneath her eyelids, muttering so low I can hardly hear her over the floor fans.

The waitress brings breakfast.

"Must be morning," says Flo, like always.

And Callie always grabs Flo's wrist, looks at her watch, then delivers her line. "It *is* morning."

We all laugh.

Merle slathers grape jelly on her toast, then swirls more jelly around in her eggs like ketchup. She never fails to eat like a horse after a fight.

"You boys be good," I tell our beaux after we're full. I slip my sandals back on. "I'm fixing my face, Callie."

This is one of my favorite parts of the night, when me and Callie squeeze into the ladies' for a quick pee and face repair before we walk home.

"You could drown in the Lysol in here," Callie says from behind the pumpkin-colored bathroom stall. "But I guess Merle gave that one what for."

"Mmm," I answer, giving my lips little pops to spread the lipstick. Pink. I don't go for the hot reds anymore. They make me look like an over-the-hill lady of the night. I get up on tiptoe and bend over the sink to get a good look in the clouded mirror. The porcelain, curved like a hip against me, is cool. Soon me and Merle will be under our cool sheets.

Callie's behind me now, peering at herself over my shoulder. "I don't understand why it always happens to you, Tiny. I mean, not that you're not dynamite to look at, but what do you do, lead them on?"

Twenty years ago in high school, Callie and me used to pretend we were boy and girl making out—for practice. I've learned a few things since then. Callie still has a lot to learn.

"You know I don't."

"Then does Merle do something to get their goat?"

"Yeah. She exists." I let Callie have the sink. "She's top dog in Morton River. These Upton types come up here slumming and strutting, thinking the hicks are going to swoon at their feet. They have another think coming when they run into Merle." I go in to use the toilet and call over the stall, "Not that I can't take care of myself. I think she does it to save her honor, not mine."

"What do you mean, girl?"

I stretch over for the last pieces of toilet paper on the roll. A lot of the nail polish graffiti is gay: *Ronnie'n'Doris, Lisa'n'Al, F and C Forever*. Flo and Callie can't write out two female-sounding names.

"Where else can she be king of the roost?" I ask.

"Home with you?"

A lot to learn about who's really in charge at home. I say nothing, bending to straighten the seams in my nylons.

"Flo says Merle's top producer at work."

"That means a ton in a man's job, doesn't it?" I ask, slamming the stall door open. "She still gets paid a dollar an hour less than the men, plus she's wrecking her body proving herself all the time. All the time." I don't say this to Callie, but it used to be that Merle made love to me most of the day on Sundays. Now she soaks in the tub and lets me rub her back.

Merle and Flo are at the register when we finish, chitchatting with the waitress Merle used to date. Merle takes a toothpick and flicks it around on her tongue till it falls into the right spot in a corner of her mouth. She slings her jean jacket over her shoulder.

"Get the lead out, girls," Merle tells us in that take-charge way of hers. I can't help a glimpse back at that poor waitress who didn't know enough to hang on to Merle.

"What do you two do in the little girls' room?" Flo asks when we're out on Railroad Avenue again. "Clean the place?"

"It needs it," Callie says, laughing that high clear laugh of hers, like a glass wind chime they can hear in the houses on top of the hillside.

The moon's so bright it lights the windows of the old brick factories across the street. There's no traffic at this hour. The running river is the only sound except our footsteps. It seems like the four of us are alone in the world. A damp breeze finds us. Merle shrugs into her jacket.

"Is your kid home tonight?" Flo's whispering in her foghorn voice. She thinks we can't hear.

"Yeah," Callie whispers back. "Your folks?"

"They're going up the river tomorrow, but it's still too cold to sleep in their cabin."

"I wish you could stay the night. You'll walk me home?"

"Oh yeah, baby. I'll walk you to the ends of the earth."

"I wish we could at least hold hands."

"How about—" We hear them rustling behind us. "It's nobody's business what's in your pocket," says Callie and sounds her chime laugh again. The heat from the two of them comes barreling along the sidewalk at us like a steamroller.

I suck in a deep breath. "You could take the couch, Merle," I whisper, trying to be fairy godmother to the new couple. "I'd sleep on the old daybed so they can have our bed."

Merle flicks her toothpick to the other side, eases her hands into her slash pockets, thinks it over. I hope she's remembering how Tiger and Marjorie—Tiger's dead now, from emphysema, and I visit Marjorie in the nursing home, though she doesn't know me anymore—used to let us have their place for a few hours on Saturday nights while they went to the movies.

Finally, Merle says, "They've got it bad." She turns on a dime. "Hey, you two lovebirds," she says, walking backward.

Flo's and Callie's hands fly out of Flo's pocket. "Nothing like scaring the pants off us."

Merle cocks her head and brags from the side of her mouth, "I never had to scare them off a woman yet."

I have to swallow a laugh. If I didn't love my butch like I do, I'd think she was too much.

She spits the toothpick out. "Ask them," she says to me, turning back.

It's not an order. Merle gets gruff when she's feeling shy. I say, "Why don't you two come over to our place for the night? You can have the bedroom."

It's like Lucy and Ethel, the way their mouths fall open at the same second. Lucy and Ethel if somebody told them it's okay to jump each other's bones right there and then.

Then Callie groans. "I can't leave my kid overnight. She's seventeen, so a few hours are okay, but what kind of example is that, not to come home till morning?"

Flo's face falls. "When are we going to get a night together, baby?"

"I can't not go home, Flo. It wouldn't be right. She'd think I don't care about her. I might have been married at her age, but inside I was a girl-child still, and so is she."

Flo nods. "You're right. You're a hell of a lot better a mom than I ever had. I'm not used to it. Come on, you two, stop getting our hopes up. Anyway, the kid won't be home tomorrow afternoon."

I tease them. "Remind me not to call Callie's place tomorrow."

"Aw," says Flo.

Callie stuffs her hand back in Flo's pocket. "Don't be embarrassed—they do it, too."

"Who says?" Merle asks quick, giving her crooked smile, the one that shows her missing tooth.

Callie gets me back. "I know Tiny."

"Hey," says Flo, "I've got a new elephant joke. Why do elephants have wrinkled knees?"

"Because their nylons are sagging," says Callie, yanking at her pantyhose.

"No. From playing marbles."

We groan like we're supposed to at Flo's corny riddles. Then we tell more jokes, clown around, hush for the long steep climb past dark houses. A dog-day cicada rattles off its heat alarm, but all's well with my world. We're in a moonlit bubble of contentment. Didn't we have jobs? Didn't me and Merle have seven whole years together? Weren't Flo and Callie brand spanking new, like birthday presents to each other? Life really is good.

Merle brushes a hand across my back like she's flicking off a bug or something, but I know, in a better world, she'd be putting her arm around me.

Then Callie yelps real loud into the dead silent night. Something falls at her feet. She's staggering, falls against Flo. There's a stream of blood down Callie's face.

"What the—?"

"Where—?"

"*Run.*"

"I can't—I've got Callie. Baby, are you okay?" Flo whispers.

Callie straightens. "Ow," she wails. "It hurts, Flo."

This stuff happens, and I turn into an animal, all ears, wanting to run like hell, but I can't—it's Callie. "Can you walk?"

Another rock slashes by and hits the hedge behind us.

"I'm not staying around here." Callie sobs and shuffles up the narrow sidewalk.

"Fuckin' lezzies," comes a male voice. Other men laugh, young from the sound, white. Men without women on a Saturday night.

Merle's like a pointer dog. "Come on," I tell her.

But she yells, "Where the hell are you, scum? Show your ugly faces."

"Talk about *ug-lee.* What're you going to do to us, runty lez? Huh?"

"They're drunken monsters, Merle. Don't let them get to you." My voice sounds to me like I'm talking along a quivering string between tin cans.

Merle pulls away. She kicks at a tree stump with her square-toed boots like it's the whole communist army. Except, I'm thinking, people like us don't need to go to Russia to find trouble.

"You're not at the Edge, Merle," I tell her, attaching to her arm. Her body is tight as a scream you have to swallow. "You can't protect us. This is dangerous."

Merle pushes away from me. "I'm sick of this crap. Go on home."

Just like that I'm not scared anymore, only icy cold to my core. Pressing my purse so tight against my chest I hurt, I say, "I am not leaving your side."

Nothing happens for so long it's like the twilight zone. I'm meantime smelling the cut grass in the yard behind us. Someone—say, while I was fixing our cold cut supper—was mowing a lawn in the twilight, listening to the kids call back and forth playing street hockey, racing tricycles. Then maybe the mower stopped and someone struck a match to a cigarette. I smelled the sulfur, watched the light fade, heard screen doors slam and the last jingle of the ice-cream truck. And then it's dark.

A hoodlum smashes a bottle. Four of them step off the porch of a three-story house. In the moonlight I can make out moss growing between the shingles. One man makes wet-sounding kissing noises. "That your girlfriend there, lesbo? Give her to us, we'll show her a good time."

"Merle," I plead, "Merle, come home."

Merle pulls away. She starts toward the men, striking the metal taps on her heels extra loud on the cement. I catch at her sleeve. The four men talk about what they'll do to me. Merle strips off her jacket. She lurches toward them, chin up high, letting loose a stream of curses like a growl.

Flo comes out of nowhere and grabs Merle's arm, jerking her back. I've still got hold of the jean jacket and grab her wrist. Together we walk Merle a step backward, away from the men.

"I thought you'd want in on the action, buddy," Merle taunts Flo.

"Callie might need a doctor," Flo says, voice forceful, though her face is sick-pale. "We need the phone at your place to call a cab, Merle."

"Take them home, Tiny."

"Don't be stupid. Not without you."

"Come here, bull dyke. We'll be glad to give you a turn. After we get through with your girlfriend." Their laughter is like chalk on a blackboard. I feel the hairs on my neck shiver.

"Merle." It's all we can do to keep dragging her. Merle's arm is damp with sweat. She strains forward.

"They can't get away with this," she's saying, her voice like a file, hiding tears. She's too slight for Flo's bulky strength and knows she's losing ground. "Don't you get it? I couldn't ever show my face again."

From an open window someone screams, "Shut up, I'm calling the cops." The window slams down. The men laugh and strut back to their porch. Merle lets herself be wrestled over to the tree stump, shakes us off, then leads us farther up the hill to where Callie is moaning on someone's chipped flagstone steps.

"How am I going to explain this to my kid?" Callie asks, holding up her bloody hanky.

Merle snaps her fingers over her shoulder, like the whole incident is behind us now. "Come on. Flo, don't leave her sitting there."

They ease Callie up. Me, I'm like a dishrag by this time. It's quiet again. Nothing is moving but the three of them hobbling ahead of me in the moonlight, like a refugee family fleeing without its belongings. I can hardly keep up.

At the top of the hill, they turn into our alleyway. In the backyard I see that the upstairs neighbor left limp white sheets on the line. The squeal of the pulley bringing them in will wake us to the bright hot day.

Inside we can see Callie better. The bleeding stopped, but is there a concussion? I'm so tired, and so glad to see home, smell home, be safe home. I clean Callie in my bathroom, replacing her blouse with a towel like in high school, when we fixed each other's hair.

"That rock must have hit a vein or something," I tell her, sponging the wound. She bites her lip at every touch. "You've got a good bump, too."

"I don't want to go to the emergency," Callie says. "I won't, so don't tell me I need to. I've got to get home."

There'd be too many questions, names. What if a cop was hanging around? "I don't think you need stitches, Cal. You feel dizzy or anything?"

"A headache from hell."

I scold, "That's from the last pitcher of beer."

Callie laughs, then groans and puts her hands to her head. "Exactly what it feels like."

"Okay, then. Put your shirt on. We'll get you home by cab."

"But Flo will never take a cab from my place. If those guys see her alone, they'll kill her. I'm so scared, Tiny." Callie presses herself against my middle, hooks her arms around my waist. "I'm going to miss our walks."

This tired, I can't help getting sharp. "You think this will keep Merle home?"

She pulls away, looks up in surprise. "I wish we could hide here with you two forever."

After the cab leaves, after every light is out but the moon, Merle and I squeeze under the covers in her twin bed. Merle's pajama top is open. I find a soft white breast, lay my lips on it. Here, not far from the reservoir, the tree frogs throb.

I shiver under the soft cool sheets and press closer to Merle, who feels hot as a falling star. A passing car, revving its engine, makes me ask, "You don't think they followed us?"

Merle, stiff, doesn't answer. A long freight train calls a warning at each crossing, over and over.

"I kept looking back," I whisper into Merle's breast. "I didn't see them. Do you think they could tell Flo and Callie were holding hands? Did they do it because Callie's not white?"

Merle is quiet as the grave. Her sideburns look like spit curls now, her neck and shoulders are all creamy woman, asking for caresses.

"Merle." No answer. "You asleep?" Is she breathing? I go cold again with stark terror. Have they killed her somehow? I prop myself on my elbows and in the dark stare down at her. "Merle."

Then she folds in on me, like Callie did, her back heaving, face running with tears, her poor scarred hands wringing the life out of the bedclothes.

"Oh, baby," I say, putting my arms around Merle and pulling her magnificent head against the opening in my nightgown. But I can't hold Merle as close as I want, as I need. Her pride's too tender. I hear myself singing, "I love you, I love you, I love you," until her storm subsides into a sound like the train's.

She looks up at me, eyebrows in their question mark, asking the things she'll always be too proud to admit not knowing. Voice gruff, she says, "I'm not scared."

I hold her as tight as I dare, dreading the fight she'll seek out next week at the Edge.

Originally published in *Cactus Love* (Naiad Press, 1994)

CANNON STREET

Cannon Street was as ordinary as daylight. Still, as she rounded that last corner of worn red brick sidewalk laid probably a hundred years ago, she always caught her breath. The street only cut through a neighborhood, but it was her avenue of spectacle and adventure.

There was a tree outside the beige apartment building on the other corner, and on that day the tree dangled russet leaves. From beneath it she could look far along the street and see women pulling shopping carts behind them, purses dangling from their arms, could see high school kids like herself explosive on their holiday, and men bumping and rattling empty dollies over curbs. She could see from under those last leaves the length of Cannon Street lined with parked, double-parked, and honking vehicles, past the two block shopping district with its guardian candy stores, one at each end, past the pharmacy with its lunch counter, past the new grocery store, the cleaners, the dark, coffee-scented A&P, the hushed card shop that rented cellophane-wrapped hardcover books, past the French bakery with lacy chocolate-topped cookies, pastel petits fours, and that sweet hot bread smell, past the hardware store with its bins of mysterious gadgets, its wooden floor used until each plank was cupped and sound was muffled by the old walls, past the bicycle shop packed to the rafters with fat-wheeled blue cruisers and shiny green three speeds, and red wagons, red sleds, red scooters with a dozen uniform raucous black-bulbed horns and shiny handlebar bells in the window, and upstairs along the street the signs of accountants and dentists, the old-coin dealer, the costume and tuxedo rental shop—she saw from under the old beech tree how the street stretched out of sight to the fusty old cannon perched at its far end, forever poised for one more salute.

There were also a barber shop and two hairdressing salons on

Cannon Street. When she was a small fry, the barber sufficed, and she would run her fingers around the swirling, glass-smooth red, white, and blue striped pole on her way in, but a year and a half ago she'd become a teenager, and her old-fashioned mother switched her over to the Elegant Beauty Shoppe. Mr. Jack, with the hairy arms and balding head of a barber, owned the business with his wife. He prettied up Ericka's Dutch Boy cut, feathered it and shingled it and gave her itty-bitty pointy sideburns as if he wanted to make a pixie of her. Each time she walked out of the nauseating odors into the fresh air, her white sneaks and bobby socks were as heavy as cement shoes. Each time she lost her footing, and it took a few blocks to find her own walk all over again.

Today her mother gave her cash and told her to say hello to Mr. Jack. Hands in her pockets, whistling jaunty tunes for courage, she hugged the buildings across the street from the Elegant and counted cracks in the slate sidewalk, avoiding the eyes of every shopper that passed, hoping it was too chilly for Mr. Jack to be lounging outdoors with a cigarette. There was a dazzling new display of baseball cards in the window of her favorite candy store, and the doughnut delivery man happened past with a trayful that smelled like the cinnamon sugar crullers Grandpa dunked in his milky coffee.

Afterward, she'd come back.

Before she knew it, she was past Snip'n'Shape, the other beauty salon. She panicked, stopped, felt conspicuous, went on. If she turned around and went in, they might have noticed she missed the shop on her first try. As it was, a woman she recognized as the mother of a ninth-grade classmate smiled at her. She tripped on a deep sidewalk crack, fled into the deli, and pretended to look around. In this palace of German sausage and tins of crackers in alien languages, of loud orders in a foreign tongue, of hanging bolognas and hard salamis sliced paper-thin, of sawdust and a wooden pickle barrel, she played with a fifty-cent piece of her own in her pocket. She uncovered the barrel, took the cold steel tongs from the side, and fished a small bumpy green pickle from the brine. Everyone called the aproned counterwoman Gerda. She owned the deli with her husband, nicknamed Mr. Gerda for his less dynamic presence. Gerda nodded and smiled at her choice as she snapped open a white waxed paper bag. "Don't spend it all in one place," Gerda commanded, returning a quarter, dime and two nickels in change.

She never waited until she was outside but crunched into the dripping gherkin while still under the aromatic spell of the deli. Once she was in the daylight, mouth full, dabbing juice from her chin, she realized she goofed up. Now they'd think she'd gone past on purpose to eat a garlicky old pickle before her haircut. She'd reek.

With great reluctance she set the pickle in the trash can on the corner and wiped her fingers on her red dungarees. A bent old woman in black coat, black shoes, and black babushka *tsk*ed as she passed. Ericka found one remaining Chiclet from a two-pack her father brought her from a subway machine, and she cracked its white coating to spread the mint in her mouth. She was going to do this.

Where once the heavily accented man with smelly hair tonic swept the sidewalk outside his Mala Strana Salon, now each morning as she passed on her way to school, she saw a woman sweeping. One Sunday morning the woman washed the plate glass window, loudly whistling "There Is Nothing Like a Dame" as she stretched to reach the top of an arch of brand-new gold letters that spelled Snip'n'Shape. She'd been impressed by the whistler's brisk thoroughness and by her haircut, kind of swept back with a dip in front and shaped to a point on the neck. No feathering. No prettying up. Her mother would hate it.

The sign in the window that said No Appointment Necessary was still there. She pushed the door open, eyes to the worn maroon linoleum floor. The shop smelled as bad as the Elegant. Dark nylons and white shoes appeared in front of her. She looked up. The beautician, her height, wore a tight white uniform and held out her arms, hands open, as if Ericka was a long-lost friend.

"Hi, honey. Here for a cut?"

Ericka stopped breathing. The woman's long, narrow eyes were dark as semisweet chocolate and welcoming under angular eyebrows. Her nose was noticeably yet elegantly curved, her dusky brown hair waved into ruffles. Her broad, keenly etched lips smiled, dressed up in a grapey lipstick.

She looked quickly away when she noticed, behind the comely hairdresser, a row of three ladies under silver space-helmet driers staring past magazines at her, cigarettes between index and middle fingers.

Another beautician, this one tall, bent over a sink to scrub an old woman's white hair. Ericka saw no sign of the whistling woman who washed windows like a proud shop owner.

Her beautician was never still. She swung a stiff transparent cape over her as soon as Ericka was seated, then led her to a sink where, with an excess of movement that made a performance of her attentions, she washed Ericka's hair.

Back at her station, the beautician asked, "Like this again?" She held up a hank of the overgrown pixie styled hair. She smelled of a kind of flowery powder that Ericka's mother patted on with an oversized puff. Did she cut the whistling window washer's hair? Ericka's insides quivered.

She got chills as the beautician, warm fingered, refastened the cape at the nape of her neck. Her heart worked like a bongo drum as she answered, "No."

"Okay. Like what?"

The only style in her mind was the whistler's. They must be very good friends to go in on a shop together. While Ericka searched for words, the beautician bent down until they were virtually cheek to cheek in the mirror and asked, "What's your name, honey?"

She'd practiced this three hundred times or more before her mirror. She put herself to sleep chanting it. *Ericka*s were blond, and tall, and swam like fish, rode with men in sports cars, wore cocktail dresses, and used those huge powder puffs. "Rickie," she announced.

"Say that again?"

She was used to whispering it. "Rickie," she barked, then cleared her throat to show that she hadn't meant to be abrupt. "Rickie Deigh."

The door opened, and the whistling window washer strode in, hands in her pockets. "Angela," she said, in a bark of her own, and waited by the register.

"Tam," called the beautician. She turned back to Rickie. "Do you want to look at some photographs I have of hairstyles, honey?" Angela gave her a loose-leaf notebook of eight-by-ten black-and-white portraits in plastic, then patted her own ruffled hair and hurried to Tam.

Glamour-pusses, she thought, flipping pages. Not for her the bouffant, the permanent wave. She lingered over a petite model so pretty she couldn't bear to turn the page. In the mirror Angela listened to the whistler. Rickie studied Tam's trim, jaunty haircut as the woman flung out her arms. They raised their voices over the roar of the driers.

"Thirty days," Tam said. "We pay up in a month or we're up the creek without a paddle."

"You can't work two jobs and keep this place going, Tam." Angela spoke quickly, in the barbed way of New Yorkers like Rickie, but there was a syrupy quality to her voice, as if it came from some rich source in her chest. "Give it time. We're pulling in more customers every day." Angela indicated Rickie with the flutter of a hand. Rickie wrenched her eyes down to the pretty model, but back up in time to see Tam looking her way.

Rickie burned with a second-degree blush. Tam looked like herself, in her dreams. Angela might be the friend Rickie danced with, in her dreams.

Tam shook her head. Her voice was not high, but not like a man's either. It was subdued, strong. Rickie wondered how to make her voice like that and quietly cleared her throat, lowered her chin. Tam announced, "I'm going to take the job. Till we're over the hump."

Angela, semisweet eyes pleading, stood very still and whispered, "But I'll never see you, hon."

Rickie would keep Angela company. She'd sweep and wash windows. Put up advertisements all over town. Save her allowance to pay for extra haircuts. Across Cannon Street a truck ground to a stop, idled. It drowned out Angela and Tam. If she earned a million dollars, she'd bow and present it to Angela, who'd say, *You've saved the shop.* Instead of studying haircuts, she dreamed. Angela took Rickie's hands in gratitude. Rickie saw herself cracking a joke, drawing herself up full, then gently, then firmly, press a hand to Angela's back, lift her delicate arm, and, under a velvety starlit night, dance her down Cannon Street.

Angela, darting back, startled her. "Find anything you like?"

Tongue-tied still, she stared at Angela in the mirror. She was dizzy. Stiff as a wooden dummy, she handed Angela the album. "I don't want to look like them," she said, her voice uncontrollably loud in her effort to lower it to Tam's timbre. Tam looked up. "I want to look like her."

In the mirror, she watched Angela follow her pointing finger to Tam. Angela's whole face changed, eyebrows lifting, eyes widening, mouth going round with an *oh* only Rickie heard.

Angela's hands on her hair were lacy warm waterfalls. Each time Angela touched the back of her neck, Rickie shuddered like she did at the feel of the delicious warmth of her blankets on chilly nights. What was going on? From her heart down she was molten. Whenever hair was not falling into her eyes, she watched Angela's face in the mirror. There was a grown-up flirtiness to her. Her hands did not seem to move so much as beckon. Her eyes, checking her work, kept smiling a knowing smile at Rickie. Her fingertips brushed hair off Rickie's cheekbone, forehead. Sometimes Angela's soft belly pressed fleetingly against a shoulder. Rickie felt like she would explode, like at night when she practiced with her pillow how to kiss.

She was about to soar away but, at the same time, sat more and more still for Angela's deft touches and feared that Angela saw her heat waves, like the ones that rose off the asphalt ahead of her as she roller-skated to Cannon Street on a hot summer day. And if Angela did notice? Would Angela laugh, keep cutting, keep touching, keep her soaring and sitting happily ever after?

Tam stood at the window reading a comic book. Lucky Tam. Did she and Angela go home to one of those new buildings down off Main Street? What if she, not Tam, lived with Angela, in a big sunny apartment with shiny floors and tall potted plants to dance around. What if she lived with Angela in a place where, at night, they saw the whole city sparkling like diamond rings. What if they went to the park together, tulips awakening at their feet as they walked around the lake, holding hands. And what if sometimes Angela waited for her outside school for everyone to see. Or if Angela fixed her hair every day, fingers swift and sure and attentive, like this.

Then it was over, the gentle fingers withdrawn, Angela's snipping dance done, the lusciously cloying scent of her powder removed. She gulped air.

"What do you think, Rickie?"

It was the first time she'd heard her name from other lips. She stared in the mirror and saw nothing but Angela's big tender smile. "I love it," she managed to say in her new low strangled voice.

Angela clucked with her tongue and swung her around in the chair. "Tam. Showtime."

Tam walked with a faint swagger, like a movie cowboy. She approached slowly, leaned her arms on the back of the next chair. "Hot stuff," she pronounced in that murmur of a voice.

Tam was teasing her. She couldn't bear the humiliation in front of Angela and swept the cape from her chest.

Angela put a light hand on Rickie's shoulder, and Rickie leaned in to it, enough to memorize the touch. "Come back in a month, six weeks, Rickie. We'll work on it some more, until it's perfect. You'll be irresistible."

She caught the affectionate smile between Angela and Tam, slid off the chair, started for the door feeling mad, feeling pleased, weak from imagined passion, not knowing what she felt.

"Oops," she said and whirled back around, pointedly not looking at Tam, searching her pockets. Into Angela's soft hand she carefully laid her mother's money along with her own quarter, dime, and two nickels.

"Thanks," she coughed out, making it to the door, then stumbling on the welcome mat as she glanced back and saw that Angela's warm gaze followed her.

Cannon Street, her avenue of dreams, throbbed with clamorous possibility. The daylight dazzled her; the fumes of a passing bus were the offering of a rose garden. She peered toward the cannon, cocked an ear for its salute, noticed that the sidewalk floated far below her and that everyone wore Angela's smile.

"Come back," Angela said.

She mooned over the florist's window, giddily pleased to have nothing left in her pockets but her hands. Cool air touched the new bare place on her neck. In the florist's window she saw Angela's touch, her hair kind of swept back, with a dip in front. She felt the cowboy swagger in her own walk.

Originally published in *Cactus Love* (Naiad Press, 1994)

FRUIT STAND

I: Oranges Out of Season

My mother would give me an orange, as big to me then as an orange summer moon is now, and a green lime which I'd name Baby, and I'd use them to set up housekeeping under this row of wooden shelving here. One side of the fruit stand was the bedroom, another the living room, and another the kitchen. This front area here was the yard. The orange was Mama.

Oh, I know it sounds silly, Curly, but that's why I say I've been in this business almost half a century. You think I'm kidding? By the time I was five, I worked after school, after kindergarten, dragging out bags of trash or empty crates. My father would give me a nickel for the afternoon. One day I asked for five pennies instead of a nickel for the gumball machine at Izzy's, the ice cream shop over there, across the street, see? Between the cleaners and the bakery. And he started me off waiting on customers right then, making change.

Oh, my family's been here a long time, Curly. Long before I took over and started hiring lazy baby dykes like you. I pay you to help me, and all you want is to hear stories about this place, the neighborhood. You know, people say all the time things are so different, but how do they say it? The more things change, the more they stay the same, am I right? Yeah, the kids still come by, like I did, from the Sister school, in plaid pleated skirts and white blouses. Can you believe I was ever that small? Um-hum, till I was about thirteen, I was a regular shrimp like you. Then by the time I'm seventeen, I'm five foot eight. Never did gain the weight to go with it.

Look up there, middle of that next block, that's where I learned to shoot baskets. Now if I was seventeen and five eight, I'd probably get a scholarship to one of the colleges snapping up girl basketball players. So I'm teaching the youngsters how to get snapped up. Yeah, I coach a team. Ten-, eleven-year-olds. Call themselves the New York Nukes. I know, I know, it's a crappy name. Doesn't even sound like a girls' team, but they voted for it. Give 'em more spunk, anyhow—can't beat the deadliest team in Queens. Am I right?

I got the fruit stand from my mom and dad. He died when I was twenty. I'm supposed to look like him now my hair's gray. I stoop like him. From lifting these crates you should be heaving. I had to come in and help. If I hadn't, my mother would've killed herself trying to pick up the fruit at Hunts Point four o'clock in the morning, then set up, run the store till six at night. She wouldn't have lived on another ten years after she lost Dad. I was only supposed to be helping her. But, hell, she was sixty-three; she couldn't handle it.

Yeah, I was born real late. She had seven before me. Practice makes perfect, you know. What—I'm not perfect? You're fired. How do you like that? Contradicting the boss. Here, let's at least fix up these pears. Poked half to death from the fussy housewives. Wait, that one's a mess, can't sell it, put it on the damaged stock table with the overripe fruit; some poor soul will be glad to get it free.

No, we were all girls. None of us was expected to help out here. I liked it. Loved it, as a matter of fact. They sent me to business college after St. Joan's, and I learned bookkeeping, so I worked a year in the city, which had its good points. It wasn't home, though, if you know what I mean. I wanted to work here. But my mother, she wasn't ready to retire. "What would I do?" she always asked when I mentioned it. Oh, and complaining she didn't have a son to take over the business. I told her I wanted it, but she thought I was going to be like my sisters and be a full-time mother. Can you imagine? Every damn one of them, housewives on Long Island.

What are you laughing at—you that I picked up from the gutter. Seven straight sisters and then me? You're right, it is funny. And they're real short. A bunch of cackling bantam hens. Stop it, stop it, Curly, you're making me cry I'm laughing so hard. There, see, you dropped a pear, and here comes Mrs. Gonzalez. The rush is going to start, wait and see.

❖

Yesterday wasn't bad for your first day—believe me, it wasn't, Curly. Sometimes it's so slow, I think I'm going bankrupt, then out of nowhere, we get twice as many customers, and I don't know how I'm going to handle it. That's why you're here, for all the good you're doing me. Did you see that big blonde with the short hair? Reminded me of Sophie, my old partner. No, no, I'm not going to tell you about her till we get some work done around here.

What's to do? Lazy Brooklyn dyke. They didn't teach you to work over there? No wonder the Dodgers moved out. They were embarrassed to be from Brooklyn. Only kidding. I got nothing against Brooklyn. Only glad I was born in Queens. Come on, start hauling that fruit out from under the stands. No, no, the apples first. Here, put the green ones here, the customers have to pass them to reach the eating apples, then they'll think of making pies. That's called merchandising. Sophie taught me that. Right side up, you backward Brooklynite.

Sophie? She was almost a real partner. Fought her off tooth and nail. She'd say, "Henrietta…" I was named for my father. They figured I was the last chance for a son. And Sophie always called me that when she was going to lecture me. Anyways, she'd say, "Henrietta, you need vegetables in here. And to run your vegetables you need a partner." And I'd run her out of the store, even though she was working for me by then. This is where I met her, too, I tell you that?

The Delicious next, the Red Delicious. Or should we go green, yellow, red? No, use the contrast. Put up the Red Delicious. Then the yellow. Here comes the milkman. Sophie's the one got me to put in the milk and bread, too. Thank goodness. I put it in a whole year before Nicky, who runs the vegetable stand two doors down, came. The ladies got in the habit of buying here, and Nicky had to give those items up after six months. Didn't Sophie gloat then.

Oh, she was gay all right. Sophie was, but I wasn't. Well, okay, maybe I was, but I was the last to know it. When you were nine? Impossible. Now Sophie, maybe she could have come out that early. She was something else. I didn't know she was gay at first, but I knew she was real special.

First time I saw her my heart kind of heated up, you know how it is? Why am I asking you? You're too young to know anything; you think you know it all, smart aleck. Shut up, maybe you'll learn something. This is what I get, hiring a seventeen-year-old dropout. What are you sitting on the orange crate for? You can't work if you fall and break your ass. That thing won't hold you. As a matter of fact, I'm putting you on a diet starting now. When Kathy brings lunch around, I'm telling her to lighten up on yours.

Yes, Kathy that I was with at the bar. She always brings lunch. Before her lunch rush at the diner. Over on Roosevelt Avenue, right across from where you got off the subway. She's the cook there. Good cook. That's why I married her. Only kidding. Twenty-three years we've been together. Well, you better believe it, because it's true. And that's something else I have Sophie to thank for. Learning to work hard at loving.

Anyway, I'd look up from this table of fruit we used to have right here, parallel to the front—it was all open then. I'd sit behind it to wait on customers. The scale was there, and paper, the books, knives. It was my office, but there was fruit displayed on it, too, whatever was out of season, to catch the customers' eyes.

That was my father's idea. He'd always call one thing out of season, even if he couldn't get anything that week that was really out of season. He thought the ladies would splurge on something special. And it worked.

That week, I was using navel oranges. They're never really out of season if they grow in the right climate with the right care. But they were sure out of season for this neck of the woods. I'd cleaned off every one of them, and they were sitting there shining—rough, bright orange balls, a surprise at Christmastime. And I'm leaning down behind them, doing the books or something. It was a slow time of day, and I look up through this orange kind of glow from being surrounded by the oranges and working on them and all, and there's this short-haired blonde, almost tall as me, with big gold hoop earrings. She was…misty looking, is the only way I can say it, with the orange haze around her and this real physical look about her. She looked like the word *sensuous* sounds. With these full lips like you'd right away think about kissing. And blue eyes, hungry looking, behind her almost-matching blue glasses frames.

What are you laughing at now, ignoramus? Remember we're talking nineteen fifty-seven, near thirty years ago. People wore glasses like that then. Yes, even lesbians. Sure, she was wearing a skirt. Women wore skirts in those days. Besides, she was visiting her grandmother. Sophie was on Christmas layoff from the factory where she worked. A sewing machine operator. No, it was a lousy job. Hour after hour bent over the machine. One of those heavy industrial ones. Stitching leather. Now, that's a tough job. And getting paid lousy. She'd gotten fired a lot of places, that's why she was working there. But I didn't know that then. She was shopping for her grandmother who was sick over Christmas. Sophie was, oh, caring. Do anything for you. Shopped here every day of her vacation, bringing her grandmother fresh fruit on her way from the subway.

Well, of course we got to talking. I can feel now the two oranges I picked up and played with while we talked that first day. I was nervous and I juggled them, dropped them, and ran my fingers over them the whole time she was there. The skins were textured; all the tiny grooves and pits and ridges were smooth and pleasing to my touch.

I remember my father used to hawk the fruit on the sidewalk like when he started as a peddler. "*Awrenges* outta season," he used to call. They'd think I was crazy if I did that now, but sometimes I wish I could. I guess that's what they call nostalgia.

Hey, you're goofing off again. And you've got me doing it, too. Naw, Kathy won't be here for another hour. What a teenager. You think about nothing but your stomach. I've been up since three, you know, and haven't eaten since then. Have some fruit if you're hungry. Careful, gently—don't bruise the other bananas in the bunch, the ladies won't buy them. One big stomach at your age. That's all you ever think of. All right, all right, almost all, you dirty baby dyke. Am I right?

What did we talk about? That day I guess we talked about the neighborhood. I don't know for sure. Mostly I remember what she looked like and the oranges. Touching them was like touching her. I never thought of that then. I mean, she didn't come out and say, *I'm gay, come home with me.* No, we must have talked about the neighborhood because she'd been visiting her grandmother here all her life. She was a few years older than me, maybe twenty-three, twenty-four. Poor thing, she was from Brooklyn, too, across the bridge, what's that section called?

What do you mean, what do I have against Brooklyn? I'm teasing you, you ragamuffin diesel dyke. You're so touchy. Hit me again and I'll make you wait on Mrs. Muller. She's rough, man. Oh, she'll plow right through our stuff, leave a mountain of poked, peeled, and smashed fruit and every display undisplayed. Oh, I think that's what I'll do to you, to see you apologize to her after she's made a mess and bought half a dozen of the eggs we have on special and absolutely nothing else. If she ever bought enough to make it worthwhile, you wouldn't mind what a kvetch she is, but she does that to every one of us—Nicky, Frankie the fish man, the butcher. Even poor Nora who runs the florist's across the street—on the corner, see? She even manages to paw her flowers and leave them wilting, though Nora doesn't have to put up with her every day.

Now Nora's nice, too. She and me got together a long time ago, after Sophie left and before I met Kathy. But she couldn't handle it. Ran off and got married a couple of months after we broke up, divorced him three kids later, and moved back to the neighborhood to get fat. That's her uncle's shop—Nora runs it. Salt of the earth. She has us over for coffee a lot. She's the kind of person who's only happy single.

You want to know why Sophie left already? I didn't even tell you why she stayed. She did come back after that first day, I bet you guessed. Well, anyway, every day we'd talk longer, and pretty soon she was telling me she was gay. I guess I backed off and got kind of cool because she didn't come by the next day. Or the day after. And then it was Sunday and we were closed.

I took my mother to church on Sundays in those days. Then out to eat. That gave her a thrill. Usually, we went to the diner, but you'd think it was Lindy's or someplace fancy the way she got so excited. That's how I got to know Kathy, taking my mother to the diner.

That particular Sunday, I took her to an Italian place, tiny, stuck under the El, it's not there anymore. Trains rumbled your teaspoon. I loved it. Italian places always seem so exciting to me. Romantic. Chianti bottles on the table. Red and white tablecloths. The whole bit. I caught myself being jumpy that day, though. Looking up every time the door opened. I was looking for Sophie in the only romantic place I knew. It scared me, but it made me realize I missed the big blond queer. That was a funny feeling. Like the time me and my best friend in eighth grade, Ana from Czechoslovakia, held hands during a movie in the school auditorium. *The Man Without a Country*, it was. Don't ask me why. Maybe because she was foreign and feeling like she didn't have a country. But that wasn't what I was talking about.

The next day Sophie comes by again, bouncy like she never left, and I say, "I thought you had to go back to work."

"Decided not to," she says.

"How are you going to live?" I ask. "Moving in with your grandmother?"

"Maybe," she answers, looking mysterious, almost like she knew what I was thinking in that Italian restaurant. And she takes off.

Well, at the time my mother was still working with me, and that day believe it or not she decides to fall. On a banana peel of all things. One of the bananas in that shipment was rotten and slimy, and she dropped it when she took it off the bunch, then forgot about it waiting on a customer. She used to wait on the ladies those days, and I did your work. So anyway, to make a long story short, she's in the hospital and then home for a long time with a broken hip. You know how older people's bones are. I didn't know then, but she was never going to get better. Pneumonia, you know, and the whole route. Had too damn many kids if you ask me. Not that I'm ungrateful she waited for me.

Sophie hears this the next day when she comes by. Then around time for the rush, which is coming up now if it doesn't start snowing any minute—Doesn't it smell like snow? Come here, stick your nose out in the air. Oh, you're chicken, afraid of a chill. I'll take you down to Hunts Point some morning with me. That's cold. So, Sophie shows up at rush time. Hanging around while I'm going crazy. And I see she's starting to leave. Well, you know I didn't want that to happen.

"You want to help out?" I yell.

She walks over to where my mother's apron is hanging, one of those bibbed white ones like I'm wearing, and starts waiting on customers, talking up a storm, pushing fruit like she owned the place. I'm amazed. After, I asked her did she ever work in a market before. "Sure," she says. "My uncle's got a candy store. I worked at the fountain for years."

"But how do you know enough about fruit to handle this?"

"I make it up," she says, winking.

You know, our sales went up like crazy with her there. 'Cause of course she started coming around every day for the rush. Wouldn't take a cent. After about two weeks of this I told her I wouldn't let her go on bringing more money into the store without getting paid. "Make me your partner," she says.

It was so promising. I mean, I said no to the partnership at first, but I knew it was worth a try. Sophie had so much to give. And I think at that point I would have paid her to keep her around. She made me laugh so much. I really had a crush. No, it was more than that. I loved her. As a friend. Real deep. You know plums? The deep purple ones always with a thin cloud over their skins, like royalty in lace? Well, that's how I felt about Sophie. She moved me, you know? Way inside. It was warm being with her. I felt like we could make anything work, the two of us.

Anyway, to get back to it, she asks me to make her my partner, in charge of vegetables. Her grandmother will even put up money for her. Seems she's been talking to her about it. I don't want to change my father's way of doing things, and Nicky, the veggie man up the street, he opened a few months before and I like him, I don't want to cut him out. But Sophie, she works on me, and finally I say to her, "Okay"—wishing, maybe, I was giving in to something else—"bring in a couple of veggies. Maybe potatoes and onions. Something we won't lose our shirts on. And no partnership. Let me see how we do. Anything you bring in extra you get a percentage on. And we'll go on from there."

Well, Sophie went at it like her life depended on it. Later, I found out that it did. She came with me to Hunts Point every morning whether we needed the potatoes or not. "To see how the market's doing," she'd say. Of course, it was only a matter of time before she'd be running over to me with a deal on string beans or a deal on squash. You know. Sucking me in to it because she knew I couldn't resist the bargains. And it wasn't long either before she brought this girl into the stand and introduced her to me. "My sweetie," she called her, though I don't know why when her name was already Cookie. She was about nineteen, scrawny, and real femme. Black hair teased up like a pineapple top, eyebrows ripped out and drawn on again in incredible arches, white ghoulish lipstick. Only about five foot. I swear, she looked like a kid dressed up as Snow White's wicked witch or whatever she was. But Sophie, big Sophie who dressed in black, from her pointed ankle-high black boots to her short belted black vinyl jacket, would parade her Cookie around so proudly. They moved to the neighborhood to make it easier for Sophie to take care of her grandmother and go with me to Hunts Point.

Well, yeah, Curly, I was jealous and I wasn't jealous. Sophie was so proud of Cookie, but she was so...butch, like she owned Cookie, you know? I felt really deeply about Sophie, but I didn't want to be owned by her or by anyone. That's why I wasn't married like my sisters. It was exciting for me to know I'd be with her every day, and I guess we kind of, maybe, teased each other because it gave us a good feeling, but you know, I was convinced I wasn't gay because I didn't want to live with Sophie or to take her away from Cookie. I mean, Sophie used to tell me about these butches fighting over femmes and all that, and I knew I wouldn't fit in to it. You, you're lucky, with the liberation movement you don't have to be butch or femme, and nobody thinks twice about it. Right up till Kathy, I tried to be like a man.

What are you laughing at? Sure, I was butch. When you're tall and not pretty or nothing, that's what you are. As soon as I came out, I went and bought myself a pair of boots like Sophie's. Only brown. Do you believe that? Right, it is kind of sad. But so is the shape these bins are in. Here, you're finished with sweeping. Straighten that fruit out while

I get the bookwork started. Oh, and we need to run this money to the bank before it closes. What time is it? That's good, after the rush we'll get dribs and drabs of customers till suppertime.

Hmm? Quiet? I'm not being quiet. Concentrating on these numbers. Yeah, I can answer a question while I work. What? How come I have no vegetables now? I don't know. I was happy when the store was a fruit stand. I didn't really need a lot more money, and after Sophie I had no taste for veggies. I was never really comfortable with them. People mess them up. Pour sauces on them, slather them in butter or sauce. Fruit is a miracle. You might have to peel it or wash it, but when that's done, it's ready—perfect and whole for you to taste, juices most likely running down your chin, your eyes closed from the tartness or a groan coming out of your mouth from the sweetness.

Hey—Mrs. Marseglia. Look sharp, Curly, they're starting again. Eh, Mrs. Suarez, look at what we got, your favorites—peaches. Yeah, and nice ones. They're going to cost you, out of season, and still I won't make a cent. But I couldn't resist when I thought of how much you love them. And look, I've got this here basket of spoiled ones real cheap for your pies—you like? I thought so. Hey, Curly, walk Mrs. Suarez and her peaches home, will you? She can't carry all this.

Yeah, I know she's great, my Kathy. But isn't she a good cook, too? Where else have you worked where you get lasagna for lunch, huh? Now you know why I want you to work hard, to earn what you're getting. And speaking of earning it, how'd you like that Mrs. Muller? Boy, didn't Kathy ever laugh when she saw you follow Muller around. I'd love to see her in the diner. Kathy says there she's completely different. Thinks she's queen. Orders more than she can eat and tips like crazy. Doesn't even ask for a doggie bag. I can't figure it. Yeah, I think you're right, she must use everything she saves to eat out. Tuesday nights, every week.

I could go for a nap now, but we better clean up this mess or we'll never get out of here later. Am I right?

Sophie? Oh yeah. Here's a broom. You want to know what happened to her. Ah, I don't even want to tell you. She disappeared. All of a sudden, no Sophie in the morning. I drove off to Hunts Point expecting her to come running after me like she had a few times when she overslept. But she didn't. And she never came to the stand. Her veggies wilted. Her potatoes grew eyes, luckily, since mine were wearing out looking for her. Sorry, vegetables make me corny. When her section, which had grown quite a bit from two items, began to smell, I dumped it, cleaned it out, and left it empty. It looked like I felt: abandoned. I'd been up to her and Cookie's place a couple of times for dinner. They were very uncomfortable evenings with Sophie playing the loving husband, getting waited on. Anyway, I knew from those visits where she lived, and I went up there the first day she was missing.

Cookie was there. She was a mess. "She tried to kill me," she whined when I asked what happened. "Your good friend did this," she yelled, pointing to a gap in her teeth. "And this." She pointed with her long red nails to her black eyes and bandages. I must have looked as if I didn't believe her because she started screaming, "Get out of my house. Go ask your friend, your good old partner what she did. What did I do to deserve this? You tell her that, closet case. Now you can have her all to yourself."

Of course, I'd never heard that term, and I was scared of the yelling Cookie was doing. I mean, I was only looking for my friend. Anyway, she scared me so much I forgot to ask where to find Sophie.

Luckily, Sophie had mentioned the name of the bar they went to most. I knew it was in the Village, and that Sunday I hopped a subway and went down there. I found a phone book and looked the name up and then asked people along the way how to get there. What a narrow alleyway it was in. I didn't know what I'd find inside, but there were a few short-haired women sitting around. The place was pretty dingy after I'd been outside on that bright winter afternoon. I ordered a beer. The women ignored me. And why not? I looked like them. So I asked the bartender, a hard-faced, good-looking woman who wore her hair slicked back.

"Sophie? You a friend?" She gave me a real suspicious look. "We don't want nothing to do with Sophie, do we guys?" she said, walking over to the butches. One of them got off her stool and hitched up her black denims. I felt like I was watching a Western, Curly—I mean it. I remember their words because it was like watching a play in slow motion.

This one says, "Who're you?" and lights a cigarette. Then she stands there with it hanging out of her mouth. Finally, they told me that Sophie was probably almost across the street from the bar at the Women's House of Detention.

I practically ran out of the bar, really thankful I wasn't gay. You're not laughing this time, Curly—what's the matter, you don't like this story? You're right, it doesn't have a very happy ending for Sophie. I found an entrance and was told that Sophie wasn't there anymore. She'd been violent and got shipped to Bellevue. Well, I thought, at least it's Bellevue, glad it wasn't the big state hospital, Creedmore.

I hit visiting hours and was directed to her ward. You've got to go through heavy, locked doors, and all these guards or nurses or whatever check you out through thick glass. By the time I got to the lounge and saw the depressed, wandering, bedraggled women, I was ready to crack up myself. I felt sick to know that strong, beautiful Sophie was locked up with them. I wondered, too, why they let her be with these women if she was supposed to be so violent. I'd persuaded myself it was some temporary problem already resolved, when I saw why they could trust her.

Sophie was sagging. She shuffled over to me and gave me a brave smile, looking like she had a mouthful of Novocain. Then she sat as if she was exhausted. Drugs, I thought. Sophie was on some powerful drugs on purpose, to keep her calm.

She told me what happened. Cookie was spending too much time with another butch. Sophie beat her up, didn't even realize how bad. She hung her head and shook it slowly. Somebody called the cops because it would cause more trouble to have another butch defend Cookie, and they thought she might be hurt too bad for them to handle. The cops locked Sophie up because she had a record. Of beating people up, being in fights. That's why she lost so many jobs, she told me, I guess thinking that I knew more than I did about her. Worse, she'd been beating on Cookie for a few weeks.

"I was good a long time, Hen," she pleaded with me, as if I could make it better. "Ever since we started, you and me. I figured with a hand in a business I could straighten out and fly right. I had a great partner, a great woman, and a great job. I could respect myself, you see? I was like everybody else. Nobody could put me down. I wasn't a misfit, a queer, anymore."

"Then why didn't you keep it up?" I asked her.

"Cookie was making eyes at this chick. I thought she was going to leave me. I was scared it was all going to fall through." Her black clothes, the same ones I guess that she was wearing when she was arrested, looked gray, were wrinkled, and there were stains on them here and there. Cookie's blood?

"'Cause she looked at someone else?"

"I warned her. She talked to the bitch on the phone, saw her at the bar. I warned her how it would be. She didn't listen to me. She didn't stop. She didn't care."

Sophie cried. I couldn't take it. She was always laughing.

"I can't explain it, Hen. It's my pride. Everybody'd know if she left me. I couldn't face them. I couldn't face you. I had to show them I could control things. That she wanted me most. She did like me better, you know."

Sophie's crying and talking kept getting louder, and a male nurse came to lead her back to her room while another nurse told me that it wasn't good for Sophie to be upset, I'd have to leave. She said there wasn't anything I could do. I left my address and number. I don't know if they didn't give them to her or if Sophie was too ashamed to get in touch. Anyway, she never did. Hey, you better let go of my hand. There's a customer at the door. You wait on her. I don't want to right now.

That was quick. What did she want, milk? Yeah, I saw Sophie once more. No, leave the rest of the work for a minute. Why am I telling this whole story to a tough brand-new dyke like you anyway? Because you're so tough? What does tough get you? What it gets you is Sophie. Or a life like hers. She thought being gay meant she was no good. She had to prove herself, and she thought it took acting like a man to measure up. It's not hard to see things her way. In this world all we're told is that a dyke is shit. We're perverts and there's laws against us. Oh God, what the world does to us. What it did to Sophie. Am I right?

Anyways, Kathy and me went to a bar out on the Island a few years ago to celebrate one of our birthdays. We were sitting watching the women dance. I must have seen Sophie out of the corner of my eye without knowing it because I was already thinking of her. I often think about her in the bars anyway, and this time I was wondering if I'd taken her on as a partner whether she would have felt she had more of a stake in succeeding and maybe felt better and not started taking things out on Cookie. We watched the women dance—we only dance the slow ones now, at our age—and the song stopped. When the floor cleared, there she was, standing at the bar in her old pose. The Sophie stance where she looks like a Texan who struck oil five minutes ago. I was so glad to see her I told Kathy and started to get up.

Kathy put her hand on my arm and kept watching Sophie. I looked at her, too, and watched her order and down three shots in a row. Then she picked up a beer chaser. She turned toward us. She was wearing a hokey black leisure suit and boots like the old ones, only square-toed with stacked heels. But she looked washed out. Like a stick person someone had hung a stiff new suit on. I wondered if she was dying of cancer. She looked like her vegetables after she left and they started to rot. I nodded to Kathy and decided to get drunk. We were halfway there anyway.

But I couldn't stay away. I went over to the bar, knowing Kathy was there if I needed her. Oh, I'd always wanted to touch Sophie, but now when I reached out to do it, I pulled my hand away because she was repulsive to me. But for the sake of what she'd meant to me, I stood there till she looked around. The lively clear eyes I'd known were cloudy. They didn't show any light at all. I wondered if I'd made a mistake and this wasn't Sophie. But when I told her who I was, she kind of started, patting me on the back in a hearty manner and talking loud, introducing me to the people at the bar.

I could tell this was the nicest thing that had happened to her in a long time by the way she carried on. It was like she was showing all the people at the bar she really did have a friend and a life beyond them. I wasn't sorry, I didn't regret having come over. It was the least I could give her, the first woman I had loved, the woman who really brought me out, without touching me.

We went back to my table and I introduced her to Kathy. My warm, loving Kathy who told me later that she felt a chill when Sophie pressed her hand. But the night is wavy in my mind, like there's a screen of heat between me and it. I guess that's my emotions, huh, Curly? Sorry about you having to get the customers. At least there's not many.

Sophie sat there, and we told her about our life, our great love and how peaceful we feel, and about the neighborhood and the business. She smiled and nodded. She asked questions. But, Curly, she wasn't there. I was sure of it, that she hadn't heard a thing we'd said when we asked her what she'd been doing.

"Well," she said, her lips kind of slack, not full anymore, "they sure cured me. Cured me of love. I haven't been with a lady for these many years." I couldn't tell if she spoke with bitterness or not. "But I'm still gay," she boasted. "They can't take my gayness away from me. Still spend my time in the bars. Read the new gay books and magazines. Things have changed. Sometimes I wonder if I've changed. But I don't take chances. I stay out of trouble. I don't hit no more. 'Cause you know," she warned, trying to look wise, "if you love, you hurt. Ain't no way around that."

I don't remember how Kathy got me out of that bar.

My partner. My real sister, not like the hens, Curly. My real big sister. Couldn't I have saved her? Kathy says no, she was too far gone even back when we met. I was still looking for myself then. She would've taken me under with her, taught me her ways. Kathy says I should thank my lucky stars I came out my own way. I know she's right.

Hey, are you crying? That's okay, kid. I cried, too. Sophie's sad, but I figure without her, maybe my life wouldn't have been as good as it is. It's like everything here in my fruit stand. It all grows, right? Some sweet, some sour. Life isn't always sweet to us. A lot of it is sour because we don't get much sun. Sophie came along in an ice age, as far as sunlight goes. And she didn't know how to help herself grow. Knowing what she went through, I worked at being different.

Speaking of sun, it's going down. Look, you let those Sister school kids make a mess in the nuts. Heaps of shells on the floor. Better get the broom. Ah, I'm stiff. It gets harder to stand up from these crates every day. Clean out the scales, too, will you? Hey—here comes that good-looking cook from the diner, done for the day.

Hi, Kath, what's cooking? Besides you being tired of that joke. The kid? She'll do fine. Cares about the fruit, real gentle with it. Real gentle.

Originally published in *Sinister Wisdom* 18 (Fall 1981)

II: Honeydew Moon

You know that song, "That's Amore," about the moon hitting your eye? That's what the moon was like on our honeymoon, only it wasn't a pizza pie, it was a honeydew. A fat juicy honeydew, perfect, like I sometimes get for my fruit stand, almost white, with the tiniest bit of yellow to remind you about the sun that grew it. That moon was hanging loud in the night sky, looking like it would fall right into our laps. If it did, it'd pop right open, split clean in half—half for her, half for me. We rolled back on the cool night grass on the edge of a sand cliff like we were the only people in the world, lay back for a while on the edge of our lives together, practically sucking sugar from that honeydew moon.

Now what got me started? Right, you want to take your girl away for the weekend. You definitely should. New York might be the greatest city in the world, and Queens the greatest borough in the city. Still, fresh air and the ocean…You remember that, am I right, Beanpole? Okay,

okay, I'll tell you about my honeymoon. First, it's late already, hand me the broom. You start weeding out the fruit that's too manhandled to sell full price like I showed you. Ouch, stooping's not as easy as it was back when we took our honeymoon, Kathy and me—here's the spoiled fruit crate for the food bank. Those squished berries will make nice muffins or pie.

Would you look at that sky? I swear, if they made syrup out of gold, this is what it'd look like, the way the sunrays hit the street in the late afternoon. Did you ever see anything prettier? Gold syrup. That's why I need you to keep the windows clean—everything looks prettier, more open, with the windowpanes clear as air for the gold syrup to pour on the fruit. My dad had this closed in with wood. I put in plenty of windows, maybe from that taste of open-air markets I got on our honeymoon. I wanted something that resembled the country, where fruit comes from. Not food warehouses like the supermarkets.

You're thinking about taking her to Atlantic City? The beach is okay down there, but too crowded. No place to cuddle in some lonely spot. How about the Cape? Or out on the Island? I hear there's lot of good restaurants on the Cape, and you need them. Never mind you want to do that with your girl all weekend. You take her to a good restaurant and feed yourself. Skinny as a rail. I don't know how you lift these crates, except you have to if you want to keep your job. Am I right? Newborn dykes like you are a dime a dozen, Beanpole. You put some weight on your bones or you'll keel over someday and I'll sweep you out with the old straw.

Yeah, me and Kathy went to Long Island for our honeymoon. Way out near Montauk, the Hamptons. Of course, they let us in, there's working people out there. Who do you think makes life easy for the rich people? We stayed with friends—stop asking questions. I'm not telling you another story until this place is clean. Look how the light's shining on those Golden Delicious apples, like they're going to catch on fire any minute. What a sight.

I'll tell you what, why don't you come have supper with us, and Kathy can fill in what I leave out about the honeymoon, and we'll feed you. No, don't worry; we're practically vegetarians, too. I'll make you something nice and fattening, right out of this store, what do you think of that?

❖

Okay, Beanpole, how does dinner look? Is Kathy talking your ear off? Ah, she's boring you with the picture albums already? No, we didn't have a camera on our honeymoon. They weren't as easy to come by back then. Now I have two. Wait, let me get the Polaroid and take your picture with Kathy and the fruit salad. I'll call it Fattening the Beanpole. You don't like me calling you that? Too bad, you're Beanpole to me.

Look, I made strawberries in gold syrup, or the closest I could get with the sun already down. Soaked in honey instead of sugar water. Over chunks of watermelon, cantaloupe, fresh coconut, pineapple rings, banana slices. And here in the middle—I cheated, this isn't from my store—some sherbet. Now that ought to fatten you up. Let's eat before it melts.

She wants to hear about our honeymoon, Kath—you want to help me tell it? Wish we had some May wine. Kathy makes good May wine, learned from Monica, one of the women we visited on our honeymoon. She died real soon after her lover. Don't look sad, Beanpole. They had a good long life. Am I right, Kath? They lived into their eighties. That made them, what, sixtysomething when we stayed there.

This was after my folks died and left me with the fruit stand. I was selling fruit in my sleep, Kathy said. Refusing to take time off. Kathy was determined to get me away on a honeymoon. Said she was tired of falling in love and breaking up in a month or a year. She had this idea that when she found the girl she wanted to spend her life with, if we did some of the things straight people do to tie the knot, maybe we'd have a chance of staying tied forever. You know, since the religions won't bless us, she thought up other ways to make what we promised each other real important, so we'd take it seriously when things got rough.

You bet it worked. Twenty-five years. I'm glad you're impressed. Some of these dykes today think it's not such a hot idea to stay together, to have a rock in your life you can lean on. As far as I'm concerned, except for my stand and my girl, life wouldn't be worth living. I'd probably die on a barstool. It's rough out there. Didn't you find that out yet? Wait, you'll see what I mean.

Me, I wanted the whole package including Niagara Falls. Kath was right, as usual. Hey, what's with the dirty look? Can't I pinch my girl?

Maybe Long Island wasn't the perfect honeymoon spot. At least we weren't stuck in the middle of thousands of squares showing off how straight they can be and staring at us because we weren't like them.

See, we visited Monica and Johnnie. They lived right on the beach, and we rented a cabin nearby. Who were they? How can I explain them to you? In the old days, queers had it even worse than now. Johnnie had a really bad time of it, and she found her own way to be safe.

You ever hear about women who dressed like men, pretended they *were* men? No, it's not disgusting. Sometimes that was the only way you could be queer and get along. Johnnie wore men's clothes when she couldn't get a job any other way.

Monica told the story. She said Johnnie had no trouble being mistaken for a man. I guess you'd describe her as burly, and she had rough features. She'd be called ugly if she dressed like a girl, and she was mean-looking in men's clothes. Had a thick, raised scar on her chin that healed red because she refused to see doctors after listening to their comments when she stripped for exams. Professional? No, Monica said there's something about a woman who looks like a man that makes otherwise nice doctors get nasty. On top of all that Johnnie had a beard. Really, she had to shave. Dressed as a woman, she'd shave every day to hide it—not when she pretended to be a man.

The worst thing for Johnnie? She was mute. Could hear, didn't talk. Couldn't explain herself. You see why she had a hard time? Yes, she really was a woman. It was only the world said she wasn't. Monica told us the older Johnnie got, the gladder she was to be a woman. Acting like a man, she saw a lot women wouldn't usually see. She came to hate men. Wanted to start a women's army and someday take over the world.

Meantime, she had to earn a living and kind of fell into the gardening business. She was from an upstate city and didn't know much about growing things. She looked for any kind of work at all, got knocked around by the men who found out she was a woman, laughed at by the women who found out she wasn't a man. Then she saw a card on a supermarket bulletin board for an assistant gardener. It didn't pay much, but it didn't need any talking, and the guy let her bunk in his garage.

He thought she was a mute boy and took a liking to her. She learned everything he had to teach and would have stayed on except it turned out he was gay. He was married, see, and pretty soon Johnnie figured out why he went downtown one night a week. He showed up at the garage drunk, looking for a guy, and discovered Johnnie wasn't one. He's the one gave her that face scar, when she snuck back for her belongings. She got away with only a picture of her and her mother wrapped in some underwear.

Johnnie hit the road again, spent a bad winter cleaning johns, and ended up on Long Island, doing odd jobs at a mansion. It was spring, and with no friends, Johnnie wandered the grounds, taking care of the plants and trees out of love. Her luck changed when the gardener quit. The rich people from the mansion had noticed her skill. To keep her around, they let her fix up an unused cottage on the beach. She wouldn't make a salary off-season, but she wouldn't have rent either. Around the cottage she grew her own garden and learned from the cook how to preserve fruits and vegetables. This was the second happy season of her life. She had a job, a home, and nobody bothered the strange mute gardener who lived by himself in the cottage by the beach.

Hey, Beanpole, eat up, your sherbet's melting. No, you didn't have enough. What's the matter? The story's upsetting you? Hey, this is the way it was, count your blessings.

Anyways, here's Johnnie living on the beach in back of this mansion, happy as a peach pit about to grow a tree, lonely as the last apple in an orchard. She thinks about a girl back home who used to walk with her in the woods. And kiss her.

Then, on a trip to town in the gardener's truck, she notices the new girl at the feed store. They always had a man before—now the sons were off fighting the war. Johnnie used to dread visiting town once a month; now she went weekly. There was something about this girl.

Next thing Johnnie knows, she's sitting outside her cottage after dinner, watching the birds fish, when the girl comes walking up the beach. She's in pants, like Johnnie, and that was unusual then. Johnnie pulls her kitchen chair out of the cabin and they sit together awhile, the girl chattering enough for the two of them and making Johnnie laugh. The girl returns that Sunday, and Johnnie pulls the chair out again. By the third visit Johnnie's bought a beach chair at the junk shop in town. She's suffering, wondering if this girl is like the one back home. By the flush on her cheeks when she looks Johnnie's way, she might be. Does she have a chance with a pants-wearing girl who thinks Johnnie's a man?

One night the girl, Monica, shows up early. Johnnie's still inside washing her dinner plate. Monica wanders around the cabin. She picks up the picture of Johnnie as a young girl, bow in her hair, holding her mother's hand. Johnnie figures it's now or never and points first to the long-haired girl in the picture, then to herself.

Monica smiles, sets the picture back, and walks over to Johnnie. She puts her arms around Johnnie's neck and presses herself to her. "I know," the girl says, kissing Johnnie.

Will you look at this table? Picked clean. Beanpole could do with a good feeding once in a while, am I right, Kathy? Let's clear it off and put up coffee. You want what? Herb tea? No, we don't have any of that stuff. What's the matter with you, Beanpole, you've got to be different? Yeah, I heard caffeine's bad for you—I need my fix. Wait, I know what we'll do. How about fresh mint leaf tea with gold syrup honey? Go sit. This kitchen's not big enough for three. And yes, I'm getting to the honeymoon. You had to know the whole story.

No, Monica's folks weren't upset. Johnnie and her ran off to New York City and came back saying they were married. Nobody asked to see a license. Monica's folks were disappointed she didn't get a man with money and looks instead of a mute gardener, but Monica was happy as a robin on a spring lawn. She thought her mother envied her, living such a simple life right on the water, instead of taking care of five sons and an ambitious husband.

They never did find out Johnnie was a girl. Monica worked at the hardware store till the war ended and her brothers took back their jobs. She took a job housekeeping for the people in the mansion. Years later, when Johnnie and Monica were too old to work like they had, they got a small pension and the cottage for life. What more could they ask?

Give me the dish towel. Kath, I'll dry. Your coffee's almost ready. Beanpole, this tea's pretty weak stuff—no wonder it's good for you.

How we got to honeymoon out there…Kathy met Johnnie and Monica through some friends. It seems Monica was not exactly innocent when she put her arms around Johnnie that night. She knew a couple of women like us through work. Those women knew a couple more and on like that till there was a circle of them having parties at their homes. Monica and Johnnie didn't let on about Johnnie except to a very few who visited on the q.t. One of them brought Kath, and how could they resist her?

Umm. Gold mint water. I think I'll start a company: Henny's Mint Syrup. Healthy, refreshing, dull as a hothouse tomato. You don't think it'll catch on?

When we met, Kathy hadn't seen Monica and Johnnie for months.

We decided to honeymoon out there. Besides, you kind of thought of them as your family by then, am I right, Kath? She wanted their approval. Goodness knows I was nervous.

I closed up the stand that Saturday night. We didn't want to spend the money calling long distance for a room, so we slept outside Johnnie and Monica's in the panel truck I used for hauling fruit. Kathy thought to toss a couple of blankets in the back.

Yes, that's where we spent our first honeymoon night, Beanpole, locked in the dark truck, lying on tarps and hopsacking over straw we spread on the ridged metal floor, covered by smells like cantaloupe rind, strawberry juice, lemons and limes and bananas, like a dream. I called the truck Cornucopia. Kathy was my new treat, and I had a feast. Oh, stop blushing, Kath, I didn't mean that. Besides, Beanpole knows the facts of life.

In the morning we met two of the finest human beings on earth. I thought Kathy was a magician to have stayed in touch. Monica was this grandmother type in a faded bib apron with flour up to her elbow and hairpins sticking out of her gray hair. Johnnie was still pretty solid, though stooped from gardening. She had a kind of rough way about her like people get when they have a hard time being understood. Once you caught on to how she talked—with her hands, with Monica's help, with scraps of paper and shaky, old-fashioned printing—she was shy and gentle as could be. Birds picked crumbs off her big palm, am I right, Kath?

The grounds around their cottage, despite the sandy soil and saltwater, were a picture postcard. Johnnie had flowering vines trailing up and around their porch, rose trellises, fruit trees. You could see why the rich people were letting her live out her life in that cottage: she'd planted much of herself in it.

And the way they were together, their eyes still shone when they looked at each other. They were so patient and appreciative you would have thought they were the ones on a honeymoon. I mean, who ever thought of two old ladies loving each other? I could see me and Kathy twenty, fifty years down the road. Being gay had always meant being young, fooling around, going out. Now I was looking at the happiest people I ever met, and they didn't fit any of that. We had a future.

What a week it was. The pretty cabin we stayed in down the road was open to the wind and sun. It was painted white outside; inside was rough wood that, warm, smelled fresh-cut. One whole side of the beach bordered the monastery next door. We had it all to ourselves and, mornings, ran along the water's edge as far as our breath held, holding hands and hugging. There were low sand cliffs above the beach with short trees and tall grasses and we'd lie there making out, always alert, because we would've killed ourselves if we gave Johnnie away.

Since they'd given up driving, we made a big shopping trip into town to save them the bus ride. Johnnie put on a tie and Monica a hat and dress. It was a small, shady town, after that white beach, and we carried their packages. Along the roads were produce stands. I had to stop at every one. That's where I got some ideas for my place: straw on the floor, the light, bushel baskets. Tricks like that make people feel they're in the country, think the fruit is fresher.

In town I saw for myself what Johnnie gained by playing a man. I was like you, because though I liked her a lot, it really bothered me: the shaving, the haircut, men's clothes down to the boxer shorts Monica hung on the line. It seemed perverted. I suspected Johnnie liked playing a man and Monica didn't really want a woman. Then I saw everybody they met on the street stop and say hello, smiling and passing the time of day. I could see the appeal for shy Johnnie.

I once asked Johnnie if she'd rather be a man. She rolled her eyes at me and shook her head no until I thought she'd scramble her brain, all the while making a face like she smelled something that disgusted her.

"I guess not," I said. "Me neither." We hugged.

I mean, twenty-five years ago Kathy and I were careful not to be seen on the street too much, afraid people would put two and two together and quit shopping at the fruit's fruit stand. Lucky Monica leaned on her lover's arm, wore a matching wedding band, in that small, stuffy-rich town.

So don't put Johnnie down, Beanpole. If she looked like you, they might have killed her, wouldn't have employed her for sure. Her life would have been bare bones. They compromised back then. You may not be afraid with your marches and your bookstores. Don't forget, there are plenty of Johnnies left.

That day, the four of us were happy as bananas grinning on a tree—us two on our honeymoon, those two enjoying the fruit of their long years of hard work and caution.

We got back to their cottage exhausted and sat around talking. You'd think me and Kathy would want to be by ourselves for a while. No, we had a whole lifetime to do that, and every minute with those old people was too precious to waste. They gave our honeymoon something nobody who goes to Niagara Falls will ever get. We even talked about setting up a farmers' market and lunch counter near them. Kathy was waitressing and knew the ropes. Now and then Johnnie's eyes would brighten and she'd put in her two cents, her hands going a mile a minute in her own kind of sign language, and Monica keeping up with her.

After a while when the ideas were flying fast and it really seemed like me and Kathy might move out of the city, this big silver car pulled up in the driveway.

Monica threw her hands up. "It never rains, but it pours."

Though she hadn't mentioned any problems to us, we recognized their fear. Johnnie sat tight and tense. The lawyer talked smooth and polite and slimy at Monica, said he represented the monastery.

Monica hadn't wanted to worry Kathy on her honeymoon. The rich people from the estate died, and their kids planned to cash out to the monastery. Monica and Johnnie said there were signed papers saying the cottage was theirs to live in all their lives, rent-free. Nobody gave them copies of the papers, the church people claimed there never were any such papers, and the lawyer was there to tell them they had to leave.

Me and Kathy sat there speechless while the lawyer said he'd be back with the final papers ordering them out. The Brothers offered to put them in a senior citizen project.

Monica cried. "Johnnie accepted the cottage instead of enough money to pay rent. We won't be able to grow our own food and stretch our dollars."

Until this afternoon, they hadn't been too worried. One of the things pretending to be straight had done for them was to make the church respect them like the townspeople did. They figured the priests were too naive to see past what the world thought. They'd been praying up a storm, sure they'd be saved in the end. Now it looked like religion wasn't all it was cracked up to be.

Didn't they have a lawyer, we asked. No, they didn't want to make a scene with the church, lawyer talk was over their heads, they weren't the kind to hire lawyers, how would they pay him? What if somehow because of this Johnnie got found out?

We four spent the rest of the day trying to find a solution.

Nothing worked or suited them. The threat of the monastery was over us all night, like evil. After the lies and pretending, the hard work and fear, this would wipe out their efforts toward a decent life. They might as well have been out in the open from the start.

"That's okay, girls," Monica said. "All we ever had was each other. And the good will of the people on the hill."

By the time the lawyer showed up the next day, I was mad as hell.

"What's the matter with the Brothers?" I shouted at him as got out of his slimy silver car. Someone had to speak up for these women. "Are they afraid of the real world? Let them come throw the old people out themselves."

Monica and Johnnie watched me, Monica's eyes frightened, Johnnie's face creased with worry.

"Why can't your so-called Christians let these old people stay? The priests don't need the damn cottage."

He claimed they'd love to let them stay, but their insurance made it impossible.

"What you mean," Kathy says, "is they don't want to spend the money insuring these owners who've always lived on the water and now might all of a sudden fall in?"

Monica managed to laugh.

Silverslime didn't like our tone at all. He pulled himself up and said he could make them one final offer.

"We're listening."

He wanted to move them into the caretaker cottage on the monastery grounds. If they were employees, and not as endangered by hurricanes, the problem would be solved.

The old people looked interested, but not happy. Seeing that, I couldn't help myself, I risked everything because I knew they were right. Except for being queer, they lived a godlier life than anyone I knew. Their world was full of peace and love and kindness and, poor as they were, charity. The God of flowers and fruit and sea and sun had claimed this piece of land for them, and big old Henny was their appointed priestess. I couldn't help it.

"No, they're not going to settle for changing their whole lives this late, mister. Johnnie paid for his home with years of his labor. It's not much reward. You know how small his pension is. He and Monica own something here. You can keep them from selling it, from passing it on. Take it away? Wrong. I own my business in the city, and I know about your games. They've got me in their corner now. Get yourself and your papers back in that car and get out of here. Their lawyer will contact you."

Silverslime huffed up, looked like he was either going to give me a speech or have a heart attack, and I didn't much care which. At the last minute he oozed back into his slimemobile and roared off.

Maybe I was being hasty and getting involved where I didn't belong. Maybe I was bluffing some to prove to the priests that I could match their firepower. Maybe it was my sense of fair play that was offended. What did I have to offer them if we lost? My parents' old apartment where Kathy and I already lived? Damn it, I wanted that home for them. For all those years they'd had to swallow their pride and their own natural ways, for all the things they did without to get what they had, for all the queers who lived half lives to get any peace at all, I wanted that home.

So our honeymoon took an unexpected turn. We didn't run along the beach that day, or make love that night. I wanted to call my lawyer. Monica said she'd call the one who first drew up the papers on their house. I said we'd pay him, and she accepted with tears in her eyes, despite Johnnie's gruff headshake no. Monica kept putting off calling, like she was still waiting for that church to fix things up.

When two of the brothers from the monastery came to the front door that night as Johnnie was building a fire in the woodstove, I wondered if Monica's faith was paying off. How could priests order such frail good people out of their home, once they met them? An hour later they were gone, whining at not getting their way.

"Faggots," Kathy declared, and we all laughed except Johnnie, whose eyes laughed for her.

In the morning we found a formal letter in the mailbox. The sheriff was coming to evict them.

Kathy persuaded Monica to call the lawyer immediately. I paced around outside watching to see if any busybody sheriff dared stick his nose into our business. Kathy called me in. Another setback: The old lawyer had been dead for several months. His daughter took over his practice. A woman. Monica and Johnnie were old-fashioned. They were dead set against using a lady lawyer.

Things were at a standstill again. Hell, I decided, I'd gotten them that far against their obstinate wills. I called that lady lawyer. Once she heard who was involved, she got very interested. Their benefactor's daughter had been her best childhood friend, and she remembered the family's affection for the old couple. She would check her father's files.

We sat down to a cold supper of homegrown vegetables and baked chicken, worried this might be the last dinner on the beach, these last homegrown vegetables ever. Would it kill Monica and Johnnie to move up to the monastery? It would be better than wandering around Queens, living a new life among strangers, depending on us.

After they went to bed, Kathy and I sat on the front porch, watching the dark waters. Near midnight we were startled—there was a sound inside the cabin. It was like a child's cry, or the whimpering of a hurt animal. Kathy put her hand on my arm.

We heard Monica ask, "Johnnie, are you crying?" The bedroom was right behind the porch, and light burst into the night. They must have thought we'd gone to our cabin.

"I don't want to leave this place," said a dry, rasping, high voice. I went cold with shock. Kathy's hand leaped across her open mouth. It was Johnnie. Talking.

"Something will happen." Monica was trying to comfort her. "If we do have to move to the city with the kids, why, then you can be yourself at last. No one will know us or care about the way we are."

"Have we been wrong to live like this? Maybe we're being punished. If only I could use my voice. I'm ashamed, Henny having to do this for me. If anyone fights for our home, it should be me."

"Johnnie, say it with me." Like a prayer they must have prayed many times, they said, "Don't you forget, whatever happens, we still have each other."

There was a smile in Johnnie's voice. "That's most important, I know." The light went out.

Kathy and I held hands in the dark. The voices went on for a while, Johnnie's breathy, unused. It gave me the chills because it was female as could be in a body I didn't think of that way and because we never guessed she had a voice at all.

We waited about an hour after the voices faded and very carefully snuck off the porch, down the road to our cottage. Too stunned to talk, we held each other and cried over Johnnie's girlish sobs, her few rusty words. How terrible it had been for Johnnie; she'd given up her voice to mute the ordeal of living in her body. I was bowled over thinking how awfully, awfully strong she'd been all those years, how she'd stayed as true to herself as she could and kept loving Monica and lived the whole time like a tomato plant without a stake, holding herself up by sheer will. If she lost everything she'd earned by giving up her voice…

By eight o'clock that morning I was at the lady lawyer's office. The sheriff might come anytime, I told her, and I insisted on helping in some way.

She was a pretty lady, very straight, and looked at me like I was a new kind of beetle about to attack her rose garden. "No need," she said, waving a folder. "I found this in Dad's personal files at home with a few closed cases."

She handed me a sheet of paper. It was the original notarized statement giving Johnnie and Monica the cottage and a half acre of land around it. "Hot dog," I yelled, and before she knew what hit her, I hugged her.

The lawyer dropped out of my arms to her seat. She produced two copies. "Dad got sick and never made it back to the office. These were never mailed out."

She thanked me for calling her, both for the old couple and for her father's reputation. She would deliver the papers to the monastery lawyer. "The Brothers might still fight it, since the cottage wasn't mentioned in the sale of the property to the monastery. We'll work something out."

She smiled big, and I ran off to show Monica and Johnnie that beautiful piece of paper.

They clapped their hands and, arm in arm, did the tiniest bit of a square dance swing, crying in relief—Monica loudly, Johnnie silently, though Kathy and I listened hard for a familiar whimper. The lady lawyer called later to say their problems were over. Out of respect for their parents' wishes, out of a sense of responsibility because her father's office was at fault, the children of the rich people and the lady lawyer would make a donation to the monastery to be used to pay insurance on the beach cottage.

Hey, Kathy, will you look at the grin on Beanpole's face. What's the matter? With friends like me and Kathy, you needed to worry?

Our honeymoon? Oh sure, we got back in the mood, what with all the celebrating we did that night. We were exhausted from our scare and from the royal battle. We collapsed the last two days.

I kept hoping Johnnie would thank us by breaking her silence. It was okay that she didn't; they gave plenty. Like what? Their example: staying together, enduring. It was like having parents to look up to. We wanted to live like them, to be as decent as they were despite what they went through. We wanted to stay together forever, like they did, because we could see how happy they were.

Yeah, Beanpole, like me and Kath are now. Like you're going to be someday.

Don't get me misty-eyed about it, though. I saw you and Kathy looking for tissues. Here, it's late anyway. Take these pastries and get home to your girlfriend. Don't stay up late looking for honeymoon dew. I need your eyes open at work tomorrow.

What's honeymoon dew? Look at Kathy winking at me over there. It's something we discovered on our honeymoon. You'll figure it out.

Originally published in *Old Dyke Tales* (Naiad Press, 1984)

III: True Love

Did you see that moon last night, Bookworm? Looked like a Sunkist billboard up there, a jumbo painted fruit, all orange and full. I wanted to peel it, see what it is about the moon that drives people nuts.

My guess is we're going to be busy as the dickens later. First off, the moon makes the customers hungry. If they can't have true love, they want full bellies, am I right? The other reason, remember this day last month? You college kids—your memory only goes back as far as your last meal.

Oh. Your last roll in the hay. Knowing you, that's not very long at all. How many girlfriends did you go through so far this year—and you're only a freshman? You work harder at finding your true love than anyone I've ever met.

Anyway, it's food stamp day. And it's Saturday. The customers will start late, but once they come there won't be a lemon or a grape left on the shelf. I'll ring the register, you restock. And no dumping things in the bins please, Bookworm. Make the oranges look like full moons and the kiwifruit like candy, so they'll buy them for treats. That's how you make a profit in this business, the extras, not the staples.

What about who? You think I remember who I was talking about yesterday afternoon? No, I'm not getting decrepit—I have more important things on my mind. So give me a hint.

Kathy's cousin. The gay one. You're a great help. Do you know how many gay in-laws I have? There's Adele and Irene and Mike and Mitzi and Steven here in Queens, for starters. If all Kathy's gay relatives were talking to one another, they could rent every square inch of Cherry Grove for themselves and their lovers and ex-lovers and no one else would fit.

The pretty old lady with the rings who was cruising you by the overripe bananas last week? That's Mitzi. She lives over on Eighty-Ninth Street. Nice prewar building, rent-controlled. She's been there forever. She retired from her job at a hospital on Welfare Island, a licensed practical nurse who worked with people who were never discharged. Almost never. This was a long time ago.

You have to be a certain kind of person to deal with that, with kids who wouldn't get any care at home even if they were a hundred percent so they have to live in the hospital to stay alive. I always wondered what kind of life that is to stay alive for, but I guess if it was what I was given, I'd take it with thanks. Mitzi also took care of adults too sick or hurt to care for themselves. And old people without a clue who they are anymore and nobody wants to clean their diapers, but they don't have the insurance for a nursing home. Which is just as well, the way some of those homes are run, am I right?

Anyway, Mitzi is Kathy's mom's cousin, Kathy's second cousin. Yes, there are dykes even older than me, Bookworm. I'm only fifty-six.

She never hid what she is either. Kathy had Mitzi to run to the first time she fell for a slick butch in boots and a ducktail haircut. Mitzi was seeing one at the time, as a matter of fact. Mitzi's butch was there on a day Kathy stopped by and about knocked Kathy's socks off. It was the style then, you know, cool as ice, never a smile, but eyes that promised the Garden of Eden if you gave her one dance.

No, I wasn't ever like that. Kathy had some sense knocked into her by the time I found her. She wanted a solid woman who wouldn't skip out on her if the going got tough. And I haven't; we celebrate our thirtieth anniversary pretty soon. Right, it *is* awesome.

But Mitzi taught Kathy the ropes, femme to femme, you know, and was there for Kathy to brag about her lovers, or after breakups, or in between girlfriends. She was fifty or so by the time Kathy dragged me over to Eighty-Ninth Street to meet her. I polished my boots till you could see your face in them. I knew I was getting inspected, and I wanted that stamp of approval like I never wanted anything before in my life. Except Kathy.

Of course Mitzi looks like an old lady. What do you think, femmes are exempt from wrinkles? Well, yeah, she is exempt from gray hair. She didn't make much money, but she knew how to use the riches she was born with. That auburn hair comes down to her calves, which isn't that long considering how pint-sized she is.

We visit her now and then, and Mitzi makes sure she sits at Kathy's station at the diner every morning for breakfast. Kathy told me about Mitzi the Femme: life of the party, dancing till dawn, the siren of Greenwich Village. Even as a kid, she hated her plain-Jane name,

Miriam, and pestered the family to call her after vampy Great-Aunt Mitzi.

What do you mean, is that all she did with her life, nursing, seducing butches, and combing her hair? What are you doing with your life except breaking hearts? You're eighteen and you have no plans. Anthropology? What kind of work is that, going around collecting stories like Mitzi's? You should be a doctor or a teacher, help somebody. What good will it do to write books about old femmes?

For your information, though, Mitzi did make a difference. It was hard work she did at the hospital. She went in every holiday to make the days special. And why not? Her girlfriends went to their families, and of course they couldn't bring a gay lover home to Mom. So Mitzi spent the days with her patients and, if there was time, spent the evening with her family. She still goes to the hospital with presents even now. She loves those people.

Maybe more than was good for her.

She was given a ring by nearly every lover she was with and wears them, all at the same time, to this day. The men were always after her, but she was a woman's woman, am I right? She was looking for her true love.

Darn, where are the customers? We should have a few early birds at least. Maybe the mail was late; people will have a hard time making it till Monday if it was. Yeah, I give credit, but it's not such a hot idea. The day the stamps come in, they buy stuff they need even more and don't have anything left to pay their credit here. I have to wait for the welfare to come. But the old people save me. They get their pensions earlier, and they always pay cash. I scold them for carrying it on them. They tell me they don't want to pay the bank fees, so what else can they do except risk the muggers? It must be hard getting used to the world turning out so rotten, like watching a kid grow into a criminal.

Right, we were talking about Mitzi. She stopped going out to the bars and parties. Now this is before I knew Kathy, before I even knew I was gay, so I'm getting it secondhand. Ancient history. The stuff you won't find in books.

You're going to write books about Mitzi—and me? All right, all right, you are. Maybe I should start calling you Dreamer. I definitely won't switch to Dreamboat, though. What do the girls see in you?

You're going to be famous? Who ever heard of a famous archeologist? Anthropologist then. Margaret Mead? Never heard of her. Is she gay?

I was saying, Mitzi drops out of sight nights. She catches the subway every morning, but she comes home at weird hours, still in uniform. Eventually Kathy's mom goes to see her, but Mitzi's not talking. Kathy's mom grabs Steven, figuring one of the gay cousins might get more out of her. He strikes out. It's Adele, who's only sixteen at the time but has been with her true love two years by then, who finally gets through.

Adele goes alone after school to the hospital. She gets home and Peppie—you know her, she's the one who runs numbers over at the cigar store—says Adele looks like she's seen a ghost she's so white. Kathy heard the whole story from Peppie.

It seems like Mitzi is seeing someone at the hospital. Not staff either. I mean, she couldn't find some lady doctor and set herself up good, could she? No, she falls for a patient. A mostly paralyzed, terminal patient. Why do people get themselves into situations that can only end—can you answer me that with your college education?

What doesn't end? Good answer, Bookworm. You think it's easier knowing the end like Mitzi thought she did, than making believe it won't come? No? Then what? Maybe you're right—human beings live off hope. So tell me, is true love the one that lasts, or is it the one where your hopes go as high as that bright orange sun?

Bett was Mitzi's age exactly and, from the pictures Peppie showed us, a good-looking woman. Way too thin, of course, and tense, like someone who needs to be angry but has no energy. Still, that old butchy magic hadn't disappeared. Mitzi combed her hair back for her, and Bett posed with the cigarette Mitzi put in her mouth, like Bogart. Bett would squint over it and could blow smoke rings out of one corner of her mouth at the same time as she held the cigarette in the other side.

How'd she end up paralyzed? Hit-and-run accident. She was the only woman in the garment district not sewing, but actually hauling clothes. You know how the guys do it, dashing across streets, walking with the traffic, pushing those racks on wheels. Count your blessings that we don't have to peddle fruit along Roosevelt Avenue like my father did starting out. My insurance would go higher than your hopes.

Well, one day Bett was out there crossing the street with an empty, and this car comes screeching around the corner and brakes, but way too late. Bett's down, her spine hurt real bad, and a knock on the head from the fall. The driver backs up, pulls around her and takes off. Nobody saw the license, nothing. From the bang on the head, Bett's out cold for months. She doesn't carry ID, no driver's license, nothing.

See, she was passing. You know, pretending she was a guy so she could get work that didn't pin her down to a sewing machine or a typewriter. She was paid under the table, no questions asked.

No one comes looking for her. Once she wakes up about all she can remember is her first name—at least, they thought it was her first name. They called her Leah. A couple of months later it came back to her. She was Bettina Sola, but the hospital social worker couldn't find relatives.

Meanwhile, the cops talked to people at her job, thinking it might not have been an accident. Everybody said she played it real close, like she had something to hide. Then this one guy said he saw her—him, he thought—going in and out of a building in his neighborhood in the East Village. It wasn't exactly trendy down there then. The landlord told the cops that Bett shared a one room cold-water walk-up with another woman, and they took off without paying the rent. *The girly one probably went home to Missouri where she should have stayed in the first place, away from these deviants*, the cops quoted in a report.

Meanwhile Bett was getting back bits and pieces of her past. In July, the calendar picture was of woods. A couple of weeks staring at that and she remembered growing up in the Bronx, near Pelham Bay Park. Missouri triggered something else. She remembered the woman she lived with, but there was no way she could even start to find her.

Legs and arms dead, the only blessing of the accident was that she could talk and, after a while, read if someone turned the pages for her. A lot of good it did her to talk, though. She was scared to death to tell anyone that she and Missouri were lovers.

They'd been together a year and a half, with enough high hopes to beat the band, were saving money to look for work down in Jersey, somewhere in the country. Bett thought she could get a job as a house painter, though she couldn't now remember why. Missouri would be a store clerk, like she was back home. They needed a car and then they could start looking for an old farmhouse to rent.

They planned to stay together forever, but after the accident, Bett figured, Missouri must have thought she found someone else. Bett also thought it was all the same. She wasn't supposed to live long, something about the brain injury. I never understood it, Bookworm, but I felt for the gal.

The pits is right. It could happen to anyone, but if it's one of us, especially if the authorities assume it's a man who turns out to be a woman, and there's no such thing as a marriage record, and no blood relatives who care enough to go looking, well, there's nothing they can do but pop her in a place like Mitzi's hospital.

There were times she couldn't even breathe on her own. They were afraid to give her therapy because of the risks. Mitzi was assigned the hardest cases. While she rested up from her transfer, Bett lay there, getting turned every couple of hours.

One day in the spring Mitzi went to change her sheets, and Bett smiled at her for the first time. Mitzi told Adele she almost keeled over from the power of it. Like walking into a room and there's the noon sun grinning at her.

Afterward, Mitzi claimed she already knew. They wheel in this woman with short curly hair, no trace of family, and worldly goods consisting of a comb, a pack of cigarettes, and one of those old Browni radios, the Cadillac of transistors. Plus, she gets this faraway look in her eyes if a Lesley Gore song comes on.

Mitzi couldn't be sure. You take a perfectly good butch type and throw a hospital nightgown on her, take away her swagger and her hand talk, and how's anyone supposed to know who's in that bed?

Until she smiled. Mitzi said it hit her right in the you-know-what, down there. Don't use that word. It's dirty, that's why. I don't care if the Queen of England is reclaiming it. Which I doubt. It doesn't belong in a palace any more than in a shop. Shh. The customers might hear you.

Mitzi jumped to attention at that smile. The Browni was singing a love song in the background. Then Bett gave her the look. I'll bet even you can't seduce a woman with nothing but your eyes and a smile.

First Mitzi started spending her breaks with Bett, then her lunch hours. She always gave her all to any patient but was professional; she knew better than to give her heart away to people who couldn't stop themselves from leaving her.

After a while she started cooking dinner at home the night before and heating it up at the hospital to eat with Bett. Then Mitzi started going over there on her days off, staying after her shifts, arriving early. When true love came, it hit hard.

Outside, she'd been seeing this woman known all over the bars for her jealousy. The woman stormed the hospital. "You're not breaking another date with me or I'm breaking somebody's leg."

She found Mitzi reading *The Girls in 3-B* aloud to Bett. The jealous lover was quick.

"You don't play fair, Mitz. How can I break her leg?" She glared at the two of them. I don't know who was more helpless, the woman or Bett, cool as a cuke with her motionless hand in Mitzi's. "You better keep this quiet, bitch. I don't want any of my friends wondering what she has that I don't."

The hospital staff didn't seem to mind. Mitzi never hid her life choices, and well, whatever comfort another human being could give Bett, more power to her was the attitude. Wouldn't it be nice if the whole world thought like that? It's a hard life, Bookworm, as you'll find out, college education or not, and why people want to deprive themselves and others of some loving words and tender touches I'll never know.

Whoa, a customer. She's good for seven apples, some garlic, and two pounds of greens anyway. Mrs. Marseglia, come on in before the crowds pick it over. What? Maybe it'll come in today's mail then. You bet, I'll see you later, no rush. If you haven't gotten yours, no one has.

What did I tell you, Bookworm? It's the mail. Or the government. I suppose you want me to move my business into Forest Hills where people live on cash, not stamps. Don't you forget your roots, education or not. Don't you forget your own kind here under the elevated, hawking apples or caring for the bedridden.

Did they make love? It was all making love, Bookworm. Mitzi made love to Bett every time she spent an extra minute at her side. Bett made love to Mitzi with her words, her eyes, the songs on her radio. Adele visited sometimes and told Peppie she'd never seen anything like it. Mitzi would caress Bett's cheek, and Adele swore Bett's lashes could flutter like Cupid's wings. Or Mitzi would take her hand, and Bett's eyes would stroke Mitzi's breasts. Bett could kiss, too, though they never did that in front of Adele.

Mitzi piled on the glamour. Uniforms were required at work— dresses, back then—and she festooned herself till she looked, Peppie said, like an Easter bonnet. Flowers, perfumes, glittery pins, makeup like a model's, and of course her hair, her long flowing glowing hair tied up with ribbons or bright barrettes. She took Bett's limp hand and stroked her own hair with it by the hour. Bett told her she could feel it, but no one really knew. I guess it didn't matter. It was making love, am I right?

If I couldn't love Kathy the way I'm used to, I'd do it any way I could. But I'd want the same things with her that I have right now. Living together, for instance. Mitzi and Bett were like anyone else. After they were going together for several months, Mitzi wanted to bring Bett home. I know, I know. Bett needed constant care, but they wanted to be alone together, too, not stuck on a ward with a bunch of other people. Mitzi persuaded the administration to move Bett into a room with only four beds, but at least one of the others was always occupied. Bett longed to be in an apartment, with her bed up to the window, raised so she could look out at birds or the street. And Mitzi wanted to spend some time at home again; she was always at the hospital.

If Mitzi finagled to bring Bett home, one of Mitzi's cousins, who was a nurse, promised to help care for Bett while Mitzi worked. Other cousins and their partners came forward to offer their time, including me. Mitzi, excited, went to the hospital administrator.

"I heard you were dedicated," the gruff man told her. "Don't you think you're going too far?" She couldn't persuade him that she wasn't overworked to the point of obsession, or trying to do a patient out of an inheritance.

She didn't let up. Mr. Gruff investigated and smelled something queer. Very queer.

"Keep this up and you'll lose your job," he threatened her. "We can't have this kind of thing going on here. We have the hospital's reputation to uphold. If the public gets wind that you've been corrupting the patients, we'll have no choice but to let you go. Now stay away from the Sola woman or you'll be on the unemployment line."

The idea of staying away from her lover was as stupid to Mitzi as the idea of selling raspberries from a bin of tomatoes is to me. Mr. Gruff might not know she was the top LPN in the city, but her supervisors knew to protect her. They looked away when she was with Bett.

Then it occurred to Mitzi that if she was related to Bett, no one could stop them from doing whatever they decided. She tried to find a way to marry her but couldn't do it legally—though what harm they think it'd do, I don't know.

Somebody made a joke about adopting Bett. Mitzi thought that was the best idea ever. Mitzi's brazen past came up, and they dropped her application like she was out to murder Bett, not love her.

By this time Mitzi's tired, damn tired. She's still totally in love with this woman who would charm her with compliments and tales of her sexy past. Mitzi said she never felt so appreciated in her life. But she wanted to come home to Bett at night, not sneak in to see her at odd moments and leave at the end of visiting hours, which the supervisors insisted on after Mr. Gruff laid down the law.

Her next scheme was to find someone in Bett's family. The authorities considered Bett incompetent ever since the coma. All Mitzi needed was one blood relative with a sympathetic ear to sign her out, and then Mitzi would take over. Was that too much to ask? Bett was no help. Whole parts of her life were missing, like what schools she went to, who her friends were as a kid.

Mitzi followed the earlier path the police took and came to the same dead end. There was only one other avenue she could try: Missouri. If Bett was such a storyteller now, talking and talking until her memory stopped her, maybe she'd been that way with Missouri, and maybe Missouri would remember a family connection. Maybe she kept Bett's Social Security card and stuff.

But almost two years after the accident, Bett couldn't remember Missouri's name.

Adele went with Mitzi to the landlord. He didn't want to cooperate with them, but Mitzi was desperate. Adele said Mitzi flirted and pleaded and wouldn't give up. Finally, the landlord scribbled something on a piece of paper. Adele said Mitzi's hands were shaking as she looked, outside on the crowded sidewalk, at the information. "Leah Seals," she read aloud. "One twenty-one Oak Street, Baring, Missouri. We have hope again."

These days I suppose you'd call the woman and get it over with. Back then long distance was still a kind of expensive magic to us all, so Mitzi went home and wrote her a letter on hospital paper she *borrowed* for that purpose only. Adele helped her compose it. It was the bare bones, not a word about love. Mitzi went to the hospital and read it to Bett. Then she crossed her fingers.

She crossed Bett's fingers, too. This was their last resort.

Over a week went by. Mitzi asked Leah Seals to write directly to Bett. Every morning Mitzi went through the patient mail before the candy striper distributed it. On the tenth day, still nothing. On the eleventh day, a Sunday, they could only wait for Monday.

Or so they thought.

Visiting hours were over, and Mitzi was getting away with staying later since staff was low on Sunday nights. They heard a commotion at the other end of the hall. "Must be one of the kids acting up," Bett said with a laugh. Then they heard a voice outside Bett's door.

"I've come all the way from Missouri. You better let go of me."

The nurse on duty rushed into the doorway, trying to block the way. She looked over her shoulder at Mitzi with horrified eyes.

"Bett," cried Leah Seals. "Oh, Bett, Bett, Bett. Why didn't you tell me? I thought you walked out on me."

The nurse and Mitzi were holding Leah Seals back.

"You could kill her," they were yelling. "She can't be barged in to."

Leah stood still, chest heaving, eyes pouring tears. Bett looked from Leah to Mitzi as if they both were trying to kill her.

"I'll be careful," promised Leah.

She was a slender woman with pale skin and a wrinkled dress under a cardigan. She put a worn canvas bag on the floor and moved toward Bett, pushing nondescript hair from her eyes. Mitzi could tell that fixed up she was pretty.

"My heart has been broken for two years," Leah told Bett. "I went home and moved back in with Mom. I didn't have the spirit for cities anymore, or for love. Tell me what happened." She turned to Mitzi. "Tell me what I can do. Can I kiss her? Can she talk?"

Mitzi, still in uniform, moved backward toward the door. She couldn't say a word. It never occurred to her that Leah would want Bett again, like this, after all this time. Bett watched Mitzi with her eyes pleading. But for what, Mitzi wondered. For Mitzi to understand that Bett would have to go with Leah now? Mitzi left.

Mrs. Suarez, I'm sorry. We were talking and didn't notice you were ready. Did the mail come at last? What can we do for you?

Yes, beautiful mangoes this week. They'll cost you, out of season like this, but I grabbed them. I know my customers. You want the full ten pounds of oranges? I'll put them right in your shopping wagon. And there's your neighbor, Mrs. Avilla, and Mrs. Kho.

Look sharp, Bookworm. The day has begun. The end of the story? Quick, before they get to the register, come here.

Leah brought a letter from her mother, using who knows what threats, saying Leah was Bett's sister. Don't ask me why Mr. Gruff took their word for it, maybe to end a bad situation for the hospital. He didn't like a staff member being involved.

Bett decided to leave.

Why? Because she couldn't choose between them. She told one of the other nurses that she hoped the trip would kill her because she didn't want to decide. Remember, the doctors said complications could do her in. They wanted her to stay put. It wasn't, the note she dictated said, that she didn't want to be with Mitzi, but she hated being a burden on anyone, and the end would be quicker this way.

By the middle of the next week Leah took Bett, Bett's radio, cigarettes, and smile to Missouri. Mitzi hoped Leah would at least let her know when Bett died, but lo and behold, the first letter was from Bett herself. She dictated it to Leah's mother.

The doctors were wrong. She'd been moved plenty, she said, and she wasn't dead yet. She missed Mitzi, but things were easier in the country, and Mrs. Seals took care of her while Leah was at work. Mitzi could have a real lover now, like she deserved, wrote Bett. Mitzi disagreed. She meant every forever promise she made to Bett, and she planned to stay true. Personally, I believe her heart was too broken to mend.

Baring, Missouri, Bett said, was like heaven. She spent her days in a wheelchair out on Mom's porch. Leah clerked at the general store, then came home and cooked pies and huge country meals for her. She was getting fat watching the hummingbirds drink sugar water and listening to the robins serenade the world.

Mitzi? Her heart left with Bett. She never added another ring to her fingers.

Originally published in *Cactus Love* (Naiad Press, 1994)

IV: Riding Lesson

It's about time you showed up for work, Bookworm. Five minutes? More like fifteen. What happened, didn't this big red sun come downtown to wake you? You grabbed the express by mistake and had to double back from Woodside Avenue? No? Then maybe we'll read about it in the paper, how Bookworm's train sat in the tunnel for half an hour on the one day she was going to get here early to meet Kathy.

Sure she was by—didn't I tell her my new assistant was drooling to meet her? She grabbed her break, the boss hollering and all, and you're not even here. I need you to unload some more of those crates off the truck on the double. That sun's not cooling down any. It looks like July in the city for sure today.

You finished unloading? Talk about slow. If it weren't for my back creaking and groaning inside like the old Third Avenue El, I'd have them on display by now. Never mind did Kathy help me throw my back out last night. What do you think, we've got one-track minds like you?

Now what put me in mind of the El like that? I'll bet I haven't thought of it in years. Seems like there was a lot less crime then, though, having some of the cars out in the open like that. Am I right?

Why, me and Dagmar—that was it, Dagmar Allen. Kathy waited on her yesterday.

Yeah, yeah, I'll tell you about Dagmar, but I want you on that sprayer pretty constant today, you understand? I'm glad we caught the refrigeration problem in April instead of waiting for the heat. I can't believe Dag and me used to go into the city to get cool. We could have gone to an RKO right in Queens, but was that good enough for us? No, we went to Saturday matinees on Broadway when her dad snapped up discount tickets. Lucky for me he was a stagehand, or I might never have discovered the shows.

Dag? She was a classmate at the Sister school. We were the tallest in our class and were always put together at the back of the line.

Hey, don't forget, extra mist on the apricots. They wither up faster than a subway rider on July third. Did I tell you? We're shutting down on the Fourth. Didn't even sell a pint of strawberries for shortcake last year or the year before, and Kathy's restaurant's closing, too. We thought we'd take a bus out to the stables, nose around. No, I won't ride with my back like this. Besides, I never thought it was exactly right, people using animals to get around. I mean, who do we think we are? It'd mostly be to see Dag again. Kathy says she hasn't changed a bit.

From what? From that great tall adventurous girl in jeans and a work shirt, the one I used to ride the subways with. From the tomboy kid who couldn't sit still in school and taught me to ride horses. From the long-legged girl in a plaid skirt, knee socks, and white blouse with a Peter Pan collar who used to shoot hoops with me and one of the nuns.

What did I know from queer at that age, Bookworm? No, we never did anything together except play like two wild things unleashed from the classrooms. After school Dag would tear off her skirt first chance she got. "I feel like a sissy in it," she always said. We saw *The Teahouse of the August Moon* on Broadway that year after passing Dag off as a guy to get her in. Women in pants weren't allowed.

What are you trying to do, kiddo, drown the poor nectarines? Pay attention to what you're doing. Here, dry them off with this. Then go on up to the Korean market and get me some prices. Let's make sure they don't undersell us today. It's easier to keep the customers than to win them back. Am I right? And you don't need to bring a paperback to work; I have plenty of stories. Take Dag, for example.

That was quick. I should've figured—you want your story. Let me see that list. Bananas. Go mark down the bananas. And let's do a special on the cherries. I got a good price, but the way you're misting, they'll rot with the nectarines. Yeah, yeah, we'll get back to Dagmar. Are you playing anthropology student again? And who said you could stop for batteries on fruit stand time? You know I hate that darned tape recorder.

Dag Allen was pretty wild for a girl in the fifties. We were supposed to grow up to look like Mamie Eisenhower. Have you seen pictures? Permed hair puffed out around our ears, skirts to our calves, clunky black shoes, and girdles to keep us in one place. Dag was a rebel like James Dean. No other girl got away with wearing jeans. I tried to persuade my mother, but you'd think I'd declared World War III, which we were waiting for, by the way. We had a million air raid drills at school. The horrible clanging bell would go off, and the Sisters would herd us into the hallways where we sat on the floor, heads down, hands across the back of our necks, like prisoners.

I suppose you're right, we were prisoners of the cold war, Bookworm, but Dag and me, at the end of the line, poked and giggled together. We were tomboys even at sixteen. The ugly things in life weren't real to us. Yet.

About once a month I'd go home with her. She lived half a block from a pint-sized stable. Dag was head over heels with those horses. She'd hung around since grade school, helping Jack, the owner, clean out stalls, learning everything she could. When she got tall enough, Jack hired her to give children pony rides. In exchange, she got to ride whenever she wanted. She took to horse life like berries to the sun. Instead of this big gawky girl with an old-fashioned braid, Dag was like a cowgirl, pitching hay or riding across North Hempstead Turnpike into the park, braid tucked under a straw cowboy hat.

I felt like her greenhorn sidekick, bouncing up and down on my saddle. Fruit I knew, but only rich people rode horses in the city. I finally was allowed my first pair of jeans to go riding. It was worth it, if only for that.

Even after the summer when she changed like a caterpillar to a butterfly—in reverse as far as I was concerned—she had a style no one came close to. Even when she joined the hoody seniors and wore makeup and short skirts, she walked like an actor in drag through a crowd of extras. What she did, she switched best friends to be with this jazzy gal Charlotte Hogan, the leader of the girl hoods.

Charlotte Hogan was interested in boys, boys, boys. She'd lipstick hearts and initials inside the bathroom stalls. The *C.H.* always stayed the same, but the other initials changed faster than you can sell cranberries in November. I started seeing Dag's name up there, too. The initials inside her heart were always Charlotte's hand-me-downs.

Now, I knew how Dag felt about guys. They weren't very smart. They were too big. They smelled bad. They called her horseface, then tried to cadge rides from her. I told her they weren't all bad, but nothing doing. Then, practically overnight, came the change. How could she stoop to dressing up for them? Going out with them? She couldn't have liked it—because am I right, Bookworm, deep down inside you know when a woman's one of your own. Even in ribbons and lace, you still know. There was only one reason I could imagine Dag changing her tune. She did it to get close to Charlotte.

Speaking of ribbons, we have a couple of gift baskets to make up. One for a customer, but I want you to do one for Fred—he can't come by these days. HIV. Yeah, I miss his dumb jokes. I'll take it by on my way home, catch him up on the neighborhood dish.

I really missed Dag. She didn't shoot hoops anymore, she skipped school half the time, she didn't even go by the stables. I know because I went over there and talked to Jack. "Like that," he says, snapping his fingers. "She's here one day and gone the next. If you ask me, she's in love."

In 1954 I'd never heard the word *gay*. All I knew was to laugh at people like Fred, with their antiques and poodles, and to laugh at women truck drivers. But now my best friend Dag had a crush on Charlotte the size of a prize-winning watermelon. I could see it in her eyes, in the way she'd bend to talk to the girl, like a guy would his date. It got my wheels turning, am I right? Dag went on dates to get close to Charlotte, maybe they doubled. Maybe she liked making out with boys who'd touched Charlotte. Maybe her and Charlotte compared notes, and things got steamy between them. Maybe they practiced. Maybe I wished I could get steamy with Dag.

You know how it is, having those queer shadows in your head, knowing this stuff, and running as far as you can from it? Hey, nice basket, Bookworm. Add some cherries to Fred's, will you? We used to see who could spit the pits farthest. I hate that he's so sick. Sometimes I hate what life brings to us, take it or leave it, no money-back guarantees.

One day in June I go into homeroom late—Dag and Charlotte and me were in Sister Adelaide's room—and there's this whispering, giggling, and staring going on. I'm surprised to see Dag and Charlotte aren't in the middle of the ruckus. Charlotte's looking at her nails, the floor, out the window, lips thin and tight as a customer who found a worm in her apple. Dag's bright pink in the face, scribbling in a notebook, looking more than ever like she's in costume for a stage part that's going to end. Charlotte's not talking to Dag. These two are like Siamese strawberries since September, am I right? Sister Adelaide comes in then and slaps her ruler against the desk twice to quiet the class, but you can feel the excitement like slow boiling water in a canning pot.

Later, in gym, I crowd into the bathroom with all the other curious girls. Somebody'd wiped out the boy's initials in Charlotte's heart and wrote *C.H. loves D.A.*

Maybe we were innocent parochial school girls, but somebody drew another heart next to the first one and wrote *C.H. Licks D.A.* That was the only sex ed lesson I ever had in Sister school. I can still hear the squeals as one girl explained it to the next.

"Down there, it means," says one of the hoody girls. "Ugh," she adds to cover her excitement.

Was it true, what they were saying? Or was it that pack instinct, turning on the one they sensed was different? I didn't see Charlotte talk to Dag the rest of that week. If she loved Dag, she wasn't abdicating her throne for her. By Friday, Charlotte, in her tight plaid skirt and girl's blouse over her pointy bra, had won back her place as the queen of the hoods. Dag didn't make it to that last week of school.

I craned my neck watching for Dag at graduation, feeling my tassel bob around like her braid. At practice she'd been assigned the seat next to mine. Finally, as the school orchestra finishes tuning, she marches in the door. Sister Adelaide tries to stop her, but Dag brushes her off and climbs over me to sit. Sister Adelaide reaches across me to tug on her arm. I thought it was because Dag had missed the last week's classes.

Dag wouldn't budge. The principal started her speech. The Sister gave up. Dag passed me a note. *I'm sorry, Henny,* I read. *I must have lost my mind all year. I guess I didn't want to be me for a while there, but I learned my lesson.* Then she opened her robe and I saw why Sister Adelaide was so red-faced furious. Dag was wearing her horse clothes to graduation, the jeans and the plaid shirt and boots. She smelled of stable. Delicious.

You're cheering already? Wait till I tell you this. Because of being tallest, Dag's the last girl to go up. I've got my diploma, and I'm leaving the stage. I hear a gasp, and I look back to watch Dag accept her diploma in drag. You understand, I didn't see it like that then. I stop on the stairs when I see she's tossed her mortarboard and is pulling her cowboy hat out from under her wide-open robe.

Can you believe it? In 1954? She was telling those girls they were right; she was what she was and proud.

Well, I'm stock-still as she comes down the stairs, staring, ready to protect my head when the bomb falls. She grabs my arm and lets out a whoop, dragging me up the aisle with her. She doesn't turn into our row of seats, though. She says, "I have to get back to work at the stable. Jack hired me full-time. Come by and see me." And she was gone.

I wanted with all my heart to fly out that door after her, but my family's in the audience, and we have to make a living in the neighborhood. I decided it could wait a day.

It waited a couple of weeks, to tell you the truth. See, I wasn't ready to come out. That would take a few more years. Sure, we went riding a few times. When she brought a girlfriend around to the shop, I was confused. As much as I admired Dag, I was scared to be seen with a woman who always wore jeans and had a girl on her arm.

But, like I say, Kathy ran into her the other day. Kathy used to be one of those girls on Dag's arm. So things have come full swing. Dag bought the stable from Jack. I think it's time to go on out there with a major fruit basket and tell Dag the end of my story. With Kathy on my arm.

Originally published in *Cactus Love* (Naiad Press, 1994)

THE EASTER FEAST

The Swashbuckler: Epilogue

The sun once danced for joy on warm Easter mornings. Frenchy remembered waking at dawn, filled with excitement. For days ahead the girls and mothers on her block readied their pastels, their navy blues, their patent leather shoes. Frenchy, thrilled by the holiday vibrations in the air, had been anxious to stay outside playing and anxious, at the same time, to be alone with her Easter basket of fancy-colored foils nestled in green cellophane grasses.

But that was a long time ago. Today was her thirtieth Easter, and somewhere along the line the holiday's suns grew weaker, dimmed to what she could see through the dirty subway window. She and Mercedes were crossing the East River, traveling all the way out to Jessie and Mary's home in Queens. The water was gray and lumpy, with none of the sparkle a full sun could give it. There were no girls of any age showing off in the Queens neighborhoods the train passed over—the day was too cold. The neighborhoods themselves looked wan, as if exhausted by winter.

Frenchy longed for the sun today. For the return of the giddy excitement that swept her beyond life's downers. She needed badly to shake this depression, but she couldn't quite name what bothered her. She reached for Mercedes's hand as they left the subway.

"Hey, lover, welcome back."

"I was thinking," said Frenchy, still dreamy.

They saw their bus and sprinted for it.

"Cold as hell," said Mercedes, shuddering as she pressed up close to Frenchy on the rear seat.

"That's what you get for dressing like some college kid," Frenchy said, as she admired Mercedes's button-down collar, burgundy crew neck, and black Members Only jacket. Her own blanket-lined denim jacket, corduroy collar, and black turtleneck sweater were more substantial, especially with the men's silk scarf Mercedes gave her at Christmas.

Mercedes's grin was roguish. "And how about you?" she teased back. "Us butches don't get cold, right?"

Frenchy pulled a comb from her back pocket and swept it through her black hair. "Right," she said. "I guess that makes you femme."

"Oh yeah? See if I sleep without pajamas tonight."

"I never met pajamas I couldn't get past."

They jostled each other with affection. The sun broke through the clouds, and on every street corner they passed, children crept into the brightness as if testing cold water. They left the bus and walked the remaining blocks to Jessie and Mary's, winding their way through girls skipping rope and boys exhibiting yo-yo skills. They appeared like multicolored blossoms on the sidewalks of College Point.

But then she remembered the night before, and as they waited for their friends to open the door, gray clouds drifted overhead.

Her impulse was to take Mercedes's hand, to hold on tight until the comfort of that touch drove away her stomach's distress.

Last night was perfect for lovemaking. They were rested, in fine moods, dined by candlelight. Mercedes turned her on as much as ever. But after she made love to Mercedes and Mercedes approached her, she resumed fretting. It wasn't that she didn't like what Mercedes did, or how she did it. As always, Mercedes was the best. But last night, after many attempts to let herself go, after getting so close, after clearing her head time after time only to have some disruptive thought invade it, Frenchy pretended to come. It wasn't the first time; she couldn't disappoint Mercedes that way. And didn't know what was wrong with herself.

To stop coming with a lover—what did it mean? With Pam, orgasm used to be a given. But she was never as connected with Pam Sternglantz as with Mercedes. And with Mercedes there were no problems at all. But now, when it was plain that they belonged together forever, Frenchy was no longer able to give herself up to Mercedes. And she wanted to badly.

The door swung open. "Boy, it's good to see you." Jessie threw her arms around both of them at once and talked behind them all the way up the stairs, as if the force of her words could make the climb easier.

Jessie lived with Mary on the third floor of a big old brown house owned by Mary's parents. On the first two floors lived Mary's sisters with their families.

Mary wore a ruffled apron, blue eye shadow, and gold rings. "You met Mario's wife Lisa before, didn't you?" she asked. Mario was her brother, the cop. The rest of the family was at Disney World for the Easter vacation.

"Help yourselves," said Mary, and with a sweeping gesture set a tray of crisply brown turnover-like pastries on the coffee table. Lisa, a tiny woman with soft brown hair and a sweet smile, picked one up and offered it to Frenchy. She bit into it and was surprised by the smooth and soft spinach and cheese filling, rich with garlic.

"What're you drinking, guys?" asked Jessie. Then, too excited to wait for them to notice, she exclaimed, "How do you like my new bar, Frenchy?"

She was queasy from the spinach pastry, or maybe it was excitement at celebrating Easter dinner with her oldest pal or anxiety about her sex life with Mercedes. She left the others to join Jessie. "It's very sharp," she commented.

"You don't sound impressed," said Jessie with a frown. "Remember not being able to get a drink anywhere but the Village? Waiting in line to use the bathroom?" She arranged and rearranged cut glass decanters on the swing-out counter. "This is the life, Frenchy."

The furniture, Frenchy noticed, was still shrouded in stiff plastic protective covers as it was when she first saw it several years before. "I am impressed," she said. "Your own bar. Jess, you've come up in the world."

Now Jessie could be modest. "Nah, this was only to celebrate my promotion to foreman."

"You're kidding me. Their first ever woman foreman? Go ahead and let me have a Seven and Seven so I can toast you."

They clinked glasses and went across the room to the rest of the group.

Mercedes smiled the way she always did when she was about to tell Frenchy how much she loved her. The twinge returned to Frenchy's gut. What if she found out Mercedes was faking it? She'd want to go off to some dark corner and shrivel up from shame that she couldn't make

Mercedes fly. Even worse, that Mercedes hid it from her. Lies were love killers, and faking was lying.

Without knocking, Mario entered the apartment. "Sorry I'm late," he said as he strode, short and hairy and barrel-chested, straight to the bar.

"Help yourself, why doncha?" Jessie said.

Only when he'd mixed and taken the first swallow of a Scotch and water did Mario turn to his wife. "Hi, chickadee," he said, lifting her clear off the floor in a hug.

Mary laughed. "How come you never do that to me?" she asked Jessie.

Mario poked Jessie. "Because you don't work out at the gym every day, right Jess?"

"Mario," Jessie said in response, "this is Mercedes and Frenchy."

Frenchy solemnly shook his hand. "Glad to meet you." She wasn't at all certain she was. Cops busted gays. What was she doing having Easter dinner with one? At least he wasn't in uniform.

As the others talked, she wandered to the window, pulled away by her dilemma. Was it easier, being straight? No, they went through troubles, but at times like this it was hard not to think maybe being gay was wrong, living the life too hard. Not that she had a choice—or wanted one.

Clouds floated across the sky like puffs of spring to come.

"You okay?" Mercedes joined her.

"Of course. Why wouldn't I be?"

Mercedes narrowed her eyes. "I don't know. But ever since last night—"

Panic clenched her insides like a fist. "I'm remembering being a kid at Easter. Maman made me special dresses, always tight at the waist, itchy at the neck, longer than anyone else's."

"Likewise. We called it Domingo de Resurrección. The old people celebrated all week, but Sunday was the worst. I couldn't wait for church and the big dinner to end, so I could go out and play."

Mario was ranting about the Yankees. Mercedes couldn't stay away when they were maligned.

Frenchy refilled her glass. What was messing with her head?

Out the window, the small girls in pastels wheeled doll carriages with Easter bunnies for babies. Mercedes was like her—after dinner she'd be out on the street with the boys swinging a broomstick at a Spaldeen.

Overwhelming cooking smells stormed out of the kitchen. Frenchy was too upset to eat, but her mouth watered.

Mercedes came to her. "Mario's beat is out at Queens College, where Lydia wants to study." Lydia, Mercedes's daughter, was spending this Easter back in Harlem with her grandmother.

Frenchy laughed. "At least we know she'll be safe."

Mario, after his fast start, drank 7Up. "I always need something to relax me when I get home," he said, then winked. "Being as how we're in company today, I thought the hostesses might appreciate me downing a drink more than watching a long cuddle with Lisa."

Once more, Frenchy was drawn out of herself enough to laugh. "That's what I love after a long day at the A&P."

"A cuddle with Lisa?" Mercedes asked, joking around.

"With you," Frenchy replied in a soft voice.

"What do you do?" asked Lisa.

Mercedes eyes teased. "With Frenchy?"

"Head cashier," Frenchy answered with pride.

Mario said, "That's a rough job. I used to clerk at Grand Union. You get the crazies who think they've been cheated out of a buck."

It wasn't often that Frenchy found someone who knew to be impressed by her job. She sat up straighter. "I'd rather do that than walk a beat. That's dangerous." She started to like Mario, cop or not.

"Ride," corrected Mario. "Me and my partner ride around Queens. But that's not always safe either. The other day this drunk rammed into us at an intersection. My partner's stuck in one of those whiplash collars."

Mercedes said, "I saw scads of that kind of injury at the hospital this winter." She shook her head. "It was all the ice on the streets."

"Are you a nurse?" asked Lisa.

"Nuclear-med tech," Mercedes answered.

"Even your job isn't safe," said Mario. "Watch you're not exposed to that radiation you use."

Lisa sneaked up behind Mario and hugged him. His face lit with pleasure. "This one insists on working, too, even though I offered to pay her to stay home and look pretty for me."

"I love kids too much," Lisa said. "I work at the Head Start Program."

"When you have a batch of your own, you might want to stay home," Frenchy said.

Mercedes's hand shot to Frenchy's knee, as if to stop her. Frenchy looked at her. "What?"

"That's okay," Mario said. "We're past hiding it or beating ourselves with wet pasta over it." Lisa slipped around and sat next to him. "We can't have kids. My fault. I was born broken." He laughed and put his arm around Lisa. "After I met with the doctor, I was so ashamed I didn't tell Lisa for over a month. It got so bad I wouldn't look her in the eye."

Lisa put her arm all the way around Mario's waist. "I was so relieved he wasn't leaving me, which is what I thought by then, that I realized he was much more important to me than babies."

"We've been closer than ever since I spilled my guts." He kissed Lisa on the forehead. "Man, what I almost did to us by holding out on her like that."

"Chow time," Jessie shouted. She bore a steaming, sweet-smelling ham glossy with glaze, decorated by slices of pineapples. Behind her came Mary with a glass casserole dish.

Mario said, "Wowsie-kazowie, baked ziti, my fave."

The flat was hot with cooking fumes. While the others watched Jessie carve the ham, Frenchy, stomach cramping, wandered once more to the window.

The block was nearly empty of children now; they were inside, like her, anticipating a holiday feast. A wave of unutterable loneliness swamped her as she looked down at the deserted street. Only an aged woman in a long black coat and kerchief, hauling an empty shopping cart, moved under the cloud-covered sky.

Gloomy, Frenchy worried the woman was a lesbian who ended up, as the straight world promised, alone and destitute in her old age because she lost her last lover by holding back an important part of herself. Mario faced up to the truth. There were plenty of times Frenchy lied to girls about this and that—was it too late for her to learn to be honest?

Mercedes caught her with tears in her eyes. "What's going on, Frenchy? We've been calling you to the table. You catch my crazies? Or are you getting your period?"

As a matter of fact, thank goodness, she was due for her period. Mercedes, who took meds to control the crazies of her past, was studying her eyes. Frenchy wanted to stay safe in that gaze forever, and said, "I guess it's my preperiod blues."

Mercedes led her to the table, now a forest of dishes.

Mary held up two golden-brown loaves of bread braided around hard-boiled eggs still in their shells. "These," Mary said proudly, "are my first Easter breads."

"Do you eat them?" asked Frenchy.

"If you have an Italian wife," Jessie said, "you eat everything on the table, or she's hurt to the core." There was an edge to her laugh.

Mary, defending herself, said, "Or if you're an Italian kid. Mamma used to get so hurt over Mario's picky eating."

"And," Mario said, "neither of us married Italian girls."

"Remember what Pop said about not marrying an Italian."

Lisa and Mario chanted along with Mary. "No wonder you can't have kids."

Mario laughed as if on cue. "Did he ever shit a brick when I told him it was my fault. Then Mamma pipes up—"

Mary supplied the punch line, "You never did eat enough."

In the midst of the laughter Mary said, "Mangia!" and they began.

But Frenchy's attention wandered. Why? Her troubled brain went on and on as she ate, even as she joked and made conversation. What brought on this snag? She wanted Mercedes more than anything on earth. Back when she made up her mind that Mercedes was the one for her, she ignored the warnings about butches not going together and convinced Mercedes to give them a chance. Neither of them was any less butch; neither had turned femme.

Laughter sounded around the table. Mercedes, mouth full of fried peppers, had quickly realized they were hot. "Holy shit," she yelled when she was able.

"Some hot-blooded Latin you are." Jessie's face, after a second helping, was red and shiny with sweat. She unbuttoned her cream-colored pants. She'd discarded her matching jacket while carving. "*Ohhh*," she groaned when the main course was over, "I ate too much."

Mario laughed. "You always say that, Jess. Why don't you stop when you're full?"

"You leave Jessie alone," Mary said, like some stern grandmotherly figure. "What's wrong with a healthy appetite?"

"Healthy? She's getting fat. She's proving her love to you the way I refused to please Mamma. And the way you did." He flung a cork coaster, Frisbee-like, toward his sister. "The first thing I remember in school, some kid comes up to me and says, *It's the fat girl's brother. What's-a-matter, Bones, she eat all yours?* I slaughtered him."

"I never heard another remark about my weight," Mary boasted.

Jessie looked earnest. "Is that why you like to see me eat? So you'll know I love you?"

"Don't be silly," snapped Mary, rising to clear the table.

Jessie's patter thinned but revived with praise when Mary triumphantly appeared with Italian pastries. "From Giamoni's Bakery," announced Jessie. "Only the best for our friends and family."

Later, Lisa and Mary moved to the kitchen to do dishes, refusing help from Mercedes and Frenchy. They joined a somnolent Mario to watch a football game on TV.

Mercedes stretched out on the couch, her head in Frenchy's lap. Frenchy gently, almost reverently, stroked her dark short hair, her soft dark skin. She watched night seep into the sky through the window across the room. It was still light enough, though, for the young ones to be out after dinner, shrieking, running, and dirtying their clothing with abandon. Her depression was lifting. Here was Mercedes, safe, her lover, her companion, all that she could want in a woman.

And around them, immobilized by their holiday feast and the movement of the small, brightly colored figures on the screen, were people no different from them when it came to stumbling blocks in their lives.

Lisa and Mario couldn't have children, but went on anyway, maybe loving each other better because of the trouble they'd been through. Jessie, and Mary—for years they'd been having problems around weight, and there was the time Mary had a crush on her art teacher. Every couple, it seemed, went through its tests, maybe lots of them, before passing from being in love to loving for good.

What made her think she was so special, that she could fix this problem all by herself? How dumb could she get, assuming Mercedes was going to split because something was wrong.

Mercedes stirred. Frenchy held tight to her. When had she last enjoyed such safety and love? When she was her mother's little girl in pastels, playing in the sunny streets. What happened to that joy, that love, besides growing up and choosing colors different from her mother's? She smiled. She wasn't going to lose this woman's love.

Mercedes squeezed her leg affectionately and got up to use the bathroom. Frenchy relished her butchy walk, not a man's walk at all, but a womanly body claiming its rightful place. She rose to open the window wider, to breathe in the cool air off the East River. The kids outside one by one answered their mothers' calls and fled the gathering dark for well-lit homes.

Why was she resurrecting all the old hurt of her mother's rejection? Why did she expect Mercedes to turn on her? Mercedes didn't fall for the child in pastels, but for the grown-up dyke Frenchy became.

Mercedes returned to her side. Frenchy leaned in to her. "I love you," she said, with a smile that came freely and warmed her.

"Hey," Mercedes kidded, "my girlfriend's back."

The sun had set, but it would dance many other days. And she owed it to both of them to talk openly to Mercedes on the bus going home.

Originally published in *Home in Your Hands* (Naiad Press, 1986)

MARY'S GARDEN

As I looked down the long foyer of her apartment, it was difficult to pick Mrs. O'Broin out from her accumulation of bric-a-brac. I was sure she had a souvenir there from every tenant who had ever moved out or died or parted unknowingly from some treasure. China animals faded on the windowsills. A bowlegged bulldog doorstop peeked from under a faded tablecloth. A procession of unlit gold-tasseled floor lamps stood sentry along the hallway to the great desk that severed tenants from Mrs. O'Broin's living quarters. On the desk stood the proudest of the lamps, one with a green glass shade like an upside-down bowl that once contained the clutter.

"Emmie," she'd say to herself when I went to pay the rent, "where'd you put it now?" Or she'd say before she found the rent pad or the disassembled ballpoint pen, "That wild creature of a granddaughter of mine's been into the desk and upset everything." By that time, I'd be stumbling on bits of overlaid carpet, backing toward the door, nodding while Mrs. O'Broin's voice continued and her tall white body shrank with distance, becoming, as I closed the door, a dusty, brittle fixture among all the others.

My apartment was over hers on the second floor. I had a big front window, rounded at the top like the two smaller windows that flanked it, and this triad of glass lured me from my own desk too often. I watched Mrs. O'Broin on her thin, stiff legs wobble determinedly down the courtyard steps past the splendor of Mary's long shallow gardens. She cared for the gardens herself now that Mary was dead; she surveyed their half wild growth as she passed them on her way to the bruised white car rattling at the end of the walk, in a parking spot reserved for her by tradition, not law, and her daughter at the wheel.

"Emmie ain't so young as she used to be," I'd hear Mrs. O'Broin explain to herself in summer when my side windows strained for the city breeze. And off she'd go, sailing sluggishly through the hot streets to the grocer who had known her since her husband, and then Mary, kept the building shining like a great mansion.

One day during the second summer I lived in Mrs. O'Broin's building, when the air in my high-ceilinged apartment got too fetid to breathe and the typewriter ink made me nauseous, I decided on a walk to clear my head. I took the elevator on the chance it had kept some cool air inside. It passed the lobby and went to the basement.

I have always been deathly afraid of basements and cowered in the corner of the elevator, jumping when Mrs. O'Broin wobbled inside. Her hands were covered with soot, and she clasped to her smudged bosom three jars filled with silver coins. I at once thought the jars had been buried under ash left in the unused coal furnace.

Mrs. O'Broin wore a cotton housedress, its faded flowers blue and green on a darker green. It sagged to one side of her body, and her hair sagged with it. She looked at me for a moment, a flash of brightness eerily lighting her eyes, and said, "Emmie's done."

"Emmie's done," ran through my head like a buoy's bell in a storm and sent a shudder down my back as cold as the first splash of water the wind raises on the sea. Before the elevator door shut all the way, I stepped out of it and walked as briskly as I could to the basement door. The elevator closed behind me and began to rise before I was outside. Feeling foolish, I wondered if Mrs. O'Broin guessed that she'd scared me.

I knew, of course, that it was only being in an elevator and a basement that made me feel so strangely frightened. It was a fear I remembered whole and unchanged from my childhood. Mrs. O'Broin was a pretty strange lady anyway, I assured myself as I struck off down the hill toward the intertwining back streets on the edge of a poor neighborhood. The heat must have gotten to her, I thought, along with the memories that must always be with a widow who stays on. Especially in Mrs. O'Broin's case this would be true, as she also took on Mary's work, the work Mary, in turn, had taken over when Mrs. O'Broin threw her husband out. She told me when that ninny of a husband went, the landlord ordered her out. She admitted to him she'd been doing the bulk of the work herself. She swore on her mother's grave she'd keep the place up, and demanded, after all these years she'd put into the building, that he give her and her poor daughter and the baby a chance.

The landlord, in the face of so much adamant womanhood, let her stay, and his visits were so infrequent that he never noticed when Mary arrived and took over. "My own daughter was like her father," Mrs. O'Broin said. "She never helped out at all."

But Mrs. O'Broin forgave her because almost as soon as her daughter was old enough to be of use, she'd had a girl baby of her own. Forgave her except when their screaming fights rose up the long disused dumbwaiter shaft to my apartment. After one of the fights, the car, which had lain idle since Mary's departure, was put back into use. The daughter found her purpose in life: She would be her mother's chauffeur. She would not go into the grocery store but would load and unload purchases. She refused to dress up and attend mass, but she waited faithfully outside the church, as well as the doctor's office, the dentist's. Mrs. O'Broin never learned to drive herself.

While I lived in that apartment, I often walked the area. I'd lose myself in a maze of cobbler shops, pizza parlors, and corner delis, noting the mad, fantastic architecture bred from poverty and high hopes.

Grandfathers, gnarled and brown as their stogies, worked the earth, raising the colors of their old lands out of it, hosing down tomato plants so that the greens and dull oranges and finally bright reds shone without the dust of the city on them. Here and there a chicken or rooster ran loose in a yard.

At the edge of a neighborhood a group of African American preteen girls jumped rope, chanting, *White lady, white lady, coming my way. White lady, white lady, go far away.* A small boy with a missing front tooth grinned as he flung pebbles my way. I turned back, full of sadness for the children, for myself, but the outside air was so much cooler than sweltering over my typewriter, I continued walking down Remington Street's long hill.

There she was, almost as I expected: Mrs. O'Broin in a long black dress that hung below a shorter gray coat, too warm for this weather, but her best coat. A prim black hat like a lacquered crab shell clung to her hair. Her tiny gray curls were as limp as the black veil atop the hat was stiff. In her hand a large black patent leather pocketbook on a plastic handle pulled her down to the left, while her slip fell with each step beneath her dress hem to the right. She had no nylons on long, shocking white calves, black-and-blue with bruises. She wore her usual practical oxfords. I expected her to enter Holy Rosary Church or the parish house next door. But no, she stopped at neither. That buoy rang the words *Emmie's done.*

I was glad to be out on Remington in the summer. I worked nights and walked this very same mile ten times a week, once in a blizzard, before the plows arrived. When I made it home the next morning, there was Mrs. O'Broin gingerly shoveling at the front steps. "Heaven help us if someone falls, sues Mr. Greater Than God Himself, and old Emmie didn't shovel."

I reached for the tool to take a turn. After several minutes she took it back, saying, "I can't stand by here watching someone else do my work. Give it here and scoot inside where it's warm and dry before you catch your death of cold. If Emmie can't do it, then she deserves to be booted out. And I'm afraid my time is coming, so I might as well do it while I can."

I am not one to argue with pride, and exhausted myself from working and walking, I left her there with her shovel and the daughter suddenly in the doorway. The daughter, in her nightgown, red hair hanging greasily onto her shoulders, shouted for her mother to get inside or she'd have a heart attack and then where would her poor grandchild live.

That evening, as my breakfast smells mingled with everyone else's dinner, more snow hung suspended over the city, ready to fall right smack onto Mrs. O'Broin's clean swept steps.

And here I was, in the summer heat, still worrying about the old lady as she plugged away down the hill ahead of me. Her walk, on those gangly legs, became more uneven as she reached the steepest part of the decline. It crossed my mind that she might be tipsy, but I'd only seen her in that state once, on another snow-filled evening about a year before the blizzard.

I'd gone to the lobby after my twilight breakfast to see if the mail got through. There stood Mrs. O'Broin on the inside of the double doors watching the snow come down, holding a small tooth glass of amber stuff she twirled in her hands. "Mary's been gone a year," she said. "I guess that means she is dead, though I never saw her body again. Twenty years by my side." She looked at me accusingly. "Twenty years and they took her body from me on a night like this on a stretcher through the snow."

I was afraid she would cry right there in the doorway while I watched her. "Are you all right, Mrs. O'Broin?"

"I'll never be all right till I'm at my Mary's side, and I don't care who knows it, though I think you understand," she said, giving my jeans, sweatshirt, and short hair the once-over. "She was the best friend a woman ever had." Mrs. O'Broin turned away from me. "Worked herself to death. Had a back as broad as a man's and was willing to use it. When Mr. O'Broin went, she filled his shoes five times over. And never lifted a hand to hurt me. The best thing I ever did was to let her buy my drink that night at Maloney's restaurant. And they took her from me. Back to Springfield to be buried with her family, they said. Well, they didn't want her when she was alive, says I. I loved her in her men's shirttails and out of them."

She swayed a bit, and I reached out to steady her, holding the loose flesh on her upper arm and settling the bony elbow in my palm. I'd never suspected Mrs. O'Broin and surly, sooty Mary of being lovers.

"I only wish I'd known her from the start. But now I intend to know her through eternity, God willing." She shook her arm free of my support and waved me to the mailboxes. "You can look if you want, Curly, but he never came. Not a soul came up the walk I cleared but yourself this morning. Nor went down it. Once the snow, and worse than this, wouldn't keep folks in. Now it's any excuse to do a bad job or none at all."

She stood there like a tall weathered farmer, humbly respecting nature's creations, proudly surveying her own toil, tears falling all the while. Her grief brought my own loneliness plowing into my heart like old snow, heavy and cold. I left her there before I cried, too.

Walking down the hot hill behind her now, I supposed Mrs. O'Broin thought she deserved a drink that night, on the anniversary of Mary's death and kidnapping by straight relatives. At Holy Rosary, I ran my hand along the rusting fence spikes to hold myself back. Mrs. O'Broin crossed at a *WALK* sign and disappeared under the shadow of the highway. Why wasn't her daughter ferrying her across town?

On the other side of the bridge over the thruway she stopped for another light and stood straight and still at the curb.

I continued on as she passed the new police station. She stopped for a moment, and I thought she would go in, but she hesitated by all the police motorcycles grouped pell-mell in front of the station. She appeared to examine each black-and-white oversized machine before going up to one and touching the white bar between the handles and the seat. I had a vision of her, like a Disney heroine, flinging herself onto one and riding off out of the city, free of everything, including her sanity. The door to the station opened. She hurried away at the sight of two officers.

Down the hill she continued, bag swinging one way, clothes

hanging the other, past the old homes taken over by lawyers, past the shoddy Chinese restaurant, past the welfare hotel where the daughter threatened to move if Mrs. O'Broin stopped supporting her. The street was deserted in the noontime heat except for myself and Mrs. O'Broin, lurching toward Main Street.

I thought that was her destination. Again, I was wrong. Right on she went, past the dirt-splashed windows of the coin shop, the restaurant supplier, the upholsterer, the corner spa. Across the street she went, picking up speed. Her profile was toward me, and I could see her mouth working, talking to herself. At the last of the hill, she disappeared around the corner. I feared I'd miss her rushing into a dark doorway, but she was jaywalking diagonally toward the entrance to the railroad station.

The buoy's bell rang again, and I shivered. The station was a great dark mass spilled down the hill from the city. The sun shone behind it, making it the blacker. The building and tracks were set high. Underneath were indoor and outdoor passages, with pools of shadow and shafts of light. Staircases led to either end of the station, and a ramp was set in the middle. Many a time I had climbed that ramp myself, lugging what I owned, going on some great journey, but always coming back. And now Mrs. O'Broin was disappearing from the sunlight, climbing the steel steps, leaning heavily on the rail, her heels clanging dully and slowly on the gratings.

This I had never considered. Where could the old woman, never having visitors, never visiting, be off to?

I knew the wooden door at the top of the stairs was heavy and that every draft in the old station managed to get caught inside to make getting in or out a struggle for anyone. I ran up the ramp and beat her to the door, pulling it open for her. She stepped inside, looking at me and thanking me, but showing no sign of recognition.

I almost went to the ticket window with her but stopped myself in time and sat on an old straight-backed wooden bench, looking at the tall, tall ceiling and its pigeons. Then I was up off the bench cursing myself because I'd never discover where she was going if I sat there like the head mourner.

And I was too late. All I saw was a hand pull rolls of coins inside the window. She had her ticket and was rushing to the stairs that led under the tracks to the northbound side. I took parallel stairs closer to me, but there was no mystery. She sat on a bench under a shading ledge, waiting for her train.

I was being foolish. What was so strange about an old lady taking a trip? I bent over the rail that faced the parking lot and the harbor. Nothing moved in the lot. Cars baked in the sun. There was a barge in the river going slowly, slowly somewhere. Had Mrs. O'Broin considered stealing a police motorcycle to get to her destination?

The loudspeaker announced the train's arrival and destinations. As soon as I heard it, I knew. Springfield, where Mary was buried. Of course. Springfield was the only place Mrs. O'Broin wanted to be.

The train moved noisily away, shaking the station to its foundations. I waved because it seemed someone should. Surely the old lady was only off on a visit. I knew damn well she wouldn't be back.

On my way home it seemed I was climbing a whole side of the city, going home to an empty apartment.

Had she gone to mourn Mary, to join her? What, in her overburdened old mind, did she want from her lover's grave in Springfield, from that sleeping mound? Would she call across the space of death to her lover and reach her, pushed to it because she found no comfort from this life and no one but me, a dyke stranger, with whom to share her grief?

I looked now across the thruway at my three windows over Mary's gardens and felt alone, desolate. "Emmie's gone," I said. The hillside had become another sad chasm in my life.

I resolved to start gardening myself. First there would be a transplant to a place where I'd have something more than Emmie had. Someplace lesbians were. I dreamed, as I trudged up the hillside, of founding a City of Dykes with a museum like Emmie's foyer to house bits and pieces of our lives and a great park called Mary's Garden. Suddenly, I became the head mourner, mourning Emmie O'Broin and Mary and a way of life, a solitary confinement we all suffered as lesbians.

Originally published in *Old Dyke Tales* (Naiad Press, 1984)

THE FIRES OF WINTER SOLSTICE

The fire, thought LilyAnn Lee, who was six feet tall even without her firefighter's boots, could have been worse. A big old warehouse full of furniture, an alert watchman who'd smelled the smoke despite the flask in his pocket.

It had been clear to her right away, from the smell and pattern, that the fire was electrical in origin. As soon as they controlled the flames, they began the tedious job of searching its origin and making certain it spread no farther. This was the kind of work that demanded only half of LilyAnn's mind. She drifted above the garbagy wet smoke smell, above the splintered furniture, above her light on the wall as she excavated for signs of burning wiring.

Now and then a distinct whiff of burnt cedar reached her from that stack of hope chests she and Horrigan had wet down for fear of sparks. A smell like the cedar they'd burned in Alley Pond Park last year for the solstice ritual. Her friends from the Women's Food Co-op had urged her to return this year, but damn, she'd been uncomfortable.

All those white girls, she thought, those earnest women with their dead-serious incantation of the Goddess. There was something thin and pale about their ceremony. They gathered in circles like doubting, hopeful supplicants who prayed extra hard to get past a sense of make-believe. The woman who'd learned rituals on the West Coast seemed intense and desperate, determined to perform her office exactly right, not to let any wavering spirit she called on flee in the tendrils of smoke that rose from the tiny illicit fire in the park. She wondered if Dawn and Goldie, the other sisters who'd been there, felt strange, too. Would they go back into the night to sit in this year's cold circle?

She remembered, as she worked along the wall and checked

periodically on big beefy Horrigan across from her, the promise of light in the women's song.

> *You can't kill the spirit*
> *She's like a mountain*
> *Bold and strong*
> *She goes on and on.*

It was getting smoky again. Had Horrigan found something? She couldn't see its source. She put her mask on, breathing easier, seeing somewhat better, and waved to Horrigan, who didn't seem bothered by the smoke yet and ignored her signal. He was a temporary partner, an old-timer whose regular partner, like hers, was on vacation. Horrigan was a bigot but close enough to retirement not to buck this pairing with a Black *fire impersonator*, as he called the women in the department.

She peered through the smoke to the wires she followed. Upstairs more of the company searched, heavy-booted, but as carefully. Sometimes she felt closer to these guys her life depended on than to the women at the Co-op. She partied with the women, sat in meetings with them, joined their ritual circles, but that click wasn't there, the click of bonding in the face of immediate danger. Of bonding in another way with Dawn and Goldie by virtue of the common danger of their dark skins in a white country.

While she was drawn to women's spirituality, found it closer than anything else she could accept, it didn't move her anywhere as meaningfully as the mass prayer at a firefighter's funeral, or the firehouse Christmas tree. Didn't warm her even as much as the static-filled radio insistently filling their living quarters with carols. All the firefighters, women and men, talked *bah, humbug* and complained about Christmas Day duty, but the women brought in baked goods, the guys gave out cartons of cigarettes or quarts of liquor.

LilyAnn had made a ritual of reporting for her Christmas shift early with four mince pies and cooking them in the oven at work, filling the firehouse with their smell. Last year a false alarm came in while they baked. LilyAnn forgot the pies until the truck was halfway back to the firehouse. She raced upstairs to the oven. Someone had carefully gauged when the pies were done and turned the oven off, but she'd never been able to find out who.

She was chanting to herself as she worked.

You can't kill the spirit
She's like a mountain
Bold and strong
She goes on and on.

Her back ached from holding her arms up, her legs started to tremble from the strain of walking sideways in a crouch, the mask bit into her face, which had swelled from the heat.

She worked methodically on. Crazy things happened in these old buildings: fire waiting to explode out of a wall where it was trapped, beams so weak the heat and water sent them crashing through the ceiling below. Horrigan was masked now, too—professional, thorough, like her. He'd probably dragged many a Black woman from a burning building. She hoped again that she could rely on him to rescue one more, even, she smiled to herself, this unwelcome peer.

Unlike at Alley Pond where she, Goldie, and Dawn were welcomed excessively warmly, treated with deference, even wooed by the white women who'd learned that a healthy culture was an inclusive one. The burnt cedar smell pulled her back to that night, helped her see that some part of herself longed for, belonged with the women as they lit their candles to light the way through whatever winter brought.

They'd used the cedar for purification, burned it carefully with sentries posted, knowing full well that discovery meant more than a fine for their bonfire surrounded by gallon jugs of water for safety. Celebrating the solstice was pagan; the police or the media could make much of it. Were there still laws on the books against witchcraft?

Her rebellious self would return to the fire circle for certain. Hadn't her people, after all, been as defiant? They'd salvaged their African fires and chants, bits and pieces anyway, from the puritanical wrath they found on these shores. In the solstice circle she'd sat cross-legged, butt cold against the ground, imagining the souls of those ancestors swell and fill and heat her own body till she felt like a great Amazon warrior, one of many, many daughters of daughters, gargantuan and powerful. Was this fantasy or memory, she wondered. Hadn't the Amazons come from Africa, been dark skinned?

You can't kill the spirit
She's like a mountain
Bold and strong
She goes on and on.

The warehouse was silent but for shuffling boots. She mined the world for light and heat, a lot more of both than the women's candles gave. The priestess had instructed each woman to light the candle of the woman to her left and to address the topic of power when the light reached her. How they'd gather power to warm themselves, arm themselves against the frozen wasteland of the patriarchy.

Well, here I am, thought LilyAnn, working with that very patriarchal beast, sure hot enough now. Sweat ran down her face under the mask. She couldn't mop it with her fire-retardant sleeve. Was the work making her hotter, or was she nearing a hidden fire?

She couldn't survive that African sun now, she decided. Her blood had changed. Where did she belong—the cold park, the hot warehouse, neither? The men stomped and chopped, getting noisy with frustration as they searched for embers and sparks that might not be there.

You can't kill the spirit, the women had chanted. Goldie and Dawn looked strained; their voices quavered. Did LilyAnn want this kind of spirit or the uplifting energy church gave her when she still believed? She wanted a spirit that would so move woman after woman that they'd flare into words or song and testify to its strength. Something, anything, but polite turn-taking, awkwardly recited words. It seemed that she, along with the others, chipped and chipped away at the wall between them and their spirituality, bit by bit cut into the plaster that held them back.

Fire can make a sound like a great gulp when it finds enough oxygen to swallow. LilyAnn leaped back from the box-sized inferno that exploded at her. Her training, like blind faith, took her over. She quickly, distinctly, told her radio she needed help even as she turned to summon Horrigan. He'd heard the great gulp, though, and had begun to carefully hurry across to her when another dreaded sound filled her ears. A crack, a tearing, a *No!* of surprise as Horrigan crashed through the floor.

So close to retirement, LilyAnn thought, and turned her back to the spreading flames. She made her way along what she'd later remember as a wall of candles, the flames reflected in her mask's eyepiece, toward Horrigan who clung to a metal pipe over the deep basement below. Cold air gusted up toward the flames, drawn like the firefighters rushing to contain them. She gave them the flames like gifts, trusting their skills.

Earlier she'd noted the placement of posts in the huge room and now ran to one, attached her rope, then treaded softly to the edges of the cold hole. She was big, but lighter than a running man. She prayed to whatever damn spirit would help her that the edge of the floor would hold as she lay, belly down, to crawl and stretch until she reached Horrigan.

She's like a mountain
Bold and strong
She goes on and on

Damn, she thought as she attached the two rings that must hold Horrigan's weight, damn if that vision of herself as an Amazon didn't come back to make her feel trebly strong. And damn, she thought again as Horrigan heaved himself finally over the edge and they scuttled away from the weak floor, damn if that wall of candles wasn't there in her head to guide them through the thick smoke to safety.

They both joined other firefighters to grasp hoses and help drag them close enough to train them on the fire. The hoses were bonds she could see, linking them against danger. Yet the circle whose spirit she hadn't been able to see, touch, believe, had been there for her, too, a song that moved with her, that moved her. She'd never expected to feel the joy that tingled everywhere inside her now in this rank-smelling fire site. And she'd never expected Horrigan's words, nearby on another hose.

"For a minute," he shouted, mask pushed aside, "I thought I might not be around this year to save your mince pies."

Originally published in *Cactus Love* (Naiad Press, 1994)
"Like A Mountain" by Naomi Littlebear, used with permission.

NATURAL FOOD

Lucy was so tied to the earth it seemed to pull her down from every prominence: chin, breasts, lap. The dark maxiskirts she wore dragged her earthward, as if she had to carry them around with her, too. I half expected her to complain about the weight of it all, but she never did. As a matter of fact, above the marionette lines of her face there was a lightness to her eyes, a vision of another way she had been or could be, a glow. Lonely single women, restless married women, followed her home from work after an invitation to supper at her apartment. Three months to the day working in the same department with her, I became one of their number.

It wasn't that she was a gourmet cook or that she put on sophisticated entertainments. She offered laid-back comfort to toiling coworkers. The ritual was simple. You walked in, were pushed affectionately onto the couch, had a cat settled on your lap, a glass of wine or a mug of tea put into your hand, and the TV flipped on. Maybe there were other women there, with whom you talked quietly about nothing of import, or maybe you were alone with Lucy, and under the sound of the TV, you heard Lucy's fuzzy house slippers lisping across the kitchen floor, echoing the slight lisp in her speech.

The inordinately large oak dining room table looked as solid as Lucy. She'd sewn deep green velvet cushions for her odd assortment of chairs, but never covered her table. Guests were asked to light the tapered candles.

Too busy to entertain before dinner, she communicated through the smells that she sent out of the kitchen. What she cooked was simple, natural food that never cloyed, never titillated, always satisfied.

As I dutifully scratched Cobweb—a cat, not a spider—I made

note of the stories on the six o'clock news. Table talk was subdued and secondary to eating, but Lucy liked to hear her visitors' versions of the news because, she said, it was so much more digestible secondhand. I've since sat and watched the news with Lucy and understand now why she said it—she gets as upset as a cat after a bath.

I don't think she's ever missed a peace march, a civil rights rally, a feminist or environmental protest in our city. Whenever possible, she goes to national events. Every time the newscasters speak of warfare or inequality, her face reddens and tears gather. Environmental abuse infuriates her. She is one of those people who won't pick a flower out of respect for its right to live. We need to remember that the earth is our mother, she says, and treat it accordingly.

Dinner for me, then, was a summary of the day's news and a hope that nothing would upset this woman who made me feel so good. After dinner, she would pull out a game or play records. My favorite evenings, she had a certain group of us over who appreciated her collection of rock oldies. The only racket I ever heard in that apartment came from the hi-fi's full volume while "Sally Go 'Round the Roses" revolved on the turntable. Or Timi Yuro's *Make the World Go Away*, the Ronettes, Little Anthony and the Imperials, The Temptations, and The Supremes. She had shelves of 45s from the early 1960s.

Some of her company laughed at the absurdity of the songs or grew melancholy at memories, but not Lucy. I liked that about her. It was a less serious, but somehow deeper side, which was truly moved by the facile lyrics and simple rhythms. Her eyes showed a different spirit, then, one livelier than we were used to, the light in them dancing. The music both enlivened and disturbed her.

It was hard, in those moments, to visualize her walking the halls at work, slow and very solid under the fluorescent lights, a hardworking woman who was an institution in her department. At home, listening to music, she was more like a child skipping. It made me wonder about her past. Who had been in it? Had Lucy looked the same? How did she become who she was now? I resolved to find out one day but kept putting it off, fearing to stir up more than I might want to hear.

The others seemed seldom to wonder about Lucy. She had earned their respect as a worker and friend. If she calmed them as much as she did me, I understand why she wasn't subject to the usual office gossip and judgements. When someone new asked who Lucy was, they were more likely to describe her record collection than her. Newcomers appeared to accept that was all they'd learn. Once in a while I heard how it was a shame Lucy never married, but they knew no man would want this treasure of a woman, with her heavy body and quiet ways.

As for myself, I was a scrawny kid with a lot of crazy curly hair. I liked to think I looked like Bob Dylan because I also wrote songs and played guitar. I planned to stick around until I went on either to a better job or found the clitzpah to hitch to California. Speed was my best friend, and I used it at any excuse. I'm trying to live calmer and slower now, but with speed in me, I was indomitable.

Anyway, this is not about me, but about Lucy. I was drawn to her, like the other women, because she offered comfort and shelter, even though I was different from the other women. I'm a lesbian and the raw, painful side of my life was full of women, not men. But I treated myself and the women I thought I loved as if we were men.

It was the time of the women's movement. I was busy going to this and that meeting or, like Lucy, to demonstrations. She thought meetings were a waste. My love life was an extension of that. I never had less than two lovers on principle and often three or four. Sometimes we all slept together at once.

I was so divided, so torn. I needed speed if only to stay abreast of myself. In consciousness-raising groups, we talked about women being gentle and deep and how we made love more slowly and caringly than men, but I cannot remember one relationship I would call intimate. We might have had our clothes off, or we might have spent a lot of time at the kitchen table dealing with parts of ourselves we saw as faulty, but we seldom touched each other inside. I guess the proof of that is the many women from that period in my life who now see themselves as bisexual or straight. They're still living the same kind of lives, sleeping around, committed to every cause in the world but themselves. Or they've settled with men in some kind of living group that precludes all but the most superficial privacy or intimacy.

But some of us are still out. Still resolved to finding our sources and resources as women. Some are alone and celibate. Some, like me, are in couples. Some continue to find satisfaction in free love.

Back then we were going to set the world on fire. Smash monogamy and patriarchy, and achieve wage parity. Our intentions were good, but we were self-destructive. Unable to see which of our struggles were important and which were meaningless rationalizations for avoiding the real issues.

I went to Lucy's differently from the way I went anywhere else. My visits were probably what kept me alive and sane enough to maintain my pace, though I couldn't see that then. I was poor and used that as a reason—a free meal, although I contributed when I could. Sometimes I went because of what I thought was curiosity, to see inside Lucy.

The last time I visited her it was the two of us. I didn't know until much later whether everyone else canceled, or if Lucy wanted me alone. While I scratched Cobweb and watched the figures jabber on TV, I determined to make Lucy tell me about herself. In my revolutionary-youth arrogance, I wanted to be special to her, the only one she talked to as well as fed.

"Listen," I said after dinner, "I'm tired of you communicating only through your food." I was so arrogant. "Tell me about yourself. I want to know you."

Poor Lucy sat in the recliner across from me with the corners of her mouth lifted out of their frequent droop, smiling at me. Maybe she was amused. I deserved it if she was.

"Curly," she said, with a nervous intake of breath, "I'm gay."

It was my turn to smile. Of course, I thought, surprised at the happy feeling her announcement gave me.

"I'm telling you this because I believe you are, too," she said, and when I nodded with vigor she went on. "I've been living without a lover or any contact with lesbians for a few years now. It's painful for me. When I'm with lesbians, I can't forget what happened to me. In this strange social life I've created, I can show my love for women by cooking but never have to get involved with any of you. I don't mind you knowing about me because I've kept you in the distant circle of my friends, and I think you'll be happy to stay there."

"Can you tell me what happened?"

Her first response was to again lift the corners of her lips, which this time gave the illusion of lifting everything about her. She came to sit beside me on the couch. "Of course."

That close, I felt the full force of her size. She was overwhelmingly present. I moved back and refocused my eyes as she gathered her thoughts. It was the first time I attached any significance to the pinky ring she wore. "Yes," she said with her quiet lisp, "I wear it because I'm a lesbian. I came out when we still did that, wore pinky rings. I'm a femme."

I must have looked surprised because she explained, "I didn't know how not to be. That was how it was. If you were a lesbian, you chose a personal style. I had no idea how to be aggressive, so I settled for the passive role. And I enjoyed it. I went out with two or three different butches, teased my hair, dressed sexy, cooked for them, let them make love to me. They treated me like I was attractive, desirable. I'd finally found a world where I belonged. It didn't even matter that I was big, and I wasn't as fat as I am now," she said, pinching the pale white flesh on her upper arm. "In the gay world, a woman didn't have to conform to the same rigid norms straight women do. A big woman could be alluring, could be loved." She sighed.

"Then I met Gerry. She was a precursor of the women's movement and wasn't into roles. That suited me fine. She respected me. We fell in love and moved in together. I'd never lived with a lover before. I was very happy. Not only was I a lesbian, I was a whole person, nobody's *little woman.*

"In our sixth year, Gerry was laid off from her job. While on unemployment, she became more involved in the women's movement. I couldn't throw myself into it as she did because I was still up to my ears in the peace movement."

I could tell it was getting harder for Lucy to tell the story because her eyes kept clouding with pain. I reached to her soft arm and laid my skinny fingers on it, wondering what the hell kind of comfort I thought I could give this nurturer.

"Gerry started bringing women home. Our place had always been open to friends, but these women crashed. Sometimes for a week or two. And Gerry had this fire in her I'd never seen before. She was in love half the time, plain and simple. She wanted to sleep with them. It took her a long time to tell me, and I might have taken it better if she'd simply said it, if she'd admitted to me and herself that she was very turned on to the movement and the women in it and it made her love them and want to make love to them all. But she didn't tell me."

Lucy shifted away from me in her seat. "She trailed home with elaborate reasoning about opposing the concept of forever and how it would be good for our relationship if we slept with other women. That was the last good laugh I had."

We both sat silent, mourning her loss of laughter.

"I told her I didn't want to sleep with all the lost children and disturbed adults she brought home, that I understood how she felt, but I didn't share in it. I told her we had a very close, warm, secure relationship I cherished and found satisfying. That I thought she was getting her enthusiasm for the movement confused with her love life and responding inappropriately to how she felt. She said I was old-fashioned, and she didn't want to separate her feelings like that."

Of course, Lucy could have been talking about me, quoting me, and I hoped I had never caused anyone such pain with my politics. "It went on," she said. "This argument went on. And still goes on in my head even now."

She turned back to me. The pain had receded from her eyes. "I believe the intimacy two people can achieve is diluted when you try to share it with others. I hope you won't take this as criticism if you're trying to have a lot of relationships yourself, but for me, that's a waste of time and an insult to spirit. Think of the squandered energy we could give to our causes. The human beast is such that when you start sharing those kinds of nurturing, sustaining, absolutely life-giving feelings with whomever excites you, you disturb something in yourself, some balance you need, and you go away drained instead of replenished. As if you'd gotten drunk instead of having a drink of water when you were only thirsty."

I didn't let on that I was feeling criticized. This was her night, and I didn't want to talk about myself. It wrung my heart to hear her voice falter when she said, "We broke up. She went her wild way, as she called it, and I moved here so I didn't have to agonize every time she took a new lover. It didn't last long, though." She laughed, but bitterly. I was surprised Lucy could be bitter. "Gerry decided she didn't like living that way after all, and I heard she settled down in a new couple relationship. I suppose I should feel vindicated, but I feel loss and, despite her rhetoric, rejection."

"Didn't you try to meet someone else?"

She thought for a moment, stooping to lift Cobweb. When he was settled in her roomy lap she explained, "For a long time, I didn't want to meet anyone. I thought it was pretty useless. I couldn't win. Either I was promiscuous like everyone else and wasn't satisfied, or I committed myself to a woman who couldn't be satisfied because she wanted other lovers." Lucy raised her arms in exasperation, startling Cobweb, who had to resettle himself.

She went on, "When I was more rational, I saw I was oversim-plifying things and began to think it would be good for me to meet women, but then I didn't know where to go. I'd gained this weight and felt self-conscious about the bars. Although I knew I'd be accepted, the thought of going out and being seductive in that atmosphere made me feel foolish. I knew I'd be a fat old femme to many of them. And going to women's movement functions meant dealing and struggling around those issues when I wanted to put my political energy into peace. I didn't bother."

"You were caught between two worlds," I said dramatically.

Lucy leaned over, upsetting Cobweb, to muss my curls. "You've got great hair," she said with an appreciative smile. It captivated me, that warm, charming smile, and reminded me of the delectable smells that came from her kitchen. "So here I am. Sergeant Lonelyhearts herself, pouring my heart out to you. Thanks for listening."

I felt funny about the way I was living my life, seeing it through her eyes, but I didn't want to go there.

Soon afterward I left, edgy, a bit scared that she would want to make love. And I was certain I wasn't attracted to her. She was slow and heavy and depressed. I had a life to live, a world to subdue, a revolution to win, women to love. She'd made her decision, I told myself as I returned that night to the collective I lived in. I talked about her at my next house meeting because she was on my mind. The women voiced sorrow for poor Lucy. Not long afterward I moved to Denver and never found the time to say good-bye to her.

In all those months after I moved what stood out most in my mind was the way she described feeling when we women came to visit her. How she would sit in her living room after dinner, playing the evening's game or talking quietly, how she'd wallow in the waves of sensuality she felt rolling over her from the comfort and security the women were feeling. Her home, her cooking, and her body were oases women could visit for what they needed, what their men-friends and husbands couldn't give.

That literally turned me on. I had orgasms when I was with a casual lover by fantasizing being back in Lucy's living room with her telling me about warmth and comfort and having a place to rebuild oneself. It was a pretty weird time. I even went to the bars and got together with non-movement women a couple of times, to see if being with a femme was what made Lucy stick in my head. That didn't work. And I couldn't talk about it to any of the women I knew. How could I admit I'd fallen in love with comfort and security and was scared to death my need would sap energy from my political work? I told myself—you can't have both, stop thinking about it.

I couldn't; everything had become less and less meaningful. I knew I'd had it when, not long after I moved to San Francisco, Harvey Milk was shot. I never wanted gay people to generate martyrs. The rioting was madness, a lot of inevitable craziness, because there was no core, no anchor for us. We were energy run wild, hurt animals running in circles as new wounds opened. Maybe nothing was wrong with the women's and gay movements as a whole, but I was mad with pain and frustration and loneliness. I lived with lesbians, worked with them, planned with them, slept with them, but I was empty and alone. I had nothing, not even the self I'd been so carefully developing. I needed something different.

One day, sitting looking at the Pacific, I saw plainly what a gold mine Lucy was. I couldn't get back to her soon enough.

"Lucy," I said at her door, falling to my knees before she could even ask me in, "Lucy, can we get to know each other so I can ask you to marry me?"

She'd been waiting for my return, she confessed later. She told me her story, she said, because she sensed it would have relevance for my life. It was only in telling it that she realized she wanted me to stay that night. She'd been hopeful she tied her story around my ankle tightly enough that, like a homing pigeon, I'd remember my way back.

As I knelt at her door, she laughed that great loud laugh she thought she lost after Gerry. I had a twinge of anxiety she'd learned to laugh again since I went away, but when she pulled me off my knees and bear hugged me right there in the hallway, I knew it was me who'd brought her laughter back.

Originally published in *Old Dyke Tales* (Naiad Press, 1984)

WHITTLING

"What do you think?" Jessie Malone asked the counterman where she bought her morning coffee. "I moved out."

The counterman's mouth dropped open in his red, harried face. "You what?"

To Jessie's left, someone stirred coffee interminably, clanking spoon against cup. Sickening fumes of toast and bacon emanated from the grill into the overheated air. Outside the steamy plate glass windows, a windless winter day froze the city in place. She took a deep breath and ordered a strong cup of black tea with plenty of sugar.

The counterman was still staring at her, not saying another word.

"Hey," Jessie said, trying for a joke, "life goes on, doesn't it? I have to fill my gullet with something, don't I, Morris?" Her hands shaped a napkin into a flower, and she offered it to him.

"From Mary? You moved out from Mary?" Morris leaned across the counter and whispered, without taking the napkin. "And didn't I not long ago make you that fantabulous flower arrangement for your tenth anniversary? How dare you move out on Mary?"

With his hands on his hips, his too-black hairpiece and paunch, Morris looked to Jessie like a typical College Point, Queens, fairy. He and his look-alike, Jerome, had been together almost twenty years.

"What do you mean, how dare I? She's the one who—" Her voice cracked and she thought she would choke. The words, when they came, were dry and unappetizing as burnt toast. "Who stepped out on me."

"Nah," Morris said, dark brown eyebrows almost meeting his careful black wave. "Mary?"

"Shit." Jessie stamped her feet like a child. Several heads rose from their plates and cups to take her in. She wouldn't cry.

Morris patted her forearm. "Come on in the kitchen and cry on Mama's shoulder."

"No." With a knuckle she roughly wiped one tear out from under her horn-rimmed glasses. "It may be okay for you to cry, but I'm no sissy." She rose and gathered up her two heavy suitcases, her shopping bag of woodworking tools, and the string-tied shoebox which held the miniature carvings she'd planned to enter in the art show at the community center.

"Hey," called Morris, "where are you going? What about your tea? At least let me toast you a nice bagel."

"I'd only throw up," she yelled back over her shoulder.

With small, tight steps, Morris ran out from behind the counter. She stared down at his usual spit-and-polish black leather shoes as she pushed her way backward out the door.

"Jess, Jess, let me help." His shouted whisper barely carried over the yells of waitresses, chattering customers, clanging plates and silverware.

She shoved one suitcase toward Morris with her foot. "Here. Hold this for me, will you? I'll be back for it. I think."

"A suitcase? I want to fix your life, and all you'll let me do is hold a suitcase?"

"Give it a rest."

She walked as fast as she could along the slippery sidewalk with her remaining bundles. Even the taxicabs crawled the streets with caution. Every skinny young tree along the curb was encased in ice; trash was frozen to the gutter. She'd forgotten how desolate it was, being alone.

A dense gray sky promised no melting for today. She trudged warily on, veering away from ice patches, muttering to herself. What did boys know, with the fooling around they did? Her stomach growled. The shoebox, though lightest of her burdens, was the one which weighed most heavily on her mind.

For a year she'd prepared for the College Point Art Show. Why did it have to be today? She was more skilled than last year when she entered those big rough sculptures, painstakingly balanced, and received an honorable mention. This year she was obsessed with learning careful detailing. She floated on air while she worked with those miniature pieces, using her delicate blades.

She wanted badly to spring her proud creations on the world, but Mary organized the show. Mary, from whom she carefully hid her carvings, afraid criticism would discourage her into quitting, afraid after Mary took college courses and became Arts Director at the community center, that she'd hate these primitive offerings. Jessie would have to face her in order to enter, would have to receive any prize from her. Would have to see the beloved face that no longer belonged to her.

One block up, she reached the jewelry store. She was too tired to stay angry and stood at the curb across the street, forlorn. At least it was a Saturday and she didn't have to go to work at the factory. It was no day to be a foreman; she'd be yelling at everyone. Probably get herself fired. See how Mary would like that, she thought, then remembered. Mary wouldn't care anymore.

Outside the jewelry store, Hermine, a heavy bleached-blonde in her forties, rolled back the grate with a crash and cranked down the red-striped awning. Hermine went into the shop and returned with a bag of rock salt. Halfway through spreading it, she looked up.

"Jess," she cried, stepping back.

Jessie crossed the street to her.

"Where have you been?" Hermine demanded, looking ominously oversized in her puffy pink and white ski parka. "You scared the shit out of me, standing there making like a ghost. Don't you know Mary's looking all over the city for you? Where in hell did you go last night? You've got me and Beebo worried half to death."

Jessie put down the second suitcase, the shoebox, and the shopping bag. "I was at the Y. Where else can I go when my girl finds somebody else three weeks after our anniversary? You can tell her to stop looking for me. I don't want to play second fiddle."

"You get yourself inside the shop, Jess. Beebo's in back. She'll give you some coffee. You look like you need it."

Jessie hesitated, but ten minutes later, in the back room, she was crying against Hermine's soft bosom. Her old friend's familiar flowery perfume mingled with the scent of silver polish. Beebo, nicknamed by her pals for a character in a lesbian novel, stood in the entryway, alert for customers. She was legally blind and lived with a pronounced stoop from peering at jewelry and watches. She did all the routine repairs, and Jessie typically found her leaning close to her workbench, feeling for imperfections.

"You have to work it out," Hermine said. "I don't care if she cheated on you, and where's your proof she did? What chance does it give Beebo and me if you guys break up right before we get our ten years in? You think we're the perfect couple?"

"Why? What's wrong with you two?"

Hermine looked toward Beebo, who shrugged. "She doesn't see too good," said Hermine, "but that doesn't mean this one hasn't got a roving eye."

"Beebo?"

"Lucky for her," Hermine went on, "I'm a very forgiving person."

"It was only the once," Beebo said, eyes downcast, "in the beginning. I still couldn't believe you wanted me."

"So she has to go out and prove she's lovable, right? I told you, you should come to me, I'll show you how lovable you are."

"I have ever since, haven't I?"

"You have to tame them when they get kind of wild, Jess."

"What do you want me to do?" Jessie separated herself from Hermine's sweater. "Climb into bed with them?" She sat up and shook her head. "All I want right now is to figure out two things. One, where I'm going to stay. Two, what I'm going to do about the art show." With the tips of her fingers, she held on to the cushiony bulge of Hermine's waist.

"The show," said Hermine. "We finally get to see your work. I hear you wouldn't even let your girlfriend see it."

"My ex-girlfriend," insisted Jessie, trying to get used to the idea. It only made her start to cry again.

"So you say," retorted Hermine. "And what do you expect? You won't let her near your workroom where you spend half your free time. What were you concocting in there, the atom bomb?" She glanced up at an ornate cuckoo clock. "It's ten now. When do you have to get your stuff to the community center?"

"By noon."

Beebo leaned her bent self against the doorframe, hands in her pockets, thick glasses slipped halfway down her nose.

"And they're doing awards, what time?" Hermine asked.

"Tomorrow at three."

"We'll be there," announced Hermine. "We want to see you get your first prize this time. Pam will know good work when she sees it. Imagine, all the way from California to be one of the judges. Mary's doing a good job here, bringing College Point up in the world."

"Pam can get away easy. She's single," Jessie said.

"And Frenchy will be there with Mercedes. They've got almost eight years if you can believe it," added Hermine. "That'll be interesting, Frenchy's hippie ex, Pam, meeting up with Mercedes."

She was ashamed of her failure before these friends. She and Mary were a big deal in their crowd, the earliest, longest, the forever ones. What happened?

"If I could only lie down and die," Jessie said, slumping in her chair. "Mary's whole family will be there to see this show. For Pete's sake, guys, how am I going to make it without Mary's family? They've been better to me than my own. And I can't even tell them what Mary's done." She hugged her stomach, imagining that the pain would kill her off any minute. "I can't tell them about that stinking no-talent refugee from poshy Connecticut who's their next son-in-law."

Beebo shifted in the doorway. "I thought Verne was an admired painter."

"Yeah," Jessie said, balling up her handkerchief as if it was Verne. "If you like paint-by-numbers. She's a hustler. Paints five or six landscapes over and over and sells them at shopping malls. Her newest thing is selling everybody else's work. Says she wants to open a gallery and get rich."

Abruptly, she rose. Another wave of pain was approaching at the thought of Mary with such a conniving woman. Word was, Verne recently moved out of one lover's home in Connecticut into a new lover's apartment in College Point. What brought Verne to that workshop Mary organized? Why couldn't it have stopped there, not progressed to coffee after, dropping in at Mary's office, then a trip to a museum? Then…this.

Jessie wanted to outrun the pain. She thought briefly of drinking herself into a stupor as she did a few times in their early years, but this time there was no brother-in-law Mario to rescue her. She never needed steadier hands or a clearer mind than she did now. She lifted her box of sculptures and her bag of tools. "Can I leave this suitcase here?"

"Where're you going?" Beebo asked.

She pushed the heavy suitcase under the worktable, then bumped her way past Beebo. "I don't know. Away. Connecticut maybe, where I can learn to be a skunk and hurt other people before they hurt me."

"What about the show?" called Hermine from the length of the sparkling counters.

"What about it?" She struggled with the front door. A bus slowed to a stop at the corner. She ran for it, the string around her box cutting into the pads of her fingers. She would sit on the bus and think. But it pulled out in a belch of exhaust and dirty slush before she could reach it.

She turned toward the East River. Several blocks on sprawled the garage where Del worked. That grease monkey was favored with the tightest thinking cap Jessie ever ran across, except for Mary. A lot of good Mary's would do her now. Jessie carried her pain to Del like one more heavy suitcase to be left behind.

Her fingers were numb from cold by the time she got to the garage. She saw Del working inside, a shadow amidst the men twisting, pounding, measuring, and shouting to one another in the oily smelling building. Del didn't exactly pass as a guy—she was plain and simply looked like one, all the time, in every move and gesture. She was Jessie's size, taller than average, bulky but without curves, like a nicely blocked-out chunk of wood, thought Jessie. As always, she was head-to-toe grease.

Del wiped her fingers on a filthy rag and pumped Jessie's hand. "Long time no see, pal."

"Mary's been seeing somebody behind my back," blurted Jessie.

"I told you that dame would go dizzy on you," Del responded without a pause. She stuffed the rag into her back pocket. "Didn't I tell you that? You don't give her enough attention, barricading yourself in that workshop of yours or else staying at the plant overtime."

Jessie's hand had taken on a sheen of grease. She quelled the urge to smell it, to be covered by grease or sawdust or whatever good earthy substance would soothe her pain.

"I wanted to surprise her. If she came in and saw what I was working on, she might not like this one or that one. This way, I figured she'd at least like some of them." Jessie carefully balanced herself on a stack of tires.

Del lit an unfiltered cigarette. "So you kept all of them from her, not to mention you kept all of you from her. So she went out looking for hands that wanted a woman, not wood."

Jessie came up in a crouch, fists squeezing tight on every ounce of rage inside her. "Fuck you."

Eyes narrowed, cigarette between her lips, Del held Jessie at arm's length. "You come to me to get a pretty picture or what? You're the highfalutin artist. You go whittle yourself what you want to see. Me, I look at the insides of things, what makes them go."

Jessie stopped glaring. She rebalanced herself on the tires, the rubber threatening to collapse and spill her into the deep center hole. Del always made her mad; Jessie always ended up thanking her.

Del went on. "Mary's a good girl, don't get me wrong, but she's had it easy since she was a kid—first her old man at her beck and call, then you. She thinks she's been playing house with you all these years. What do you expect? You shut her out, she's going to find another playmate. She has no way of knowing yet that broken hearts hurt like hell and can't always be welded back into one piece."

She drew smoke in for such a long time, Jessie waited for it to come out her ears.

"So what do you want?" Del asked, finally exhaling. "You giving up for good, or you trying to scare her, hauling your baggage to hell and back like hearts on your sleeves?"

"I don't know yet. First, I have to find a place to stay. Second, I have to figure out by"—she looked at her Timex—"noon, if I'm going to put my stuff in the art show Mary organized."

"I got the invite. Planned to go see if there's any photos of old cars this year. Remember that Kaiser picture I bought? I got it framed. That's my kind of art. You still doing those weird boxes?"

Jessie stroked her carton. "I've been trying mini carvings. There's a couple cars in there I thought might be up your alley."

Del stomped on her cigarette until it was shredded. "Let's see."

"No." Jessie pulled the box to herself, fingering the rough hairy twine. "I don't need more bad luck, showing them to people." Even as she said this, she knew herself to be making it up. "Holding them back is a habit now, but I guess I wanted Mary to see them when I was ready. It wasn't anything personal against Mary."

Del laughed. "And her side affair probably isn't anything personal against you either."

"That's different," Jessie sputtered.

"Hey. She doesn't have wood to carve." Del craned her neck toward the office where her boss was at his desk. "I have to get back to work. I'm not saying it was right, what Mary did or didn't do, I'm saying it doesn't have to be the end. Listen, I'll see you over at the community center."

"I might not go." She gripped her stomach again.

Del heaved a large sigh and once more glanced over at the office. "What's the matter? You have a bellyache?"

"Yeah," replied Jessie, sweat forming on her forehead. "It's like I've got Mary inside me, carved down to a nub that got stuck in my gut."

Del gave a short gruff laugh. "You whittled her down to size, huh?" She picked up some tools and motioned for Jessie to move to the car with her. "Look at this."

Jessie stared down into the depths of the car as if its guts were her own—rusted, leaking, complex. She closed her eyes against the pain.

"Me," said Del, "I learned not to get a dame mixed up with this vehicle's insides." She hitched up her pants and bent over to dismantle something. "Donna may be heaven for me, but this here is earth."

"So what would you do? If you were in this car-fixing contest, and Donna was giving the prizes, but she did what Mary did."

Del stood, blinked at her, smirked and shook her head. She brushed herself off and set her tools by the side of the car, then lay flat on her back on a low dolly.

"You mean I'd have a choice? Hiding myself under a bushel basket or showing Donna my best damn work? She'd be looking at the very best of me?" Del wheeled herself under the car, laughing.

Jessie stepped to the open garage door. It was eleven thirty now and icicles everywhere were dripping, then crashing to the sidewalks. The service bells sounded as cars pulled in and out of the station. A pump jockey leaped from island to island. The factories were quiet today, but the parking lot at the grocery across the street was packed, and a man with a hot dog cart wheeled quickly toward College Point Park. She could smell the remains of Hermine's perfume on herself.

All her friends wanted her to stick it out. She had no heart for it earlier, for registering in the art show, for seeing Mary again. She'd never forgive her if she did it with that Verne person, but maybe it wasn't all Mary's fault. Maybe she whittled away at their life together the last few years and ought to look inside to figure out why.

She called back to Del in the shop. "Can I leave my tools with you?"

"The shopping bag? Right here by me, Jess. I'll put them in my car on my break."

A sharp wind came up from the river, but the sun quickly tempered it. The smell of toast and bacon stayed in its wake. Her mouth watered. She lifted her shoebox into her arms and cradled it. Was she going to throw this away?

Originally published in *Cactus Love* (Naiad Press, 1994)

AT A BAR

I: In the Morning

Sunrays fell like cobwebs through the dusty bar window. The small room held several round Formica-topped tables between the short counter and the window. On one side of the door to the back room stood a shining new jukebox whose flashing lights made it look like a visitor from the future. On the other side of the door, garishly painted women in bathing suits posed on an old pinball machine with an out-of-order sign.

Sally the bartender, skinny as a bar rail and tall, with a cap of short blond hair, leaned over the bar on her elbows to stare past the Café Femmes window sign. She smiled to see Gabby's short, bobbing figure beyond it.

"Hah!" breathed Gabby as she pushed through the door, sounding the cowbells that hung there to warn Sally of customers.

"Hah yourself, Junior."

Gabby protested indignantly, fists on her broad hips. "What's the matter with you that you call me Junior every morning now, Sal? I'm pushing forty like you." She took off her plaid wool jacket and climbed onto a stool, shaking her sweatshirt away from her body and her worn work pants. "Got hot out there. I'm sweating like a pig."

Sally smiled at her. "You looked like a Junior, coming past that window, hurrying home."

"After my night on the town?"

"Where'd you end up last night, Gab?"

"Here." Gabby sighed, looking bored. "Liz said it was your night off."

"What'd you do?"

"What I'd like to do more of right now, Sal."

"Ten a.m. fix coming up. By the time your unemployment runs out, you're going to be a real lush."

"Why the hell not?" challenged Gabby, downing the shot and picking up her beer. "Hair of the dog, like they say."

Sally ran her rag over the top of the bar, picking up the circle of moisture left by Gabby's beer.

"Nobody in yet?" Gabby asked.

"You're first, as usual."

"Come on, Sal. Meg's here before me."

Sally stretched her long body and yawned.

"You working all day, Sal?"

"Somebody's got to keep you high."

"Thank goodness for that. Couldn't stand it otherwise."

"Can't you get into some unemployment program?"

"And do what, clean the streets? I'm not ready for that, no matter what the politicians think."

"It'd keep you away from the sauce a few hours a day."

Gabby's face closed. "Lay off me about that. This is my life."

"Sure, sure. You know I don't want you to end up like Meg. She used to be so sharp and funny. She'd come in here Fridays after work in her business suit and have a mixed drink or two."

"You know I'll get back on my feet, Sal. I'll get a job. I'll find a girl. I'll get a decent place to live. Right now, I need a vacation."

"From everything?"

"Don't you ever feel so damn tired you can't lift your head off the pillow in the morning? The only reason I get up is because there's a Café Femmes to come to. I'll get my energy back, Sal. Haven't I always before? I'm tired of falling in love, then breaking up; finding a job, then getting canned. Making an apartment nice, then losing it along with my girl or my job. You can talk—you've got this place here."

"Which Liz and I worked damn hard for."

"At least you had the wherewithal to get what you wanted. Not everybody can own a gay business." Gabby set her glass down hard. "Let me have another setup."

As she poured, Sally said, "Liz said Meg cadged more drinks than usual last night. She shut Meg off, but we can't do anything about people who keep buying her more."

"What could happen to a rummy like that?"

"What happens to the other rummies on the street? You think she can't get sick or hurt because she's a dyke?"

"No. Maybe? She's getting like the guys on the Bowery, isn't she."

"One step away, Gab, that's all."

"I can't believe that."

They fell silent. The mailwoman, Jenny, pushed through the door and sounded the cowbells again. "Sounds like I'm down on the farm when I come in here. How are you today, Sally? Gab? Where's Meg?"

"I don't know," said Sally. "We've been talking about her. You see her around, tell her to drop in, okay? Want a shot?"

"Love it, honey, but that's all I need to do—get caught smelling of it. I'll take another rain check?"

"Sure, sure, anytime," Sally said, sorting through her mail. "We'll see you later, right?"

"Could be—it's Thursday." The door slammed behind Jenny, rattling the bell. Thursdays, Sally and Liz extended happy hour.

Gabby rose, taking her beer, and wandered to the pinball machine. She said, "Friday's a lousy day to look for a job, too, you know."

"Any day's bad from what you say."

"Really, Sal. Friday the bosses are looking to sail their boats, not start someone new. Especially not someone who looks like me."

"How you look doesn't matter with the kind of jobs you're after."

"It shouldn't." Gabby pushed aside the out-of-order sign and put a quarter in the machine. "You haven't fixed this yet?"

"The repairman is supposed to come today."

"One stinking ball for a quarter."

"Keeps you on your toes. You need to do really well on one quarter. Here, take some replacements." She spilled some coins onto the bar.

"No. Never mind. I'm not in the mood. Too much work."

She watched Gabby walk to the window.

Gabby spoke toward the empty street. "You know how many damn girls I thought I'd be with forever? Five. Five damn girls. Maybe it's me. When it comes to making it work, I don't have what it takes. Falling in love is fine. I have that down pat. But when love starts to be an uphill battle, I only know to take off. Unless they leave me first. If only I could keep a job. Or if we could adopt kids—that would make us work to stay together. Even if we had families who'd get upset about us splitting, it would help. We come down here, and what is there? A bunch of chicks looking to make it with somebody, no matter who or who it'll hurt. And like a damn fool I can't resist them. It's so easy to cheat on your girl. Plus, when you're high? You don't give a rip. Until she finds out. So why try settling down? What's the sense?"

Sally was dusting the bottles behind the bar. "Love has its good points," she said, thinking of Liz coming home that morning and slipping naked into bed with her.

"And jobs. I'm not smart. I'm not good-looking. I can't get a job in an office because I come off too much like a dyke to fit in. I can't get a job in a factory for anything but minimum wage because I'm too small, too much a woman to do men's work. I used to give my all to get ahead in a job, but I never had what it took. Going at top speed on piecework earns me enough for a few more beers and a sore back. I tried everywhere. And I know I'll get something eventually, some crappy job at the end of a subway line. But who wants it?"

"So you drink."

"Why the hell not," Gabby said again, returning to her stool. "How about I go across the street and get us burgers? Might as well make myself useful somewhere."

"Sounds good to me."

"No sign of Meg out there."

"Why don't you stop at her place on your way to lunch?"

"Where's she live?"

"Around the corner. One thirty-six. Top floor."

"That flea trap?"

"At this point she's lucky to have that. One of her ex-lovers helps with the rent."

Gabby shook her head. "Wow. I didn't know she was that broke. How about a beer this time? Then I'll take off. Maybe she'll show up while I drink it. How high is this top floor?"

"Only five."

"Shit. That's a long haul."

They sat watching the bright street outside the window. The sun had moved overhead, and its light no longer reached them. Passersby would see two figures inside, shadowy and still. Only the bottles shone in the mirror behind them.

"Sally," cried Jenny the mailwoman as she flung open the door. The cowbells thudded only once and tonelessly.

"Is it Meg?" Sally asked, knowing in her gut that it was.

"And is it ever. They found her early this morning. She fell down the stairs."

"All the way from the top?" Gabby asked, her voice filled with horror.

"She must have stumbled into the banister. It collapsed, and she fell to the fourth floor."

Sally was hustling out from behind the bar. "Is she—?"

"She's not dead. Weak as she is, the neighbor said she was alive when the ambulance took her." Jenny's laugh came out bitter. "You can keep us down, shut us up, make us hide all our lives, but we're damn tough to get rid of. She was asking for a drink when they put her on the gurney."

"A drink," Sally said. "Sometimes I hate this business."

"I better go visit her," Gabby said, heading for the door. "See if there's anything she needs."

"Could need a lot," said Jenny.

Sally grunted. "Don't we all."

"She's at St. Vinny's," said Jenny. "I'll go over when I finish at work. You want to go with me, Sal?"

"Definitely. How about that hamburger, Junior? Before you run out on me."

Gabby stopped as if Sally had yanked on a harness. "Sorry, Sal. You're stuck in here. I'll bring it right back."

Jenny stared after her. "I haven't seen Gabby move that fast in months."

Smiling, Sally said, "It's sure nice to see her all lit up about something. It's the wake-up call she needs."

Jenny gathered up her mailbag. "I'll come by for you, Sal."

"About six?"

Several minutes later, Gabby rushed in and slid the burger along the bar's polished top to Sally. "See ya."

Sally ate in short-lived peace and quiet. Why did the kids continue to buy Meg drinks? It was cruel.

Once more the cowbells made their jaunty, raucous sound, as four women and a large pizza crowded through the doorway.

"Hi, ladies," Sally greeted them, setting up glasses for four beers.

"Want some pizza, Sal?"

"Thanks, no." She accepted their money. "Gabby brought me a burger."

"Yeah," another woman said as she fought to control a string of mozzarella. "I was looking for her. Where's Meg?"

"Well," she answered slowly, smiling. "Meg had a fall. But Gabby's on her way now."

Originally published in *Common Lives/Lesbian Lives* 4 (Summer 1982)

II: The Jersey Dyke

The sun shines again through the big window of Café Femmes. It sparkles through a new generation of bottles lined up behind the bar. Habitually, Sally the bartender leans her tall thin frame over the counter to wipe it with a damp rag. Her blond hair falls over her forehead brightly, covering blue eyes somehow too wide and clear for such a tiny and normally dim bar.

But in daylight, before the first customer rings the cowbells by opening the door, the lingering stale smoke is more obvious. It is a film on the windows, a fuzziness in the air. Sally's nose is more sensitive to it this early. And the pinball machine—even the new space-age game— looks tawdry in the light.

Sally watches workmen across the street load and unload trucks from the platforms. She reads the backward lettering of her bar's name on the window, then reads the company names on the trucks, then the name on the building. Every day she looks at this same scene, except Sunday, when the street is deserted. The men sweat and swear and struggle on the loading docks. The trucks wheeze and groan, entering and leaving the street.

She can't say exactly why, but Sally finds this all comforting. It's familiar. She has her place in it. She bends to pull a bottle of cold white wine from the crushed ice. She pours some into a wineglass. It's a habit she should probably drop, but all day she stands behind the bar and waits for what life will bring her. This is her treat now and then through the day. At night her lover, Liz, does the same, but she drinks other things—whatever her first customer orders, that's her game. Sally sees Liz when their shifts overlap, so she knows what liquor Liz will smell of when she joins her in their bed after closing up. They spend Mondays together, the one day the bar is closed. They never drink that day but try to get away from all this, at least to Central or Riverside Park, somewhere open and airy. They blink in the full sun those days and find the straight people scurrying about the city very strange. By Tuesday they're glad to return to their bar, to the lesbians, to their accustomed life.

Jenny, the mailwoman, startles Sally as she opens the door and rings the cowbells. Sometimes she'll talk over the bar for a minute, discussing what happened in the course of the night—news Sally otherwise doesn't get until Liz comes in. But today Jenny has a busy time of it; she explains quickly that Sunday is Mother's Day.

The workmen across the street knock off, running to the tiny lunch stand down the block or emptying lunch buckets their wives have prepared. Sally can see them examining this and that in disgust or with smiles and boasts. In a few minutes, her own lunch crowd, dykes who work in the neighborhood factories or offices, comes in. She's told them to bring their lunch bags, their subs and pizzas, even if they don't want to drink. She keeps cold sodas on hand for them. She likes their company. After a while they go back to work, dragging their feet, leaving the smell of pizza behind.

A stray long-haired straight man, an artist from one of the lofts, has been drinking beer at the far end of the counter, but he too leaves. Good—she was afraid she'd have a drunk on her hands.

The sun is still out as the workmen begin again, but it no longer shines brightly through the window. At two o'clock Café Femmes is still empty. It's one of those afternoons that make Sally wish she ran a bar in Mexico—she'd close for siesta each afternoon. She pours herself another wine and takes it around to one of the tables where she sits sometimes to test the feel of the place.

After a while a woman comes in, a stranger. She's almost as tall as Sally, but on the heavy side. She shambles to the bar, maybe depressed. Sally takes her wine behind the bar, which she wipes down needlessly. The woman asks for a Michelob, in a New Jersey accent.

Sally takes stock of her without seeming to while she readies the beer. She cards the overgrown sulky child. Her jeans, plaid shirt, her high school jacket all look loose, as if she recently lost weight. Oddest of all, she doesn't check the mirror as most of the kids do first thing, to make sure they're looking sharp.

Neither speaks, but now and then the newcomer, a baby-faced twenty-three, glances at Sally from under heavy eyebrows as if to measure her interest.

Hurt exudes from this woman like an injured animal fallen at

Sally's feet. When the other's pain too acutely reaches her, she carefully wipes down each bottle again to distract herself. Then she works on the books awhile, but she can't concentrate.

Finally, the newcomer, looking down into her beer, says, "My girl killed herself."

Sally tries to think of what to say, but the girl takes care of the silence.

"Do you mind? It's been two months now, and I couldn't tell anybody. Oh, I don't mean nobody knew, they all knew she killed herself, but nobody knew we were, you know, together like we were, because she was so pretty and popular." She pushed forward her Michelob. "You better give me another one of these. My name is Julie."

"Sally."

Julie holds out her hand. Sally can only shake it and go on listening.

"We live—lived in this town in New Jersey. It's real, real small, but close to Somerville, which is bigger. Only by close, I mean you have to use a car to get there, which I don't have. My folks drive theirs to work, so I needed to make some money. I got a job in town, at a dry cleaner. Yeah, I know it's not much, waiting on customers, tagging dirty clothes, but they won't hire me anyplace else. Look at me. I'm fat, and they think I'm a guy anyway when I go look for a job. Everybody knows me at the cleaners now—they put up with me. We're closed Wednesdays. The owner was driving to the city, so I got a ride from him. I'll meet him at seven to go back.

"See, I had to tell somebody. I don't know anybody at home I could tell. She had friends, lots of them. She was always dancing and laughing and had the lead in the school play—she was a senior this year. Her parents thought she was great. She got accepted at Rutgers and was going next year. But me, I only have a couple of friends, from high school. You know, from the ugly crowd. We used to ride the school bus together, but they're secretaries now, spend all their time trying to get prettier so some man at work will marry them."

"Do they...know?" She feels compelled to ask, if only to stop this rush of words.

"That I'm gay? They might've figured it out by now." She looks self-conscious. "Well, how can I tell them? What if I lose them, too?"

Though Julie speaks so quickly, time in the bar seems to speed up, the workers across the street slowing as their break approaches. Sally sees them lounge more and more frequently against the portals of the loading dock, smoking. She wonders if she'd like the kind of work where kids weren't always spilling their guts out to you.

Julie has fallen silent. Sally decides she could at least ask a question. "How did you get together with this girl?"

Julie looked up at her in surprise, as if she'd never asked herself this. "I guess because I was gay."

"You really think you're the only queer in town?"

Julie lets out a choked laugh. "I guess we both thought so. Otherwise, why would she come to me? She was so pretty."

"Did she give it all up for you?"

"You mean the dates, the parties, the football games?" Again, she looks at Sally in surprise as if this possibility, too, has never occurred to her. "No, man, you got it wrong. She had to have all that stuff. She wasn't the kind could give it up for love. I wouldn't ask her to. That's what I don't understand. She had it all. She had a girl lover, and she had boyfriends. Everybody liked her and looked up to her. Why would she kill herself?"

Sally doesn't have an answer. She looks around the empty Café Femmes and smiles inwardly. No matter how shabby, it's hers. She goes over to plug in the game machines; she'd forgotten before lunch. Their lights pop on, flashing.

"If only she'd thought to ask me, we could have made a pact," Julie said. "You know, to die together."

Sally walks back to the bar, wondering if the girl might yet join her lover. Perhaps she should refuse to serve her. Liquor would do her no good. Even now, after two beers, her speech slurs, like she isn't used to drinking. But who was Sally to decide what was good for the kid? Could be this is the only way Julie could let it out of her system before she returns home.

"I've got to tell you," Julie says, facing Sally, not looking sulky now, but suddenly radiant. "This one day, we went to the Shore. She got hold of her folks' car and we drove and drove and drove. Touching, you know, all day. We'd never been able to do that before, never had the privacy of a car for so long.

"Oh, and the sun was shining, and we ate fried clams at the beach and drank beer, and walked by the water, along the rocks, holding hands. This was last fall, and it was already nippy, so the beach was pretty empty. We found some rocks we could lean against where it wasn't windy, and we smoked cigarettes and held hands, and once in a while she would let me kiss me right out there in the open."

Julie sighs. "It was beautiful. I always tried to figure a way we could have a day like that again, when spring came. But spring never really came. For her."

Sally looks over, but the Jersey girl doesn't cry. Probably she's so used to hiding her tears they won't come out anymore.

"I feel so...kind of empty. You know?" She isn't looking at Sally.

"Did you ever come into the city together? To the bars?"

"Us? No. She wouldn't like that. She was a nice girl. We went for walks in the woods. Or hung out in her parents' family room when they were upstairs. We never went anywhere else together, except that one time."

"And you didn't want to go to college?"

"Me? Sure. I got into Rutgers, too, by the skin of my teeth. But I wanted to stick around. I mean, she was really special. I told Rutgers I needed to wait a year, financially, which was true, but I wanted to go when she did. I guess I was kind of counting on it. But without her there, I don't want to go anymore." She begins to bite her nails.

She asks for another beer. For the next hour, she alternately chews on her fingernails and drinks beer. Sally moves around quietly, getting ready for the evening, asking no more questions, not because she can't think of any, but because a bartender soon learns that to express interest can be interpreted as taking a kind of responsibility in another woman's life. She couldn't help all the needy kids who came in.

The workmen unload their last truck. They glance at their watches, as if hoping no one would drive in at the last minute and make them work overtime. She hears the loud slam, finally, of the sliding metal doors closing on the concrete platforms. The men drift off the street like a fog, echoing good-byes at one another. Julie bites her nails in silence.

Soon the after work kids drop by for drinks before disappearing into the subways. The light inside the bar is dimmer, even though it's still daylight outside. Late afternoons, the dark seems to close in early, which is good for business, as the kids party earlier. Those who have a reason to go home leave. A few return as they walk their dogs; more locals stop in. You don't get many outer-borough kids during the week. The bar smells of pizza again. There's a constant turnover of drinkers.

Liz appears. Shorter than Sally and with slightly darker, slightly longer hair and glasses, she greets Sally with her eyes. Sally throws the bar rag at her. Liz laughs, catching it, and throws it back. It doesn't take her long to notice Julie, now sitting like a liquor-sodden lump, staring at nothing. Maybe she's bitten her nails down to the quick.

Abruptly Julie stands up. Bang goes her fist on the bar. The glasses rattle. "It's not fair." If she's trying to shout, her voice is too hoarse. She turns and leaves the bar, slamming the cowbells behind her.

Liz and some of the kids at the bar look to Sally. "Her girl killed herself," she explains as she runs the rag over Julie's place.

They shake their heads. There is silence for a while. Then someone plays a slow sad song on the jukebox, like a dirge, but when it stops, a fast dance song comes on and the bar noise picks up.

By the time Julie returns, darkness was closer to filling the cavity of the street outside Café Femmes. Most of the kids are huddled at the space-age pinball machine, watching someone top the highest score. Sally is getting ready to go home. She looks at her watch and confirms Julie hasn't left with her seven o'clock ride to New Jersey.

She sets her up with a clean glass and a Michelob.

Julie's face, when she looked up to thank her for the first time that day, looked different. Maybe she's finally been crying. No, it's a face washed of stifled anger. Has Julie never gotten angry over her girl's death before today? Over the unfairness of her situation?

Maybe. Sally nods to herself as she walks to the door. She well knows, when you're the only one in town, you don't think you have any business being angry. You're out of step, so it's your own fault.

"Hey," calls Julie.

She looks back.

Julie lifts her beer in a toast. "To my girl."

Sally stands in the doorway. "L'chaim," she says, unsure she wants Julie to hear.

Julie smiles, a little bit. "To life," she quietly agrees.

Originally published in *Old Dyke Tales* (Naiad Press, 1984)

III: Sally the Bartender Goes on Jury Duty

Afterward, when anyone would mention jury duty, Sally would shudder, as if reminded of a nightmare. Yet it started well enough.

It had rained all day, and Café Femmes was by turns crowded with kids escaping from the weather, and empty because few would venture into such dampness to hang out anywhere. Sally longed to be home under the covers with Liz. But they had a bar to run, and it was Sally's shift. She served the drenched women who took refuge in her shelter and did some cleaning, ordering, what have you, when she was alone. She absently wiped the counter and watched the workmen across the street. They stayed as far back on the covered loading docks as possible, filling and emptying trucks with unusual dispatch. The sky was gray, like the warehouses themselves. But the bar had a cheery feel to it, especially when Sally remembered to switch on the game machines with their bright flashing lights.

Late in the afternoon, Sally saw Liz rush by their plate glass window, her bright yellow slicker streaming under the April downpour. A moment later the cowbells over the door sounded, and Liz came in, shaking her short dark hair like a wet dog. As usual, she hadn't worn her hood because she hated the way it looked. Sally peeled the wet coat off her and took the dry mail Liz removed from her pocket.

"What's this?" Sally asked. "Are we in some kind of trouble?"

"With who, or is it whom?" Liz stood on her toes to peer closely at the envelope. Severely myopic without them, she wiped steam from her glasses.

"Some court."

"Betcha it's jury duty," Marian said. She was from the Bronx and had recently taken to hanging around the bar. Liz guessed she was hiding out from an ex, as Café Femmes was pretty out of the way. But Sally thought she was trying to meet somebody to bring her out, because she looked too straight to be in the life yet.

"Oh no," said Liz.

"I got one of those a couple of years ago. In an envelope like that one," Marian continued.

"Open it, Sal. Let's see what's up."

"Go take care of Gabby then. She probably wants more ice for her Coke."

"How'd you guess?" called Gabby.

"'Cause it doesn't cost a thing, tightwad." Sally stopped laughing when she opened the envelope.

Liz was back. "So?"

"So, it's jury duty."

"That's what I thought," Marian said, somewhat boastfully.

"What the hell are you going to do?" Liz.

"Go, I guess."

"Go, she says. What about the café?" Liz liked to call it a café. She'd been to Europe once, a college graduation present, and had fallen in love with Paris. Especially a lesbian bar to which she would steal at night when her mother and sister were already in bed. She swore someday she'd open a Parisian bar for lesbians in New York. But first, there had been the years of bracing herself to tell her parents she was gay, then the years it had taken for them to adjust to that. Then the time to get them to lend her the money. She and Sal were paying it back, too.

"I know it won't be easy, baby. We'll need to switch shifts, but I've got to go," Sally said.

"Why?"

"Well, first off, because it says I'd be fined or put in jail if I don't."

"Tell them you have a business to run."

"What. A gay bar? I bet they'd think we're real essential."

"So? Who cares what they think? It's how you earn your living. When do they expect you to sleep?"

Sally put the notice down and pulled Liz to a table out of earshot of the others. "Listen, Liz, I ought to do this. It's my civic duty. I mean, I live here. I have the right to a jury myself if I get in trouble. I ought to be willing to give them some time."

Liz looked at Sally. "What a baby you can be. Forty years of age and still with that long skinny runner's body, that fair, fair skin and hair. My innocent, upstanding citizen, as if ninety percent of the people who get jury duty notices didn't try to worm out of them. Okay, we'll get by."

Sally knew that Liz knew not only was it useless to try and dissuade Sally of anything once her mind was made up, but Liz admired her determination. They were pretty close politically, except for the big holes in Liz's family because of the government where they'd been citizens before they were, horrifyingly, victims. She gave her a kiss and, standing, pulled her head against her breasts for a second or two. "Maybe Deveta will take over for you. I don't think she's working."

"Is she still drinking heavily?"

"No more than she was last time she helped out. She's okay behind the bar. It gives her a feeling she belongs somewhere so she doesn't need to drink as much."

"I'll ask her."

❖

On her eighth day of jury duty, as on every other day, Sally sat slumped in a molded plastic chair with metal legs as thin as her own. Liz said her legs looked like toothpicks with doorknobs for knees, but when Sally offered to keep them out of sight in bed, Liz quickly uncovered them and reached between Sally's legs, stroking her as she said, "Don't you dare. They're half the reason I fell for you."

"And you mean that literally, don't you?"

Liz cracked up.

The courthouse wasn't air-conditioned, and the jury waiting room was hot. Sally straightened, feeling as self-conscious about her legs, in their floppy, worn bell bottom cords, as she'd begun to feel about all of herself. Did the other jurors think her legs were another weird thing about her?

By her second day, she was bored out of her skull. Jury duty, such a simple normal thing. She stood and walked to the window, half glowering at the other jurors in case they should look at her, should whisper and giggle as they had the first day. A bunch of them were wandering in from a case settled out of court at the last minute. At least they'd been chosen. She'd acted as respectably as she knew how, saying *yes sir* and *no sir* until she felt obsequious, but still they hadn't wanted her. So she sat in the plastic chairs, reading bartending manuals, small business guides, and the *New York Times* she treated herself to every morning. When she became restless, she looked out the windows at the traffic below, the storefronts, the hurried pedestrians, cabs, messenger bikes, police cars, corrections vans. When no one was around to make her feel self-conscious, she paced.

The first day, she'd been excited. Here she was, wearing the navy-blue pantsuit she'd bought long ago for a funeral, a businesswoman with enough money to live as she wished and a lover she'd been with longer than a lot of straight marriages lasted. The city had deemed her respectable enough to serve on a jury. She proudly gave her name to the clerk of the court and smiled at the prospective jurors around her, all talking nervously among themselves. When they gave instructions, she regretted having nothing to jot notes on so she would do everything right. They'd gotten out early that first day, and Sally, feeling good about doing her civic duty, the rain letting up for the afternoon, had walked all the way to her apartment and had woken Liz. The sun was even shining in their window. They'd made love until it was time for Liz to go downtown to take over from Deveta.

For the next few days, Sally's nervous excitement continued as she went through the selection process over and over. She became used to rejection. One by one the other jurors didn't return to the waiting areas. Then, one day, Sally was the only one in the lounge. She was sent home early again.

When the others returned from their various assignments, they'd formed bonds among themselves, even though they scrupulously avoided discussing cases.

"Still not picked, dear?" asked one blue-haired older woman.

Sally smiled. "Not yet," she said brightly.

Old blue-hair looked her up and down as if to determine why she hadn't been chosen, smiled minimally, and moved to sit with a young woman in a dress. Later, Sally saw out of the corner of her eye that they were talking about her. She blushed and casually went to the rest room.

Another time a man, middle-aged, neatly dressed and always complaining he should be at work, spoke to her. "You work?" he asked.

"Sure," she said, glad to talk.

"What do you do?"

"I run a bar in the Village."

He drummed his fingers on the arm of the couch. "You're losing money, being here."

"Maybe, but somebody's got to serve on juries."

"Where's this bar of yours?"

Sally told him.

"Maybe I'll stop in sometime. I get down to that end of town quite a bit on business."

Sally was torn between being friendly, in which case she'd have to welcome him to the bar, and warning him that it was a women's bar.

As she hesitated, he nodded, as if to say, I thought so. He made elaborate preparations to smoke a cigar. Sally moved away from the smell.

No one else spoke to her. She was now too self-conscious to start conversations with any of them. There was one woman who Sally thought might be a very feminine dyke, the way she stared at her. If she was, though, she was determined to pass because she responded curtly to Sally's overture and never sat near her again.

On Friday of the first week, Sally had been once more summoned for selection, the criminal trial of someone accused of burglarizing several apartments. When they brought the defendant into the courtroom, Sally's heart began to pound. She was a very young black woman. And Sally could almost swear she was gay. She walked like a dyke, sat like one when she forgot to sit up straight with her knees together and her hands folded, and looked all wrong in the skirt and blouse the lawyer had probably brought for her to wear.

Sally was determined to get on this jury. Not because she wanted a gay girl to go free. Familiar as Sally was with some of her customers' experiences at the Women's House of Detention, she knew the defendant might be guilty. She wanted to be sure Jonelle Browley really got a fair trial by a jury of at least one real peer.

Sally cringed with the selection of each juror. Blue-hair. The man with the cigar. A black man in a three-piece suit who was never without his briefcase and work from the office. Another man who liked to tell dirty jokes to the ladies who would listen, although he'd never tried with Sally.

When Sally was questioned, she sat up straight, but not so straight she would look too tall, and she met the questioners in the eyes. Maybe that was her mistake, she thought on her way back to the lounge. Maybe ladies didn't look judges and lawyers in the eye. Or maybe she was marked. It did seem almost as if she wore a sign around her neck: this one can't be trusted to think like us.

Once more, she was dismissed early. The sky threatened rain but held on to it. This time she tramped first to the East River, then to the Hudson River. She crisscrossed the city for hours, until she was too tired to be angry anymore.

She fixed herself some dinner and watched TV until she couldn't stand it either. Every program was about some dumb straight family or a bunch of straight men acting tough. She was tempted to get drunk on the white wine she and Liz kept in the refrigerator, but wine was something she drank when she wanted to celebrate because everything was right and she was in tune with the world. She did not want to celebrate this Friday night. Never mind, she told herself, it's the weekend, and she didn't have to go to court the next day.

She went to bed early to be fresh in the morning but kept thinking of the young Black dyke so much like herself and fell asleep to dream of her: The smug jury judged her guilty before her meek lawyer was given time to defend her. The dyke went crazy, attacking the cops, the judge, the witnesses. The judge threatened to increase her sentence. Then she turned to Sally who was tied and gagged on the evidence table, and the Black dyke spoke softly to her, touching her gently, untying her ropes. "It's not your fault," she said, but Sally woke up mumbling into her pillow that it was, it certainly was because they would've let her on the jury if she'd worn a wedding dress. Then she lay awake, terrified of sleep, until Liz came home and soothed her.

Monday, she returned to her molded chair. Blue-hair and the young straight woman were the only ones left in the waiting area with her. In a flash she was furious again. Maybe not everything about running a bar was legal, she thought, but at least the people you dealt with treated you according to the way you did your job, not who you loved. The guys who serviced pinball machines, or delivered beer—they didn't drop their teeth when they looked at you.

The clerk of the court told Sally she could go home for the day. She shoved her hands in her pockets and left the building, walking head down, butchy, shouldering out of her way anyone in her path. What the hell good did it do to look respectable? You didn't fool anyone. To them you were only a goddamn queer. Maybe that's what the sign around her neck said: queer.

❖

Halfway through the last week, Sally was released for good. By this time her anger fit around her like the molded chair. She said good-bye to no one.

She walked into a fine May day. Last month's rains had washed the city clean. Delicate white or pink petals fell silently to the treed crosstown sidewalks. One more time, she was free to walk the daytime streets. Why go back to work? Why not enjoy the spring for a few more days, since Deveta was already counting on the income. The separation between jury duty, with all its depression and anger, and her normal life might do her good. Then she laughed, right out loud on the sidewalk. Normal? She wanted nothing to do with normal ever again.

Try as she might, she was not able to veer away from downtown. Soon she stood in front of Café Femmes. She could taste the white wine she knew sat cold in a bottle under the bar. Should she go in where she was wanted? Begin her life again and maybe do some good?

Deveta looked up at the sound of the cowbells. "Hi, stranger," she said cheerily from behind the bar. No one else was there.

"Hi, Deveta, what's happening?"

"Dead day. It's too nice to be inside. They'll show up later."

"Would you rather be outside?"

"Most of the time, no, but I took Marian out last night, and I'm itching to finish what I started." She winked. "You know she's never come out?"

Sally congratulated herself on her instincts. She knew her own world well. "Why don't you give her a call now? Go pick her up?"

"You mean it? You don't have jury duty?"

"It's over."

"Forever?"

"Jeez, I hope so."

"You don't need me?"

"Listen, you can finish out the week if you like, because that was the deal. But if you want to take off, that's okay, too. We'll pay you."

Deveta was slowly zipping her sweatshirt. "What if I take today, see how things go, then let you know later about the rest of the week?"

"Fine with me." One nearly negligible gesture, that's all she had to give. She couldn't repair this damaged world, but a lifetime of such gestures might be better than nothing at all.

On her way out the door Deveta stopped. "Hey, Sal?"

"Yeah?" She was already behind the bar pouring a glass of cold white wine.

"This Marian, did you know she's got kids?"

"I thought she might." Sally wet a bar rag.

"She left her old man a long time ago, but she still has the kids with her."

"You can handle it, Deveta."

"You think so? She makes me feel wanted, like she needs me in her life. You know what I mean?"

Sally ran the clean bar rag over the counter.

"I do. I know exactly what you mean."

Originally published in *Old Dyke Tales* (Naiad Press, 1984)

IV: White Wine

Once, when Sally the bartender was least expecting it and certainly didn't want it, she fell in love.

Never mind the details of the long, silent courtship. Roxanne came into Café Femmes, caught Sally's eye, and Sally, try as she might, could not look away.

It was during those early spring nights that have a cold edge to them, when the darkness still belongs to winter, when people scurry from one circle of lamplight to the next, impatient for brightness. Sally, sensing a hint of warmth in the air, was impelled toward spring, her whole being pointed toward it, suspended.

She stood behind the bar and, more restless than usual, ran her bar rag over and over the countertop. She and her partner and lover,

Liz, recently installed new overhead lights. Half of the originals were beyond replacement, and for a few years now, Café Femmes was dim enough that it took the two pinball machines and the jukebox to brighten it up a bit. Now the lights shone on the counter, exposing every stain. They illuminated the gay kids that hung out there in such a new and revealing way, Sally saw them clearly for the first time. She, too, was exposed by all this new light, flushed out of the pleasant daze in which she usually worked.

It was about this time when Roxy first began to frequent Café Femmes. What was it about her? Sally couldn't quite put her finger on it, on what made her heart flutter when that woman ordered a white wine in her Southern accent. Of course, the accent made her different, more noticeable, but she'd never been drawn to a Southern woman before. Maybe it was her knowing smile, confiding in Sally from the very start a wonderful secret, a connection.

Roxy was tall, but not as tall as Sally; thin, but not as thin as Sally. She was graceful, unlike Sally, in the way she opened her arms to the women in the bar, as if to embrace them all, and in the way she walked, as if with every step she might sink down beside some woman on a bed.

Her hair was light, but not blond like Sally's, and long. Her eyes flared now and then like streetlights in darkness. A dimple formed above Roxy's lips as she gave Sally that wise smile and said something in her slow voice like *Come on home with me, sweet Sal* when Sally was running a lemon around the rim of a glass, when anyone could hear. Sally's hand would shake, and she'd stare at Roxy's hands, wondering what their touch would be like if she did go home with her.

Gabby, one of the regulars, teased her about her crush. Sally was panic-stricken because it was too strong, because she couldn't end her obsession, couldn't hold in her high emotions, and wasn't at all sure, if the opportunity presented itself, that she could keep from falling on Roxy, from devouring her with her hands as well as with her eyes.

Sally was thirty-eight then. She also drank white wine, but when Roxy came into her life, she quickly switched to mineral water. Each time Roxy was near, she drank bottle after bottle of the stuff, trying to douse the fire inside rather than inflame it with liquor.

As for Liz, their shifts overlapped briefly. Besides, Roxy came into the bar at different times and flirted with many different girls. At home, Sally pushed Roxy out of her mind. At Café Femmes no one, knowing Sally's and Liz's devotion to each other, took Sally's infatuation seriously.

One night about three weeks after Roxy first appeared, Sally stepped out of the bright bar after her shift was over. The season remained spring/not spring. Earlier it was too warm to put on a winter jacket, and now she was chilly.

The warehouses that lined the street stood bulky and dark, blocking the sounds of the city. Sally walked from pool of light to pool of light. She stopped beneath a streetlamp, realizing this was one of those rare moments when the city fell absolutely silent. The quiet was a vibration in her flesh, a bell tingling after its audible sounds faded.

A lone car turned onto the street. Its rattle echoed between the warehouses. When it slowed, Sally began to walk again, afraid it might be a queer-basher or any man. But inside her body the vibration continued despite the car, despite her motion, until she knew it was fear no longer, but excitement. Roxy had mentioned that she drove up from the South. Could it be Roxy's car? Could it be Roxy? And if it was, what then?

❖

"Damn this traffic," said Roxy, inching her light blue Comet forward. It was rush hour on the Brooklyn Bridge. Two or three times a week for the last few weeks, Roxy picked Sally up around the corner from Café Femmes to hurriedly drive with her into Brooklyn, where Roxy had settled.

"The bastards don't care how short of time we are," Sally said, putting her hand on Roxy's thigh.

"Umm," Roxy said, moving as sensuously as any woman could on the ripped vinyl seat.

Sally withdrew her hand and covered her eyes.

"What's the matter, sweet Sal?" Roxy asked.

"I can't stand it, wanting you like this." Her clitoris must be twice its normal size and was becoming irritated as it throbbed against the seam of her pants.

When they got to Brooklyn, they couldn't go to Roxy's place. She had a live-in lover, too. Luckily, one of Roxy's friends worked second shift and offered her apartment. They were headed there now, under the darkening exhaust-filled sky, suspended over the water. The bridge lights came on.

Roxy was able to advance a few feet. The breeze as they moved cooled Sally's flushed face. "Talk to me," commanded Roxy. "It'll make the waiting easier."

"Roxy, Roxy." Her slightest look was intoxicating to Sally.

"Talk to me, sweet Sal."

"How's your cat?" Sally croaked.

"Ol' Orange Blossom? She's as sweet as you. When I can't be with you, she curls up against me under the covers and purrs your name all night."

Oh my gosh, Sally thought. This woman can't be for real. Does she honestly care this much for me? If she does, why aren't we talking about leaving our lovers?

"How about Spot?" Roxy asked, moving slightly farther toward the end of the bridge.

Sally couldn't for the life of her think of anything romantic to say about her dog. "He doesn't understand why I don't come home as early nights."

Roxy slipped her hand under Sally's leg. The car moved steadily, but slowly. "Where are you going nights, sweet Sal?" she teased.

Sally's heart pounded harder, and her mouth was dry, totally dry. She licked her lips.

Roxy watched her tongue.

"To you," Sally managed to say.

Roxy put the brakes on quickly, and the Comet stalled. She started it again with difficulty. Traffic stopped once more. Silently, Sally panicked. What if the vintage bomb overheated, and they never got to the apartment? After all, the car was nothing but Mercury's version of the Edsel. What if she was stuck atop the Brooklyn Bridge for hours, hungry for Roxy, inches from her, and never got to make love with her? She wouldn't be able to stand it.

But they moved again. And soon they reached the friend's extra bedroom. Sally was relieved both of her frustration and of her fear that she and Roxy would run out of things to say, that Roxy might find Sally's penchant for silence, her habit of few words, boring and drop her.

Another time, they spent a mere hour at Roxy's own apartment. No place else was available and their urgency was so great they risked her lover's unexpected arrival. Sally peered around as they entered, trying to glean glimpses of Roxy's life. What did she expect to see, anyway? Some revealing Southern memento of the life Roxy left behind? A clue to her relationship with her lover? Closing the curtains, Roxy led her firmly to the bed, turning on only a small night-light, as usual. Roxy liked to trap them in pools of light, usually one which lit only the bed they were on. Nothing was real but themselves, their touches in the silence of a strange place, and the unknown darkness around them. The light, the dark, intensified their time together.

They finished—if they ever were finished—and hurriedly left. Roxy drove the Comet out of her neighborhood fast and stopped in front of a park. Endlessly wanting, they embraced, kissing in a fever of tongues, made more ardent by the smells left from their hour of privacy. It was not unusual for them to do exactly this, pull over and make inadequate love, unable to wait until they were alone together, or unable to bear parting.

A police car drove slowly by. Roxy pulled back, her fingers lingering on the crotch of Sally's pants. When the cop was out of sight, Sally reached under Roxy's shirt to play with one breast beneath its bra. They stared at each other, watching their eyes turn muddy, brighten, finally smile. "I'm hungry," said Roxy.

"Me, too," replied Sally.

It was still early, and the dark sky held some light. Roxy started the Comet and tore up and down a few streets, finally struggling into a parking space on Flatbush Avenue. They walked across the wide street without touching, to a brightly lit restaurant.

"Ever been to Junior's?" Roxy asked.

"What is it, a hamburger place?" Sally seldom ventured into Brooklyn.

Roxy laughed. "More. Much more."

They entered a flood of light and noise and motion. The place looked like an enormous luncheonette to Sally. Her hunger increased with the pungent smell of pickles set out on each table in a dish, and steamed pastrami.

Sally grasped that she would remember this experience all her life. More vivid even than their lovemaking was this hour at Junior's, tasting things together, surrounded, for once, by ordinary people, as if they were ordinary lovers. Their color heightened from lovemaking, their eyes shadowed and brightened alternately by their fervor, they were as excited as if on a holiday.

They split a bowl of matzoh ball soup and a pastrami sandwich, rudely presented by a shuffling waiter.

"They're like that here," Roxy explained, feeding herself half of a pickle. When their cheesecake was served, they savored it slowly, once feeding each other a forkful, making quiet animal sounds of appreciation and laughing, something they seldom did in their passion.

Around them the shouts of the waiters continued, punctuating the rising and falling drone of the customers, a love song of sorts. It was as if she'd entered the heart of Brooklyn, her lover's adoptive land, and she watched everything that went on around them while Roxy smoked a long, elegant cigarette. When they left, darkness was complete. The low roar of the city was a kind of silence, as if they'd walked out of the world. The bridge glowed beyond them, an intricate pathway back. Their arms went around one another; they didn't want to go back. Roxy pulled Sally into a doorway and ran her hands down her body, pulling her buttocks closer, then kneading them rhythmically as they kissed.

Wet lipped, they broke apart and crossed to the car. They didn't say a word. No one passed by. The not-silence was thick as fog as they pushed their way through it. The light blue of the Comet shone like a beacon.

All this time Sally was more, rather than less, attentive to Liz. Not to cover up what she was doing, which she couldn't seem to deny herself, and which had nothing to do with their life together, but because she was at such a height of stimulation. It didn't matter that Liz wasn't Roxy. Liz was familiar and soothing and quieted, for a moment, with her gentle knowing hands and mouth, Sally's fire. This was real and long and utterly good, what she and Liz built together.

But that same afternoon Roxy would enter the Café Femmes and they would plan their next meeting.

Could it be Roxy's very unfamiliarity that fired up Sally? Did she trail her uncommon Southern origins like a scent behind her? Too, unlike Liz, she was a supercharged femme. Her come-hither eyes broadcast her demanding sexual presence. And Sally longed to meet Roxy's every demand, forever.

In bed, Roxy was, at first, all submissive female grace. Until Sally found herself uprooted, on her back, submitting to touches she'd be too shy to bring home to Liz. Touches so stirring, the very thought of them turned her on. Touches so intimate, Roxy marked her soul. And it was not like down-to-earth Sally to think something like that.

So again and again, in a pattern that varied slightly from one time to another—and that variation was mostly in the ways they found to enhance their sensations—Sally found herself driven as fast as possible to Brooklyn, then faster back into Manhattan, rattling past streetlights in the blue Comet. Often, she sang Johnny Mathis songs to herself, embarrassed to sing them aloud. The breeze through the car windows was an extension of Roxy's last caress, especially as they went deeper into spring and the breezes grew warmer.

Stopping at Sally's apartment building, they would look at each other, filled with the tragedy of a future of partings. Sally would step out of the car, watching and listening as Roxy broke their dome of silence by accelerating into the night.

She wondered where Roxy went. Home? To Café Femmes? Another bar? Perhaps there was a second, a third late-night lover? Perhaps Roxy, unlike Sally, was accustomed to a double life.

But really, when she was alone, Sally didn't care. She shivered in pleasure, remembering yet another response Roxy elicited from her an hour before.

Another time, the lovers fled to an Italian neighborhood in Brooklyn. Young men milled about the stoops where neatly dressed girls sat and giggled. The small apartment they borrowed boasted floor to ceiling white-framed windows and textured red wallpaper. The bed was covered with a satin quilted comforter. Plush low modern furniture was arranged around a woven straw rug. It was only one room, and a tiny kitchenette, but Sally loved its opulence. Undressing Roxy, she couldn't help but pose her on the furniture, move her from place to place to experience every texture on their naked bodies. When they heard music through the windows, they were not too carried away to wrap themselves in the cool silky comforter and see what was outside.

It was dark. The buildings on both sides of the street were brownstones, their stoops filled now with whole families. Solemnly, slowly, down the middle of the street, marched a procession in white. A priest came first in his robes, scattering blessings to the onlookers. Small children marched among women in virginal white gowns. Boys in white suits played the few instruments. Every free hand held a candle. The whole procession, which was not long, looked like a moving island of lights, except when streetlamps shed light on their set, devout faces. Toward the end, four older boys carried a statue of the Virgin Mary on a platform. Votive candles burned around it.

Sally and Roxy stared in wonder at this primitive march through the Brooklyn street. How mysterious were the ways of people who clung to such pomp, how different from themselves. Yet it should be Sally and Roxy worshipping the virgin female. They celebrated themselves differently, stepping away from the window, letting the comforter fall, and looked at each other naked a long while before they lay on the bed and made love slowly.

She couldn't have said why, but the procession disturbed Sally. She was compelled to reassert her own reality, to exaggerate their own celebration, over and over and over.

At some point as they made love, Roxy whispered, "Look." A full moon shone its light through the huge windows. Roxy switched off the lamp over the bed, and they saw each other for the first time in moonlight. Sally's uneasiness disappeared. She emerged somehow blessed, purified. Still, it was one of their last times together.

Sally, behind the bar, opened a bottle of mineral water but wasn't into drinking it. She looked over toward the jukebox and the pinball machine, knowing she should have plugged them in long ago. Instead, she went around the bar to wipe down the empty tables. Outside she saw the workmen getting ready to knock off. It was daylight savings time, but newly, and she was not yet used to a bright sky this late and in such contrast with the darkness of the bar. She hadn't yet flicked on the new ceiling lights either, to postpone surrender of her dark silence.

It was a very slow day. Not even Roxy came in—her mother was in town from the South for a few days of visiting and shopping. Or so Roxy said. With a twinge of guilty doubt, she thought Roxy might simply have found a new passion. In the end, these few days without Roxy weren't as bad as she expected, and to tell the truth, she was relaxed for the first time in months.

There went the workmen. She really needed to turn the lights on now. But as she moved to do so, she caught sight of a cab pulling up. Liz emerged. Something was wrong. Not only was Liz early, but without fail she took the subway to work.

"Liz?"

"Oh, I couldn't stand it any longer," Liz said, running her fingers through her dark bangs as she rushed inside.

Fear struck Sally. Did Liz find out about Roxy?

"I wanted to get here early to install it." Liz said, pulling objects out of her pockets, not noticing Sally's concern. "Every night I come in here and wince under these glaring lights. They give me headaches, Sal. I mean, it's one thing to work during the day like you do, when you can keep them off, but at night I can't see to mix a drink without some light, and our new ones are too strong. So here's my brainstorm for today. We'll install one of these dimmer gadgets, since the lights all work off one switch, and then we can adjust them exactly the way we want. Okay?"

Sally was vastly relieved and didn't give a thought to the solution of the light problem. She pulled Liz to her and rocked her, saying. "I'm sorry, I'm sorry."

"About what?" Liz asked, pulling back.

Sally looked down into her distracted face and experienced a surge of warmth, and more relief. "That I didn't tell you how much I hate them, too. Every day I wait longer and longer to put them on. If I'd mentioned it, I might have spared you some of those headaches. But I thought you were attached to the new lights."

"They were your idea."

"Because you complained how dark it was at night."

They stopped and laughed at themselves. Then Liz went to work.

A few kids trickled in on their way home from work, Gabby among them. Sally, bouncy with relief, joined them at pinball.

At one point, when Liz was in the basement fooling around with the electric panel, Gabby said in a low voice across the bar to Sally, "It's good to see you laughing and happy for a change."

"Haven't I been?"

"Not hardly," replied Gabby, pushing her glass forward for another drink. "I was beginning to think the rumors might be true."

"What rumors?"

"About you and Roxanne."

Sally slopped the foam from Gabby's beer on the counter. She hoped Gabby thought her red face came from stooping to get her bar rag. "Me and Roxanne what?"

"You know, that you've been seeing each other."

Sally got faintly hostile. "No, I didn't know."

"Hey, I'm only letting you know. Listen, you tell me there's nothing to it, and I'll beat the shit out of anybody who says I'm wrong."

Sally didn't know what to say. She couldn't lie to her friend. Luckily, some kids came in and called her to serve them. While she worked, the lights came on, and she squinted against their glare. Then

Liz came running upstairs, wonderful Liz, and grabbed the knob she'd installed on the wall.

If that rumor had gone any farther, wondered Sally, would Liz have heard? Was it worth all the hurt she would have caused her? The lights dimmed and lit up again as Liz turned the knob one way, then reversed it, back and forth to the beat of the music, a proud grin on her face.

Maybe Sally should confess to her. Maybe Liz would take it well, and she could see Roxy once in a while.

The lights were down as low as they could go. Almost the only light came from the blue glow of twilight outside the window. Everyone in the bar applauded. Liz bowed, giving the knob its final setting. The bar turned—almost—back to its former dim self.

The cowbells sounded over the door, and Sally saw Roxy come in. Funny, even after three days her heart didn't do its usual flip. Hell, she knew things were slowing down anyway. Why hurt Liz? Why not call it quits while the good vibes remained from her fling with Roxy?

Sally felt free. Liz came behind the bar to work with her for a while. Gabby got up, and Sally caught her before she left. "You tell them," she said. "Tell them there's nothing going on."

Gabby looked relieved. "I can always count on you and Liz to stick it out when everybody else gives up the ghost. It kind of gives me hope for myself."

"What was all that about?" Roxy asked, taking Gabby's seat. She looked tired. Not from the strain of a visiting mother, either, Sally suspected.

"There's a rumor going around about you and me."

"Shit," said Roxy. "And we were unbelievably careful."

Sally noticed her use of the past tense. Liz came by and bumped into Sally affectionately.

"Hi, Roxanne," she said, cheery from her triumph over the lights.

Roxy became subdued with Liz's proximity. As a matter of fact, Sally realized, Roxy never came in when both she and Liz were on. Was this another hint of change? "Maybe we ought to lie low for a while," Sally suggested in a mutter.

"Exactly what I was thinking," agreed Roxy.

Their eyes met. It was over. How simple. Where were the teary scenes? Where was the passion that burned a few days ago?

Never mind, this turned out exactly right, and she dared smile at Roxy. "A white wine?" she asked.

"If you please." Roxy smiled back.

Sally poured, then reached for another mineral water for herself. No, she decided and poured the wine. She'd been keeping a bottle chilled, the way Roxy liked it, and it tasted good. She opened a beer for another customer and went back to her wine.

As she sipped, watching Roxy talk with someone, she sipped an essence of Roxy, so often had she tasted white wine on her lips. But no. it was more the essence of her infatuation with Roxy. It was exciting, this cool liquid, but delicate, graceful going down, until it heated the depth of her. And made her want more. But not too much more. She drank just enough before she went home at the end of her shift.

Originally published in *Old Dyke Tales* (Naiad Press, 1984)

V: Summer Storm

Content advisory: racism

At the height of that summer, when Sally the bartender gazed out the plate glass window of Café Femmes, the afternoon shadows cast by the warehouses appeared part bleached and didn't cool the street at all.

Sally had stepped outside earlier to escape the air-conditioning. Sometimes all that air filtered through a machine drove her outside to breathe the sooty, real air of the city. As she stood on the hot sidewalk, tall and blond and skinny as a bar rail, the heat rose through the rubber soles of her sneakers. The cobblestones in the street, after a few minutes, became bubbling lava to her eyes. She went back inside, and Café Femmes was a dark, cold relief. Through the plate glass window, she watched the workmen wipe their brows as they loaded and unloaded trucks across the street.

When the gay kids began to come in for lunch, they were wrung out. Their slicked back DA haircuts, their short-sleeved shirts or halter tops, were all damp. Teased hair had collapsed. More often than not they paid Sally with soggy bills carefully pried from damp pockets.

That was the first day the five Black dykes made their boisterous entrance. Sally couldn't hear the cowbell over their fun.

"Woo-ee!" said a woman in glasses, named, Sally found out later, Dovie. "This place feels like the North Pole."

"About time someplace did," grumbled a woman with a thick Afro as she collapsed into a seat.

"Even the packing line's cooler than the street," said another of the group.

"How you doing, sister?" asked Dovie, who ordered drafts for all of them.

"I'm doing fine," Sally replied as she wiped the bar and started to draw the beer. She liked seeing new faces in the bar. "I'm lucky. I work in here."

"Sure wish I was in here with you," Dovie said with a laugh.

Sally explained to Dovie how, if they were going to be in the neighborhood, they were welcome to bring their lunches in and she'd serve beer or soda, whatever they wanted.

"Sounds good," Dovie said, after delivering four of the beers to her table. "We ate down the street already, but it'd sure be cheaper for us to bag it. Rate they pay over at the factory, we're barely making our subway fare here. If they put us on piecework, it'll get better."

"When did you start there?"

"Last week. One of the white gay girls told us about your place. She doesn't come in here days, she says, afraid someone'll see her, but if the someones who see us don't already know, they're too dumb to figure us out anyway." Dovie laughed again.

Sally saw what she meant. Four of the five she would peg as butches, the one with the Afro and two, like Dovie, short-haired. The thinnest butch walked like she meant business; her femme, straight hair to her shoulders, never left her side.

"What a sweatshop that place is. But you know how it is, you work where you can. When Randa was hired—that's Willie's girl."

Sally nodded at the femme.

"Right. She brought Willie down the next day. Since they didn't bat an eye at Willie, the rest of us applied. They have a lot of girls quitting, 'specially in the summer. Most factories shut down two weeks come summer. Not this one. These bosses going to squeeze every penny out of our asses they can. Then they'll hang us up to dry and catch the drippings. And there's plenty of them in this heat."

Sally found Dovie's laughter infectious.

Dovie leaned over on her elbows and lowered her voice. "I can see you play okay, but you think we'll be hassled by the trade?" she asked, indicating with a nod of her head the white kids who were leaving to go back to work.

Sally viewed the room. These were all kids who'd been coming to Café Femmes for years. She liked most of them. They seldom caused trouble unless they were very upset, and then the fight was taken outside. Her eyes traveled to one of the regulars, Betty Marie, and she worried about her for a moment but shrugged. What could one bitter drunk do by herself?

"It's hard to say," she told Dovie. "We never had any trouble like that. We have a few Black women who come in. They live around here or go with white girls. Most of our regulars are pretty nice."

Dovie's expression was hopeful. "Reason I ask," she said, "this job is bad. Real bad. I don't know if we can stick it out without some kind of nice thing happening in our days. This Femmes bar is that kind of thing."

Sally understood. After all, she hadn't always been half owner of a gay bar. Before she and Liz went into business, she worked in an office surrounded by straights. She remembered how hard it was to go in there every day and to stay there without punching somebody in the mouth. "Liz and I will do what we can to keep it comfortable for you."

"You're a pal." Dovie laughed. "For a honky."

Sally laughed back and extended a hand over the counter. Dovie soon gave up on teaching Sally to follow her complex handshake and settled for a simple shake.

The bar was eerily quiet after the lunch crowd left. More so after the five Black dykes who, because Sally wasn't used to them, came across as bigger than life. Betty Marie remained, steadily sipping at her second or third gin and tonic of the day. But she was over by the window, watching the activity on the street. Sally poured herself a chilled white wine and tipped it to her lips, toasting the five, as she was already thinking of them. Dovie had added something extra to an otherwise dull day, and she appreciated that. She hoped they'd come back.

Later, Betty Marie moved to the bar for a refill. Sally drained the last of her wine and wiped the countertop, knowing she was in for a long afternoon.

Betty Marie had only recently returned to Café Femmes. She moved in cycles, from one bar to the next, wearing out her welcome wherever she went, disappearing unerringly before she was kicked out for good. A few months later she'd slink back in, banned elsewhere, more full of rancor and sarcasm than ever. Every gin and tonic fueled her anger.

Sally, being the softy she was, pitied her. She let her come back, though Liz declared she couldn't stand the woman. Liz was a Jew, and the Jewish people—along with Blacks, illegal aliens, liberals, and atheists—were some of Betty Marie's favorite targets. She quickly learned to clam up in front of Liz. Sally tuned her out, knowing she should shut her up instead.

Today's topic was to be expected: the five African American dykes and how they were going to take over Café Femmes, New York City, and anything else Betty Marie believed was hers to protect.

Betty Marie was a small woman, about thirty-five, with large gray circles under her eyes, chewed fingernails, and frizzy dark hair she straightened when she had the money. This was not one of those times, and smooth the hair down as she might, up it would spring. Often, after a long day of drinking, Betty Marie's hair was an electrified halo.

As the woman spewed her hatred, Sally couldn't help but remember other long afternoons.

"Maybe I do have a chip on my shoulder," Betty Marie said one day, "but I have my reasons." She dipped into her glass like one of those trick plastic birds Sally saw in novelty shops: dipping and filling, back and then forward, moved by nothing but the weight of the liquor. "I went to parochial school, see, but I passed the public school to go home. The colored girls went to public school, but they lived in the projects on the other side of my school." She closed her eyes, and a faint shudder ran down her frail body.

"I fought my way to and from school almost every day. *Girlie*, they'd call at us, *hey, girlee*. We'd be in uniform, and there they'd be in their bright colors. Your Black people have their taste in their toenails," she spat. Sally warned Betty Marie she would be thrown out for using offensive words, and she knew it. "Then they'd say something about our uniforms, or about Catholics, the heathens. Or they'd make fun of our looks or of our families. Pretty soon they'd get us going, and we'd go at them, tearing their hair, pushing them down, you know how girls fight. Somehow, though, always us white girls were blamed."

"You mean you didn't do anything to provoke them?" Sally asked, skeptical.

Betty Marie ignored her at first. "No one believed the colored girls were at fault. If it went down on the way to school, the Sisters would yell at me in front of the whole class, then slap me and put me in a corner. And, sure, we called them names, too. Wouldn't you?" she asked, her eyes unfocused. "No, maybe you wouldn't. You're such a

Goody Two-shoes. They were too different from us and talked nasty enough you couldn't help talking back. But they always crossed the street to start something with us, I swear."

As Betty Marie continued muttering, Sally shook her head and moved away. Perhaps someone else would come in and free her from Betty Marie. At times she took the paper and read it by the window, pretending the light was better there. What could she do? Betty Marie needed someplace to go, maybe more than a lot of the kids. She let her be.

The five came in every noon for the rest of the week. There were some stares, some elbow nudging, but for the most part, the kids were cool. When the five didn't come Saturday, Sally assumed she'd seen the last of them that week, but Sunday morning, when Liz came home and slipped under the sheets with her, she told Sally three came with their girls.

"How'd it go?"

"The kids will get used to them. No one hassled them. You could tell they weren't really welcome, though. I tried to make up for it without being conspicuous."

"I know what you mean," Sally said sleepily. "You don't want to treat them differently, but you want them to know you like them coming in. Was Betty Marie around?"

"Oh shit, don't tell me she's back."

Sally yawned. "No question about it. Wonder why she wasn't there."

"I don't know, but she doesn't have to explain her absence to me as long as she stays away. Do you think she hates Blacks as much as she hates Jews?"

"At least," Sally said, pulling Liz toward her, intending to show her how much she herself liked a certain Jewish woman next to her in bed. But the next thing she knew the sun shone in the window, and she dressed to catch the subway and open the bar. Before she left, she watched Liz sleep, golden-colored in the sunlight, soft and vulnerable without her glasses. She wondered if she would have loved her if she'd been Black, but that was silly. Liz would be a different person altogether.

The sun was as strong as it had been all week, but somehow, perhaps because it was Sunday and the street deserted, the heat was softer, more merciful. Sally sat outside on a barstool for a while, sipping white wine and soaking up the rays before the kids began to drift in, discussing cures for their hangovers. She indulged in her perfect cure: a glass of white wine, chilled, whenever you wanted it, up to two times a day. The kids called her a teetotaler and ordered Bloody Marys or shots of whiskey.

Betty Marie came by soon enough, and even before she ordered her first gin and tonic she said, "I hear you were recruiting for the NAACP again last night."

Her tone, like the day's heat, was light enough for Sally to kid her along. "That might not be a bad idea. A gay chapter of NAACP."

"You two would be full-fledged members, that's for sure. Give me a G and T, will you?"

Sally wanted to say, *If you behave yourself,* but what was the sense?

Betty Marie leaned over the bar to watch Sally make the drink. She asked speculatively, "Liz did wash the glasses last night?"

"Of course, why?"

"You never know who was there before you."

It took a moment for Sally to realize what Betty Marie was not saying. She didn't believe this woman could be serious now, in twentieth century New York City, and she eyed her as she put the drink down and took her money. "What's the matter, you afraid being Black's contagious?"

But she only half listened to Betty Marie's answer and the complaints that went on and on.

"If the Sisters or my mother weren't yelling at me, my father was," Betty Marie whined. "Before I was enrolled in school, I went to the playground down the street. One day, I made this new friend, Wayne. He let me ride his bike. At lunchtime, I invited him. I always dragged kids home with me—my mother rolled her eyes and fed them. We rode double all the way there, and I loved it.

"My dad was laid off at the time. When I walked into that kitchen with Wayne, Dad acted crazy. 'Course I know why now. Didn't mean anything to me then that Wayne was Black. Dad bellowed for Wayne to get out of his house, then started hitting on me for bringing him home." She took a sip from her glass and smacked her lips.

"I mean, I didn't know. Nobody ever explained these were the people my father and his friends talked trash about. When Dad calmed down, he explained how Wayne's father took his job because he worked cheaper. Said you didn't need as much money to live like those people did. And he told me there were other ways they could hurt us, asked me if Wayne touched me at all."

Sally was fed up.

Betty Marie didn't stop. "I'd rather be a queer than Black any day," she said. Sally, sickened, realized Betty Marie must hate gay people, too.

She should say something. Maybe no one ever tried reasoning with her. "Black people aren't poor by choice, you know," she started.

"Don't give me that bullshit about them needing us to make exceptions for them."

"That wasn't what—"

"Go ahead and call me Archie Bunker," Betty Marie said proudly.

How could you argue with someone like that?

Sally left Betty Marie to herself and watched out of the corner of her eye as various of the kids now and then talked to her. A few nodded. Betty Marie was a waste of a good lesbian, riddled with hate as she was. Still, she had to serve someone full of rancor as long as she didn't hurt anyone else. But she wondered if she, herself, might be hurting a whole lot of people with her live and let live attitude.

At the beginning of the next week, the heat relented a bit. Everyone's mood improved, including Betty Marie's. She didn't come by at all Wednesday, and Sally hoped Café Femmes' turn to host her simply ended sooner than she'd anticipated. Strange, even without Betty Marie's obvious, exaggerated prejudice around, the other kids became hard to handle.

"I don't care about Rosa coming in here," Gabby, a regular, said on Wednesday night. "After all, she lives right around the corner. And I think Dolores is nice. I'm kind of tight with Almeda. But Sal, doesn't it kind of scare you—a bunch of them moving in like that? I mean, they have their own bars."

Sally argued with Gabby and thought she brought her around. Then she contended with everyone else's comments. She couldn't ignore the situation anymore, but as long as the five didn't come in on weeknights, and Betty Marie wasn't around, at least she didn't have to upset Liz by talking to her about it.

By Thursday, though, both the heat and Betty Marie were back. At lunch, Sally watched Betty Marie, to see how she acted and to avert any confrontations. But the woman was on her first drink of the day and did nothing more than cast hateful glances when none of the five were looking.

Sally remembered a night, during a bad snowstorm, when almost no one came into the bar. Betty Marie had started on bombs and how sending men into outer space upset the weather, and before long she fully launched into blaming everything on Black people.

"Once I had a chance to run in a city race," Betty Marie said. "I belonged to the Police Athletic League."

Sally observed the small woman. At one time she might well have been swift and agile, but certainly too small for much of a future running.

"The PAL planned this field day. I won most of the races at school and figured no sweat. I didn't count on all your Black friends being there. This was my big chance—I could be a real champion. Maybe of the city. Definitely of Queens. But I forgot how fast the Black girls ran. I mean, it isn't fair to let them run against white girls. It comes natural to them, and we have to work really hard to beat them. I lost the very first race. And if I couldn't beat them that day, I knew I'd never be able to—they grew taller and I stayed a runt. Running was the one damn thing I did good."

Sally thought Betty Marie would cry, but she ordered another gin and tonic and toasted her lost fantasy career.

"Come on," Sally couldn't help saying. "Aren't you making kind of a big thing of this?"

Betty Marie had perfected the evil eye, and Sally backed down, but not before deciding to close early. No one else was coming in through that blowing snow. The bitter, self-defeated woman at the bar drained her drink and left mumbling that she knew when she wasn't wanted.

Today, too, Sally wished she could close early. Instead, she went outside to stand in the blazing heat and burn off the despondent mood Betty Marie put her in. Across the street, the workmen were red-faced with exertion and heat, slick with sweat.

"Wish I had your job today," called one to Sally.

She laughed, shading her eyes against the glare from the sky. "No, you don't," she shouted back. She turned and walked back inside. It wouldn't do at all for straight men to grow comfortable with visiting the bar. Then she'd have another eviction problem.

Betty Marie held court at a window table with two kids who worked nights. Sally lounged behind the bar, enjoying the chill of drying sweat under her white shirt and succumbing to the familiar rhythm of a late morning at Café Femmes.

Friday remained the same, unbearably hot, with Dovie and friends coming in at noon. Betty Marie grumbled; the other kids eyed the Black women like they posed some kind of threat.

Sally and Liz talked about it finally and decided it would be best if Sally hung around that Saturday night. What with the heat, the continued presence of the new women, and the growing hostility of the regulars as Betty Marie egged them on, anything could be stirred up. Besides, Sally liked to stay nights once in a while both to enjoy the bar and to spend more time with Liz. Usually on those nights she would treat herself to dinner out.

That Saturday she walked over to Little Italy and her favorite restaurant, tiny and unimpressive except for a rich red sauce and perfectly cooked linguine. She wanted to ask who supplied their delicate pastries but found herself too shy. The girl who served her appeared to be the family's eldest daughter, and she, too, was shy. As usual, they smiled obliquely at each other when Sally left.

On her way back to Café Femmes, Sally carried with her the acceptance behind the young girl's smile as well as a takeout order of linguine for Liz. Why couldn't life always be this good, she wondered. People acting nice to one another. Sally was obviously queer, but the girl treated her with respect. If Dovie walked in, would she be treated well?

Despite her leisurely walk, Sally sweated. It was one of those hot city nights when the day's air never left. It fit over the city and over Café Femmes as snugly as an observatory roof.

Most of the kids arrived early to enjoy the air-conditioning, and their noise level rose as high as the cold. The jukebox roared, the game machines clamoring. Betty Marie sat at the same table under the window, and a group hung on her words, supplying her with drinks.

Later, four of the five, with their girlfriends and a couple of other friends, came in. Sally could tell from their partying mood, as well as their unsteadiness, that Café Femmes was not their first stop.

She'd almost forgotten the heat outside until they opened the door. The day's sticky, breezeless air came in with them. Sweat formed on her upper lip—from heat or anxiety? She and Liz locked eyes. They periodically glanced at Betty Marie only to find her scowling bitterly at the Black dykes. She turned toward Sally and Liz as if to say, *I told you so. I told you they'd take over.*

Ignoring Betty Marie, Sally helped Liz meet the haphazard and high-spirited orders. She found herself laughing again with Dovie, glad the women acted unaware of the relative silence their entrance produced in the bar. But then, she thought, maybe they were used to it.

The dance floor proved to be the undoing of the evening. Small, occasionally it became too small for the regular crowd, some of whom would sit out a dance to make space for others. At one point a particularly fast song with complex rhythms began to play, one the kids normally sat through. The Black women cheered and jumped up to dance.

The air conditioner noisily pushed icy air into the bar, the kids talked and laughed, admiring two of the dancers who were particularly good. The lights were dim, everyone was served for the moment, and Sally wiped the bar with her rag, enjoying the dancers, considering an unheard of third glass of wine because things were going well. But Liz leaned worriedly on her elbows across the bar.

Betty Marie never danced. Nor did she move when the four white women at her table did. The whites pushed their way onto the dance floor and, once there, danced stiffly, obviously not for the joy of it. Sally, almost unconsciously, began to roll up her sleeves. Gabby came to the bar and stood near her. Betty Marie watched the dancers, smiling.

On the floor, a white couple stumbled in the path of a Black dancer, then offered an exaggerated apology. It happened again, with the other white couple. The Black women, finding themselves edged toward the tables, were frowning.

The record stopped, but instead of returning to their tables, everyone on the floor stood her ground, as if to yield it at this point would be some sort of defeat. When a slow song came on, Sally tried to relax. Perhaps this would cool things down and the tension would pass. She remembered another Betty Marie story. Did any of these women remind Betty Marie of her lover in prison? Is that why she was particularly vindictive tonight?

"I'd never done time before," Betty Marie had told Sally, rambling through an afternoon. "I was in for passing bad checks one too many times, and I heard enough on the street to know I better watch my p's and q's around everybody, guards and prisoners alike.

"So what's the worst thing can happen to me inside? This Black girl in for manslaughter and tough as nails has a thing for me. She gave me the creeps. I was scared to death she'd kill me if I let on I didn't want her. I played hard to get, flirted, pretended I wasn't out yet. She's gentle as a lamb, patient as a saint with me. White, I bet I would have loved her, she was that good to me.

"So it went on like that for a while, and pretty soon she's mad. But to tell you the truth, by that time I was enjoying it some. Knowing she liked me, knowing I wasn't going to give in to her, knowing what a hard time she was having wanting me and not getting me.

"Then one day in the yard one of her friends comes up to me. *Listen*, she says, *you're really driving her up the wall. I don't like to see her hurting like this. What do you want from me?* I say. *Don't lead her on. Leave her alone. If you don't want her, let her down easy. Stop torturing her.* I say, *Why? You have a soft spot? Could be*, the girl says, and I'm thinking this is getting more interesting all the time. Now there's two of them hung up because I won't give in and I won't let go. I pulled out my trump. *If I tell her I don't want her, she might hurt me bad.* The Black girl shakes her head. *No way she'd hurt you or anybody she loves. She's in here for going after a guy who tried to rape her, not someone she ever cared about. Nothing she could do to you would hurt you as much as what you're doing to her. And I can guarantee she won't touch you.* How? *Me and my friends, we'll watch out for you.* I thought about it, trying to figure which I'd enjoy more, leading my 'lover' down the garden path a while longer, or dropping her so hard she'd never forget it."

Sally's stomach churned to hear the cruelty in her voice. Betty Marie had continued. "So I told her okay, thinking the whole thing was a waste of energy, and I might as well ditch her now while I had protection. The next day out in the yard, in front of her friends, making sure they were there for me in case I needed them, I told her. And boy, did I tell her. I didn't hold a thing back. I was telling off the girls who beat on me and Wayne who got me in trouble, and all those runners. She went creeping away from me like I broke her in two.

"And then you know what her friends did? The ones who were supposed to be protecting me? They turned on me. Took me behind this wall and hit me over and over till I puked on one of them. They turned on me, the bastards, when I trusted them."

In a way that remained Sally's favorite story, because of the ending. Remembering, it decreased her own desire to grab the baseball bat from behind the counter and go after Betty Marie. She wondered again, as she watched her stare at the dance floor, what made Betty

Marie tick. What kind of life she lived with this hatred inside. How she'd become twisted.

The funny thing was, what occurred next was really an accident. While they were dancing all jammed together. Randa, the long-haired femme who was Willie's girl, stepped on a white femme's foot. Both jumped back as if a shot had rung out.

Now, as well as a matter of territory, it became a matter of personal pride for the two butches, each of whom thought she must protect her girl. The white butch cursed the Black femme's clumsiness, using a racial epithet. Sally saw Dovie's conflict. If she threw the first punch, she risked getting kicked out of the bar. That would be the easiest way for Sally and Liz to react. And since her friends would back her up, none of them would be able to return either. On the other hand, if she did nothing, she would lose face with her girl and her friends and probably be banned from the bar. It would simply take longer. Which mattered more to her, her Black friends or some white women's hangout?

Dovie yelled at the white femme. Betty Marie's cohorts were ready for her. The other whites weren't about to see their own pushed around; the other Blacks reacted the same.

While still in the stage of shouts, threats, and some shoving, Sally ordered Betty Marie out of the bar.

Stumbling and laughing, knowing she'd win in the end by driving the Blacks out, Betty Marie left. This distracted everyone from the fight, so when Sally politely asked the white dancers to follow their friend out, no one moved except Sally and the two couples. Without their leader to egg them on, they went willingly enough, stomping, threatening to meet the Blacks outside, vowing never to return.

Things went back to normal. The five, as if to prove their courage, danced. Dovie nodded her thanks to Sally. The white kids went back to their conversations, but none of them danced as long as the Blacks were on the floor. Dovie and her friends weren't comfortable either and went outside. Sally followed them into the muggy night, shaking hands with Dovie on the way, telling her to come back, apologizing.

There was no sign of the two white couples, but Betty Marie leaned against a lamppost across the street, swaying under the electrified halo of her hair. She taunted the Black women as they made their subdued way past the hulking, sleeping warehouses and factories, up the uneven pavement toward the subway. The women saw her, heard her, ignored her—perhaps the most courageous thing they could do as they walked, hand in hand, stoic and silent as the night.

Betty Marie's cries echoed off the buildings and bounced back at her. Was she disappointed when they didn't beat her up? Would their blows have proven her own worth? If they'd abused her, she was wronged, deterred, kept from being all she could be. Now whose fault was any of it but her own? What ending could she give this story to cast herself in a sorrowful light? Who would take pity on such a bully?

Sally, bitterly sad when she locked the door later, behind the last of the kids, wanted nothing but to take off and go home.

"Come on, Liz. I'll clean up in the morning."

Liz stopped sweeping. She leaned on her broom.

"Come on," repeated Sally, switching off the air conditioner, turning off the bar lights. The streetlight shone in the window. Liz stood under the shadow cast by the words ƧƎMMƎꟻ ƎꟻAƆ.

Tears ran along the shadows on her face, glimmered behind her glasses. "Someone like that," Liz said as Sally put her arms around her, "ruins everything."

"I know." The machine-cooled air was seeping out of the bar. Sally drooped.

"She's full of hatred. The same hatred that led half my family into the camps." Liz raised her voice, crying into the empty bar. "Why does she have to bring it here?"

Sally answered sorrowfully, "She knows we can't turn a dyke out into a world that hates her."

Liz laid her head on Sally's shoulder. "That's what paralyzed me," she explained with a sigh. "What if someone tried to push me out? Where would I go? Will Dovie and her friends ever come back?"

"I can think of better ways for them to spend their Saturday nights."

"Then we have to turn that monster out for good."

"You think that'll keep hate out of our lively bar? Banishing her? It's in all of us."

"You're right, you're right. It wouldn't have gone that far if only Betty Marie was prejudiced." Liz held on to Sally. "What are we going to do?"

"Talk to the kids maybe, one by one. That's what Betty Marie did. If we show them we want the Black women to be here…"

Sally and Liz wore tiny smiles as they left the bar.

At the end of their ride uptown, they emerged from the subway to the sound of thunder rumbling in the distance. They cheered quietly; a summer storm would break this heat wave.

"It doesn't have to be a storm," said Sally. "A little rain might be all we need."

Originally published in *Old Dyke Tales* (Naiad Press, 1984)

VI: Winter Sun

It happened toward the end of the worst winter Sally the bartender could remember. Other years had been colder, but you could dress to defend yourself against those; and there had certainly been stormier winters, when snow would fall and fall upon itself until it seemed it would seal shut the door of Café Femmes forever.

When did this particular winter begin to go wrong? Perhaps it was that heavy snow followed by a melt, then a freeze, which left small glaciers stuck to streets and sidewalks.

People continued to have accidents on that ice, which like everything else left on the city's streets too long, turned filthy with grime. She stared at the ugly cold patches that seemed to keep winter anchored in New York. Sally was fed up.

Day after day her startling blue eyes squinted into the weak sun which dared to pit its powers against the ice. She felt like shouting, *Come on*, as if to a losing team. At that point, she'd have another drink from the bottle of red wine under the bar, to thaw her own impatience and anger at this standoff between winter and spring.

She couldn't quite remember when she'd switched from two glasses of white wine for special occasions to the red wine which seemed to flow so much more easily into her glass—and to disappear more quickly, more often. Come spring she'd switch back to the white. Or stop altogether. She'd watched too many fine gay kids go down under a flood of the liquor they thought would ease their way.

It wasn't pretty anymore, this warm red stuff that sometimes seemed as sticky as vein-clogging blood. She didn't like, either, the way she and Liz brought their drinking home. Until lately, they only drank at the bar, except for celebrations. Little by little, they celebrated the small things. First Sally thought it was because they were bored and needed to brighten their lives. But lately she feared that it was a need for the alcohol itself. Despite everything she knew about alcoholism, she'd gotten into the habit of toasting the new day as soon as she got to work. Or having a quick one if she saw that queer-hating beer salesman, the one who shouldn't have a route anywhere near a queer bar, coming to do an order.

She wondered if he was the one behind the rumors that when funds from Albany became available to renovate the neighborhood, Café Femmes would be pushed out. A woman from the spanking new art gallery up the block—until recently a repair, parts, and sales shop for rebuilt meat slicers and grinders—filled her in when she came to invite Sally and Liz to the launch of the business association. The owners of the warehouse across the street wanted to convert their top floors into fancy co-op apartments; a gay bar in the neighborhood was not part of their plans. Liz made an appointment with her father's lawyer and was certain they would be all right. They'd toasted to their future in Soho.

A couple of kids came in to fortify themselves on their way to visit an ailing friend. She told them about the rumor and joined them to toast Café Femmes remaining right where it was. When they left, smoke from their cigarettes hung in the air, and she coughed till her throat hurt. Had it been months since she'd really breathed? Or years. More and more often she scared herself wondering about things like that, worrying about her increasing sensitivity to what she and Liz called occupational hazards.

Hell, she thought, it'll be better next month when we can open the door. What, after all, could she and Liz do that was anything as agreeable as running a lesbian bar?

The cowbells clanged, and she felt a quick surge of irritation. Those bells were cute at first, a friendly warning that someone was coming through the door. But now...sometimes she wished the kids would stay out, especially those who drank in the mornings, who couldn't get through the day without a drink.

But it was only Gabby. She'd given the stuff up a while back and came in now because she could be herself at Café Femmes. As she watched Gabby take a stool, Sally couldn't help but remember when Meg fell down several flights of stairs, drunk, and how Gabby ran to her aid. Gabby visited for hours at a time in the hospital, then, to earn rent money for both of them, found her current job.

Meg drank herself fuzzy for so long she lost her job and health insurance. Injured, she couldn't get to a city welfare office, much less subsist on what they might pay her.

Gabby learned by Meg's mistake, stopped drinking, and hung on to the job, even when Meg became well enough to walk—and did walk, as far as a bar, a liquor store.

"Never," Gabby said at Café Femmes the night she discovered Meg's backsliding, "I'm never going to get like that. I want you to kill me first, Sal, if you ever catch me with a drink."

Today Sally shook overgrown blond bangs out of her eyes and wiped down the bar with a wet rag. "What are you doing out of work so early?" she asked Gabby.

Gabby didn't answer right away. Her eyes were hidden by shades, her chunky fists beat a nervous rhythm against the bar. When she looked up, it was not at Sally, but behind the bar, at the bottles.

Sally felt a constriction in her chest, as if sweet red wine was gumming up her heart.

"What've you got good?" asked Gabby, looking half challengingly, half coyly out from under her bangs.

Sally was silent. She wasn't going to help.

"How about some of that Wild Turkey?" Gabby suggested as if she were kidding.

But Sally saw the dead-serious determination to have a drink. "What happened?" she asked tonelessly, not moving.

The sun disappeared behind a cloud and the bar looked dingy. Gabby's cold-reddened cheeks were fading to the same pasty-white color most of the white kids at Café Femmes wore these days.

"Gabby," prompted Sally.

"I got fired," her friend mumbled.

"Oh no."

"It wasn't my fault this time, I swear," Gabby said quickly.

"I didn't say it was. But you kept this job so long. What happened?" she repeated. There was a feeling of doom about Café Femmes today, which made her shudder. Maybe it didn't belong in this neighborhood. Gabby worked hard at her jobs. When she stopped drinking, Sally assumed life would get better for her.

"You've seen me bring Sue here. She's the bi girl I work with?"

Sally nodded.

"This new foreman came on and he started dating her, too."

Sally sighed. She knew what happened. "Didn't Sue stick up for you?"

"Maybe, I don't know. Why should she risk her neck for me anyways? She's got one foot in the safe camp."

How many times had Sally heard this story? She groaned. Gabby looked up at her, at the sound of her pain.

It was the conflict that hurt. It grew more and more clear to Sally that she must decide what was right for her. Yes, it felt good to be with gay kids all the time. And yes, the kids needed a place to be together, to be away from straights and guys, a place where they weren't stared at or laughed at or thrown out for being themselves, a place to go when they were fired. But was Café Femmes the best place for them?

Spending so much time in a bar, they naturally drank. When you drank—it was beginning to dawn on Sally—you drank more. She always harbored doubts about that part of running a bar. She and Liz talked about it off and on, especially lately, as they poured the stuff while the kids got older and drank more.

"How are we any better than street corner pushers?" Sally asked Liz one painful Monday, their day off, as they walked their aging dog Spot on the East River Esplanade.

"Of course we are," rationalized Liz. "People don't OD on booze."

"They don't?" Sally stopped and faced Liz, all too aware of her own hangover. As they searched each other's eyes, Sally named this one or that one, who got sick, who disappeared, who was put away.

Spot had tugged at her leash and they dropped the subject yet again. Sally couldn't imagine leaving the bar. How could she ever fit in to an office again? Besides, the bar was Liz's dream.

This pain, reappearing at the bar, was corroding her insides, doing as much damage, she imagined, as the liquor she drank to soothe it. She searched for her wine. What else could she do?

"Hey—customers first," said Gabby.

Sally's pain grew muted as she drank. Then she wiped the bar down again and poured Gabby a mixture of seltzer and grape juice, dressing it up with a slice of lime, a slice of orange and plenty of crushed ice.

"What is this shit?" Gabby demanded.

"My newest blend." Sally turned her back and pretended to be busy.

"Hey, Sal. Pal. You don't give it to me and I'll go someplace else."

Sally's pain returned. She picked up her wine, then set it down; to drink would be rubbing it in. "I can't, Gab."

"Why the hell not?"

"I don't want to get you started drinking again."

"It's my life."

"It's my friend's life."

Gabby's face was red with anger. "Friend? I come in here after being fired, and I need a damn drink. A friend would give it to me."

As usual, Sally stayed calm. "Not the way I see it."

"So save all the other kids. Why pick on me?"

"I'm not the Salvation Army. I'm one gay bartender."

"Then maybe you ought to go join the Salvation Army and not be a bartender."

Sally wanted that wine. So what if she rubbed it in? No, that would make Gabby mad enough to find a drink elsewhere. Clearly, the only thing to do was to give her the stuff. But how could she?

The Wild Turkey was so seldom used it was dusty. Too expensive for these kids. "One," she said, "on the house. To show you how much you hate it." She pushed the shot glass toward Gabby and slammed the bottle back on the shelf, still dirty. She hated it. She hated every bottle and never wanted to see them sparkle in the sunlight of Café Femmes' window again.

Gabby downed it, choked, then sighed. Sally knew that warm feeling of release, of relaxation. She reached for her wine as Gabby pushed the shot glass and a five across the bar, looking warily up at her.

That groan came out of Sally again. Her hand stayed on the neck of the wine bottle. "I said *one*," she growled.

"What's the matter, Sal, feeling guilty about feeding our habits all of a sudden? Don't push your guilt on me."

Sally's rage warmed her veins. She needed no wine. As a matter of fact, she needed much more than wine, and she knew what it was she needed to do. Fearfully, trembling, she began.

Slowly, she lifted the wine bottle high above the bar, lifted it till the bottle began to spill its stream of red onto the floor, lifted it until it was empty and then—then smashed it on the edge of the bar.

Gabby's eyes widened in horror.

Sally held the jagged neck toward Gabby. "I'll smash a bottle every time you take a drink." Then she lifted the Wild Turkey off the shelf and filled the shot glass.

Gabby hesitated, put it to her lips. She sipped, her eyes glued to Sally as if searching for her calm, slow-moving ways.

Sally smashed the Wild Turkey bottle. She threw both bottle necks to the floor and reached blindly for another bottle.

"Sal," said Gabby, rising, glass in hand.

"Drink, you ass."

Gabby, as if hypnotized, drank.

Sally smashed the next bottle, a clear white rum. This time she cut her hand. Blood ran onto the next bottle she picked up.

Gabby put her glass down, then snatched it up quickly, as if to fortify herself.

Smash went the blood-smeared bottle.

Gabby moved back slowly, cautiously, from her stool toward the door.

"Going to another bar?" snarled Sally.

Gabby nodded.

Smash.

Gabby put her hand on the doorknob.

Smash.

"You're crazy," said Gabby.

"Finally," said Sally.

Gabby slipped out the door.

The cowbells echoed over and over in Sally's ears. She drowned them out by throwing a bottle of blackberry brandy at the mirror over the bar. A long crack appeared in the reflection of *Café Femmes*. Sally wanted to methodically smash every bottle in the bar, but she wasn't feeling methodical.

It must have been a call from Gabby that brought Liz so quickly, in a cab. Except to chase out a kid looking for a drink, Sally played pinball all that time, paper towels wrapped around her cut hand. Through the window she saw Liz, Gabby, and the kid, staring in at her.

"Listen, I'm sorry," Sally said as the anxious group entered. "I guess I went a little nuts."

Liz was behind the bar already, saying, "Oy, oy, oy," her hands to her head as she surveyed the damage.

Gabby, standing gingerly a long way from Sally, stared at her.

"Want another one?" Sally asked her. She was crying now, her long body slumped against the pinball machine.

Liz went to her, wringing her hands, looking closely into Sally's face. "What is it? What happened? You decided you don't want the business anymore?"

"Gabby's drinking again."

"It's all my fault?" Gabby pointed at herself emphatically with her thumbs.

Liz glared at Gabby. "You stay out of this." She turned back to Sally. "So Gabby's a fool. You have to be one, too?"

Sally knew her whole demeanor conveyed defeat. "What's so damn foolish about being sick and tired of watching our friends turn into alcoholics? Maybe we should let the neighborhood association push us out," she said. "Maybe they're right and we don't deserve to exist at all."

"I'm no alcoholic," protested Gabby.

Liz glared at her, and the kid steered Gabby to a table by the window.

"This is your fault, that they drink like fish?"

"Come on, Liz." Sally was standing, her shoulders stooped with misery. "You know what I mean. We've talked about it enough."

Liz surveyed the damage pointedly. "We never talked about tearing down with our bare hands what it took so long to build."

Sally hung her head. "I said I was sorry."

"Oh, Sal," Liz said, taking her in her arms. "I'm sorry, too. We should have talked more. Done something. You need some time off."

"Time off? How about forever."

"I think that's a terrible solution," said Liz, leading her to another table by the window.

Sally felt the tears well up again. Never again to watch the seasons pass outside this window? Never again to stay open Christmas Day so that the kids would have someplace to go? Never again to hear another sad story and watch it turn out right? Never to realize their dream of running a lesbian bar with a difference—a gay bar that cared?

"I've been thinking about alternatives, Sally." Liz showed her a small notebook. "I carry this with me, adding ideas as I ride the subway."

Sally clenched her fists. "We could turn it into a straight bar and watch *them* become alcoholics."

Liz tapped a foot. "That's not on my list. You want to hear this or not?"

Someone tried the door. Sally could see it was the two women who'd toasted Café Femmes staying in the neighborhood.

"Gabby," Liz said, "find the Closed sign in all this mess, will you?"

"What'll I tell those two outside?"

Liz looked at Sally. "Tell them we're making alterations," Liz said. "Tell them not to go away forever."

Gabby bustled till she found the sign, then strode to the door as if she carried the fate of the kingdom to the crowds. When she shut the door she said, "They want you to hurry because this is the nicest bar in town. And if the neighborhood gives you any trouble, they'll help you fight back."

Sally's eyes avoided Liz's.

Her voice heavy, Liz began her list. "A juice bar."

"They don't make money."

"A game parlor."

"What I always wanted. To wear a change apron."

"A restaurant." Liz looked particularly attentive, waiting for Sally's response.

"Why don't we start a Lavender Julius franchise?" Sally answered sarcastically.

"You're being negative."

"You know what the failure rate is for restaurants."

"Not when they're part of an established bar."

"I guess I don't really want to close Café Femmes."

"Close Café Femmes?" shouted Gabby, rising and striding to their table. "What would we do without Café Femmes?" Ignoring Liz's look, she went on, "You're burned out, Sal, that's all. We need this place. You guys are doing us good, not harm. Think about it."

Gabby looked so earnest, put on such an air of proprietorship, that Sally laughed. "First off, I said I didn't want to close Café Femmes."

Gabby lowered her gaze and sunk her hands into the pockets of her corduroys.

"Second," Sally continued, "without Café Femmes you'd be drunk by now."

"See?" said Liz.

"Yeah," Sally replied. "But look what I went through to keep her sober."

"I'm sorry, Sal," said Gabby. "You were right. I didn't need the drinks. I guess I need to be here, not drink here. It's because"—she flung her short arms out helplessly—"you know how hard it is for me to get a job someplace where I fit in."

More women came to the door, and Liz motioned for the kid to take care of them.

"And third," Sally said, stretching her long legs out from under the table, "you're right. I need time off. Lots of it. I need something more," she said, turning to Liz, "than the bar and walking Spot on Mondays with you."

In a soft tone devoid of expression Liz asked, "Do you want to be the Café Femmes representative to the neighborhood association?"

Sally looked at her in amazement. "I thought we didn't want anything to do with that bunch looking to fancy up the area."

"Today was the day I met with the lawyer."

Sally was seized by a moment of fear. What would she do without Café Femmes? "I forgot about that. What did he say?"

Liz spoke absently, as if continuing an internal conversation. "I've been trying to figure out where we'd get the time to join. When I saw you like that today, I worried I couldn't handle this, too. But you may be the solution."

"More like the problem."

"He advised us not only to participate in the Business Association, but to become important in it. Show them we have something to give the street. Something unique."

"Like me," Gabby burst out, doing a short tap dance. She was back to her usual upbeat Gabby self.

Liz laughed, then leaned forward. "Sally, we are unique. Look at the historic cast-iron facade on our building. We're the only bar on the street. We're the only gay business. We bring people into the neighborhood who otherwise would never come here. They buy from the pizza place, the Mexican restaurant, the street vendors, and the boutique shops moving in. The lofts are filled with not-so-starving artists. We're the only establishment that serves a completely social function."

"So?"

"So? Oh, boy," said Gabby. "Don't you see? What a lunkhead you can be, Sally James. You could be the—What do you call it? In the middle of everything?"

"The fulcrum," said Liz.

"Yes. The whatever it is. You could have meetings in your back room. You could do a lot of extra stuff with all the time you spend alone in here, in this time off you want. You could sponsor a softball team."

"She's right, Sally. Most of the people are perfectly willing for us to stay. We have a real place in the community—they need us, want us here, and the people who don't like us would lose any power to hurt us."

"They'd want a gay bar?"

"No. They'd want Café Femmes. A café. The way I've always

dreamed it would be. With coffee, sandwiches, French pastries, along with the liquor. And tables on the sidewalk—a few—with pretty tablecloths under an awning."

There was a silence so profound in Café Femmes it was as if the very building was astonished to think of itself prettied up like that. The kid lounged at the bar. Gabby stared at Liz.

Sally remained skeptical. "Can we afford it? To work fewer hours? To get the licenses we'd need, the equipment, the furnishings?"

"If we keep it simple, try to retain the same feeling we have. The awning and the serving station, along with a server, would be the biggest expenses, but we could have our name printed on the awning and forget about the neon sign we planned. And, because we're improving the business, we can apply for a low-interest loan from the neighborhood development people. Best of all, we can write everything off, including your salary for working on the improvements."

Liz paused, breathed deeply, watched Sally's face. Gabby nobly controlled her excitement, betraying it only with occasional jingles of the change in her pocket.

"What color?" asked Sally.

Gabby stopped jingling.

"What color is what?" asked Liz.

"The awning."

Liz smiled. Sally smiled. They watched each other's eyes as they reached to hold hands across the table. Liz peeled the paper towel from Sally's cut. The bleeding had stopped.

Into the silence Gabby's excited words sounded like a cannon shot. "Lavender!"

"Oh no," said Sally, dropping her head into her hands. "It *is* a Lavender Julius."

Liz said, "We're going trendy."

"Not very," cautioned Sally.

"No, not very with Gabby tending bar and running the food counter."

"Gabby?" asked Sally, as if trying on the idea.

"Gabby?" asked Gabby. Then, quickly, "Me?"

"You said you needed a job," Sally reminded her.

Gabby whirled in place. "Gabby the bartender," she cried. "This calls for a celebration."

Sally looked suspiciously toward her.

Gabby flushed red. "Not Wild Turkey."

"There is no Wild Turkey," Sally said sternly.

"What you made me before," Gabby explained, licking her lips. "With the lime? And the crushed ice? And the orange?"

Sally rose, eager.

"Only, Sal," asked Gabby nervously, "would you add one other thing?"

Sally hovered threateningly. "No liq—"

"Would you put a cherry in it, too?"

Originally published in *Common Lives/Lesbian Lives* 17 (Fall 1985)

VII: The Florist Shop

The bar was closed for two days that week. One for repairs, the other to give them a real day off. On that second day Sally and Liz were so rested they woke at dawn.

Rising early in the morning gave shivers of excitement to Sally. On Mondays they often lingered in bed together, long blond Sally and soft dark-haired Liz, enjoying their bodies under the tangled sheets, reprieved from the usual tearing apart to enter the day.

It wasn't that they were weary of running Café Femmes. Sally still enjoyed the daily subway ride downtown, where the warehouses were long awake, working at a pace that seemed designed to bring the lunch hour on even sooner.

But today they were on their own, adventures before them. They planned nothing in particular, yet before they'd said a word, Sally was kicking the covers off her long legs and pulling Liz up with her into the shower where they quickly washed, and more slowly made love, Liz worrying about wasting water, before bursting out of their apartment building into the sunlight. The crisp spring morning was delicious, the sun bright enough to throw sharp shadows everywhere; they passed from the cavernous darkness of tall buildings to the glory of a circle of yellow daffodils in Central Park and warmed up with the morning as they crossed the Park and found warm, buttered blueberry muffins, crusted with sugar, in a coffee shop on Sixty-First Street.

By ten o'clock the uptown boutiques were opening and gray-suited businesspeople raced one another into and out of the buildings. Sally and Liz walked off the heaviness of their meal, but they'd begun to tire.

"Do you want to go back to the Park?" asked Liz.

"Or to a museum?" asked Sally.

"See a movie?" But they shook their heads no to that. Who'd want to spend the afternoon inside on a day like today?

"The Cloisters," Liz suggested.

"Too far," answered Sally.

"Gallery-hopping."

They agreed, laughing, and turned back to Madison Avenue. Once before, because they'd found themselves in the neighborhood, they'd invented a game in which they were rich and snobbish art buyers. In their jeans and Café Femmes jackets, looking like refugees from a softball team, they'd taken the galleries by storm. This painting wasn't quite right for the sunken living room, that photograph would look gorgeous by the door to the penthouse patio.

Anything under forty thousand was cheap, anything over, pretentious.

"We may get kicked out of this one," warned Sally.

"With our chutzpah? Who would dare?"

"Look at the flowers," cried Sally. She set their course for a spot bright with color half a block away. "I'll buy you some, and no one will be able to tell you from a lady."

Liz looked over her glasses, eyebrows together in a stern frown. "And ain't I a lady?" She was doing her Barbra Streisand imitation.

"Of course you are," laughed Sally, stopping to nuzzle Liz in broad daylight. "But you're my kind of lady, not theirs."

Mollified, Liz nuzzled back. "Do I see violets?" she whispered.

They both sighed. Violets were their flower the night they admitted their love.

From a cart outside the florist shop, Liz chose a bouquet of yellow daffodils, their flower of the day, and Sally went inside to pay.

She struggled to recall the face before her. But it wasn't the slack-muscled face with its heavy eyebrows that she remembered first, it was the feel of the woman. Tall and ungainly, as if she'd once been heavy and never got used to losing weight. She exuded hurt.

"Julie." She turned to Liz. "Remember? The girl from Jersey whose first lover—" She hesitated to say it.

"Killed herself," Julie finished in a flat tone. "I got over that, with your help. I could see how it was for her, everybody telling her how great straight was when inside all she wanted was gay."

"Yes," Liz said, "I remember well. I'm glad you're doing better."

"Hey, it's been what, almost two years now. I hope I grew up some."

"What're you doing here?" Sally asked.

"I manage the place."

"Great. You move into the city?"

"Not at first." Julie moved to her worktable. "I have some orders to get out," she explained and placed six faintly pink carnations on wrapping paper, along with six fluffy white ones. "Remember the cleaners I worked at in Jersey? The owner's brother has half a dozen flower stores. We got to talking one day, and I told him about me and flowers."

She smiled and shrugged, glancing, Sally noticed, past them and out the window. "I guess you wouldn't take me for the type, but that's always been my thing. Learned it from my mother, how to grow and cut and display flowers. She has seventeen varieties of roses in our backyard, and we're only talking roses."

Again, she peered past them out the window. Was that how she checked on customers at the carts? "He'd heard about my troubles, about losing my friend and being depressed and all, so he offered me a job here. It wasn't as manager, not right away. I was the helper."

Sally could see now that Julie was looking beyond the carts and up. Sunlight blanketed the yellow, red, and purple flowers outside, but the shop was chilly. "I loved it from the start, handling the flowers, meeting new people who didn't remind me of anything in my life. A lot of secretaries come in here to order flowers for their bosses to send, and we talk. Some of them are even gay." She flashed a frankly proud smile. "I don't hide it now, you know. Not since I saw what that can do to people, being scared of what they are."

But that hurt look returned as she spoke, like the first time Julie came to the bar, lost and bitter and alone. Sally recalled how that one day's connection with other gays began to turn Julie around, helped her focus on something besides pain and anger.

Julie finished wrapping the order and stepped to a refrigerated case to choose some blossoms Sally didn't recognize. Liz slipped her hand into Sally's, squeezing tightly the way she did when frightened or uneasy. As soon as Julie returned, she looked up and out again to the shaded side of the street.

"To make a long story short, I did move into the city, into a studio apartment across the Park. And since I didn't know anybody—I'm still not good at making friends—I hung around the shop. I used to walk all over the city, too, getting ideas how to display our flowers, what better services we could offer—you know, building business. The owner liked my ideas so much he gave me the store to manage after only a year." She finished her arrangement and looked up at them, then quickly back down, as if expecting disapproval. "So, here I am, talking your heads off again."

"It's a nice shop," said Liz. "Clean and bright." But still her cold hand clung to Sally's.

Julie was looking outside. "It's got to be. On Madison Avenue, we wouldn't sell a thing if we didn't fit in."

Sally turned to look out the window. Up and down the street were tall gray and glass buildings, mostly newly built. But directly across the street there was a hole in the frontage, a wrecker's ball hanging over the cavity. The first floor of an older building was all that remained standing. Was it this that fascinated Julie? The desolate picture of a wrecker's ball poised to finish its destruction? "What was that building?" she asked.

All three looked where Julie gazed. "An office building no one wanted anymore. Art Deco period. The landmark people fought for years to keep it standing, but some big company finally won out." She paused as if uncertain whether to go on.

Her heavy brows were pulled forward as if she was in pain. Liz squeezed tight on Sally's hand.

"I guess you caught me at a bad time again," Julie explained. "Things were going so good, too." She bit her lip and nodded toward the wrecker's ball. "I met a girl. She worked there. Every Friday she'd order flowers for her boss's girlfriend."

Across the street, in the plate glass window to the left of the dying building, Sally saw a reflection of the flower carts, all distorted.

Julie said, "She was only a gal Friday. And she wasn't pretty or anything, but maybe that's why I liked her. Curly was so different from my first girl. I guess I thought she was tougher, could take the gay life better. That she'd be safe for me to love. We were always together. She practically lived at my place the last couple months."

Men drifted back onto the demolition site; lunch was over. An operator climbed into the cab below the wrecker's ball. The sun had shifted; it fell straight down onto Madison Avenue, between the flower shop and the remains of the condemned building.

"I knew she wouldn't be around forever anyway. She was saving money to go to school somewhere out of town where she could live cheap."

A customer came in, and Julie was transformed. Smiling, she became a thoroughly professional saleswoman. The man left with an Easter lily for his mother and a quickly assembled corsage for his wife. "That's how you've got to be to keep the profits up," Julie said, explaining her other side. Her features slackened into melancholy as her gaze returned to the window.

"Her boss announced that the building was going to be torn down. Curly came across to tell me. It was pouring cats and dogs, and she was soaked." She laughed quietly. "Her hair always got frizzy then, like tiny flowers curling up in the dark. She said as long as the job was going, she thought it was time for her to move on. Two weeks later she was gone. To a school in Ohio where she has relatives."

Sally tried to think of something to say but only managed to go on squeezing Liz's hand.

Outside, the ball began to rise on its heavy cable. Julie looked more lost and helpless than ever. "Am I cursed, always getting myself into dead-end relationships?" The ball struck once, then again and again. A shudder seemed to pass through Julie's body with each blow.

"Maybe you guys showing up in my life again is a sign. Maybe I have to make another change. Do you think I should follow Curly to Ohio?" Her eyes swept the shop, its flowers, its shininess, its stack of orders on the table. "Since I got here, we added another refrigerator to handle all the new stock I sell every day."

They watched her lay ferns against paper, set flowers deftly into place, wrap them. She stapled cards to each batch and placed them in a standing cooler with others.

Sally was desperate to be back out on the street. Here was Julie, stuck again. She'd surrounded herself with dying flowers and synthetic light and now stared fascinated at a wrecker's ball. As if that wasn't bad enough, virtually the only lesbians she'd met in two years happened to walk into her shop. Didn't she learn anything that first time?

"How come you never come by Café Femmes?"

Julie looked at them both, then out the window. "I never find time, with the store and all."

"It's spring out there, Julie," Sally said, concealing her impatience with difficulty.

Julie looked hurt by her tone. She finished the bouquet. "I kind of lose track of the seasons. In here it's always spring."

"Or never spring," Sally said.

Liz dropped Sally's hand. "New York City is the gay capital of the world," she said gently.

"You mean I should meet people." She drew her brows together again. "But what about Curly?"

A crumpling sound drew all their eyes to the window at the same moment. The building was down. Nothing was left but rubble.

"I guess she's a lousy excuse. She moves a lot. This is her fourth college." Julie laughed derisively. "You know what? I must've thought I was safe as could be tucked away on Madison Avenue behind my flowers. Maybe no place is safe. I was hiding, and what good did it do me?"

Sally put the demolished building out of her mind. A fountain of sun now poured through the space across the street.

"Hey," Julie said. "I don't want to keep you from where you're going. Listen, how about tomorrow night? Can I deliver you some flowers at the bar? When will you both be there? My helper can close up for me."

Sally and Liz exchanged smiles. "If you'll hang out for a while. Make it around seven. And consider that a standing order," said Sally, as they made their way to the door. "Once a week—at least."

Originally published in *Home in Your Hands* (Naiad Press, 1986)

VIII: The Long Slow-Burning Fuse

Sometimes, as she watched the slow, subtly changing seasons through the plate glass window, Sally the bartender could barely contain her excitement. Today, it was as if beneath her bad mood there was a long, slow-burning fuse inside her that would not explode, and she moved restlessly about, cleaning, serving, stocking, wiping down the bar with a fervor more suitable to an Olympic event.

Even Gabby wasn't around to tease and cajole her out of her mood; she'd worked Thursday and Friday while Sally ran around the city applying for a neighborhood renovation loan and for licenses to serve food at Café Femmes. The same cab driver who'd been stopping by to play pinball all week was at it again today, the only customer in the bar. Sally had never seen her before, but her cab was parked out front and she was becoming a fixture.

It had been a dim Saturday morning. About the time the cabbie arrived, the sun broke loose as if running toward spring and made the street warmer than it had been for months. Sally had switched then, from mineral water to 7Up, remembering times she'd been sick as a child and her mother had brought her a glass, sweet and stirred to weaken the carbonation; it had made her feel better.

"Quarters," said the cabbie, coming up to the bar. The accent was Boston. "Jeez, it really is spring," she added, looking out at the street.

Sally had propped open the door of Café Femmes, and a bunch of kids from Little Italy were rolling by on skates.

Sally wasn't encouraging any conversation today. She nodded. Up close, she could see that the cabbie was nearly her age. She wore olive chinos, a gray sweatshirt with sleeves pushed up to the elbow, and a tweed cap.

Sally's grumpiness started to subside with her curiosity, and with the bright warm day.

"You're never on at night," the cabbie said, lingering.

"No," Sally answered, her voice rusty from disuse. She hadn't known the cabbie was a night customer, too.

"What is it that Gabby drinks at night, with all the stuff in it?"

"Grape juice and seltzer with slices of orange, lime, a cherry, and plenty of crushed ice."

"Let me have one of those, okay? I have to go back to work soon, and I don't want to smell like I've been here."

"One Lavender Julie coming up," said Sally.

The cabbie laughed. Sally joined her. Why, after all, should she hold on to her mood? Because the woman Liz had had that quick hot affair with in Paris had moved to New York? Because Liz had spoken of Marie-Christine for years as if she could walk on water? Because the woman had made magic with Liz's body in a way Liz had never forgotten? Because, lately, there had been an excitement about Liz way beyond what a renovation scheme should inspire?

As she got older, she had learned, deep into one season, to recognize the signs of the next. In winter, this winter, she rejoiced at each extra moment of light that extended the afternoons. And in Liz, with each new season she anticipated the next and the next spent together, closer and closer.

Or was Liz, restless with restrained enthusiasm as she arrived for her shift at Café Femmes, the source of this new light, rather than the more and more reluctantly setting sun? In their eighth year, Sally's love for Liz only grew more passionate. But was Liz restless, stirred by memories and ready to enter a new season in her life?

"How much do I owe you for the Lavender Julie?" asked the cabbie.

"Since it's your first," Sally said, returning to the present, "it's on the house." She smiled despite her mood. "To encourage you not to drink and drive."

"Don't worry about that. I like my job. I want to keep it."

Sally wiped down the bar and poured herself more 7Up. They sat companionably, gazing out the window and the open door.

"There's something about this place," said the cabbie. "When I started seeing my lover a year ago, I stopped going to any but piano bars. But I missed Café Femmes. It's perfect for lunch when I'm downtown. I don't get to be with many dykes in my business. The ones who can afford cab fare can't afford to look like dykes, so I don't know who they are."

"Why don't you bring your girl down here?"

The cabbie took her hat off, then set it on her head again. "I will." She swiveled her stool to look at Sally. "You and Gabby own this?"

Sally shook her head. "Liz and me. The other bartender. Gabby's a friend." She laughed. "A regular who turned into a permanent."

"She tells me you're going to serve food."

"A sidewalk café. Liz got the idea for a lesbian bar long ago, on a graduation trip to Europe. It came back to her when we got together. At the time, we couldn't afford to make it into more than this." She indicated the small dark space with her arm. "Now, with a neighborhood association and government money, we can't afford not to."

"My lover might like a sidewalk café. She grew up over in Europe."

The skaters clambered by in the opposite direction. One fell, laughing; the others picked her up. The long-skirted woman who operated the art gallery up the street walked by, waving, then stuck her head through the open door. "Beautiful day," she called.

The cabbie stood. "I have time for one last game. Want to play?"

Sally liked this woman. She seemed sure of herself and affable, easy. Unlike so many of the lesbians who came in, she wasn't much of a drinker but seemed comfortable, as if she belonged right where she was, wherever she was. "Okay," she said.

The cabbie held out a hand; her grip was warm, steady.

"The name's Annie. Annie Heaphy."

"You're from Boston?"

"North of. Chelsea."

"*Nawth.* Got to love that accent."

When Sally left Café Femmes that night, she dreaded going home. There weren't many topics she could discuss with Spot, the dog, and after that she knew she'd brood about Liz again. She called a neighbor to walk and feed the dog, then went over to her favorite restaurant in Little Italy. She ordered her usual dish of linguine with a rich red meat sauce.

But thoughts of Liz and Marie-Christine invaded, her mind a battlefield. Maybe Liz was seeing her again. And so what if she was? That didn't mean that what they had this time would be good. Look what had happened with Roxy. The affair that flared up between Sally and her had lasted no more than three months and had disappeared so quickly it hadn't left a dent in her life with Liz. As long as Liz got it over with fast and didn't leave, she thought she could take it. But if she found so much as one curly blond hair on their pillows, she didn't guarantee her behavior. She bit savagely into a hunk of garlic bread.

Half an hour of twirling the delicate homemade linguine on her fork and savoring the sauce on her tongue calmed her. She ordered a cream-filled pastry and a white crème de menthe. She could always console herself with food if Liz left, after all. She was beginning to feel guilty because she hadn't told Liz she was staying downtown. All she had to do was go home now and it wouldn't matter, she wouldn't feel as if she was sneaking around checking up on Liz. But when she paid her bill and strolled around the neighborhood awhile to help her digestion, she spotted a movie theater. The film would be over by ten thirty. It would be the most natural thing, then, to stop by the bar.

The hero's name was not Marie-Christine, but he was tall and blond like her. He was not French-speaking Swiss like Marie-Christine, but he was suave and debonair as she must be. Marie-Christine: butchy, with the graceful hands of a lover, the manners of a royal prince, swaying over a woman—her Liz—on a dance floor. The hero, the successful seducer. The cad, she cursed to herself, folding her arms and slumping down to sulk in her molded plastic theater seat.

When she left the theater and walked back to Café Femmes, the closed warehouses rested in silence along the dark street. If she could only store her heart as the businesses of the city stored their goods. Pad it, box it, till she was certain it wouldn't bruise.

She could hear noise at Café Femmes long before she reached it. After all, it was a Saturday night. Saturday night in New York City and Liz was enjoying herself with—

The music was so loud she could barely hear the cowbells as she hit them with the door. Café Femmes was packed.

"Am I glad to see you," said Liz as Sally moved quickly behind the bar to help her. "I've been trying to get you or Gabby down here for hours. I think it was the spring weather that brought everyone out tonight."

She couldn't believe it. Was everything all right after all? As she worked, she scanned the crowd. No sign of anyone with curly blond hair. In any case, it felt so good to be home, with the pinball machine sounding its buzzers and bells, cigarette smoke filling the room like a cloud of Saturday night excitement. The kids laughed, talked, argued, danced to the blaring jukebox. Her most welcome sight was Liz, dear Liz moving around her and with her to the same rhythms they'd always shared. Her heart peeped out of its warehouse, drawn by the warmth of love.

But then the cowbells on the door jangled rudely, and there she was, a tall woman with curly blond hair, looking at Liz as if she'd been presented with the world on a silver platter—and expected it.

"Marie-Christine." Liz rushed into her open arms.

Sally's heart, retreating as fast as it could, began to rip.

"Hi there, Sally the bartender," said the woman who'd entered with Marie-Christine. She was shorter, wore a tweed cap. It was Annie Heaphy, the cabbie. "I guess they know each other," Annie said, grinning.

"You?" Sally said in astonishment. "You and Marie-Christine?" She was staring at Marie-Christine in her lilac woolen cape, long gold earrings, stylishly baggy pants, high boots, and a silky scarf around her crazy curly yellow hair.

"You know her, too?"

"No. I mean—" Sally couldn't stop herself from saying, "I thought she was butch."

Annie laughed. "Marie-Christine butch?" She shook her head. "Sometimes," she said close to Sally's ear, "she's so femme I think she's a drag queen."

Sally laughed with her, but mostly in relief. She began to work again, and Liz joined her, radiant. "Did you see who's here?" Liz asked.

"I noticed a commotion," said Sally calmly, as if the commotion hadn't taken place in her heart.

Marie-Christine, in a charming accent, ordered a bottle of champagne for the occasion. Sally was entranced by her large blue eyes, her style—but she couldn't imagine why Liz had fallen for her.

"What happened in Paris?" she asked Liz during a lull. "Was she your type then?"

"Oh no," Liz said, laughing. "But then Paris was another world. I was another woman. My head was turned by everything over there. I was captivated by the women. And"—Liz's mouth went soft, her eyes sultry—"she taught me a lot I didn't know."

Sally looked Marie-Christine over once more. For all the times she'd heard of the woman's expertise, she'd never quite imagined herself intrigued by it.

Liz paused and thought a moment. "But then I'd only been to bed with a straight college girl. I hadn't even met you yet." She gave a jump for joy and then went into high gear filling orders again. "It's so good to see her. Like finding a dear one-time friend."

"And this is the first time you've seen her?"

Liz raised her eyebrows as if surprised. "I've only talked on the phone with her once, last month, briefly. She gave me her number, but I haven't been able to find it again since."

Annie was at the bar, ordering another Lavender Julie. "Marie-Christine ate the fruit out of my first," she said, shrugging. "We can't get near your pinball machine tonight."

Marie-Christine slid onto the stool beside Annie.

Sally said, "I'll tell the kids it's reserved for you between midnight and one."

"No, please, we can wait our turn. I want to talk with you, too, and with Liz. My Annie says she's been haunting your bar." She pouted. "But she never brought me until I threatened to come by myself. It's true you're making it into a restaurant with outdoor tables?"

There was something about Marie-Christine, like Annie Heaphy, that made Sally comfortable. But with Marie-Christine she also felt a stirring of the long slow fuse inside her. She tore her eyes from the woman's face and noticed her hand nestled high up between Annie's thighs. The sight made her stammer when she answered, "Yes."

Annie sat, coolly closing her thighs against Marie-Christine's hand to the rhythm of the music.

"Would you like a suggestion?" Marie-Christine asked. "If they were my outdoor tables?"

Liz had reappeared to draw a draft. "Yes, yes," she said, "but wait till I can hear it."

"Marie-Christine studied art history in Paris," said Annie. "You ought to see her apartment."

"I love Annie's drink," she said, picking it up with one hand while switching the other into Annie's back pocket.

Annie seemed completely comfortable with such intimate public touching. Her eyes watched Marie-Christine pull a peeled orange slice from the Lavender Julie with her lips. Heads close together, they shared it. "God, I love you," said Annie.

And Sally could see why.

"Orange," Marie-Christine called to Liz as she came near them.

Sally started to reach for another orange slice.

"Orange tablecloths," Marie-Christine said. Sally surreptitiously put it back. Was she really so captivated by Liz's long-ago lover?

"And yellow wrought-iron chairs. And small violet flower vases and fresh flowers," said Marie-Christine. She turned those blue eyes on Sally. "You are planning a lavender awning?"

"Yes," Sally said hurriedly, trying to please her. "A dyke florist brings the flowers we use now."

Annie's hand curled lovingly around the back of Marie-Christine's neck. Now and then Marie-Christine rubbed against it. Occasionally she looked at Annie's lips and licked her own. "Yes," she said, "the flowers brighten Café Femmes very much."

Liz bumped Sally as she grabbed a bottle. Sally stopped her, hands on her soft upper arms. "I love you," she said, pulling Liz to her, holding her tightly, briefly.

Liz started to break away after the hug, then seemed to notice Sally's urgency. She pressed against her, offering those soft lips, speaking with those sultry eyes. Sally remembered every reason she'd fallen for Liz in the first place as she imagined her through Marie-Christine's eyes, younger, and in Paris. It was a long kiss, and they had a lot of orders to catch up on afterward, but, Sally thought, noting Annie Heaphy and Marie-Christine cavorting at the pinball machine, it was the season.

And still later, in their own bed, Liz was saying, "God, you're good," her voice deep and velvety with satisfaction as she pulled Sally to her. In the dim glow of dawn both their mouths shone slick with each other's juices.

"Better than Marie-Christine?" Sally asked. She hadn't planned to, but she was all too aware that their excitement had been more intense than usual.

"Hmm," Liz said, as if comparing them.

"Liz?" asked Sally nervously.

Liz laughed, sliding her wet mouth back and forth against Sally's. "Better than Marie-Christine," she said firmly, a second before her tongue touched Sally's lips. "Sal." Her voice was as tense as her thighs.

Sally held Liz tightly with one arm. The second time, Liz moved against her fingers and, with a quiet sputter, was asleep in her arms.

But Sally couldn't sleep. Though she knew she'd have to get up in a few hours to open the bar, she was still too aroused by Liz, too excited by the night. Her mind was filled with pictures. She pulled Liz to her, kissed the soft graying hair. She remembered the warmth of their parting from Marie-Christine and Annie.

"I love you, love you," said Sally again into Liz's hair. Liz stirred, groaned sensuously, pressed her hot, now loose, thighs against Sally. Should she wake her for more lovemaking?

"Umm," Liz moaned.

Sally found she was hugging her as she had hugged Marie-Christine at parting. It was an entirely different sensation without clothes. She gasped to feel Liz's hand between her legs, to realize Liz had come very wide awake.

Liz moaned again. "You're so ready," she whispered into Sally's ear.

Sally felt Liz's hand slide easily on her, inside her. And she remembered, just before she gave herself entirely over to the sensations, how many hours her long slow fuse had been burning. How near to explosion she must be.

At the window, the sun's progress matched Sally's. By the time she cried out finally, loudly, light filled the window. Sunday would not be dim.

Originally published in *Home in Your Hands* (Naiad Press, 1986)

IX: Halloween

The two skinny trees the neighborhood association planted outside Café Femmes were decked out in reds and browns, greens and yellows. When the breezes stirred their leaves, they waved and fluttered as tall blond Sally the bartender laughed at the thought that they might be flirting with each other. They reminded her of so many of the kids coming into the bar in bright boisterous colors, preening in search of a mate. She'd gone through it with Liz, and now they were like denuded winter trees with each other, down to their bare graceful shapes, lovingly familiar and polished by caresses.

"Boy oh boy," said Gabby, jangling the cowbells behind the door as she burst in to make lunches for Café Femmes' new sidewalk restaurant. The light outside was as bright as the trees, but the bar, nestled between warehouses, didn't get much sun this time of day in the fall. "What a difference those trees make out there," said Gabby. "You can tell what season it is, even in Soho."

Sally laughed again and wiped down the bar. The lunch crowds would start soon; Gabby's, to sit at the sidewalk café and munch fancy sandwiches of cheese and avocado, watercress and anchovy; her own, with their take-out pizzas from up the street and their pitchers of beer. Gabby was slicing and singing already as she made preparations. Sally laughed once more, but to herself. Gabby had taken to wearing bright-colored overalls at work, with contrasting shirts. Today she wore loud gold overalls and a red shirt. She'd changed her hair recently, too, letting the bangs grow out and sweeping them back. The gray it revealed added character to that cheerful, round-cheeked face.

"You figure out your costume yet?" called Gabby. Halloween was fast approaching and Café Femmes always held a contest.

Sally was installing a new washer on the faucet. "How about a bum?"

Gabby groaned. "You came as a bum last year."

"Then what did I do two years ago? I'll be that again."

"Robin Hood? In that dumb green mechanic's jumpsuit?"

"And the pointy green hat with the feather," she protested, giving a last twist with the wrench. "What was wrong with that?"

"It didn't make it, Sal," Gabby said in a disparaging tone. "You looked like you stepped out of 'Jack and the Beanstalk.'"

"Humph," she said. She'd thought she looked really good. "What do you suggest?"

"I thought you'd never ask," said Gabby, striding to the bar. "Let me have my wake-up Julie."

She felt Gabby's eyes watch every move as she assembled the grape juice, seltzer, orange slice, lime, and cherry that went into a Lavender Julie, a drink Sally had devised to keep Gabby on the wagon. "Here's your drink—give with the costume idea." She added a second cherry as a bribe.

"You forgot the straw today. I don't know, Sal. You always forget something. Cheers."

Sally lifted her bottle of Perrier.

"Dee was telling me about this woman who's renting the shop over her magic store. She thinks she might be a dyke."

"What's that got to do with the price of tea in China?"

Gabby sipped noisily. "It's a costume shop." She paused as if for dramatic effect. "I was thinking, where she's a dyke and all, maybe you and Liz ought to invest some of the profits in dressing your staff right for Halloween. There's going to be a neighborhood association prize for the best-dressed business this year."

The cowbells chimed and six women entered bearing pizzas, speaking Spanish. One called, "You want some, Sal?"

"Never touch the stuff before noon," she replied.

"Come on, Gabby. We don't even have to ask you."

Gabby headed for the pizza but stopped and turned back to Sally. "What about it, Sal, want me to check out this costume shop?"

"Let me talk to Liz." She pushed two Cokes and a pitcher of beer toward a factory worker, then waved to three middle-aged women in pantsuits who'd settled at an outside table. The day had begun at Café Femmes.

On her next Monday off, the one day of the week Café Femmes was closed, Sally agreed to go with Gabby to Dee's Magic World, and then upstairs to the costume shop. Normally, she spent Mondays with Liz, but once in a while she liked being footloose and fancy-free in the big city while Liz visited her family—as long as she had Liz to go home to at night.

She stood on the Avenue of the Americas. There were a few bright trees in sight, leaves fluttering beside the international flags which furled and unfurled in the crisp fall breezes. The leaves and flags went limp all at once, and the air felt warmer; she closed her eyes a moment to bask in the sun.

When she opened them, Gabby was in sight, sauntering toward her in red denim overalls and a multicolored tie-dyed T-shirt, hands in her pockets. They set off toward Dee's, which was located on a side street below the Village. She served many of the professional magicians in and around the city and had built a hefty list of mail-order customers.

A block farther on, Gabby looked at Sally; smells of fresh bread and French pastries stopped them in their tracks. Sally nodded. It was the right kind of day to munch on sweets as they walked through the sunlight. But then they thought they should bring something for Dee, something for Dee to take her lover Willa, maybe something for the new lesbian at the costume shop.

"If she is one," said Gabby, whispering before the glass counter of baked goods.

"Even if she isn't."

They arrived in high, if glutted, spirits at Dee's Magic World carrying two bags each, one of cookies, two of pastries, another of petits fours, which they had almost emptied.

Sally jumped, as she did every time, at the wild maniacal laughter that greeted their entry. Gabby clapped her hands in glee, saying, "Like the Laughing Lady at Coney Island when I was growing up." She shut and opened the door to trigger the laugh again.

In the small shadowy shop Gabby and Dee threatened to replace Café Femmes' cowbells with the laugh. The walls were covered in foil, and its folds and crinkles reflected all the different colored lights Dee had placed on counters and shelves. She didn't use the overhead lighting at all.

"So, is the girl upstairs gay?" Gabby asked.

"As gay as they get. She's been over to dinner," Dee answered. Her long red hair glowed against her white shirt.

"Couples' night?" asked Gabby, one eyebrow cocked.

Dee raised her red eyebrows. "As a matter of fact—"

"I figured. She's taken, too."

"Nope." Dee shook her head so that the long hair brushed back and forth against her shoulders. "She's very single and lonely. You want the whole story before you go up?"

"You bet," said Gabby.

"She was living in Vermont, some hippie colony. Making costumes for a small-time local theater company. She moved back here because her grandmother's going blind, and she wanted to help keep her out of a nursing home."

"A hippie?" Gabby asked with a grimace.

"An ex-hippie."

"What's her name?"

"Amaretto."

"What?"

"She can't help it. Her mother worked for a hoity-toity shop, buying hats. Rubbed elbows with the rich. Thought a classy name would snare her kid a classy guy."

"No wonder she turned into a gay hippie," muttered Gabby.

Sally picked up a stack of wooden blocks attached by two strips of fabric. "I remember these," she said, lifting and flipping them so that the blocks fell and turned without leaving the length of fabric. "My grandma gave me a set."

"Amaretto's grandmother—she likes to be called Nanny—is cute as a button. She supported herself and Chandler, Amaretto's mother, making hats before she became a buyer."

"Chandler," scoffed Gabby. "They run in that family, those crazy names."

"Nanny named her after her lover at the time."

Still flipping the blocks, Sally raised her eyebrows. A grandma with a lover?

Gabby broke into a wide grin. "I'm in love."

"Amaretto's upstairs, waiting for Princess Charming," said Dee.

"Amaretto? It's Nanny I want," Gabby replied, bustling to the door. "Cute as a button—that's what you said, right? Had lovers even back then? Supported herself? Come on, Sal. I've got to get an introduction to this woman."

The steps to Amaretto's Costume Shop were narrow, and at one point right-angled, giving the effect of a winding staircase. Sally couldn't help thinking, after Dee's comment about Princess Charming, of the castle where Sleeping Beauty lay. She experienced a shiver of excitement for Gabby. Maybe Gabby would end up with a grandma-in-law.

"I thought she was on the second floor," said Gabby, huffing.

"Stop acting like a forty-year-old."

"I am a forty-year-old."

The shop was a full loft and was at least three times the size of Dee's Magic World and stuffed with rack after rack of costumes. Light from large windows along one wall fell in wide swaths across the reds, the blue-greens, the golds and blacks and purples. The floor had been stripped down to the original wood and highly polished. One wall was all mirrors, framed by dressing room lights. Facing the mirrors stood a slight woman in a white princess gown, sleeves puffed, skirt billowing. A few other shoppers were searching the racks.

"I'll be right with you," called the slight woman, making adjustments to her costume.

"Like a bride," said Gabby in a hushed voice.

Sally looked at Gabby from the corner of her eye with satisfaction.

The woman twirled toward them, the air currents from her gown setting in motion several ceiling-hung mobiles alive with shining stars.

"Can I help you?" The voice was unexpectedly husky.

Sally waited for Gabby to explain their purpose, their friendship with Dee; but Gabby looked dumbstruck. Amaretto's hair was as long as Dee's, but all salt and pepper against an almost unlined face. She wore wire-rimmed glasses, half-tinted blue. She wasn't exactly beautiful, but she was striking. In the gown she looked regal.

The silence continued. Sally looked at her friend. Gabby responded by opening her mouth. "Uh…" she said.

Sally took over.

Amaretto welcomed them, gave them herbal tea. Sally set hers aside, hoping Amaretto wouldn't notice. Gabby drank hers as if it was nectar.

She saw the costumes she wanted for herself and Liz immediately. Amaretto folded and pinned till Sally's fit nicely. Liz would have to come in for a fitting as well.

"And you," said Amaretto, turning to Gabby. "You're so quiet and shy, we'll have to dress you in something dashing."

Gabby squared her shoulders. "Have you ever been to Café Femmes?" she asked, her voice small and dry-sounding. When Amaretto shook her head no, Gabby cleared her throat and went on. "I run the restaurant."

Sally had never seen Gabby blush before.

Gabby looked up quickly, as if to see if Amaretto was impressed by her announcement.

Amaretto seemed to be waiting for more.

"So, you know, I need something I can wear during the day, when the straight people are around. And then something at night, more, you know, more like—"

"Dykey?" Amaretto supplied.

"Two costumes?" asked Sally, who had agreed to pay.

"Maybe one," Gabby conceded, "that could be added to."

Amaretto looked Gabby up and down with a professional eye. "A sailor," she concluded. "Even little girls wear sailor suits. I could put you in a middy blouse during the day, and a full-dress uniform at night. I think you'd look quite handsome in both."

"You do?" asked Gabby, astonishment in her voice. She'd often complained that her chunky body wasn't capable of handsomeness.

The phone rang then, and Gabby pulled a comb from her pocket while Amaretto's back was turned. But the comb never reached her hair.

"Nanny?" Amaretto shouted into the phone. "Nanny, what's wrong?"

But apparently there was no answer. She hung up and looked desperately around her. "My grandmother—I need to get over there fast."

Gabby, shyness and flustered manner gone, whipped her comb back into her pocket. "Close up, Am. I'll get a cab." As she dialed, her eyes followed Amaretto. Sally had seen her like this before, especially helping to get rid of troublemakers at the bar. "Can I come with you?" Gabby asked Amaretto.

"What?" the distracted shop owner responded. "Of course. I may need help."

At the door downstairs, Gabby turned to Sally. "You get stuff from Dee to make a sign that Amaretto's is closed for an emergency. I'll see you later."

Sally stood silently on the sidewalk, confused. Usually, she was the one who told Gabby what to do. Amaretto took Gabby's hand and squeezed it. Gabby put a comforting arm across her shoulder. Then the cab pulled up and they were gone.

❖

It was Halloween night. Often, in the two weeks since their trip to get costumes, Sally stood absently, wiping the bar with a rag, remembering the two shops. Dee's, with its mystery and air of good magic; Amaretto's, with its enchantment and color. She had wanted to transform Café Femmes for Halloween, to give it all those same qualities.

"The crazy laugh," Gabby had suggested. And Dee had offered to rent her a tape for the day.

She'd accepted, but that wasn't quite what she was after.

By the time the neighborhood association judges arrived Halloween Day, the laughing tape had startled several vendors. The lights were covered by orange Japanese lanterns. A ceiling of foil reflected the orange. The plate glass window was completely painted thanks to Pam Sternglantz, a local sidewalk artist who frequented the bar. Sometimes, she'd sit in a corner of the bar sketching. She turned the window into a ballroom, and women who might have frequented lesbian bars in 1920s Paris now danced across it in long black skirts, half-masks held to their faces. It all looked good, but Sally knew Café Femmes wouldn't win the neighborhood contest.

How could Halloween decorations be judged in daylight? Only now, after dark, when the costumed lesbians and a few gay men crowded the bar, did the atmosphere look complete. The crazy laughter interrupted Anne Murray, Barry Manilow, Linda Ronstadt regularly. The real dancers jounced and swayed before the window mural. Night shadows deepened between the glowing lanterns. It was still Café Femmes, but everyone was transformed. Sally, like Gabby, had gone home to dress but was already back behind the bar serving drinks in her samurai costume beside Liz the geisha.

"You guys look great," shouted Gabby, the crazy laughter announcing her entrance.

Sally lifted one of her two swords in salute and Gabby saluted back in a white uniform of vaguely naval design, including a peaked cap. Liz raised her eyes to the ceiling as she passed Sally on her way to deliver a drink. Sally smiled and shook her head. She knew Liz was making reference to the new couple. Gabby, in her shiny black elevator shoes, was almost as tall as Amaretto, who was still dressed as a princess. They looked like radiant angels in their whites. Holding hands, they seemed immensely pleased with themselves and each other.

Gabby let go of Amaretto's hand, moved quickly to a short elderly woman who had come in with them. "Nanny," said Gabby with a bow. Nanny wore a red sequined dress, a wide-brimmed feathered hat, and a harlot's bright makeup.

"What," Sally asked, "are you dressed as?"

Nanny thrust her chin up. "A whorehouse madam," she said firmly. Her voice had the same huskiness as Amaretto's. "I always wished I could be one for a day. When Amaretto gave me the run of her shop this afternoon, I thought, now's my chance."

Chuckling at both Nanny and Gabby, Sally replenished someone's beer glass, made change. Gabby must have been planning this entrance every minute of the last two weeks. She hadn't said another word about Amaretto, except to mention that Nanny's emergency had been a false alarm; her fall had resulted in a bruised hip, but no broken bones.

"A bar?" Nanny was saying when Sally returned to the group. "This feels like a party, not a bar." Nanny saw in shadows only.

"I'll go get someone to give up their table for us," Gabby announced, self-importantly, fitting her officer's cap more tightly to her head.

"Don't you do any such thing, young woman," Nanny said. Gabby stopped in her tracks, tiptoed back beside Nanny as if pretending she'd never left. "I've been sitting at bars all my life. It'll be good to get on a stool again."

Sally smiled. The love that shone from Gabby's eyes onto Nanny's. And into Amaretto's, when their eyes met over Nanny's head.

"And how long has this been going on?" Liz inquired in an amused voice, grinning at Gabby.

"Gabby wanted to surprise you," Amaretto explained in her low voice. "Since the shop was already closed the day we went over to Nanny's, it seemed silly to go back to work. Gabby, once the emergency was over, turned out to be so much fun. We visited with Nanny for a while, then went over to Gabby's and drank Lavender Julies through the afternoon while we talked." Amaretto looked at Gabby. "She made me laugh more than I had in years. And I'd seen her other side, too, when she'd done exactly what I'd needed her to without stepping on my toes." Amaretto tossed back her graying hair and imitated the door tape's laugh. "In those funny, funny red overalls."

Sally brought them a round of Julies, except for Nanny, who insisted on a highball. When, Sally wondered, had she last seen Gabby in her red overalls, or the gold ones, or her turquoise painter's pants? The flagrant colors had fallen as they fell from those skinny trees out front, from trees all over the city.

"To your cozy bar," toasted Nanny, lifting her highball toward what must have been a shadowy Liz and Sally. Sally wondered if Nanny's very lack of sight injected the notes of mystery and enchantment she'd tried to achieve in decorating the bar. Nanny went on, "And to lovers, finding one another, everywhere."

Originally published in *Home in Your Hands* (Naiad Press, 1986)

X: How They Got Together

There were violets, clusters of them, drooping delicately over the edge of a clear cordial glass on Liz's glass coffee table, their shirred purple petals tissue thin. Sally arrived earlier than the rest of their friends, as Liz asked her to.

She touched the violets tentatively with her fingertips. "Where did you get these?"

Liz laughed low in her throat. "In the flower shop downstairs. They were a terrible splurge. I don't know what I'm going to do. Every time I pass that shop, I can't keep my hands off the flowers."

Sally thought, I'll buy the shop for you. She lifted one slender flower and laid it across her palm. It was as weightless, as heavy, as a spirit entrusted to her. She became aware of her heart. Was it pounding? Or stopped?

Liz slid from her chair and leaned toward Sally, hands on the glass table, watching her.

Sally looked at Liz, then at the violet in her hand. "You have a nice place here," she said, indicating the coffee table. She noticed her hand was shaking.

"Hand-me-downs," explained Liz.

But the room became no more than background for Liz. Sally glanced at the ancient stand-up radiator in front of the window. In winter, heat would rise off it in waves that changed everything beyond it. Lifting the violet and running it across her own cheek, she wondered if Liz was feeling what she was feeling. Or did Liz think she was a bore? And why was this happening?

Why Liz? Why this room, this city, this day? Did love, like heat, rise because it had to?

She replaced the violet, her fingertips dipping into the glass, coming out dripping. "Liz," she said, not meaning to.

"Sally," said Liz and Sally was startled, like a deer surprised against the snow.

Liz's dark eyes burned behind her glasses. Her lips—were they swollen in anticipation?

Sally stood, walked carefully around the glass coffee table, the deer again, thirsty, cautious near a frozen pond she might fall into. It took forever to clear, to face Liz. She was afraid to draw breath because it might be a groan. Liz swayed toward her, tentative, head down, long dark hair hanging.

Sally raised one hand, then the other, until the heavy hair lay on her palms like the violet. She leaned to kiss a handful of hair, leaned back, became still, watching, waiting. Liz's eyes came slowly to hers, and Sally could see the desire, the honest, clean, potent desire in them. Then she was sure of Liz, and they kissed.

They moved slightly apart when the doorbell rang. All Sally wanted in the world was to keep kissing that face, every inch of it, the rest of her life.

But Liz rose. "They're right on time," she whispered.

When Liz swung back the door, Gabby, Bonnie and Mona, Theresa and Rickie, and Sue, were harmonizing "Up on the Roof," clapping and stomping. They immediately quieted.

Stiff with passion, exuding heat, Sally stayed where she was.

"Are we interrupting something?" asked Dixie.

Liz gestured them inside.

It took a moment for the group to enter, peer around, and relax before they regained their rowdy mood. The noise increased as Sally and Liz, eyes locked, got into their jackets.

Simultaneously, Sally and Liz found excuses to go to the kitchen. They stared at each other, hesitant to grab, to press, to kiss, but desperate to somehow touch before separating.

Rickie, good-looking and tanned despite the cold outside, found them like that. "Can I get a drink of water?" she asked, seemingly unembarrassed.

Liz, silent, pointed to the sink.

While Rickie opened cabinets in search of a glass, Liz and Sally went on staring, eyes frankly exploring each curve and groove of face and neck, their hands finally reaching to touch clothes, cheeks.

"You want us to go ahead without you?" Rickie asked, watching them as she drank.

"If it wasn't Bonnie and Dixie's farewell party..." Liz pulled herself away from Sally and buttoned her jacket.

Sally followed her back to the other room. Grinning, Rickie fanned her face to show their friends how things were between them.

As they left the elevator downstairs, Mona asked Sally, "When did this start?"

"About half an hour ago," answered Sally, looking for Liz. When she found her, she took her hand, looking her full in the face, signaling with her eyes how this touch moved her.

❖

At a bar, Gabby was telling a story. Sue, a straight girl from the warehouse where Gabby worked who'd asked to come along, sat chin in hands, listening, apparently fascinated. The others drank, smoked, watched the moving crowd on the dance floor. Liz and Sally watched each other across the table, smiling and occasionally nodding toward Gabby when they remembered to be polite.

"It's true," Gabby asserted. "The first time I saw Sal, she was in a skirt."

The friends laughed. Sally shrugged toward Liz, who smiled in understanding. It was an experience common to both, wearing skirts. Their eyes shared it, the oppression of having to wear them, and the excitement of going under a skirt to touch a thigh. I'll wrap you in long purple velvet skirts, thought Sally, so you'll feel like a violet.

"And she's a mean typist," Gabby was saying. Liz looked impressed. "I can't even hit one key at a time, with these sausage fingers." Gabby held her fingers up, then brushed ragged bangs off her pudgy face. "But Sal? When I went in there the first day, her fingers were flying so fast, they were a blur."

Rickie typed across the frizzy-haired Theresa's chest until Theresa brushed her away, laughing.

Liz examined Sally's fingers, long and slender like her body. Sally, embarrassed, curled them into her palms, but Liz reached out like a drowning woman, straightened and clung to them.

"Did she sit on the boss's lap, too?" big Bonnie said in a teasing tone. She usually was the one who teased, in her deep voice.

Sally's eyes hardened, and Liz glared at Bonnie.

"Sorry. I was only kidding."

"The boss was a lady, you jerk," Gabby said with a laugh.

"Wish I had a lady boss," Rickie said, motioning to the waitress to bring another round for everyone but Sally and Liz. Their glasses sat untouched since the toast to Bonnie and Mona.

"You don't wish this one was your lady boss," said Gabby. "At least not if she ever found out about you."

Mona wanted to know how she found out about Gabby and Sal. A PE teacher, she was worried about exposure.

"It was my fault," Gabby admitted. "Completely."

"No." Sally wrenched her eyes from Liz. Everyone looked at her. "The boss had a problem being who she was. You didn't. That makes it her fault."

Liz sighed, apparently at the firmness in Sally's voice. Sally heard the sigh and ran her fingers over Liz's hand.

"Her problem, my fault," Gabby compromised. "I should have stayed where I belonged."

Sue, the straight girl, was eying Liz and Sally; perhaps unconsciously, she slowly adapted her posture to Liz's until her hands lay before her on the table as if waiting for Gabby's touch. "What happened?" she asked anxiously.

"See, the boss dressed fancy. Flirted with the men bosses. Everybody thought she was really straight."

Gabby looked down at Sue's hands. "Like you," she said, smiling at her. Bonnie winked at Rickie as if to say, *Sure she is.*

Gabby went on, "Skirts were required where I worked, too. I figured I wasn't as obvious in them." The friends hooted at Gabby, a bull dyke if there ever was one. "So when I heard about this high-class bar near where we worked, I thought I'd drop in one night on my way home."

Theresa groaned. "You went into one of those uptown bars and thought you'd fit right in?" She always brought the group right back to earth.

Now Sue glared at Bonnie, who was laughing.

Gabby didn't seem to mind Sue's protection. "You wouldn't believe how many women you see on the street in high heels and suits and furs and makeup who are gay. It makes me wish I could tell the whole world."

Theresa interrupted a second time, scowling. "They sacrifice us to stay safe in the closet themselves."

"What do you mean?" asked Sue.

"All those damn movie stars and writers and businesswomen. If they'd only tell the world they're gay, too, we wouldn't have such a hard time." Theresa's voice was bitter.

Gabby shrugged and reached to pat Sue's hand in an affectionate way. "It's not so bad as all that."

"Yes, it is," Rickie said. "Not only do straights look down on us, but the high-class gays do, too."

"But being gay has its rewards," Gabby insisted, gesturing with her head toward Liz and Sally. The friends smiled. Gabby left her hand on Sue's and Sue licked her lips as if they had suddenly gone dry.

"So," continued Gabby, "I'm sitting there watching these women at their tables and booths, wondering if I got a good job and spent my money on clothes, could I ever be with one of them?"

"What would you want with one of them?" Sue asked, her eyes narrowing.

"I was younger then and didn't know any better."

Rickie grinned at Mona, who was looking at Sue's hand, still under Gabby's.

"And then the boss walked in," said Gabby.

"Oh no," squeaked Sue.

Sally broke in. "You guys don't really want to hear this moth-eaten story at your farewell party."

Mona waited until the waitress served their drinks and made change. Then she said, "Why not? First off, this is about the third farewell party you guys have set up for us. Second, I want it to be like it always was—the bunch of us sitting together at a gay bar, having a few drinks, a few dances, and Gabby shooting her mouth off the whole blinkin' night."

"Hey," protested Gabby.

The friends laughed. Sally pulled Liz up with her as she said, "Speaking of dancing, and since I already know this particular story, I hope you'll excuse us."

"Can't hold out any longer?" Bonnie shouted after them.

Sally held Liz to her in sheer relief to be touching once more. Liz seemed to melt into her. They spent half the dance standing still, looking into each other's eyes.

"I suppose we have to go back," Liz said on a sigh as the music ended.

Sally touched her lips with her own, briefly, longingly, and they returned to their friends.

Sue watched their return, her eyes dreamily half closed. She looked toward Gabby as if wishing she would ask her to dance.

"I wonder how long you two will last," Theresa mused aloud, not expecting an answer.

Sally smiled confidently as she sat down.

"Give them five years as good as ours," said Rickie, "and they'll be the luckiest gals in the world." Her face was flushed.

"Oh, Rick," said Theresa. "You're such a sentimentalist."

"Wish someone was sentimental over me," Gabby said and sighed.

Hope gleamed in Sue's eyes. She patted Gabby's hand tentatively. "Somebody will come along," she said, beaming.

"You think so?"

Sue nodded. "Somebody who likes to listen to stories."

Rickie was nuzzling kisses up and down Theresa's neck. "Remember when we were new?" she asked.

"Do I ever."

"I hated being new with Bonnie," Mona volunteered.

"Why?" asked Rickie.

"Because I wanted it to be over. The lust that interfered with everything. How obsessed I was by her. I wanted to be settled down in a co-op apartment with money in the bank and a lifetime of stories to think about."

"My sobersides," Bonnie said, squeezing Mona to her.

Mona scooched closer. "It isn't over yet."

"So here you are, running off to San Francisco," Theresa said.

"We're not exactly running off," Bonnie and Mona said at once. They laughed and linked pinkies. Everyone knew they were wishing themselves luck in their new life.

Another slow song came on, but Sally and Liz didn't return to the dance floor. Gradually, they scooted their padded chairs together, the metal tubular legs squawking, and Liz lay her head on Sally's shoulder while Sally encircled her shoulders with an arm.

"But what happened at the high-class bar?" Sue urged Gabby.

Everyone turned to look at the bright-eyed, very young Sue. "Why don't we dance and I'll tell you?" Gabby suggested in a low voice.

"I've never heard the end either. Don't dance yet," Rickie pleaded.

Gabby fixed an evil stare on her, then turned back to Sue. "Will you dance with me after?" she asked gently.

Sue blushed. "To think, this afternoon we were standing together picking and packing at the warehouse. That's almost dancing."

The friends tried to hide their smiles. Gabby took Sue's hand and stroked it, while Sue watched as if she'd never experienced human touch before.

Gabby took up her story. "At the bar, the boss totally ignored me. But back in the office she practically stalked me." Sue looked concerned. "I was nervous and started making mistakes. The more she monitored me, the more nervous I got, and the more mistakes I made. I started drinking heavier because of the pressure. One night I drank too much and slept through the alarm in the morning. When I got to work, she was waiting for me. She let me go."

"Couldn't you appeal it?"

"There wasn't a union. Besides, I knew there was no way I'd win. The most I could accomplish was to expose her to the higher bosses, but I don't believe in doing that. I'm not like the uptown queers. I think we have to stick together."

The waitress distributed more drinks. "But it was Sal who made the difference," Gabby said. They looked over to the lovebirds who leaned against each other, only half listening as they stroked and kissed. "I told her what happened before I left. She'd been cheering me on, but we weren't close or anything. All the same, you know what that big lunk did? She quit. She wrote a letter to the bosses on their own typewriter and told them off about what a good honest worker I was and walked out." There were tears in Gabby's eyes.

"Wow," said Sue, apparently ready to lay down her life for Sally, as well as for Gabby.

"We've been tight ever since, her and me," ended Gabby.

"I never knew that part of it," Mona said in awe.

"It's what you expect of Sally," Theresa said. "Those high ideals of yours. What did they ever get you?"

"Our respect," said Rickie.

Even Theresa nodded with the rest while Sally gave a goofy smile. The poor woman was besotted. She'd smile at anything.

Gabby put her arm fully around Sue. They looked like two bear cubs cuddling.

"So did you get Sally and Liz together?" asked Sue.

"No," Mona answered for Gabby. "They met at our place last month."

"And haven't seen each other since then?" Gabby looked over

at them, her eyebrows raised. Whispering to each other, they noticed everyone staring and broke apart.

Bonnie sighed. "I don't know if you want me to say this, Liz, but you wanted to call Sally so bad you scared yourself into not calling until today, when you were going to see her anyway. And from the looks of it, I'd say it was the same for Sal."

"Their restraint is sure being rewarded tonight," Theresa commented dryly.

"Good for them." Rickie squeezed even closer to Theresa. "Want to come home with me tonight, baby?" she asked her dour lover.

Gabby said, "Rickie enjoys a challenge. Let's all have a dance." She looked into Sue's eyes. "It could be our last dance before you guys leave."

"I doubt it." Bonnie and the rest of the group teased Sally and Liz onto the dance floor with them.

Sally saw the violets in their glass first thing. Nothing had changed in Liz's living room in the past few hours. Except for the white cat on the couch.

"Cheri," Liz called in greeting. "She was in the bedroom earlier."

Cheri stirred, then tucked her nose under a soft white paw.

Sally said, "Is she suggesting we'd prefer her bedroom now?"

Liz teased. "And is she right?"

A lot had passed between them since the beginning of the evening. Still, Sally colored, shy in spite of her bold words.

"Would you like some coffee?" Liz asked, hanging Sally's jacket in the closet next to her own.

Sally was moved by the closeness of their clothing. "Maybe a sip of wine. To get rid of the taste of smoke in my mouth."

"If I owned a bar," Liz said as she moved toward the kitchen, "I'd make it no smoking."

"You wouldn't have a bar long."

Liz poured red wine into a cordial glass identical to the one that held the violets. "Shall we join Cheri?"

They sat on the couch, to one side of the elderly cat who opened an annoyed eye.

Liz passed the glass. Sally sipped and passed it back. She put one hand on Liz's thigh and began to stroke it casually.

Liz's eyes immediately glazed over. She held the cordial glass with two hands while Sally's fingers began to seriously caress.

Then Sally leaned to the glass and waited for Liz to tip it toward her.

A trickle of wine ran down her chin. She removed her hand from Liz's leg to catch it. Her glance wandered to the violets, and she reached for one, this time running it gently across Liz's cheek. Liz's eyes fluttered closed.

Sally dipped the violet in the wine, then held the flower to Liz's lips. Licking the drops of wine, Liz swayed.

The wine was now a barrier between them. Sally dropped the single violet into the wine, then slowly, firmly, took the glass from Liz and placed it on the table, by the violets.

They moved together, simultaneously pausing to listen for a repeat of the doorbell's ill-timed chime.

Liz whispered, "Cheri says if we're going to carry on to get the hell off her couch and into the bedroom."

Sally laughed quietly. She moved with Liz toward the bedroom, turning in the second before Liz touched the living room light switch.

There, in the cordial glasses, she saw their two passions. Sally's blood thrummed—clustered violets in water, poised to spill over the edge. Liz was the single intoxicating flower, floating toward her now.

Originally published in *Home in Your Hands* (Naiad Press, 1986)

XI: Christmas at a Bar

Tuesday

You'd think the sky had given birth to a baby sun after a long labor, so elated was Sally the bartender at its appearance. She watched its weak wintry rays crawl over the rooftop of the warehouse across the street and rubbed her hands. She'd been chilled to the bone on her trip to work. The cobblestones warmed to friendly glowing purples and blues, and when the warehousemen opened their mouths, it was to belch laughter, not clouds of vapor. Next Tuesday would be Christmas Day.

An hour later, not one customer had come in. Sally finished her cleaning, her restocking, and waited for the kids who brought their lunches to Café Femmes. She polished the aged wooden bar top with lemon oil. Then she dusted the menorah that sat at its center. On one side of the menorah was a miniature Christmas tree, on the other, her grandmother's glass-enclosed underwater world. She picked it up and shook it till snowflakes whirled around the tiny village inside. The figures on the sleigh, a top-hatted man and a woman wearing a bonnet, smiled despite the sudden snow. Their two sturdy gray horses pulled them past the church. She set the globe down and watched as the snow slowed and settled gently on the ground.

She thought of the kids who came in and out of Café Femmes crying, or in love; frightened, or exultant. If only, she mused, everyone was as placid about life as that couple, those horses. Time after time their world was shaken. Time after time storms raged at them, and time after time the shaking magically stopped, the storms ended, and everything went on as before.

Wednesday

Wednesday was bitter cold.

Sally was rubbing her arms for warmth when the door flew open and whacked the cowbells that jangled her still thawing nerves to their roots. Underneath the cowbells was a less familiar jingling bell sound.

"Ho, ho, ho," bellowed the small, sturdy Santa who slid a red velour bottom onto a barstool.

"Gabby, I ought to ban you from Café Femmes in that costume."

Ignoring her, Gabby preened her long silvery-white beard.

"I don't know what gets into you every time you dress like that, but you're rowdier than ever."

"You need to serve hot chocolate in this joint," Gabby said. "I'll take a Coke meanwhile. Need my caffeine fix for the hour—I have work to do."

"You don't act like you need much caffeine, Santa."

"Things are rough at the pocketbook factory. They can't keep up with the orders this time of year, and I can't take this avalanche of overtime plus my part-time job." She tugged off her Santa cap and slammed it on the counter.

Sally scooped up some ice and grabbed the handheld dispenser to fill Gabby's glass from the fountain.

"Don't worry, Sal. I'm not going to quit. Think of the dykes of the future who'd have to sit on some dirty old man's lap otherwise. Besides, I enjoy them."

"Gabby."

"Don't worry. I'm no pervert. I enjoy the boys, too. The youngest ones are incredibly tiny. Can you believe we were once that size?"

Sally looked down at her own lanky body then at Gabby's rotundity and cocked an eyebrow. "Life plays a lot of tricks on us." She wiped the counter again.

"Yeah," said Gabby. "Like poor Dee and Willa. What a breakup scene that was last night."

"You think Willa's really going back to her husband's farm in Indiana?"

"Sure. Roxy put her on the bus and came back down here to comfort Dee."

"So she's halfway home now."

"Home," snorted Gabby. "Home's here, with Dee."

Sally poured herself some white wine, changed her mind, and poured it back. "Home for Willa, Santa, isn't what you want for her, but what's in her heart."

"A man? And two leftover boys from his first marriage?"

"Sometimes, all home means is *easy*. Maybe she wanted it easy again."

Gabby frowned. "Like you're able to swallow your own queerness and not choke on it. Like she won't be seeking out another girl next year. How did she ever come out anyway, with a husband and his kids around?"

"Some woman, traveling through town in a classic Studebaker, turned Willa's head. The family caught them together and married Willa off to the first taker, to make sure it didn't happen again."

"And Dee's going to spend the rest of her life missing the woman?"

"Or missing what feels like home."

"Thinking she can't have both."

"Maybe she can't."

"Maybe she can," challenged Gabby. She got off her stool and hitched up her wide black belt. "Time to go play with the kids."

"They could be Willa's husband's children."

Gabby, a small, thoughtful Santa, turned back to Sally on her way out the door. "She can have them. I wouldn't trade a good butch like Dee for all the kids in the world."

Sally always tried hard to take the gay kids for what they were, whatever they might be. But she dropped her eyes and shook her head. "Yeah," she agreed sadly.

Thursday

It was one day closer to Christmas. Last night, Sally was determined to finish buying and wrapping every present; she tied the last ribbon minutes before Liz got home from the bar. This morning, Sally still felt chilled to the bone and worn out. As the sun peered over the warehouse, she was too tired to be cheered.

Jenny the mailwoman entered with another stack of cards to add to those already strung across the plate glass window. "Never saw a bar receive so many Christmas cards," Jenny grumbled, shaking her head as she bundled up to go back out into the cold.

A moment later the cowbells sounded again, and Dee stomped in. She wore a cutoff green sweatshirt over a flannel shirt, jeans, and heavy work gloves. Her cheeks blazed red. "Motherfuckers," she growled. She removed her watch cap, and long red hair tumbled down her broad back. "Short beer," she told Sally gruffly. Dee often spent her breaks at Café Femmes. She was the only woman in the crew at the warehouse across the street.

"Ho, ho, ho," shouted Gabby as she shoved through the door, jangling the cowbells an extra time and brandishing her own jingle bells.

Sally rubbed the fatigue from her eyes. "Only four more days," she muttered.

"Those creeps," Dee was saying.

Gabby slapped her on the back as she climbed onto a stool next to Dee.

"Where's your Christmas spirit?"

"Where's theirs?"

Sally served them and wiped the trail of foam she'd left on the counter. Gabby swung her stool to Dee.

"A warehouse full of Scrooges. They kept me out on the loading dock all morning. If the weather is nice, you-know-who swelters inside. I'd be frozen solid if I wasn't heaving tons of materials around."

Even Gabby was silent. Dee's job got worse and worse.

Draining half her beer, Dee punched her right hand over and over with a tight left fist. "I don't how I'm going to hold out till the layoff at Christmas."

"Listen," advised Gabby, "if you're getting laid off anyway, why are you hanging in there now, working your ass off?"

"I can do it. I know I can. They'll see I can and call me back at the permanent rate before some of these loafers."

Gabby said, "Sure. They're going to call you back before the men."

"Shit, Gab," Dee said. She swung to face Gabby, her eyes half filled with tears. "I told Willa I'd do it—hold a job and not fuck up because my heart wasn't in it. If I quit now—"

"Keeping that lousy job won't bring her back," said Gabby, laying a white-gloved hand on her arm to comfort her.

"But if there's a chance, if she should consider it…Besides, if I can't open a magic shop, I have to work somewhere."

"Wait," said Gabby. "You're telling me, without Willa holding you back because she's too scared to take the risk, you're still not going to open the shop?"

"You think I'm a real magician? I can't do it alone any more than Sal and Liz can run this bar without each other."

At once, Sally didn't feel tired. "Magic," she said, grinning. "This is a magic season. You'd think with your magic tricks you'd be able to lure her back."

Dee shook her head, the long red hair brushing back and forth across her shoulders. "Magic is illusion. I have no illusions about me. I can't give Willa the life she wants. As steady as I work, I get nothing but women's pay and laid off at Christmas." She stood and stuffed her hair up under the green cap. "No. Willa was right to go. And I may be wrong to stay at the warehouse, but at least I can come over here and bitch at you guys." She almost smiled.

Gabby rose too and adjusted her beard. "I'll walk out with you. Wouldn't my boss be surprised if I was on time today."

Sally wiped down the bar after they left. "Magic," she repeated in a dreamy haze of weariness.

Friday

The sky seemed to glow over the city, as if storing great quantities of white snowflakes for a special occasion. Tons of snow insulating the world, thought Sally, as she decided it was warm enough to walk to work.

She reached the bar later than usual. Dee was in the doorway, huddled as if she'd drawn the bitter cold of previous days inside herself. Sally unlocked the door.

"It's not what you think," Dee said. "I didn't quit." She hugged herself and shivered uncontrollably as Sally turned the heat on and pushed a shot glass toward her. "Why does everything go wrong as soon as your period starts?" She downed the shot. "Yuck. What was that?"

Amused, Sally informed her, "Blackberry brandy."

"I don't drink that shit."

"It'll warm the cockles of your heart."

Dee raised a gloved hand to the general vicinity of her heart and seemed to test the area for heat. "If you don't gag on the taste," she conceded, "I guess it does the trick." She'd stopped shivering. "I never was able to sleep till Willa was home safe. With her not there, I barely sleep at all. And the cramps this morning."

Sally poured another shot.

"No," said Dee.

"Shut up and drink it."

Dee eyed the glass with suspicion but drank the brandy. "This stuff works on cramps?"

"Absolutely."

Sally stayed busy behind the bar.

After a while, Dee took off her jacket. "So Benny, the boss, was riding me today. I don't know, maybe he had a clue I'm having a hard time—maybe his wife gave him a hard time last night. But he's pushing and pushing and I'm trying and trying till something in me goes snap. I start yelling at him. Telling him what sons of bitches they've been to me. Telling him what a creep I think he is for the way he treats me. And on and on. After a while I notice it's very quiet in there. I notice the guys are working real slow, completely cowed. *I didn't know it bothered you,* Benny finally says. *Didn't know?* I yell back. *Aren't women human, too? Go cool off,* Benny says. *Take a walk. I won't dock you. We'll talk after you come back.* So here I am."

Sally nodded in understanding as she polished a glass.

"Maybe I'll be canned. Maybe they'll keep me on till the end of the season. They sure won't call me after this."

"I don't know," Sally said. "Sometimes the truth is the best magic there is."

Dee pursed her mouth sideways, as if puzzled.

Sally picked up her grandmother's world and shook it. "You shake people up," she said, "and they can see more clearly."

"What is Benny going to see all of a sudden?" Dee asked. "That

I'm worth two of some of those guys? I only want to make a home with Willa she doesn't have to be afraid of losing. Why won't they give me a chance?"

"You have the capital. Why don't you give yourself a chance with the store?"

"Because if I did, Willa would never come back. Listen, I made a choice, Sal. It was her or the store. Until I'm sure I lost her, I'm going to stick by my choice."

"But she left anyway."

"That was separate, because of my moods."

"Nothing's separate," Sally said. But she wasn't sure Dee was listening. Raising her voice she asked, "Want more brandy?"

Dee grimaced. "You kidding? No, I better go face the music."

The cowbells barely stirred as Dee left quietly, shoulders slumped, head down, diminished.

Saturday

All the parties were scheduled tonight. Even if sleet hadn't been assaulting the dark streets as if to make up for Friday's calm, Sally and Liz didn't expect a crowd at Café Femmes. Sally stayed on after Liz arrived, loath to leave Liz and venture onto the wet, slippery sidewalks.

A few couples at tables watched the lone couple on the dance floor. Two singles sat at opposite ends of the bar. Now and then, someone would play a spate of songs on the jukebox. Sleet stormed at the plate glass window.

Dee returned soaked through, her face ruddy with damp cold, her red hair wet where it had escaped the green cap. She strode to the bar, and out from under her jacket she pulled a perfectly dry, loudly purring black kitten.

"Anybody need a last-minute Christmas present?" she asked. The kitten was small enough to sit in one hand. Setting it on the countertop, she peeled off her wet coat.

"Where'd you pick up this bit of black magic?" asked Sally.

"All jammed in the corner of some subway stairs, trying to keep warm. I almost missed her."

Liz cooed at the cat. "How I miss my Cheri. She died last year, at eighteen. What are you going to name her?"

"Name her? I brought her here to find a home for her, not to saddle myself for eighteen years."

Liz was nuzzling the kitten with her nose and lips. "I thought you wanted a cat."

"We did. But what would I do with a cat?"

"Umm," said Liz, kissing its head. "You could love her," Liz answered.

One by one, the other customers came to exclaim at the kitten. Soon a group stood at the bar, as verbose as they'd been silent earlier. The kitten mewed loudly and the group was suddenly full of advice, concern, suggestions. Liz bustled away to return with a clean ashtray filled with milk.

"Put something in it to warm her up," joked one of the kids.

"How about a twist of lemon and an olive?"

Unperturbed, the kitten lapped and the group drifted away. But the couples pulled their tables together, and the singles both sat at the same end of the bar, though a seat apart. A disco group sang Christmas carols.

"If Sally ever, God forbid, left me," said Liz, "the first thing I'd do is adopt a cat."

Dee brightened. "You didn't replace Cheri yet?"

"I'd take this one," Liz said quickly, "but we have the dog."

Dee's face fell. "What am I going to do with her?" She was silent a moment. "What am I going to do with me?"

Sally kept going to the door, peering out in hopes the sleet let up.

Liz nodded. "It's a hard time to break up."

"I can't believe she's happy there. But she'd stay from pure stubbornness. And," Dee finished with a voice full with tears, "because she'd have nowhere else to go."

"Have you called her?" asked Liz.

"Hey, Liz, the woman left me. She doesn't want any calls from me."

"Hey, Dee," Liz replied, stern and mocking, "what do you want to do with yourself, make sure you feel lousy?"

Dee glared at Liz. "Of course not," she said.

"Then take this kitten home, name her, and call Willa."

"I can't," said Dee, whining like a six-year-old.

Liz shrugged. "So, okay, you can't. Ask me if I care."

Sally watched the game of ping-pong words.

"She'd hang up on me," Dee said.

Liz flicked the kitten's tail, tempting her to chase it.

"She'd only say no and I'd feel worse."

The kitten lunged at her tail and almost fell off the counter. Dee caught her.

"What if her husband answered?" asked Dee. "I can't think about her—and him."

Liz caught the kitten this time. "You know, young woman," Liz said to the kitten, "you have a long glorious life ahead of you, and the first thing you have to learn is to take care of yourself." The kitten sighted the miniature Christmas tree and made for it now. "Oy," said Liz. "There goes the Hanukkah bush."

"Hanukkah bush?" questioned Dee.

"Sure," Liz replied. "For Sally it's a Christmas tree, for me a Hanukkah bush. And you," she said as a tiny black paw batted a tiny bulb. "Which is it for you—a catnip plant? Listen, whatever you call it, the important thing is to keep your own tree lit." She pulled the kitten's paw away from the hot light. "You like the brightness? Don't be putting out your own light."

Sally moved to the back of the bar and hugged Liz from behind. "It's only raining now," she said. "I'm going home to bed."

Liz smiled a pleased sensual smile as she rubbed against Sally. "Leave the Hanukkah bush lights on, will you? I love to see them shining when I get home."

"Will do," said Sally. "If you promise not to bring any kittens with you."

"You drive a hard bargain," said Liz, watching Dee, who'd picked up the kitten and was petting and talking to her.

Sunday

A light snow fell on the cobblestones outside Café Femmes on Sunday morning. Liz woke Sally the night before, excited by the tree lights, wanting warm, loving sex.

Sally was yawning but happy to see Dee.

"So?" asked Sally.

"She kept me up till three a.m.," Dee replied.

Sally thought of Liz. "You picked up a woman?"

Dee bounced on her stool. "Yeah. Her name is Silent Night."

"Look," said Sally. "I know I'm tired, but—"

"The kitten. That's her name. That's who kept me up half the night."

"I get it now. Why that name?"

"Two reasons. One, every time I'd drop off to sleep, she'd cry, and I'd have to wake up and hold her or put more food in her dish."

"And the other reason?"

"Because it's Willa's favorite carol. I was thinking you're right. Maybe making trifling magic like that will help." She was grinning, but not meeting anyone's eyes.

"If the last thing you got was a silent night, how come you're up so early?"

"I decided to go ice skating up at Central Park." She held up black speed skates. "And maybe go see the Christmas tree at Rockefeller Plaza."

"Wish I was free to join you."

"I decided it was time to do something nice for myself. I might buy myself a present on Fifth Avenue, if anything's open. Or pick up a woman. Of course, Silent Night may be as much present or woman as I can handle right now."

"Ho, ho, ho," came a voice through the cowbells.

Dee rose. "I'm going while the going's good."

"Have fun," called Sally. "Take Santa Gabby with you." She realized too late that Dee never told them the outcome of the talk with her boss. Most likely, it never happened.

Gabby fled to the rear of the bar. Dee passed the plate glass window, skates bouncing over her shoulder.

Monday

The snow fell and fell. Uptown, the heavy Christmas Eve traffic would be snarled, pedestrians choking the stores and city sidewalks. But down in Soho only the muffled sound of artists and laborers hurrying home. The warehouses let out early.

Sally stood outside the bar for a moment, fondly gazing at the warming yellow light through their large window. They always stayed open on Christmas Eve and Christmas Day, partly so the kids who might be home alone could be with other lesbians, and partly because it wasn't Liz's holiday. Word of the tradition had spread, and this year they had a crowd. Not even the couples wanted to stay home alone on Christmas Eve. Liz eventually decided it was a party they were having and sent out for pizza to feed the kids.

Gabby persuaded her boss at her seasonal gig to let her keep the Santa costume that night. Despite her two jobs, she'd been buying and making small gifts for months and tonight plopped a full red-dyed laundry bag on the bar. Sally let her carry out her plans on the condition she keep her ho, ho, hos to herself.

"Ho, ho—" Gabby began, but stopped as Sally caught her eye.

"Ho," shouted Dee.

They were gathered at the bar where Dee was describing her skating excursion. Though she sounded lighter than the day before, Sally heard a new tension in her voice, as if she was trying to swallow her hurt. "So I unlaced my skates," Dee was saying, "and walked by her. There's no way to keep your cool if you're walking on blades."

"Did you pick someone up?" asked Liz as she returned from a table with empties.

"Why's everybody so surprised? I'm an eligible bachelor," Dee claimed in an aggrieved voice.

Sally silently counted the number of drinks they'd served Dee. No wonder she was feeling so good.

Dee went on. "I told her I admired her skating style. She said she admired mine. I told her I was a magician. She got cute and said she'd like to see what tricks I had up my sleeve."

"Oooh, baby," crooned Gabby.

"But when I asked her to go over to Rockefeller Center to see the tree with me—and remember now, the girl is dykier than a roller derby veteran—she says, wimpy-like, *Oh, I can't. My boyfriend's picking me up at five.*"

"Oh no," shouted Gabby. "Describe her to me. I'll find her for you. Wrap her up pretty and throw her in my sack—"

"Never mind your sack," said Dee.

"You're blushing," Liz said, teasing Gabby.

"Wow," cried Dee, "I made Gabby blush. This is a night for celebrating."

"What else are you celebrating?" asked Liz.

"I rented a store today."

The group was shocked to silence. Someone was waiting to be served at the other end of the bar, but neither Sally nor Liz budged. As word flew from table to table, the cheering began. Gabby stomped around in circles shouting, "Ho, ho, ho. Merry Christmas," over and over.

Now Dee was blushing. "I feel so much better for doing it," she said. "I wonder how many of Willa's and my problems came from me holding myself back. Maybe she only needed me to say—*I'm opening the store, I need to do it, please help me.* I bet she would have found the courage. But, hell, I didn't know how bad I needed to do it. Only you guys," she said, shyly meeting Sally's and Liz's eyes, "only you and Gabby were the ones to see. I wish Willa had stayed. I think we had a chance to work it out."

Liz moved to Dee and hugged her. "Good for you." She asked Sally to handle the orders while she made a phone call.

Sally gave Dee a weak drink on the house.

"It better not be that blackberry brandy," Dee threatened.

Gabby scrambled in her sack. "I have to give this to you now."

Dee unwrapped a long, perfectly smooth and straight stick, painted black, with a blue tip at one end and a red tip at the other. "A magic wand?" asked Dee.

"To make your any wish come true," said Gabby.

Dee brandished the wand, saying, "I wish I was spending Christmas with Willa and my friends." She set the wand on the bar. "If only it were that easy."

"Oh, Dee," said Sally, picking up the wand, wiping it and the counter. "I wish you'd believe in your own magic, in all of our magic. Loving is a magic, and lovers are magicians. I wish you believed that you're a real magician."

Tuesday

Christmas in the city. Lanky kids bouncing new basketballs in the snow-wet playgrounds. Girls in heavy coats and shiny new roller skates playing outside their apartment buildings. Cooking smells in every hallway. Fifth Avenue shop windows filled with holiday displays—and the crowds gone home.

Sooty heaps of snow obstructed the sidewalks in Soho. At Café Femmes the kids drifted in and out, going from their own celebrations to their families'. A few stayed until closing. Silent Night was the center of attention in her big green ribbon. Liz had gone out on some secret errand an hour ago, but Sally, in her new red and white striped bartender's apron and matching bow tie, had no trouble handling the drifters, the few regulars.

"Ho, ho—" Gabby started. "Aw, Sal," she complained, "I took the suit off. I can't take the words off."

"Yeah, Sal," said Dee. "Where's your Christmas spirit?"

Sally furrowed her brow. "I don't know why I put up with you guys."

Silent Night ran between the stools, chasing a wayward jingle bell. Sally thought they were pretty safe from inspectors this holiday.

With a wave of her wand Dee announced, "Zap. You now love to hear Gabby's ho, ho, ho."

"This is what you use your magic for?" asked Sally, as she checked to see who was coming through the door, sounding the cowbells over and over, as if to announce a regal entrance. Every head in Café Femmes turned.

It was Liz, and behind her...Willa.

"Holy Christmas," cried Gabby.

Willa's beautiful smile lit up her face, round and pale as a moon. When she saw Dee, the smile grew brighter.

Dee held up her magic wand and pointed from Willa to it, from it to Willa, and back again.

Sally beamed. "She appeared like magic."

Willa approached, and Dee rose from her stool, slowly, as if unsure of the part she was about to play. Willa set down her suitcase and reached into a shopping bag Liz had carried for her. She drew out a gift carefully wrapped and tied with a large red bow. "I had to come back to give you your present," she explained.

"Oh, Willa."

"Here, dummy, take it."

"Oh, Willa," Dee said again, accepting the gift. "I don't have anything for—"

"Oh, hush. Open it. I know I'm a surprise."

Dee unwrapped it, keeping her eyes on Willa. Beneath the gift wrap was a box, and she lifted the lid from it, watching what she was doing. Inside, beneath layers of tissue paper, lay a set of account books, black with gold edging, labeled *Dee's Magic World*.

"That's where I want to live, honey," said Willa. "In your world—I don't care if we have to live behind our storefront. Nothing's magic without you."

Dee grabbed her, was crying, was holding her tightly, was kissing her. And Willa was explaining, "I knew the minute I got in that house it wasn't home anymore. Secure and safe as it might be, it felt cold and empty. I ran straight to my folks, told them I was home for a short visit, and went Christmas shopping up in Indianapolis with my mom."

"Why didn't you call me?"

"Huh," said Liz. "Who's calling a pot a pot."

Dee tried to give her a withering stare, but her grin won out.

Willa went on. "I didn't know what to do. I wasn't sure I should come back."

"But you did," said Dee, enfolding her in her arms again.

"Oh yes," Willa breathed, eyes closed, beatific smile across her face. "I saw what I really wanted so clearly the second I opened Sally's Mailgram."

"Sally sent you a Mailgram?"

Sally had turned to wipe down the counter, draw a draft, empty ash trays—anything she found to do while her face blazed above her red and white bow tie.

"She didn't tell you? Here, I have it somewhere. It's so cute." Willa read it aloud: "*Dee says open sesame to her door all day, rubs her magic lamp till it shines. Abracadabra, Willa, the magic words are Dee wants you home.*"

"Sally," cried Liz in surprise.

"You didn't know she sent it?" asked Willa.

"No way," replied Liz.

"I thought, when you called me—"

"Liz called you?" exclaimed Dee and Sally at the same time.

"She was arranging to meet me at the station."

"Like she knew you were coming home?"

"Home," said Willa. "I never thought I'd find happiness at the sight of dirty snow. Now it means home."

"Home," repeated Dee. She picked up her magic wand and pointed it at Sally, who had gone to serve a drink but returned as if drawn by the wand. "With friends like you," asked Dee, "who needs magic?"

Silent Night apparently felt left out. She leaped high onto Gabby's leg.

"Yow," yelled Gabby. The kitten held on by its claws.

Dee scooped Silent Night into her arms. "Why did I say I had nothing for you, Willa?" She held the kitten out. "Merry Christmas."

"Oh," said Willa, awe in her face. "A kitten for us."

Liz had moved around the bar to stand next to Sally. They looked at each other and laughed at what they'd done separately yet together.

"There are Christmas lights in your eyes," whispered Sally.

The sound of a choked sob came from Gabby. "It's totally beautiful, what you two did," she told them, tears streaming as she watched Dee, Willa, and Silent Night.

"Magic," said Liz, picking up her grandmother's world and shaking it till the snow swirled.

"Love," said Liz, drawing Gabby into a three-way hug.

"That's what I said." Sally laughed. "Magic."

Originally published by Variant Press, 1984

XII: Hanukkah at a Bar

Great patches of clouds like assemblies of white smoke puffs filled the sky. The street was silent; cold muffled Soho. Sally the bartender, tall and blond, stood outside Café Femmes, under the lavender awning, her breath turning to steam. Head back, she watched the clouds drift by, sniffed the frozen, sooty air. Were they snow clouds, or did they only look like soft heaps of the stuff poised, waiting like the whole city, for Christmas?

No, thought Sally, as she returned to the warm bar, not the whole city. Not Liz, her lover and partner at Café Femmes. Liz and the other Jews of the city weren't waiting for Christmas, but quietly readying for Hanukkah, which would start Sunday, two days away. She picked up the bar rag she left on a table and moved around the smoky-smelling room, wiping down every surface. The lunch crowd was neater than the night crowd, but there were pizza stains, dried beer foam, sticky soda spills. Gabby, who normally took care of the restaurant business, left early for a doctor appointment and wouldn't be back till the dinner hour.

Hanukkah. It had never been a big deal before. She scrubbed finger smudges off the plastic window of the electronic game. Liz was proud to be a Jew. In their first years together, Sally had never failed to give her a present at least on the first of the eight-day celebration. But Hanukkah reminded Liz of her family and she hadn't encouraged Sally. She'd cried enough, Liz had said, over her stubborn, nearly Orthodox father's edict that she never set foot in his home again. Cried over what she'd lost by being gay. Eventually they marked the holiday only by placing a menorah on the bar.

But last spring, for the first time in the fifteen years since Liz came out to her parents, Mrs. Marks called to invite Liz to join them for

Passover. Liz—not Liz and Sally. Liz refused. Now her mother was trying again, wanting her for Hanukkah. And Liz was overwrought, sleepless, ever since, poised like the snow clouds, wanting to fall back into her family's arms, but wanting also to be her whole self. She was Sally's lover, she said, more than her father's daughter.

A voice called, "Guess I'll have to help myself."

Sally jumped, knocked out of her worried trance. Because LilyAnn Lee was tall, she made a habit of silencing the cowbells with her hand before the door hit them.

"You trying to give me heart failure?" asked Sally, rounding the bar, trailing her fingers on its polished wood.

LilyAnn Lee reached across the bar, set the seltzer hose back, and lowered herself to her stool. She was six feet tall, solid-looking, her skin an even, glowing dark brown. She crossed her legs, set her elbows on the bar, and leaned seductively toward Sally. Her fingernail polish was a shocking metallic magenta; her dangling earrings flashed in the light. A heady perfume filled Sally's nostrils. She shook her head. It amazed her how utterly feminine this big woman was. She remembered being struck by that the first time she saw LilyAnn Lee, a freshman entering during Sally's senior year. She'd been sure LilyAnn was gay until she next saw her—on the arm of a male basketball player.

"You know I don't care for those cowbells ringing so close to my sensitive ear," said LilyAnn Lee.

Sally grinned and suggested, "Stoop."

"I do not stoop for any white girl's cowbells. Not LilyAnn Lee, MBA." She grinned, too. "How's my old pal Sal?"

"You mean besides the heart attack?"

"Come to think of it, you are kind of pale."

"I am?" Sally asked, turning to look in the mirror.

"Compared to what is the question."

Sally turned back. "Very funny."

"What do you have in the nonalcoholic line?" asked LilyAnn.

"A Lavender Julie?"

"That sticky-sweet grape thing Gabby thrives on? Not for me."

"The Jefferson Lime Squeeze?"

"Say what?"

She wiped the bar top between them, grinning again. This would make up for the pale-faced routine. "You heard me."

"Don't tell me Jefferson is back in town. And not drinking? Well, my, my, will wonders never cease."

Sally filled her in on their former schoolmate, the woman athlete who finally brought out LilyAnn Lee.

"What do you call it? A Jefferson Lime Squeeze? I'll bet she likes that name. Let me try one—it must be good if it's keeping Jefferson herself off the sauce." Sally poured lime and white grape juices over crushed ice. "You tell her I'm putting fires out now, not starting them in the girls' dorm?" LilyAnn asked.

She nodded. "And that you finished graduate school before you joined the fire department." Despite her sardonic expression, she knew LilyAnn cared what Jefferson thought years later. Kindly, she conceded, "She was impressed."

"Mmm-uh," said LilyAnn, sucking in her cheeks as she tasted the tart drink. She didn't have to work again until Monday night, she told Sally, and settled in at the bar for the afternoon. Customers came and went as she and LilyAnn talked about their school days. A half hour later Julie, who managed an uptown florist shop, made her weekly stop with flowers. Sally and LilyAnn worked together, arranging them in hardy vases on the tables, indulging in their springlike scents.

"I'm back," Gabby announced unnecessarily as she slammed the door against the cowbells. Short, stocky, with graying hair brushed away from her forehead, she rushed to the counter and grabbed an apron. "Hey, Big Lil," she said as she began her preparations.

"That was a long doctor appointment," Sally said. It was not like Gabby to be late.

"I, ah, needed to make a stop."

"Did she say you're okay?" They all went to Dr. Sterne, who frequented an Upper East Side bar but promised to visit Café Femmes sometime.

"Yeah," said Gabby brusquely, making a point of being completely, uncharacteristically absorbed in her work.

Her silence worried Sally. She laid down the wet bar rag and crossed to stand next to Gabby, watching as she deftly cut salad vegetables, sharp wooden knife in her square fingers. Her eyes were red, but hadn't she this minute finished a neat stack of fragrant onions? Gabby was only forty. It wasn't anything that serious, was it?

"Shit," Gabby yelled.

Sally saw the blood spurt to the surface of Gabby's thumb, saw her drop the knife, the endive. Holding a towel against her cut, Gabby blubbered. Sally put an arm around her shoulder and awkwardly patted it. Gabby cried on, quietly, lifting the bloody towel two-handed to her face to wipe the tears.

"What's going on here?" LilyAnn asked. Sally shrugged, but LilyAnn took it in at once and in a moment tied a strip of clean cloth around Gabby's thumb. She held Gabby tight against her breasts. "You're going to have to tell somebody, Gab," she said with a soothing tone Sally imagined her using on survivors of fires. "Do you have to be hospitalized?"

Gabby shook her head against LilyAnn's breasts and managed to say, "I don't know. But I hate it, I hate it. Why do bodies have to wear out?" She sobbed harder.

"What is it, Gab?" Sally urged. "You know we're family. Have you told Amaretto?"

Gabby nodded. "I stopped there after the tests."

"Tests?" asked Sally and LilyAnn simultaneously.

"The doc thinks it's arrhythmia. It means irregular heartbeat. Or it could be nothing. But I could die."

"Oh-ho," Sally joked. "The junk food years are over."

But she felt a coldness around her own heart. Not Gabby. She was finally very, very sober, working in a job that suited her, and with a fine lover.

"Doc Sterne sent me down for more tests today. I see her Monday for the results."

Sally left LilyAnn to minister to Gabby and served a customer at the bar.

She saw through the plate glass window, beyond the backward words *Café Femmes*, that dusk had come.

She moved to the door and stepped outside.

There was an icy chill to the air that made her flesh feel raw. A lone truck was loading at the warehouse across the street, its exhaust inescapable. She coughed. With a clang, someone rolled shut the metal door on the loading dock. The city took on a sense of impermanence. Cities, bodies, did wear out. The tree newly planted in front of Café Femmes struggled to live, too. She glanced up and saw those smoke-puff clouds still hanging, still full, waiting…for what?

She sighed, tired, and went back in. She'd lost sleep, too, with Liz not sleeping. Should she tell Liz about Gabby, or did she have enough on her mind?

Out of the chilly night Liz arrived, cheeks red from the cold, a soft, pale green scarf wrapped around her neck. She moved as quickly as ever, a woman who meant business, but Sally noticed immediately the tension in her limbs, the tautness of her facial muscles, the darkness under her eyes. They entered the bar together. She unwound the scarf from Liz's neck with great tenderness. Liz brought the smell of home with her.

"How's it going?" she asked.

"My mother called again." Liz's voice was hoarse. She must have been crying, too. Sometimes, Sally thought as she drew a pitcher of cold beer and smiled automatically at the customer, sometimes it seemed the whole world was a cloud, filled with moisture, and everyone must take a turn in overflowing. She returned to Liz's side. "I asked to bring you. My mate. My companion. My chosen family."

Sally had no doubt. "She said no."

"She said my father has come a long way. That I should compromise, too. That I was wrong to want the whole schmear at once."

"And you said...?"

Liz became agitated. She was polishing her glasses ferociously. "All at once? I said to her. You're not going to be around forever, Mom. I want my family all at once, yes, and now. All at once? After fifteen years of not seeing the inside of my family home?" The Marks family owned a brownstone in Brooklyn, and Liz sometimes remembered it aloud, room by room, when she came home in the early morning and climbed in beside the already sleeping Sally, who wrapped her long legs around Liz and held her, breathing that home scent, half dreaming, half listening, until Liz's brownstone became part of her own dreams, as if she'd grown up there, too.

"You're not going."

"I asked for another day to talk to you about it."

"Right down to the wire."

"I need to know how you feel, Sal. What it would mean to you not to be there."

"Hey, I've lived without Hanukkah for forty-one years now."

"Not good enough, babe. I don't want one of your unfeeling WASP answers."

Sally shrugged and went to serve a group of office workers on their way home from work. What could she do? She'd been brought up to think of emotions as the equivalent of something you did in the bathroom. Sure, she had them, but to lay them down on the bar, or think about them much, wasn't something she was good at. Sometimes, to tell the truth, Liz went overboard. There she was now, hugging Gabby half to death, holding her hand, making much of what might be nothing. She'd have Gabby crying into her endives and sunchokes all night.

She started to leave as soon as Liz was ready to begin her shift. Didn't try to kiss her good-bye.

"Are you mad?" Liz asked, catching up with her at the door.

"Mad?" asked Sally, surprised. Now Liz was making another crisis. The office workers were singing "Happy Birthday," and she was forced to talk over them. "Why should I be mad?"

"Don't shout at me," Liz said, turning away with tears in her eyes.

Sally stood tall, unbending, and plunged into the chilled air. A web of emotions covered Café Femmes tonight—fear and conflict, longing and self-pity extending into every corner. She was glad to leave it behind. And sorry. She decided to stay in the dark, hushed neighborhood.

"Wait up, girl," she heard behind her.

It was LilyAnn loping toward her.

"Which way you heading?"

Sally shrugged again. "Wherever away is."

"Walk with me to the firehouse. I have to pick up my laundry."

LilyAnn discovered Café Femmes when she was assigned to the local station. They walked in silence, bundled into themselves against the cold, the tall Black woman, her Afro trimmed down for safety at work, and the tall blonde who knew her ears were reddening in the stinging wind.

The rest of the company was out on a fire. Sally considered the drab firehouse and wondered what LilyAnn's life was like, among these men.

"Pretty lonely," LilyAnn said later, over a red sauce smelling powerfully of oregano at Sally's favorite candlelit restaurant in Little Italy. They'd stopped at the service laundry around the corner first. "Some of them hate me. Some of them want to get in my pants. In between are one or two who respect me for what I am, who've watched me work and know I'm there for them on a fire, because that's my job, keeping lives going the best way I can."

"My job is cushy compared to that."

"You shitting me? Remember, I worked out there in that business world before I got this job. It's as dangerous as firefighting. You get burnt in different ways. I wouldn't want to work six days a week, every week of the year, put up with organized crime threats and every other racket there is. I can't believe the risks you take with your money, your security—you're sitting ducks for queer-bashers. I wouldn't want to listen to the gay kids' problems all the livelong day. Watch the love and the loss, the happiness that's here one day, gone the next. The waste. Too many of those kids don't know how lucky they are to have life. They're drinking, drugging it away, like it's some miserable sentence they have to get through. No, I'd rather go out on a fire where I know what to expect, what to do when I get there, watch people appreciate one another."

"Is that why you went with the fire department? To save lives?"

LilyAnn's eyes sparked like Liz's did when she talked about the brownstone. "You know, growing up in my part of the city was never dull. Believe it or not, the bad things brought an excitement that livened up the day-to-day drudgery of my mother making ends meet, of me fighting my way through that hard, ugly school, because she told me it was my ticket to living better. So when a fire broke out, though it scared me to death, I ran out there with everyone else to watch the red engines, the men in uniform, the commotion. The howling sirens, that burning smoky smell wasn't all bad for me. And those men, they were heroes. Time after time they saved a neighbor, a schoolmate, someone's family or pet. It made me live my inconsequential life on a higher plane for a few hours, thinking how those people were given a second chance, dreaming of living my second chance now, this day here." LilyAnn, dark eyes full of light, laughed as if to cover up her high ideals. "How, if I learned to save lives, people might be glad, for once, I was born tall. I knew there was a reason I stuck out like the Chrysler Building in a bunch of tenements."

They drank a half bottle of wine with dinner, and Sally found herself loving LilyAnn Lee, feeling close and trusting. She laid her hand on LilyAnn's firm arm and told her about Liz's brownstone, and Hanukkah. "It's okay with me if she goes," Sally concluded. "I expect to be left out. I'm not real family, I'm not the right religion, and it's one of those things you swallow when you're queer."

"Swallow? If you're swallowing it that easily, why are you crying?"

"Because of Liz. She's always making me have emotions." She dried her eyes with her scarf. This wasn't really crying, these few wine-induced tears.

"Making you have emotions?"

She nodded. "I'm fine on my own. But she doesn't stop asking what I feel."

LilyAnn was studying her strangely. "You know you're talking shit, don't you, girl? You sound like Jefferson," she said, "back when she thought she was a mental Hercules. Nothing reached her. Not cheating on her girl to get me, not bringing me out and dumping me when she was done, not smashing herself in that car accident. Took me a long time to see her trick. She drowned it in the juice. What do you do with your feelings, Sal?"

"You mean you think Liz is right? I do feel more than I know I do?"

The waitress brought them each a tortoni, but food no longer appealed to Sally. "Inside," she said, after a silence, "I guess I agree with Liz's dad. It's his home. He doesn't want an outsider there, sharing in an intimate family ritual. If I was male, I'd still be as outsider as you can get."

"Now," LilyAnn said between bites, "thanks to you I know how he feels, but I'm not hearing what you're feeling."

"But I don't care." She passed her dessert across the table.

LilyAnn took a break between portions. She stretched her legs into the aisle of the emptying restaurant and locked her hands behind her head. "I am remembering," LilyAnn began in a trancelike voice, "remembering what it felt like when I thought I was an outsider."

"You don't feel like an outsider anymore?"

"A miracle, isn't it? In this long Black body of mine. In this queerness that I love. No, I don't feel sad anymore, almost ever. I don't feel at the mercy of anyone else's emotions—my mother muttering into her glass how hard life is, my teachers' frustration with how we ghetto kids didn't learn the way we s'posed to, my friends' rage at not being able to have what they want in this white world. I stayed an outsider as long as they counted more than I did. When I learned, right after Jefferson left me, to be my own friend, to reach inside me, I became an insider. Life opened up. It's a big thing, life. And I want to stuff as much of me into it, or as much of it into me, as I can. If somebody doesn't want me around, that's his problem, he's the outsider."

They paid the check and went into the night. "I don't want to go back yet," Sally said. They walked up to Greenwich Village, past the brightly lit shops, the music spilling from dark clubs, through the noise of panhandlers, drug dealers, tourists, and oblivious natives. It felt warmer in the heat of the Village, in the midst of the many smells—espresso, pizza, marijuana, sandalwood incense. "So that's how I feel, like an outsider," Sally said.

"I stared at those big red trucks," LilyAnn responded, "and the men with their equipment, their know-how, their guts and belief in life, everyone's life, and I thought, back when I was an outsider, I'll never be able to do that."

"I know that feeling. You don't count. If the chief of the fire department doesn't think you belong—"

"If Liz's father doesn't think you belong—"

Sally stopped at an alleyway. "But I don't want to go to the brownstone for Hanukkah. I don't want to feel like a sore thumb, an intruder, an unbeliever."

"So don't."

"Oh," said Sally, searching LilyAnn's eyes and then the alleyway as if she'd found the path she'd been seeking. "Oh," she said again. "So that's what I really want—not to go. But I do want to share the holy days with Liz. They're part of her, part of us. Including her parents—we need to share them, too."

They began walking back, south.

LilyAnn remained silent.

"I want to be included in her celebration. That's why I give her presents. If only there was a way to equalize her parents and me, so the decision is not entirely in their ballpark and I belong, too. I want to be able to enjoy what we do share, not be heartsick."

LilyAnn laid an arm across her shoulders and gave her a sideways hug as they walked. "That's a Jefferson Squeeze, hold the lime," LilyAnn said, laughing.

Sunday, as part of the compromise she worked out with her family, Liz went to celebrate the first night of Hanukkah at her parents' brownstone—without Sally.

But the second night, Monday, when the bar was closed, her family kept its part of the bargain and visited Café Femmes to light two of the candles on Liz and Sally's menorah. Liz invited Gabby, who darted in after her doctor's visit, and LilyAnn Lee, on her way to work, in uniform.

"What, the fire department came?" asked Mr. Marks. "I knew it must be against some code to light Hanukkah candles in a bar." He was white haired, with Liz's dark eyes, but his thick black eyebrows gave him a fierceness.

"Just don't let me hear the word shiksa out of his mouth," Liz muttered to Sally. She came back to work from Brooklyn on Sunday, relieved it was over, that first meeting with her father, full of hope and anger at the same time. She described the changes to the home she grew up in, the food she was never quite able to replicate in their apartment kitchen. Tonight, she wore the long velveteen skirt she saved for weddings and funerals. Sally donned a pantsuit from her days in an office and could hardly breathe. Gabby chose her best black overalls and a bright pink shirt.

At last Sally was hearing the fabled interchanges in person.

"You gave her the goyish name—Elizabeth," accused Mr. Marks in an undertone.

"Quiet, Abe. You wanted her to fit in the modern world," Mrs. Marks whispered loudly.

"Not this modern."

Liz made coffee for the baked goods her mother brought. Its smell, as well as the presence of the parents, transformed the bar into something close to what Liz said from the beginning she wanted it to be, but at the same time not as close because of the nervous energy gathered in the air. As they assembled to light the candles there was a knock at the door.

"Closed," shouted Mr. Marks, obviously on edge.

Liz winced.

"It's probably Amaretto," Gabby said, bustling to the door to let her in.

"What happened?" Amaretto cried, gathering Gabby into her arms. Amaretto's grandmother, Nanny, who spent a great deal of time with the couple, came in behind her granddaughter. "What did Dr. Sterne have to say?" Amaretto demanded.

Sally felt herself shrink. The last thing they needed in front of Liz's parents was this display of lesbian affection.

Gabby caught Liz's eyes in apology.

"Gabby had heart tests, Ma, Dad," Liz explained. "She came here straight from the heart doctor."

"So why didn't she say right away?" Mrs. Marks asked. "We're some kind of monsters?"

Gabby hung her head. Pretty Amaretto, in her thrift store fake fur, kept an arm around her lover's shoulder. "I don't think—" Gabby said.

"Tell," bellowed Mr. Marks. He lowered his voice. "I have a little heart problem myself."

"I'm okay. I have *premature systoles*," Gabby said with labored pronunciation. "That's extra heartbeats." Amaretto grabbed her in a hug again.

"That's exactly what I have," said Mr. Marks. "Not to worry, so long as you take care of yourself and keep healthy. Don't drink," he warned, naming preventive measures on his fingers. "Exercise, don't smoke, and"—he poked the last finger toward his stomach—"maybe lose a few ounces?"

Gabby laughed. "That's the cheapest second opinion I ever heard."

They shook hands. Gabby introduced him to Amaretto and Nanny. Sally eyed Liz then LilyAnn in amazement as Gabby and Mr. Marks talked on about their symptoms. Amaretto never let go of Gabby's hand. They only became lovers in October and were obviously crazy about each other. Was that why Mrs. Marks went to stand by her husband and took his hand, too? Soon Nanny engaged her in conversation. Mr. Marks glanced down at his fingers interlaced with his wife's as he talked. Subsequently over to Gabby and Amaretto's hands and to Nanny, beaming and nodding, apparently completely comfortable. He scratched his chin.

"Okay, okay," said Liz, before her father took this chance to decide he didn't want to be a part of it all. "Did you two come to light the candles or to hang out in a gay bar until last call?"

Open-mouthed, eyes wide, miming penitence, Liz's father raised his right fist to his heart. Liz and her mother laughed.

Liz handed him a box of matches.

"Wait," cried Gabby. She skipped over to the jukebox and fussed with it briefly. In a moment the room filled with the sounds of "Sunrise, Sunset" from *Fiddler on the Roof.*

"Oy," said Liz.

"Tacky, Gab," said LilyAnn. "Very tacky."

"Huh?"

LilyAnn folded her arms. "Would you come to my family celebration and play *Porgy and Bess*?"

"It's okay, it's okay," said Mr. Marks. "Let her celebrate her good health any way she wants. Maybe Mrs. Marks will teach you the hora. Good exercise."

Gabby cast her eyes to the floor, but she said, "I want to feel the spirit. This isn't a funeral, it's a holiday. What's a holiday without music? After this scare, I want everything to count for me."

"Holy day," Sally corrected.

Laughing with the rest, Mr. Marks turned to the candles. "This is not the real thing," he began. "It's very ecumenical. So you can understand." The others ranged around the bar. "At Hanukkah the Jews celebrate their freedom to worship. No, we celebrate freedom of religion. For everyone." He gestured toward them all.

Sally's hand stole to Liz's. They were here, all of them, because Sally decided and said it was what she wanted. Liz thought Hanukkah at the bar was a fantastic idea. As it was turning out to be. She needed to touch Liz's soft hand and feel close. She reminded herself there was nothing wrong with showing what she felt.

Mr. Marks went on. "As we light each candle, we symbolize the growth of faith. For fifteen years my wife and I, we prayed to be reunited with our child, Elizabeth. Life is too short, like Gabby said, to lose anything we have." He reached out his hand to his daughter and she moved toward him, holding Sally's hand, pulling her along. Sally balked. Liz tugged. Mr. Marks's hand wavered, began to drop, but after Liz's mother jerked obviously at his coat, he steadied the hand, pulled Liz, and Sally, to himself. "Always, my God humbles me, teaches me through His will," Mr. Marks said, head bowed.

He faced Liz and, for the first time, Sally. She imagined this time she really was pale, like Friday when LilyAnn teased her. But LilyAnn wouldn't say a thing, she knew, because she saw the tears rolling down those broad brown cheeks. It made her want to cry, too. She swallowed hard.

"Once more then," said Mr. Marks, "as at the first Hanukkah, we celebrate a miracle of faith." He turned, said words in Hebrew, and lit the two candles.

"Tomorrow," he asked, turning back to Liz and Sally, "will you both"—and his voice sounded choked here, because the words came hard, very hard—"will you both come for the lighting, to Brooklyn?"

Sally stopped herself from obsequiously thanking him for his acceptance. She wanted an out should she choose to use it. "If we can cover the bar."

After coffee and pastries, her parents hugged Liz and shook hands all around. Outside, Liz walked them to their car. Sally stood slightly beyond Café Femmes' awning for a peek at the sky. The temperature had risen and the puffy snow clouds were gone for now. The sky would weep another day.

She stubbornly kept her eyes skyward as LilyAnn joined her. It wouldn't do to bend her head and let those tears fall out of her eyes. But

LilyAnn Lee put an arm around her shoulder and squeezed her. Sally, feeling like a cloud whose time had come, looked wetly down.

Originally published in *Common Lives/Lesbian Lives* 25 (Winter 1988)

XIV: The Wet Night

Sometimes, especially in spring, when Sally the bartender goes from Café Femmes into the tart midevening air, she is filled with wanderlust. Tired, she'll meander home for what seems like hours through the perhaps wet streets of the city, hardly aware that her red crusher hat smells of damp wool and is dripping. With strangers, she pauses at corners, where she sways enchanted by the sharp reflection of red traffic lights in puddles, or by the sight of bright moist rows of strawberries, oranges, bananas, and apples gleaming under the red and yellow awnings of small Korean-owned groceries.

Most of the time, she feels full with this feast. Now and then, though, she aches for Liz to be by her side.

Blond Sally opens Café Femmes in the morning. Shorter, dark-haired Liz closes it at night. They spend their day off together and sleep every night touching through the dawn hours, forcing themselves awake to talk a few minutes as Liz comes to bed or Sally gets up. This schedule makes their time together delicious, even after all these years.

Tonight, Sally is drawn to a certain brownstone off West Fourth Street, as she would be to a secret lover. The owners of the building have preserved lilac bushes on tiny plots of ground to either side of their steps. During her worst fits of springtime roving, their phosphorescent glow lures Sally, on clear nights, to the scent of a billion lavender explosions. She breathes them and breathes them until she is dizzy with pollenated oxygen and reels off into the night, longing to make love.

It's then that every woman on the street turns into a siren, and then that Sally walks among them like a connoisseur in a statue garden, drinking in every line.

That one with the wide splash of lipstick, blowsy, on the rakish man's arm. She wears an old-fashioned wide-brimmed hat, has hips Sally could spend a whole night kissing her way across. The woman's perfume rivals the lilacs for loudness, makes Sally sneeze, but she stares after the couple, knowing the woman will laugh a full pleased laugh as they begin, later, in a creaking rented bed.

She loves that her Liz laughs in bed, respectful of their lovemaking but not serious.

She turns onto Sixth Avenue, where there are more people, and her heart lurches after a quick-stepping fashion plate. Sally names her Nicole. Out of the Balducci's shopping bag on Nicole's arm peeps a baguette. She looks like she would not laugh during sex and would allow into her life only lovers who did not disrupt her agenda. She would use the word *agenda*. Even now she scurries to prepare a pretty, perfect platter for a midnight dinner for herself: parsley just so, bread rounds toasted an exact tan, the apricot wine chosen for its color against her delicately patterned crystal. Nicole believes it's healthy to orgasm once a day, hasn't the time to bother with more. Sally wants to stroke that prim sharp nose, pry the thin lips apart and find the lush tongue with her own. Wants this once to tear innumerable abandoned climaxes from the woman, which would leave them both sobbing and laughing and glad.

She passes a bar with an awning and considers returning to Café Femmes, where she could shadow Liz, spread her fingers across her bottom at opportune moments, steal kisses from a mouth sweet with the peppermints Liz uses to quell the taste of bar smoke.

The thought takes her back to the night, a month ago, when she woke from a seamy dream seething with desire. In it, a woman was above her, open legs straddling Sally's face, pressing herself gently, rhythmically against Sally's pursed, sticky lips and drumming tongue. Awake, her eyes closed, Sally exhaled a long breath. Her hand discovered that Liz was home, sitting up in bed. She was reading *The Sunday Times*. Not a promising sign.

"Hi, babe," said Sally, hoping Liz would recognize in that endearment Sally's state. She was rubbing Liz's thigh with a finger.

"You're tickling," Liz said, squirming.

Sally turned onto her stomach. Her legs became entangled in the lower sheets.

"You're stealing the covers again, long tall Sal," said Liz, tugging them back across her lap.

Sally reached an arm across Liz's hips, accidentally on purpose disturbing the newspaper.

"*Sa-al.*"

Finally, Liz gave her a sideways glance. Her eyes narrowed at the sight of Sally's big wide-eyed grin.

"Uh-oh," said Liz. "You're up to no good."

"You sure about that?" Sally asked, pressing herself against Liz's leg.

Liz laughed then, filling the air with the smell of peppermint toothpaste. It was a laugh so like that of the blowsy woman with the wide-brimmed hat and loud perfume that Sally's mind returns to Sixth Avenue. She realizes that she's walked two blocks uptown without seeing a thing. The rain has stopped.

She wants more this night than going home and waiting for Liz. She turns east on Eighth Street where the weekend crowds are teeming, and she joins their restless hunt for pleasure.

Sally wanders toward the sound of a woman singing. She is white and middle-aged, a long-haired street musician in peasant clothing, backlit by an open bookshop. Two light-skinned adolescent boys accompany her, one with short elegantly waved black hair and a fiddle, the other with a wild reddish Afro and a banjo. An antique hippie and her sons? The woman's long skirt sways as she sings, brushing the tops of bare feet. Over an embroidered blouse she wears a fringed leather vest dyed purple; her breasts push against it. Sally smells the spicy patchouli and is overwhelmed by the strength of it as she imagines her head between those breasts. She tosses money in the hat for the delight of looking.

"Any requests?" asks the singer.

Sally sorts through her skimpy knowledge of folk music. "'Mr. Tambourine Man'?" she asks, afraid the song was too popular for a real folkie to deign to sing. But the woman, who has no Baez voice, throws her full-throated, almost bluesy style into it as if this is her all-time favorite tune. Sally taps her feet and realizes how much she'd wanted to hear such a pied-piper song tonight.

Once, when they were new, not long before they closed the deal on the bar, Liz rented a car and they drove out of the city, without a destination, playing "Mr. Tambourine Man" and "Just Like a Woman" and "Lay, Lady, Lay" all the way to the end of Long Island, to Orient Point, where they waved good-bye to a ferry load of people who were crossing to Connecticut. As much as she'd cherished the thought of marriage to Liz—and buying that bar was their marriage oath—she remembered thinking the tambourine man in herself was on that ferry. She smiles at the thought that he never left. She edges out of the crowd which swells around the singer. "Mr. Tambourine Man" follows Sally up the street.

It's about nine thirty, long past dinner. At a deli she buys a package of apricot fruit leather in honor of the prim fashion plate and her pretty wine. She gnaws on the sour sheet of it until it seems sweet in her mouth. At Fifth Avenue, cloyed with the taste, she turns uptown to feed her other hungers.

A pack of punk girls who can't be over fifteen moves toward her. Their hair ranges from pink to light green, some of it spiked, some crew cut, some cut stark and straight edged. Like a cotton-candy chorus line, they jangle their jewelry and pop their gum and walk to the rhythm of raucous music piped from a store. Underneath the racoon eyes, though, Sally sees the same tender flesh she'd first kissed, and loved, at their age. Behind the heavy odor of pot, she knows there is the fresh scent only young girls have, when their pores exhale dreams and sex is a new kind of play. Her body recalls the heaviness of her own young need, knows her underwear will be damp the rest of the way home tonight, as it always was back then.

There is one teenager, at the very end of the cotton-candy line, who meets her eyes. She's at least partly Asian, wears jeans, and her hair is not as loud as the others'. The dyke, Sally thinks. She feels the girl's curiosity burn into her, feels the girl's desire to take what Sally knows and learn it for herself, the where-do-I-put-my-hand-and-when, and my tongue? Really, my tongue? And will you show me? Will you do it to me? Can I do it to you? Again? And again, please? Sally shivers at the thought of that slight frame, that new mouth on—not hers, on another fifteen-year-old who thinks she will die from the excitement.

Her legs are tired. The fruit leather has been her only dinner. At the next corner she walks quickly back over to Sixth and signals a taxi. The driver is a heavy Black woman who slouches against the side of the cab, one hand on the wheel, steering with a casualness Sally admires. She can see the woman's profile and wonders about her. Can someone so in control of her vehicle be anything other than a lesbian? She wishes the bulletproof barrier between them was open, so she could make small talk, probe with gay hints. Would the woman think she was trying to pick her up? If she did, would Sally follow through?

What would it be like, a one-night, a one-hour stand with a stranger? Sally had never done that. Would they go up to Sally's? Would the driver know a secret nook near the docks? Would she get in back with Sally? Would she take off Sally's wet jacket, then open her shirt? It was unthinkable that Sally could be the aggressor with this authoritative woman.

The driver, leaning against a door, would pull Sally's naked back to spongy breasts, would cradle her, talk to her in a strange baritone. She'd snake her hands around and maneuver Sally's pants down to her calves, push Sally's legs apart in order to explore her with those wide strong hands, twist Sally's head around to kiss her with a bold tongue, with a mouth that smelled of cigarettes. Sally would press against the driver's hand, her breath short, her desire for release desperate beyond any craving she normally had. She'd push against the heel of that hand with her clitoris while the fingers played around her opening. Self-conscious, she'd strain and strain. The driver, making wet sounds against her ear, would try to make her come despite the awkwardness of the back seat, despite Sally's feeling of helplessness at being so exposed, at being so passive. She'd expect to come suddenly, powerfully, at the thought of her unaccustomed passivity, abandoning her inhibitions to the majesty of the woman. But she wouldn't, too discomfited by strangeness. Finally, she'd lie weak against the driver, not knowing if she should apologize or reciprocate. The muffled traffic sounds, the sight of dark warehouses, the fact of Liz, would seep back into her consciousness. She'd turn around on the woman's breasts, really look at her for the first time, not merely a hand, and not Liz, a different real person, a stranger.

And then? Then the woman would repulse Sally's advances, mutter about not wanting to get done, drive her home, and refuse a tip. Sally would be left standing on the curb, still admiring the big woman with the deft hands and the air of command.

They reach the theater district. Sally raps on the window to get out, half afraid she's revealed her thoughts in some way, perhaps through the fantasy meter ticking away on the dashboard. Embarrassed by the intimacy she imagined with this stranger, she tips her too much. Sally steps outside the cab and turns to the driver with a sheepish smile. Without a glance at her, the driver zooms to the mouth of a theater and picks up a woman and a man. Sally feels empty, abandoned, yet exhilarated. She's experienced the pleasure of the encounter without the complication of reality. Liz need never know anything besides Sally's spillover of passion.

Marquees blink and blaze above her. She stands watching as the theaters empty and the streets fill. Then the rain comes down again. She wants to laugh, to raise her mouth to the sky and catch the plummeting raindrops. A woman squeals. A man holds a huge black push-button umbrella straight out, chest-level, and opens it with a whoosh. The umbrellas blossom up and down Broadway, slick and jouncing. Sally leaps over puddles in a private ballet, jubilant at having joined this huge party.

A lone woman in her sixties passes her. She wears a belted trench coat and a khaki-colored rain hat slanted down over her eyes. All Sally can see of her face is a fine-drawn mouth in faint lipstick under a long nose. The woman walks swiftly in sturdy low black heels, hands in her slash pockets. Sally waits a while, then sets off after her.

The rain muffles sounds. The woman maneuvers through the crowds. She calls no cab but moves up Broadway with purpose. They pass restaurants and a few small markets. Sally's stomach grumbles, her hat drips, her feet are sore and wet inside running shoes, but nevertheless, the magnet of this woman, who is probably sixty-five or seventy, draws her past crosstown streets more devoid of traffic with every uptown block. Their only company is a parking garage attendant who stands in a gaping entranceway, arms folded, watching them go by. Sally nods at him.

She will tell Liz about this woman later. About the Amazon who stalked Broadway, luring younger women through the dangerous city.

Where would they end up if the Amazon had her way with Sally? On the very private balcony of a high-rise on Fifth Avenue, she decided. They would drink coffee the next morning in the Sunday sunlight. Young couples would stroll far beneath them with baby carriages. Miniature roller skaters, joggers, would enter the park. Widowers would snooze on the benches that line Fifth Avenue, and women would chatter to one another across them.

The woman in the trench coat would recline on a chaise lounge, her hair gray white, her cheeks lined graphs around the jutting nose. Sally would reach to the woman's long robe and slide it open, letting her fingers rest on the gray hair between her legs. Their eyes would meet. The woman's lips, newly colored, would part. She'd let her legs fall slightly open. Sally would push into the still-damp nest from a shower they'd shared, and her finger, barely touching, would roll back and forth, back and forth on the woman's stiff clitoris until her orgasm came, like another ray of warm sunlight, as quiet as the rain-washed Sunday city and the swarming Park so far below.

But the woman in the trench coat doesn't turn east on Fifty-Ninth. Instead, she crosses as if going into the Park. Sally draws the line there. She does not go into Central Park at night. She wants to stop the woman, warn her, a hovering lover.

But the woman veers west, away from the Park, and Sally watches her enter the Plaza Hotel. Sally walks past the doors, craning her neck. An out-of-towner. Of course. In from Greenwich or a Jersey suburb for dinner with her lady friends and a show.

She is near home. It's almost midnight and she knows Spot needed her walk, so she plunges through the rain the last few blocks, grabs the Sunday papers, and an hour later is in bed where she sleeps soundly until three a.m.

"Sal?"

Sally tries to wake up.

"I'm home, Sal," whispers Liz, and Sally at long last feels a naked woman's body covering her own.

She can smell city rain mixed with bar smoke on her lover's hair, and peppermint toothpaste. Liz's skin feels tight from the night's tensions; her voice sounds raw from talking over the jukebox. The windows are closed, yet Sally hears a squalling baby in the apartment across the courtyard. Liz's body meets hers in every important place, softness mixed with hard curves.

"Romantic, isn't it?" she asks.

"You mean the baby?" Liz laughs softly and lies still against Sally with a sigh.

Sally fears Liz will fall asleep. She runs her hands down the curves of Liz's back, rests her fingers around her waist, then begins to stroke down Liz's bottom over and over, spreading the cheeks a tiny bit each time she reaches the bottom.

"Umm…" said Liz.

Sally reaches lower so that her spreading will pull Liz's lips slightly apart. "Do you like that?" She can't quite reach inside.

"All of it, Sal. I kept feeling your hands on me all night. I don't know what set me off."

"Whatever it was, I'll take it."

Liz opens her legs, tucks her feet around Sally's knees. This brings her higher. Sally slips one finger in.

"*Huhhh*…" said Liz. She pushes down on Sally's finger.

"Oh, you're ready, baby. Want to roll over?" Liz shakes her head against Sally's neck.

Sally moves her finger in circles, around and around inside the wet fleshy tent.

Liz sips tiny sips of air, jumps now and then. Her breathing quickens. Sally wonders if she's actually going to come, backward like this. The thought excites her so much she loses her rhythm. Liz laughs, patient. Sally tries to catch the rhythm, adding another finger, while Liz presses down harder, clasps them within herself, lets go, clasps again. Sally holds her breath for fear of repeating the break in rhythm. She realizes that the baby stopped crying, that Liz's breathing is uneven, that there is absolutely no friction inside Liz at the moment, only a pool her fingers swim in, around and around and around and around.

"*Huhhhhhhhh...*" breathes Liz in a quiet exhalation. Her tent yawns hugely, then folds down tight. "Sal. Oh God, Sal. Oh."

She holds Liz to her, feels their two hearts thump, kisses the side of her forehead. "I love you."

There is silence for a few moments. Sally wonders what her other lovers are doing and smiles into the dark. Has that cab driver quit for the night? Did the prim woman have her orgasm yet? The street musician took her sons to a coffeehouse where they were jamming. The theatergoer, has she put her sturdy heels outside her door for polishing? She feels a pang when she thinks of the punk baby dyke. She hopes the kid has a girlfriend who was sleeping over that very night. Stealthily, they explore each other's bodies, making sensations they never dreamed. She begins to stroke Liz again.

"That was very nice, Sal."

"Was it, babe?"

"I'd try it on you if you weren't too long."

"Maybe you can come up with something else."

"Think so?" asks Liz, leaning over Sally, grinning eyes and teeth faintly visible in the dark.

"You always have before." However, Sally is sleepy, doesn't know if she possesses the steam it would take. She tells this to Liz and lets her eyes close, snuggled in, content with intimacy.

She isn't sure, a moment later, if she dropped off and woke again, or if she was dreaming. Did Liz put Bob Dylan on the stereo? How can she know about "Mr. Tambourine Man" tonight? Was that really a fantasy meter in the cab? She never opens her eyes to ask, though, because it feels too good, what Liz—is it Liz?—is doing with her mouth, down there.

Sally hugs Liz's head with her thighs to tell her she's awake. Liz is blowing on her with a warm breath that feels like a Sunday breeze. Holding her open and blowing up, then down, then up again. Sally begins to throb, glad it's Liz's full lips so close to her, not Nicole's thin prim mouth, not the fine-drawn lips of the out-of-towner.

Then Liz does something she's never done before. She thrusts her tongue inside Sally, suddenly, and as suddenly, replaces it with her fingers.

"Liz," she said from the shock of it.

"What is it, Sal. Again?"

Sally wonders if the baby dyke has discovered this trick yet. "*Oooph*," she breathed as Liz tongued repeatedly. "That's an amazing feeling."

"Kind of rough on the tongue muscles, though," says Liz with a laugh.

That laugh. Like the first woman, who has probably long since let her creaking bed go silent. She can see the motion of Liz's head in the dark, moving it back and forth to rest her tongue muscles. Sally feels her own wet parts stretch up. Then Liz's head drops. Obviously, her tongue has recovered. It moves in exactly the right ways on exactly the right places, and Sally, out of steam or not, can only follow the feel of Liz's tongue and the hot waves of tension that shake her body.

Her breath becomes as short as Liz's had been. She knows she's flowing like a fountain. Her body feels like…She wants to say like it's finally home, but can home be this exciting?

Maybe it's the spring, the lilacs, the rain, the city lights, the women on the street, and her long spring ramble, maybe it's all of that she's feeling as Liz—Sally gripping her shoulders for dear life, a long *yes* at last rolling from her—as Liz brings her home.

Originally published in *Cactus Love* (Naiad Press, 1994)

PLEASURE PARK

I was young, I was alone. It was summer and hot in the smothering still way of the city. I'd moved here for a job now two weeks old. I hadn't met any lesbians and couldn't find a bar. Loneliness was beginning by the second weekend, not in any recognizable form but as an urge for a holiday, a change, some excitement.

During the week I walked to the office for exercise, but today I decided to board a bus for adventure. I remembered a bus I'd passed on my way to work whose sign, Pleasure Park Loop, intrigued me. The city roused itself around me as I walked its streets at a leisurely pace, noting details ordinarily obscured by my morning dash. A bakery beckoned, though the mock wedding cake in the window was frosted with dust. I bought two sweet rolls and a carton of milk from a short-haired woman who gave off no gay vibes. Where were my people?

At eight thirty Pleasure Park Loop pulled up empty. Two older women shambled up the steps in front of me, one leaning on a cane, the other holding on to her. I passed them and went to the back of the bus where I opened a window. For the first time in days, I felt the air moving as the bus started in the direction of the lake. I finished my breakfast and sank back on the seat, both relaxed and filled with anticipation.

The bus ringed the center of the city, passing from neighborhood to neighborhood on the lookout for passengers I imagined still in bed, satisfied to hide from the heat. At one stop I looked into a tasteful jewelry store where someone filled the windows with bracelets, necklaces, and rings, sparkling like dewdrops in their early morning showcases. Two Hispanic women entered on the bus there. Then several streets with churches led into a neighborhood of mothers pulling clotheslines of white sheets across their yards from second story windows. At these stops, we gathered kids with fishing poles, a young couple with a beach blanket, bags of snacks, and beer. I could have been on a holiday trip, not a city bus.

The area changed then, becoming increasingly well-groomed and less interesting as we approached the lake. Both of the Hispanic women left the bus, likely domestic help. I wondered if this district was Pleasure Park itself and considered whether I wanted to walk in such a smug atmosphere: manicured lawns, roomy houses. I caught glimpses of backyard outdoor kitchens and redwood swing sets belonging to people alien and sometimes frightening to me. I stayed on the bus.

Then, with the water, came a line of close-set, modest summer cottages, built earlier in the century by the looks of them. Apparently, working people from city neighborhoods claimed this part of the lake before the rich.

When the bus stopped, the kids and young couples exited, but the older women did not. I held a slim hope that Pleasure Park, with the promise of its name, was still ahead of me. We rode on for a while, and as I began to suspect the ladies had come only for the breeze of the ride, the bus took an unexpected turn into thick woods. It was nothing but a turnaround, but the two struggled out of their seats and off the bus. I lifted my backpack and descended the back door steps.

The women slowly followed an overgrown, seldom used road. They glanced furtively my way a few times, out of what I thought was the timid world of advanced years. I wondered where I'd gotten myself to. Weeds grew through cracks in the asphalt and sunken trolley tracks. Through the trees, plots of white cement, also cracked and weedy, lay ahead. Was this, then, Pleasure Park? A vestigial trolley stop, a ruined memory?

It was, and I was fascinated by it. The sun was on a course to her peak unimpeded by cloud or fog. Below her a couple of acres of the white cement warmed. A few wooden structures were all that was left of the park. They, too, were white, or were so long ago that now the cement was brighter than their paint, and they could not be mistaken for anything but what they'd become: remnants of an era that enjoyed this simple pleasure park. And the partial structures, what were their functions, once so important they were built to last into a time beyond themselves?

One, it was clear, had been a carousel, its long-gone wooden horses poised for escape under a scalloped roof. There the ladies seemed to have gravitated.

What must have been an indoor arcade lay beyond that. I explored this, leaving the women to what I imagined were memories of husbands. I stepped cautiously, unsure of the safety of the arcade boards, which showed signs of weakness and rot. Vandals had descended, leaving large-lettered obscenities over water-stained walls where the mechanical fortune teller, the flashing pinball machines, and Skee-Ball must have been. Windows were empty of glass, damaged fixtures, shutters, and awnings hung loose, doorways gaped open. The ruined gray boards under my feet held vibrations of pleasure-seeking crowds. I fled out a back exit to the deck that ringed the arcade.

On this side of the park ruined rides were scattered. I peered into the shadows they cast. There was a band shell. A platform once used for dancing showed signs of fire damage. People must have thronged here to lift their spirits in the summer heat, and I imagined benches of them fanning themselves. The music would swell from silvery cool instruments in a storm of pleasure. Then, with a sigh and hot applause, the throng would return to what they were, a town come to forget the heat and monotony of their lives, to lose the kids for a while, to remind themselves of the lost romances that led them to their marriages.

And here, I thought, were two of them. The women, finished with their perusal of the carousel's ghost, wandered off toward the woods. There must be paths through the trees that shared their memories. Eventually they returned, slower, drooping, glancing shyly toward me and toward the bench I now occupied, the only one in shade.

"How do?" the taller of the two said as they joined me. The shorter woman's eyes were closed, and she patted her forehead with the kind of hanky given to third grade teachers at the end of the school year.

"Hi," I answered like a puppy at the return of its people. I was so eager to hear about the world of Pleasure Park. Their world, I hoped.

"Never seen you here before." The tall one had a sheepish smile, and thin white hair all awry from the open-window bus ride. Her glasses had slipped down her nose in the heat. She didn't meet my eyes.

"I moved to town after I graduated from State last month. I never heard of Pleasure Park and wanted to see what it was."

"What it was…" She nodded. Then she turned to her friend whose face mirrored her sad expression.

"Wasn't ever much more," the other almost whispered. Her hair was thin and white, too, cut slightly longer. She wore a sleeveless blouse and Bermuda shorts. The tall woman was in white pants.

"Would you like some lemonade?" I asked, pulling from my bag the thermos I'd packed.

They lifted their heads, eyes bright. "Didn't expect it to be so hot out here," Tall said. "Usually get a breeze off the lake. This will go down good about now." She rolled up the short sleeves of her loose checked blouse farther in such an unladylike way I could have sworn she was as dykey as me.

"I packed a lunch, but it's too hot to stay long enough to eat. Drink all you like," I said as I filled the thermos cup for them.

Tall took it in her shaky, spotted hands and passed it to the other. "Em," she said, "this will perk you up."

"Ice cold." Em sighed after a tiny taste.

The other took a small taste herself. "I wish we had something to offer you."

"No need. I've got everything I want. You finish that, now. There's as much left in here if I want it."

They drank three cups with obvious relish.

"I'm Madge McCormack," Tall said, reaching to shake my hand while Em held the cup. "My friend Emily Rosen."

Did I imagine she hesitated at the word friend?

"Curly Singer," I said.

"Jewish." Emily nodded.

"Every inch. I'm glad to meet you both. Do you come out here often?"

"Not much anymore," Madge said. "It's a big trip for us now. Em's niece used to drive us once in a while, but she moved downstate to live in the real city, as she says."

"She thinks it's silly anyway," Emily added. "Still to be wandering around this ghost town."

I made a puzzled face, squinting and pursing my lips.

"For years we came out here to find the ring," Madge explained. "The ring we lost on our first trip here, right after we moved in together. It's what we do on our anniversary."

She searched my eyes, quickly averted hers. I left off wondering and began to conjecture. Were there really lesbian couples this old?

"We wanted to keep doing things together even after we shared a house. Why should we pretend we were only roommates and stop going out? We were in our thirties and unmarried," she said. "The hell with what our neighbors thought."

"The scandal of it," said Emily with a nervous laugh. "My family especially."

Madge said, "We were paying off the house, but back then the trolley ride was only a nickel. We'd buy some popcorn, listen to the free concert from the beach. Didn't take much to make us happy, did it, Em?" She nudged Emily playfully.

"Still doesn't, Madge," Emily answered, patting the hand that held the cane.

"Did your friends come here?" I asked, trying to make an opening for them to tell me it was a secret gay paradise.

"Why, all kinds," Emily said. She looked under her eyebrows at Madge. "Almost."

Madge took up the narrative. "It would be packed on a Saturday night. That's when we would come. Seeking some excitement after the long week of housekeeping and working."

"We both had jobs. Couldn't make ends meet otherwise," Emily explained, like there was some shame to it. "But at the factory Madge worked twice as long hours as me. I was only a secretary—and keeping house, that was my overtime." She laughed and faced Madge, this time with affection.

"Between me being dog-tired and Em being so cooped up, we figured we deserved a treat."

"If we came early on a Sunday, we sometimes rented a boat for fifty cents and rowed around the lake. We enjoyed our privacy," Em said, again casting her warm gaze at Madge. "I've always thought what a shame it was we didn't lose the ring in the lake. We wouldn't have had a hope of finding it and could let it be."

"Maybe she doesn't want to hear about the ring," Madge said.

"'Course I do." Something about their story appealed to me as much as Pleasure Park itself. I needed to get at the core of both to satisfy myself now.

Madge's and Emily's eyes met, as if deciding to risk sharing an intimate secret with me. I couldn't believe two women this ancient were sending me the same signals my contemporaries did when they're about to spill the beans.

"I gave her a ring," Madge almost whispered. "You know why, I think."

I smiled in a subtle sideways way I picked up from other dykes in the city and stretched out my red pinky ring to them. Their wrinkled faces smoothed right out as they smiled back.

Em was excited enough to dig her elbow into Madge's upper arm, saying, "I told you so." She peered at me. "I've never met another Jewish girl who was one of us."

I squirmed, afraid of getting in too deep with them, but they acted glad to add yet another kind of person to their slight collection of *one of us*.

Madge explained further, at last fully meeting my gaze. "Em wearing a ring like normal women made what we were seem all right to us, not something to be laughed at or to get us arrested."

Emily began to tell the story. "It was the Fourth of July and we'd spent the day at my brother's picnic, but by the end of the day we wanted to be off on our own. There were so many of them and only two of us. It would be the same here, but we often saw more people like us here.

"By the time the bus dropped us off, it was twilight. The day was as hot as today, and there wasn't a breeze stirring. The park was full, but hushed. Remember, Madge? The people were moving slowly, their kids whining, and a lot of them were sitting down for dinner on the benches or in the grass. Back then, there wasn't all this cement. That came later, when there were more money-grubbers than space and the owners jammed them in. Seedy, that's what it became. But that was a long time later.

"We weren't here long when the dark, which had been sneaking into the sky for a while, came on. Then the sun left the park and took its heat with it. The crowd grew in the cool, and Madge and I hopped onto the carousel. Under the pretty colored lights, the breeze was a waterfall of stars landing on us as we went round and round, full of ourselves, feeling our new love. I so wanted to hold Madge's hand, her on a white horse, me on an elegantly colored ostrich."

They smiled shyly at each other, as if embarrassed about the passion they shared. Me? I was beginning to ardently anticipate old age. It promised to be, contrary to what the straight world predicted, a happy time.

"Then we got off," Madge said, handing the cup of lemonade to Emily. "We walked around a while longer and started to cross over to the beach where the fireworks were starting. Em noticed her ring wasn't on her finger."

"I wasn't used to it yet, and I'd lost weight since Madge and I got together. I worried about how we were, what people would think."

She contemplated me as if for understanding. I met her eyes and gave her a slight nod.

"I'd meant to make it smaller with tape but hadn't got around to it yet. There were so many new things to get used to. Like being loved." And she looked that special way again at Madge. "I'd gotten in the habit of feeling for it now and then, and when it wasn't there, my heart fell to my feet. I'll never forget that moment. Like the carousel stopped turning forever, the lights went out, and the world stood still. My precious circle of gold was lost."

There was a sting of tears in my eyes.

Emily took my hand and went on, "The rest of the evening we spent not on our holiday, but searching for that shiny speck of gold in the confusion of the moving carousel."

Madge continued, "We couldn't find it and returned the next day. Under the hot sun, we searched every horse, every seat, every crack and cranny on the platform. We questioned the fellows who worked here. They said they hadn't seen it. Could we believe them? They were local boys we didn't think would spoil our happiness for a few dollars, though we heard snickering behind our backs and wondered."

"I swear, I thought our world ended right then and there, that it was a sign we were forbidden," Emily said, eyes cast down. "As if what we consider our marriage was jinxed because of my carelessness. As if what I was, what we were, was wrong, no matter how much we pretended to be like everyone else."

"And I," said Madge, "was a poor specimen of a spouse who couldn't find it for her, nor afford to buy her a replacement. I, too, feared they were right after all. We couldn't hold hands on the carousel with the rest of the crowd. We couldn't have a real marriage."

Emily's sadness was in her eyes. "Pleasure Park went on around us with the laughter, the excited screams, the romancing, the buying, the selling. Life went on while my world stopped dead in its tracks. We couldn't tell anyone what a tragedy this was for us because we'd have to explain the ring. It was the first time I really knew how outside of life we were, how much we were alone in every way."

"The attendant told us if it got into the machinery of the carousel, it might be ground down to nothing by now. We were hot and discouraged, gave up, and stopped for a lemonade. Curly's lemonade brought it back so clearly."

"But we never gave in," added Emily. "No, we came almost as often as we first did, always with one eye to the ground. It took the edge off our fun, always keeping our eyes out for that ring, that missing piece of us, and later we did stop coming. Pleasure Park wasn't meant for people like us any more than rings were. But Madge bought me a ring at the five-and-dime because I still longed for one."

"A ring that tarnished and had to be polished all the time. It wasn't like the real thing."

"Around about then we met two girls like us. For once we were not alone. We started coming out here with them—what else was there for the likes of us to do? And we told them the story. They sought out the ring, too. One day they did find a ring, a man's ring, but they turned it in, and somebody claimed it that same day. Soon after that the girls stopped getting along together, and one moved away while the other married a man. Besides, by that time they were pouring cement over every open space out here. It wasn't as pretty as it once was, and we thought, though we hardly ever spoke of it anymore, that my ring was probably under the rough concrete they set down to squeeze money from the park."

Madge poked her tongue in her cheek. "Progress, you know."

The sun marched boldly across the cracked cement toward us. They finished their lemonade and would take no more. "What a pleasant rest," they told me. Madge checked her big watch to plan their departure. "Bus won't be around again for another forty-five minutes," she said. "No use walking over to the stop yet. There's no shade there."

"Did you never find it then?" I asked, wanting more of their story. The white park blazed around us like a desert around an oasis. Our tiny pool of shade would soon be gone.

"Well, the next thing that happened," Madge said, "is that I read in the paper where the park was to be torn down. Gangs and motorcycle clubs were disturbing people and tearing the park down faster than it could be repaired. Those boys enjoyed the park so much as youngsters. What changed them?" She shook her head. "That was a shock, let me tell you. The offspring of those happy families we envied were now destroying the park."

"A part of us seemed to be going with it, even if we never did really belong there."

"After I retired, we'd go to your events—rallies and picnics. We watched you pretty young things claim your rightful place in the world."

I could imagine Madge sizing us up from a benign corner of a park, or curbside at a march.

"Or we'd go to the restaurant on our street for Saturday dinner, but if you went there too early, you were in the middle of families full of squealing young children, and if you went too late, you were surrounded by young dating couples. We saw our own families at the holidays, separately. We met no more like us around here and grieved for the giddiness coming to Pleasure Park once brought us. Ours was an uneventful life, and though happy, I guess we both considered ourselves a bit cheated, but we stuck together."

Madge paused to wipe her brow with a handkerchief. The flirtatious twinkle was gone from her tired face. The sun was about to touch me where I sat at the end of the bench. Madge said, "When I read about Pleasure Park being torn down, I thought to lie down and wait to die."

Emily nodded. "You were depressed for a long time, dear. Right into our retirement. Then one day I got the idea that if we were ever to find my long-lost ring, we might find it when they were dismantling the park."

"Sure. It was a great idea. They were disassembling the carousel. Aw, I knew there was no point getting that ring back, but the idea was exciting. I was sad for so long, living the kind of life we did. It was excitement enough to make my days new, to make me want to go on. My life was ahead of me again," Madge said, her eyes lively once more.

"We came out here the day they started." Emily's speech quickened; she fluttered her fingers. "We explained our story to the workmen. They joined right in the search, like we were their grandmas and too old to trigger their prejudices."

"Or they thought we were a couple of crazy spinsters, but what the heck, we said, maybe we'll find it, and if we did it'd be a kind of triumph after all the years." She peered at the sun. "Whew," she said, "it's a hot one. What do you say, Em, shall we make a last round?"

Emily nodded and rose carefully. "Would you like to join us?"

"Sure would," I replied, hot for the ending now. "What happened when they took it down?"

We started toward the carousel shell and its small pool of shade. "It was heartbreaking," Emily answered. "Like watching them murder some gentle harmless beast. But we came back day after day until the end."

Madge took up the story again. "Got to know the boys well, and we'd bring them cold sodas for their trouble. Took them all of a fall day to pack the carousel, which was going to a small city out west. They worked very carefully and slowly. We followed every one of those horses to their crates and watched them cover their fine, faded bodies. And we poked our fingers in every grimy machine part.

"We stood back at the end of the day, exhausted, ringless, watching the workmen put away their tools. It was gone, the park we knew. Night was coming on sooner with summer past. Most of the workmen were gone.

"We left the carousel and edged toward the woods." Madge stopped in the shade of the trees. "Right about here, wasn't it, Em?"

Em, smiling wistfully, nodded.

"A slight younger workman—he couldn't have been over twenty years old—stepped out of the woods holding something in the palm of his hand. He asked if it was what we'd been looking for."

Madge stared at her hand as if it held something. "I reached out and took it from him. Under the trees it seemed like night was falling, but to me that gold circle glittered like the sun was shining. It had kept its shine, not a scratch on it. I asked Em, whose eyes are better, if the initials inside matched ours."

"I was in shock, I think." Emily said. "But the tears started by themselves when I saw our initials."

"Where was it, how did he find it, I wanted to know. The boy was too young to have been born when we lost the ring. He often scanned the road to the worksite, and we knew he'd come in stealth. He told us his grandfather ran the carousel in his youth and had a mean streak for queers."

Clenching her wrinkled hands into fists, Madge went on. "Thief! I wanted to shout. I was close to striking the grandson of the boy who ran the very machine we'd loved. The carousel, the toy of the crowd, one of the few things we could, within limits, share with everybody else."

She shook her head. "The boy was so decent he apologized for the word he was raised to use. He said his grandfather told queer jokes and showed off the ring. He'd kept it to teach us a lesson, to teach us we couldn't be married like him. He used the ring when he married his fiancée, a real woman.

"And we'd believed that grandfather. We believed we'd been punished, like he wanted us to.

"The boy started to go. He said his grandmother recently passed on. When he heard from the demolition crew that we still searched for the ring, he took it from her jewelry box. She'd long ago become too heavy to wear it."

Madge's face was by turns happy, angry, and regretful. "I managed to thank him, and the boy told us this was only one of the things his grandfather and father did that he was trying to fix. *Like me*, he said. *They call me a pansy and you know what? I am.*"

Emily said, "We hugged him and told him to be proud of himself, gave him our address should he ever need our help."

The three of us stood beneath the trees now. There was a distant rumble and we all looked toward where the bus would come in.

"We'd better get over to the bus stop," Emily said and took Madge's arm. The story had taken a lot out of them. "Thank you so much for the lemonade, Curly." She reached over and mussed my curls.

"Thanks for telling me your story," I said, heavy with sadness.

"We haven't many to tell it to," Madge said, reviving as she leaned like a long-legged bird to peck my cheek. "Come pay us a call someday. We're in the book."

"Yes," I said quietly as I watched them venture out from the umbrella of the woods, like two ghosts weighed down by their burdens of life.

I, too, stepped into the sunlight, for a last glimpse of Pleasure Park before crossing to the lake. The white columns and wooden platforms glared at me across the wasteland of cracking cement. Green weeds were proving their strength through it, perhaps could destroy it. I'd learned what Pleasure Park was and wouldn't need to come back there. Unless to tell someone else the story, to show them how it used to be.

Originally published in *Old Dyke Tales* (Naiad Press, 1984)

THE AWAKENING

Sun splashed against the porch screen as summer breezes lifted the leaves and branches of the venerable maple tree outside. Every afternoon Momma, at times nodding off, sat on the large, thickly cushioned rocker with her two daughters on either side of her, Lillian stiffly on the edge of her straight-back chair, darting forward at each sound in the street, while Nan rose more slowly to witness and judge Lillian's observations.

"There she goes now," Lillian exclaimed, her index finger a stiff extension of the thin hard line of her body. "I told you so. Can't spend a day without him. She's a lush. Has to see him up at the corner every day or she thinks he won't come to see her at night." She clicked her tongue. "A lot she'd be missing if he didn't."

Nan lowered her limp, heavy form to the flowered cushion of her rocking chair, exhaling like an inflated pillow whose plug has been pulled. She shook her head and chuckled. "Can't get enough of him, can she, Momma?"

Momma, her permed white hair neat under its matching net said, "Tsk, tsk," and smiled with pleasure.

"Momma appreciates a good joke, don't you, Momma?" Nan asked, patting Momma's wrist in approval.

"But this is no joking matter," Lillian protested and snapped her cigarette case open. "Not at all, not at all." She tapped a cigarette against the arm of her chair and jabbed the cigarette between her lips before she continued. "The neighbors are up in arms. Madge Daugherty with her poor sick mother is beside herself with what goes on there weekends. She doesn't want her two girls to get the wrong ideas, you know. That's an impressionable age, the early teens, I well remember."

Nan and Momma looked as one away from the retreating figure in the schoolyard. Nan gave a nervous giggle. "Not us, Lil. I hope."

"Certainly not." Lillian's cigarette jumped on her lower lip as she spoke. "Shut up, Alexander," she called to the caged blue canary who had broken out in song from the corner of the porch. Lillian adjusted the gauzy white scarf that surrounded her pin curls.

Momma smoothed her housedress. "None of those goings-on in our family."

Nan shifted her weight. "If it was the one gentleman caller, I'd understand better. But it seems like a new one every year."

"Doesn't it, though?"

"And she had a perfectly good husband."

"Drove him away, they say."

"Needs a lot of men."

"Do you think so?" Nan asked. She fanned herself with a *Reader's Digest.* "Do you think it's her body that needs them? Or her mind?"

Alexander sang again, briefly, until Lillian hissed at him. "It's all in her head, of course." She stabbed the ashtray with her cigarette butt. "No one needs that much you-know-what."

"She thinks she's no good unless a man wants her. Why else entertain them all?"

"What makes that worthless bird sing, Nanette? It's in their nature. The woman was brought up as well as we were. Her poor mother would be mortified."

"Deviltry, pure deviltry." Momma chortled slyly and rubbed the few stiff white hairs on her chin.

Lillian darted forward, demanding, "Let me pluck those for you, Momma."

Momma waved her away with a fleshy pink hand. "Don't be bothering me, child," she admonished. "God put them there for a reason."

"Maybe God has a reason for her to carry on like that," said Nan.

"Who, Momma?" Lillian wanted to know. "Who?"

"The trollop. We need her kind to amuse the men and give the rest of us some peace."

Nan let her head drop to the back of her chair. Her hair was bleach-blond and thin, wisps of it escaping her pink plastic curlers. "Always touching and poking. They can't think of anything else."

"Except betting away the money," Lillian added.

"The horses," Momma said, rocking and nodding. "The horses and the drink."

"Speaking of the drink, there goes poor Frank."

"Poor Frank," Momma echoed.

Lillian craned her neck to see disheveled Frank stumble down the street. "Disgraceful," she said. "To think you once gave him the time of day."

"That was before I met Ned, Lily. I never did intend to marry that drunk."

"There but for the grace of God go I," said Momma.

The daughters nodded with vigor while the canary belted out a new refrain. Lillian turned to chide him until her eye was caught by Frank's cautious approach to a tree in a secluded corner of the schoolyard. "Oh no," she whispered in horror.

"What, what?" Nan asked, rising halfway and leaning to the screen. "He's not, is he, Lily?"

Lily scowled at Nan, shushing her and pointing her chin at Momma, who was straightening and repinning the doilies on the arms of her rocker. Nan and Lillian sat back in their chairs but kept their eyes on the man.

Momma looked up, alerted by their silence. "What is it?"

"Nothing you want to see, Momma," Lillian answered evasively. "There, it's over, you can look now." She lowered her voice. "He relieved himself in the schoolyard."

"Do you believe it?" Nan asked with her nervous giggle. "Momma could have seen. If school was in session, the little girls—"

"Never mind the girls, they'll have to put up with that kind of thing too soon when they're married. But what an example to the boys. My boys."

"They'll be like that soon enough anyway," Nan observed.

"Not my boys. If I ever catch them pulling a stunt like that, their father will give them what for, and I'll take away their precious bird once and for all. My boys will not be rummies like Frank or lose their paychecks as soon as they get them. You'll see."

"Glad I only have my daughter. I don't have to beat any of that piggishness out of her."

"Mine won't grow up piggy. You can mark my words."

"They're all alike," Momma said, shaking her head. "All alike, every last one of them."

Nan smiled and lifted her chin while Lillian sat tense with fury, tears in her voice. "I'm raising my two boys to make their wives happy. They'll be different. I don't care what you say."

"Look, look," Nan said, lording her find over Lillian. "It's the honeymooners—fighting again." A man and woman walked together down the street, glaring straight ahead, not touching.

"Fighting this early in the morning. My, my," Lillian said in a loud whisper, distracted from her mother's criticism. "Why she puts up with him, I'll never know."

"They say it's for the kids."

"All six of them," Lillian said, sneering.

"One with him should have been enough, I'd think." Nan looked at Lillian over Momma's head, eyebrows raised.

"She can't possibly get any pleasure from it," Lillian concluded.

"It's hard enough with a man who doesn't hit you."

They craned forward as the couple passed under the porch. "The language." Lillian breathed outrage like a dragon's fire. "To his own wife."

"Words I've never heard before." Nan winked at Lillian, who didn't spare her a glance.

"Shhh," Lillian admonished. "They're fighting about him going to work. He's telling her to work if she needs more money."

Nan clucked. "The nerve. Why, that's all they're good for, bringing home the bacon."

"Not a drop of good in any of them," Momma added, leaning heavily on the arms of the chair as she struggled up. Her stockings were rolled around thick ankles and spilled over low black shoes. The dark flowered housedress had bunched behind her girdle, and the silky material eluded her stiff fingers as she tried to grab and pull it into place.

"Here, Momma." Lillian rose and jackknifed behind her mother to help her.

"Here," said Nan, simultaneously flailing for a hold on the dress from her chair. "Why you still wear these girdles I don't know. You're mature enough to relax."

Momma winked. "Maybe the boyfriend will come by today."

"Boyfriend my foot," Lillian ridiculed her.

"What would you do with a boyfriend, Momma?" Nan wanted to know.

Lillian stood in the doorway calling after her. "Where are you going? Use my bathroom down here. Don't walk up all those stairs to your place." She went back on the porch muttering to Nan, "Embarrassed, I suppose, to use anybody's but her own."

"Do you blame her? After all those years living with Poppa? She finally has privacy. A bathroom of her own. A bed of her own. An apartment of her own except when you can't stand it down here and go up to her. You must spend half your life there."

Lillian relaxed and sat down after she heard her mother safely upstairs. "Thank goodness I have that refuge. When he..." She lowered her voice. "When he starts the drinking, you don't know what he'll do. He doesn't bother the boys. They protect me, young as they are. But there's nowhere else I can go. Last night, Nan, he smashed my fresh baked pie on the floor. Ruined it. After I cleaned it up, he wanted to you-know-what."

"I don't understand them, I don't."

"Don't tell Momma."

"No, no, I never do. I don't want her hearing about my fool of a man either. I'm sick of the horses. He found my refrigerator money yesterday. The money I've been saving for a new one. I think Sheila deserves something better than mushy ice cream, poor girl."

"To the betting parlor?"

Nan laughed. "Where else? Right down to Reilly's cigar store. But I couldn't say anything, you know. He won."

"Did he now?"

"He's buying the refrigerator and school clothes for Sheila. Taking her shopping himself," Nan boasted.

"Trying to win her favor after his meanness."

"He doesn't fool her, though."

"Good for her."

"She says she doesn't want new clothes," she whispered. "No plaid skirts like the girls are wearing, no patent leather shoes. I can't understand the child, Lily. She wants another pair of those flannel lined jeans like his folks gave her when we visited them in the country."

"Do you suppose it's a stage?"

"I don't remember any stages like that when I was eight. Do you?"

"No. Momma dressed us in the prettiest white starched dresses no matter how scarce money was, didn't you, Momma?" Nan asked as her mother returned to the porch. She leaned over to smooth the afghan on Momma's chair.

"He did his best, poor soul," Momma said as she sighed into her seat. "Did his very best." Her eyes twinkled. "Wonder what his worst could've been."

The daughters heaved with laughter. "Momma, you're a scream," said Nan.

"He was your father, though. Respect him. Respect the dead."

Lillian sounded indignant. "After how he treated you?"

"He had a hard time of it."

"He didn't have to take it out on you."

"Who else did he have?"

Nan shook her head. "Being poor drove him to drink."

"Like it drives some men to gamble." Lily looked significantly at Nan.

"Or to hit their wives."

"It all comes of trying to raise a family and keep a home together."

"Forgive and forget," Momma said.

"Still," Lily mused, "sometimes I wonder if we'd be better off without them."

Nan was scornful. "Don't be ridiculous. How could you raise two boys alone? How could I take care of Sheila?"

Lillian stubbed out another cigarette. "And our lovely flats."

"My nice new refrigerator."

"Grin and bear it."

"Would you like some iced tea?" Lillian asked.

"Sounds delicious," Nan said. "If it's not too much trouble. And I'll bring out those scrumptious A&P cupcakes Sheila picked out on the way over."

"Won't take me but a jiff, Nan. Sit and rest your bones, I'll bring it all out."

"You'll need help carrying." Nan righted herself on her short wide legs. "No argument. I'm helping."

As the sisters went into the house, Lillian quickly and full of purpose, Nan following slowly, Sheila at last let herself open her eyes. From the porch cot where they had instructed her to nap while they visited, she gazed at her Grandmomma's back. She never could sleep through their talk, though they thought she did. She wondered what Grandpoppa had done to Grandmomma. Was it the same stuff her father and uncle did to her mother and aunt? She hoped it wasn't worse. Quietly, she sat and looked up at Alexander the canary. He blinked at her. She winked at him. "Why do they live with men?" she whispered to Alexander. He blinked again and flapped his blue wings. "I'm not going to, bird. You can bet your sweet tail feathers on it."

Momma turned her slow bulk toward Sheila. "Awake, rascal?" she asked.

"Um-huh," Sheila answered, pretending to rub sleep from her eyes and stretching noisily.

"Cupcakes coming. And iced tea." Momma opened her arms. Sheila blundered over to her, still feigning sleepiness. She walked between her Grandmomma's open legs and let herself be enfolded by fleshy arms, against soft breasts. Sheila sighed. She had no intention of leaving Grandmomma's arms. Ever.

Originally published in *Old Dyke Tales* (Naiad Press, 1984)

THE ABRUPT EDGE

I sit on the floor in the rich circle of light cast by a study lamp. The rest of my new apartment is very dark around me. I am alone as usual, feeling empty, needing I know not what. My first job after college graduation will begin tomorrow, and I am nervously avoiding thoughts of it, rifling through mementos in a wooden chest that came over from England with my grandmother's family. I pick up three aged photographs.

In the first, two young women on wooden swings are poised to leave the ground, hands clenched around the thick ropes. I am on the left, the white girl whose birthmark, grayish in the photograph, wraps itself halfway around my face. How I had wished it had stolen over my whole face so that I could be all dark. As Dawn was.

She sits on the right-hand swing, my best friend and the only African American at camp. We'd had to plead with another counselor to photograph our friendship: the odd ones. She later gave us both print and negative, not wishing to keep our images. In the picture you can see us trying to look small, to be invisible to the staff and campers who shrank almost imperceptibly away when we were near. I had this sad commonality with Dawn to thank for the friendship that flared immediately between us, fanned by our isolations.

But I describe more than is in the picture. It only shows, in the harsh noon light, two young women, stiff and smiling almost bitterly at the reluctant photographer. We are hard to look at.

Lifting my eyes. I peer into the darkness of my apartment. Dawn seems to shimmer there like a vision, still near me, agonizingly touchable, as terrified as I was of touch—I look down to the next photograph, a sunlit one that floods me with light.

Someone caught us from the beach as we, on the lake, led a convoy of girls canoeing. In the shining aluminum vessel, my back shows first, upright, lifted paddle dripping water. The straight line of Dawn's back proves her new mastery of canoeing. Her paddle thrusts back and back and back at me. In the picture I am poised to follow her stroke with my own. The current we create flows between us. Her stroke became my stroke.

She cared as fiercely for me as I did for her. "Here come the saddle shoes," the kids would chant, for we were always together, brown and white. There, on the dark and glistening lake water, the camera reflected us, shining in white camp shirts, as we called our fantasies to each other across the bowed opening of our canoe. The camera exposed our dazzling visions, suspected our dazzled hearts.

The brightness closes my eyes now in this memory-heated room. My heart hurries in excitement as it did when we taught the younger girls to dance, by dancing before them. Slowly I open my eyes, losing a film of brightness to the dark around me.

I tingle as I examine the last image, bringing it close under the lamp. It is dark, taken at night from the bottom of a steeply rising cliff by a camper experimenting with her new camera. All I can make out is the sand of the cliff, some dangling roots, and patches of dark bushes. Perched atop the cliff's abrupt edge are the shadows of a tent luminous from a lantern within. We are not in sight.

But it was there, in the darkness, on an overnight camping trip, that we faced each other finally.

My need to touch her raged. My words strangled me, caught with emotions thick in my throat. Her almost black eyes seemed swollen as I laid my white hand lightly against her dark cheek, and she trembled, but whether from desire or fear I could not tell. She gave no other sign.

I took my hand away and collapsed in disappointment into the shadows of the tent, full still of my own tense need. Slowly, Dawn submerged the lantern wick, then faded into her sleeping bag.

"Oh," I cry aloud to myself as if in pain, "how could I have stopped?"

It is as if now, in my own first home, I have finally stepped from the edge of that cliff. I am at last ready to redeem myself from the failure of that dark night and plunge into a blinding knowledge of who and what I am. I hug myself to soothe the white-hot pain of revelation that sears through me, and the photographs spill from my hands. The pictures catch the light, shine up at me, their images engraved on my eyes, my mind, my heart. My need is abruptly so clear.

I will love a woman, if one will have me. I will see, be seen; touch, be touched; love, be loved, by one as womanly as Dawn, as womanly as myself. Searching through the chest, I find some tacks and pin the images of my life solidly to my new wall, lighting as well several candles before them in celebration. The wavering images glow at me, and I glow through my mottled face back at them.

Originally published in *Old Dyke Tales* (Naiad Press, 1984)

AUGUSTA BRENNAN

I: The Coat

It's not so bad sometimes, being old. You can rest at last. And I need a rest. I feel so tired it's all I can do to keep up with my memories. They wear me out so.

Since I got sick that's mostly what I do—remember. I sit here in my vinyl rehabilitation center chair, not in the least an easy chair, but one to which I've gotten very attached. Something about getting down to a very few things in life makes you hang on to what you have that much more. The day I came out here to the sunroom and that new lady was sitting in my chair, I could have killed her, that's how upset I was. It was my chair, my corner of the room, my patch of sunlight. The next day, she was too sick to sit up, poor soul, so I'm glad I didn't murder her over it. Wonder if they would have put me in jail. Wonder if it would have been much different. How embarrassing, to kill for a bit of sunlight.

It's safe here. Perhaps that's it. Safety in familiarity, when there is no other safety available. When I was working, I thought I'd be covered when I retired. How wrong to think a good income in 1950 would be worth anything today. So here I sit, in my tiny corner of the world, a small old lady with sparse short hair, sitting in the sun, remembering and feeling my life as if it was happening today.

Memory is safe, sometimes. You're pretty darned sure of the outcome. Safer even than the TV at night. I watch it when I'm too tired to remember. That happens more and more and frightens me. I never thought I'd give up so easily, and even now, on my best days, I've got some fight left in me. I filled out an application for the senior citizen housing the other day and made plans to share food with a lady who's moving there soon.

One of my greatest pleasures and triumphs is finally not being afraid people will notice I only care about the women around me. No one expects me to move in with or flirt or dress for a man. The men hardly even expect or want it from the patients, but the nurses are a different story. On top of putting up with the demanding, dependent ways that are even more exaggerated in feeble men, the nurses bear their coarse humor and repulsive touching. Sometimes they go home to their own men for even worse treatment. I don't see how they do it, and I wish I could tell them they don't have to.

Not that most of the ladies around me are any great shakes. But there are a few tough gals—like I was till I got sick—who aren't about to let a few years get them down. Do you have any idea how much you give up when you're my age and have no loving family to take care of you? This is when my memories are not safe. Remembering my apartment, my cat. When you're too sick to take care of yourself and no one expects you to recover enough to ever do so, others make decisions for you.

I'm lucky, though. My young friends are kind and help me. They're in a couple, as they say, and live in my apartment building. We had many long talks over tea, Karen and Jean and me, before I got sick. They dealt with putting my belongings, such as they are, in storage when I couldn't afford my apartment anymore with the nursing I needed, and took in my cat, Mackie. I'll see him when I visit them, but I'm afraid that may break my heart almost more than if they'd had him put to sleep.

Mackie's old, too, sixteen. The sleekest, proudest striped creature in the land. Faithful as can be. And dignified—he never begged like other cats, merely insisted on a partnership. He refrained from waking me in the mornings as long as I fed him on his stomach's schedule. Of course, he decided what time that would be, but then he was the cat, and as such enjoyed certain prerogatives. He'd never wake me before six fifteen. I used to think that was his way of compromising, waiting until fifteen minutes after six instead of waking me at six on the dot. I never needed an alarm clock with Mackie. He'd prod my cheek gently with his paw until I sat up, and then he'd lead me patiently to the kitchen, tail waving like a flag in a parade. I wonder if Karen and Jean let him play the same game with them. I wonder if he'll know me.

The sight of snow outside chills me. That's what's making me think about Mackie. Cold, winter, age, sadness: it goes together in my mind. But I know it shouldn't. I know there's something good in winter and in age. The snowflakes, taken singly, as they fall, are so lovely. But it's hard to realize that when the winds drive the snow into my window with a vengeance. It feels like an enemy, and I draw my blanket tighter around my lap. Makes me think sad thoughts.

Does Mackie feel betrayed? Does he understand it's my waning body doing this to us? Or is he pleased with his new life at sixteen without the dotty biddy pawing at him? I haven't had a lover in the years he's been with me. He's not used to sharing affection with someone else. Where would a lesbian in her eighties find a lover? What other timeworn woman will admit she'd like a lover?

❖

I must have dozed off there for a moment. Dreamed I was patting Mackie on my lap in the sun. And I see why now. That was a quick snow—the sun's back out. The ground is clear. It might never have snowed, the way the kids are going at it out there.

I thought it was crazy to build a convalescent home next to a school. They are noisy going to and from school and at recess, but they don't bother me. I love watching them, but I'm no demented pedophile. I have a game with a few of the girls I've guessed will be lesbians when they grow up. I wish I could protect them from the net of heterosexuality when it's inevitably cast over them. I'm going to bring them out right there in their schoolyard.

How sinister you must think I am, making assumptions about these sacred children. I couldn't agree more. That's why I'm giving them everything I've got to help them be true to themselves as they really are.

It wasn't too hard choosing them. Some of the girls were too straight already to save. The ones in their well-starched skirts with curled hair. The ones who, at eight years old, bring their nail polish to the schoolyard and put it on while other girls are throwing themselves into games. I rejected them because I don't feel strong enough to undo what's been done. I picked some easy ones: the tomboys in their checked shirts with their Band-Aided knees. The ones who play cowboy, not house, the ones who start the games. If only I could live long enough to see two of them pass by some day, holding hands. I'll have to trust in my fading powers.

The sun is hot. Maybe I can take the afghan off. Whoever thought I'd be sitting with an afghan over my knees? It's got some of Mackie's fur on it, and I'd cherish it for that even if one of my lovers hadn't made it for me.

"Sloppy cat, always misplacing your coat," I'd tell Mackie. Like that child, one of my chosen people, who won't wear her coat when she plays. She gives the teachers a terrible time. The minute she runs out of the school, there's her coat, thrown up against the fence under my window. Almost as if she knew I was in this corner watching her, and she was asking me to keep an eye on her coat. Her coat and her rebellion, because, of course, the casting off of the coat is really her way of saying, *No, I won't be like you, I won't play by your rules, I won't wear your restrictive clothing, I'll throw it away and be myself.*

I suppose I am beginning to sound a bit doddery, but she's my favorite, the strongest contender for the royal dykedom. And she looks like rambunctious Dale, my previous apartment manager's daughter. This one is round and full of energy, yelling as loud as the boys. She may have long hair, but it's wild and never stays where her mother trains it to go. Glasses don't slow her down a bit.

Dale is almost forty now. It's hard to imagine her that age. I watched her grow from ten through fifteen. The five years I lived in that building were strange. Different from any other years. I was between lovers in a town so small the nearest gay bar was one hundred and twenty miles away, hardly worth the trip unless I was desperate for lesbian companionship. I only made it there three times, if I remember correctly.

The place I lived in was L-shaped and had six apartments, built to house unskilled workers at the town factory. I was in the short part of the L in a one-bedroom on the second floor. I worked, of course, at the factory, helping set up their bookkeeping and accounting because the new owners couldn't make head nor tail of the system. Then I stayed, because they said they needed me to organize the office and train some girls. After that they wanted to expand and needed me more than ever. Well, it was five years before I got out of that country town, though I knew I should have left long before that, before Dale turned sixteen.

If I hadn't gone to the hotel bar for my Sunday dinners and

overheard the men's coarse jokes, I would have thought the town didn't know what a lesbian was.

Who else could Dale turn to but me? She followed me around soon after I arrived, when she was ten. A tomboy who refused to stay in and watch how her mother ironed and cooked, she was a lonely kid who spent most of her time with her dog Lassie. I laughed every time I heard Dale call Lassie because he wasn't a collie, but a tiny, tiny thing with black and white markings and long ears. The name Lassie made him comical. But Dale told me she'd always wanted a collie like Lassie, so when her mother let her have a dog, Lassie it was.

That kid begged me to go with her on long hikes up into the hills with Lassie, asked me to go fishing when her dad worked overtime. I should have known where it would lead. Overnight, she became an adolescent. And not a sulky, awkward kid with big feet and a bad attitude; she became a handsome diminutive woman. Still in jeans and plaid shirts and sneakers, she filled them out better. Instead of going through a pale and listless stage, there was more color in her face than ever, and she was full of a creative energy which, at fifty-three, I had a hard time matching. And I continued to be her favorite person.

In my isolation you can imagine what this beauty did to me. I'd come around the corner home from work, and oh my, my heart flipped over to see this trim young woman, one foot up in back of her, arms folded, leaning against the side of the building. She'd bought herself a men's Panama hat at the thrift store, and when she looked at me from under the shade of the brim, I fought off my feelings.

She might have been the only game in town, but I knew I couldn't play. As a matter of fact, I tried to stop her from hanging around with me. I was afraid for her. I knew I could leave town anytime, but she was too young to escape if there was gossip. I assumed she would move to the nearest city as soon as she learned she wasn't the only lesbian in the world, as I knew was inevitable. My problem was how soon she learned and what she decided to do about it, as I knew how tempted I was to teach her myself and not solely in words.

If only the sun would stay out. It seems to give me energy. I don't want to fall asleep during this memory. It's one of my favorites, and if I doze, I'll dream about Dale and get mixed up about what's real and what's not. Even now as I watch that young energy out there in the schoolyard, I get confused about how Dale looked, because I see Dale in her. Here she comes for her coat, the defiant tiger, teacher leading her by the elbow.

Oh, she smiled up at me. Has she known all along I've been at my window? Next time I'll be ready with a smile of my own. With a message in it. So she won't see some poor rickety woman, but a strong elder, someone she might eventually want to be like. An impression, that's what I want to leave on her brain. A hint that she can be different, that she doesn't have to be like the rest of them. After that she'll be on her own, do her own growing, as long as she has that assurance around her like a coat, a conviction that it's okay to grow up your own way.

What comfort, when the sun comes out from behind its cloud. How strong it is, and it's older even than me. Now that I'm not in pain the livelong day, I'm not as drained. Perhaps I'll get back on my feet yet. How I'd love to go for walks again, if only around the block. Perhaps by spring I can go outside and watch the schoolyard from there, but I don't want my aged face scaring the girls away from the warmth and goodness and confidence I'm able to send.

Does it sound as if I want to be the sun myself? Clothing them in the warm rays it wraps around me? But I do feel like that as a lesbian: special, lucky, touched by magic, and given knowledge that brings me a certain majesty and power. I think these new-style lesbians, the feminists, are learning how exceptional we are. Karen and Jean bring me books and magazines that the feminists write. My eyes aren't what they used to be, but I can read for short periods. The new lesbians come up with such insights and dig up such astonishing facts from women's history that I know I'm not crazy for knowing I was blessed from the moment I came out.

And didn't Dale look like a young sun goddess, back in her small town all those years ago. Didn't she haunt me with her magical beauty. Didn't she seem to know a coronation was due her, and didn't she do everything she could to bring it on. I'd get home to find she'd let herself into my place with a passkey. I'd allowed the little girl to do that but was afraid about the young woman doing it, too. Wouldn't she be stretched out on the couch that came with the place, Mackie stretched alongside her, and holding a bunch of brown-eyed Susans for me. Wouldn't she be poring over my books when I finally decided to leave them out to be sure she found the word *lesbian*.

Words. For the first time they became strained between us. In years past, I had long arguments with myself about Plato and Socrates and whether their love for boys was an excuse to be dirty old men or whether it was really one of the highest forms of love. I didn't know not to judge what I did by what men did. I left Plato on my coffee table in hopes that Dale would read him and make her own decision. And I gave my notice at work because I knew, whatever happened, it couldn't go on. I needed a woman I was free to touch.

Wasn't the sun strong that day, didn't it beat down on me as it does now, too bright for me to open my eyes, so I hardly knew then or now whether I'm dreaming or not? She let herself in that Sunday morning and woke me as she sat on my bed. In the second floor L, I had no near neighbors and slept with the curtains open for the sun to stream in. I was half blinded by it as well as by her beauty.

She was bursting with adolescence and her new sexuality. Her cheeks were fiery red, and her lips looked blackberry stained. Her eyes were hardly open she was feeling so much desire. The flesh of her body wanted to burst from her clothes. I heard her breathe short deep breaths as if she was strangling from all she felt. Her ears glowed red. She was embarrassed to be coming to me like this, as well as frightened. I wanted to comfort her, but oh, fear gripped me, too.

She leaned down to me, and I smelled her clean hair. The sweet young woman kissed me on the forehead and withdrew her lips, leaving her face closer to mine than before, her breath hot as the sun. Her breasts, above my hands, were so round in their red plaid shirt, so close. I touched them.

Dale closed her eyes, and her face filled with such sheer pleasure I didn't move my hands at all, let them stay around her breasts until she opened her eyes. I smiled. She leaned over my face and pressed her lips against mine. Not really kissing me, as if she wasn't sure how to do it. I showed her by parting mine and kissing her back. She caught on fast, and soon we were leaning back from each other, needing air. "Listen," I said, before she started again, "when you're fifty-three you need to go to the bathroom when you wake up in the morning. Will you wait for me?" I asked, knowing her eagerness would keep her there.

Closeted in that small bathroom I let myself waver, fear, and finally, brushing my teeth, risk. I'd still leave, for there was no possibility of a real relationship between us, although I've always wondered about that. In any case, Dale needed me then. She needed—as we all do—someone to give her permission, to show her the way, to open the door.

I wanted to plant a few seeds, too, to keep that door open, to let her know we were doing much more than going to bed together. That the ritual of women making love is one of the most powerful in the world. It shook women to their roots, us and those who would ban us. She must learn to be careful, to protect herself. The act committed women like us to lives unimaginable, abhorrent, to most of the world; she must learn to live fully despite threats and dangers. Today would open her emotions and mind like no other experience she could have; she must learn to temper her passions so that instead of being destroyed, she would be stronger from them and could use them the rest of her life.

She was more beautiful in her way than any mature woman I'd ever known. My waning body against her blooming one made her seem magnificent. Her crisp full flesh was an experience my hands never appreciated when making love at that age. Her trigger responses kept me more alert and responsive than I'd been in years. The smothered cries that came with orgasms, once she relaxed enough to have them, stirred something almost maternal in me because I was watching a young girl discover the staggering capacity in herself to experience beauty through sensation, and I remembered how overwhelming beauty is at that early age. Her orgasms themselves were taut and fast, compared to the rolling release my mellower, looser body felt. She was a flower blooming in my hands, and I a wilting one in hers.

Look at me, snoozing in the sun, nodding away over my memories, again not knowing if they're real. Had Dale come to me that day, or was I remembering a dream of her? The school is getting out for lunch. And there goes Dale, dragging her coat behind her. No, not Dale, that new schoolgirl. And this stiff body's got to heft itself out of its favorite chair, out of the sunlight, for lunch. Nourish itself. I need my strength, after all. There's work to be done. Worlds to be won, as someone once said.

Dale moved out to San Francisco to win hers. She writes to me once in a while. I picture her with graying long hair streaming wildly over a battered denim jacket, her eyes glittering with excitement, but now from a new hunger, a new hurry, to make the world fit for the likes of us. She's one of those San Francisco marchers. It warms me to know I helped put her there, that I knew her first hunger. That I live in her.

Originally published in *Common Lives/Lesbian Lives* 7 (Spring 1983)

II: The Tracks

I made it, thought Augusta Brennan with a peaceful sigh as she slumped against the white doily on the back of her easy chair. She never believed she'd survive a convalescent home, but here she was, settled in her new flat, her old cat Mackie bunching himself into a leap for her lap. They sat; her little bit of housekeeping was done for the moment.

The morning sun shone on her self-cut, shaggy white hair. To her shame, it was a bit dirty from the difficulty of positioning herself to wash it. She tried to avoid mirrors and the sight of the lines and wrinkles around the squint of her inquisitive eyes, and the flush which never disappeared, only grew with exertion or excitement. Her stout body had grown padding from every blow life had dealt it.

"You didn't think I'd come back, did you, old boy?" she asked Mackie. "Didn't think the old girl would make it." She chuckled. After sixteen years, she knew just how to stroke Mackie behind the ears, and he purred loudly and proudly in her lap. Thank goodness for Karen and Jean, she thought. If her young friends hadn't taken Mackie in, it wouldn't have been worth getting better. She and Mackie would never have known her beloved one-of-a-kind home.

Built between railroad tracks and a street, this row of narrow houses was the sum total of what an enterprising builder could squeeze in. Gussie feared at first there wouldn't be room to turn around, but the girls had reassured her and took charge of moving her furniture out of storage. Besides, the flat cost so little.

She surveyed the apartment above her contented cat. Its shape reminded her of water wings, those old inflated rubber things she'd taken to the beach for swimming when she was young. The two swollen sides were connected by the narrow neck of a foyer, closet and front door.

On one side of the neck was a bath and bedroom, on the other a sitting room and kitchenette. The sun played on the colors of her favorite possessions like musical notes in a song about her life. It shone on her bright afghan, on some small braided rugs she had admired at an auction and the girls had later given her, on her mother's faded quilt which still lay warm and soft and enormous across her daybed. The first floor of the little stone house by the railroad tracks was homey now. She puttered about in it just like an old lady, she told herself. The hot summer sun felt better than the weak winter rays in the convalescent home where she'd wrapped up in the same afghan, watching the little girls play in the schoolyard, remembering and remembering. Now she hardly had time to remember. It seemed to take an awful lot of upkeep, this little place.

A one-car train rumbled by. Most old folks, she thought, would be bothered by the regular racket of the trains, but she'd grown up next to tracks used much more than these, long before cars took over. It must be ten o'clock, she thought, time to go across the street to the market. Nan, her next-door neighbor, was coming to lunch.

She was always feeding guests. Between the shopping, the preparation, the event itself, and resting up afterward, a whole day would be gone. A whole day in her dwindling number of days. Once, her days were so plentiful she squandered them, wishing them to be over if work was boring or if she had something painful to live through. No more: she hoarded every minute. And the trains reminded her how fast her days were slipping away.

She and Nan, her next-door neighbor, talked a lot about how they hated cars. Neither had ever driven the dangerous machines which flung themselves across the country, getting everyone where they didn't need to be faster than they needed to get there. Karen and Jean spoke of how the automobile and trucking industries had used their power and riches to weaken the rail system, just as she saw cars weakening the old ways of life. Now the sound of the trains was like the lowing of the last buffalo on the western plains. Trains were yet another idea men had rejected to make more money.

Gussie closed her eyes in the sun. She was beginning to think like the girls. Next thing she knew she'd be marching with them. She imagined marching down the railroad tracks in the sun.

Mackie purred louder when she switched to his other ear. She'd lived by the tracks wherever she worked. Now each time a train went by, her thoughts drifted forward to her disappearing time, and backward to the full years she'd had. Here came the 10:21 freight train. It would be a long time rumbling by. She'd better get ready to go out.

Mackie leaped down as she rose. The cat strolled to a window where, between trains, birds gathered to peck at the crumbs she put on the sill. The train ran on and on. She moved to the window where she kept her knickknacks. She'd tried to hang a shelf for them, but the old fingers were too stiff for this task, holding a hammer an awkward exercise that produced cracks and gashes, nothing useful. The girls would help. Meanwhile most of the knickknacks fit on this windowsill and her dresser, leaving the other sills free for Mackie to lounge on.

She arranged everything symmetrically—the accountant in her—plants in twin white ceramic pots, new cuttings in old shot glasses, a miniature framed portrait of a former cat, a little watering can, a green glass vase and bowl sparkling in the sun, and several little figures bought in five-and-dimes across the country. From outside, passersby might assume the accumulation was an old lady's treasures, fit for nothing when she died but to be thrown away. But to her, this window was a joy, full of suggestions of memories, of thriving living things, of color. The way the objects crowded on the windowsill gave her a sense of a life that had always been bursting at the seams with travel, women, love. And loss—poor years, too, times when life had been difficult to take, but as a cutting might not make it, or as a pruned plant grew on, so her life continued with its bustling shoots and blossoms around the cuts and failures.

The blossoming of women in the night as trains sped by. So very many lovely women, lovely nights. But the thought of women reminded her of Nan, and she'd best get to the store or Nan would be left standing on the doorstep waiting for her lunch. She went to the closet in the neck of the house, drew a light coat over herself, picked her black purse off the doilied table, and went out the door, locking it carefully behind her.

Earlier in her hurried life her surroundings had often been a blur, but now she walked slowly, sat long hours, and was learning the art of seeing, of appreciating what she saw. She was grateful to have her sight. She touched the rough gray stone of her rental, then turned toward the store. She passed Nan's house and peered up at the lace-curtained windows, but they were empty. Nan owned her narrow home and had lived there over forty years with her husband. She had no worries but where the tax money would come from, and she fretted that to death, annoying Gussie at times with it. Gussie told her to take in a boarder.

"Some old coot I'd have to take care of?" Nan had replied crossly. "I can barely take care of myself. I'm seventy-seven, you know."

Not so old, Gussie had thought.

She passed the travel agency perched by the railway line. She often stopped to read the posters in the window on her days of leisure, when no one was coming to lunch. A couple of big old rooming houses came next where the tracks veered farther from the road. Then the little luncheonette where she and Nan went now and then. At the corner where she crossed to the store, she admired the old fire station, made out of red stone, whose painted towers and cool dark musty smell made her heart race almost as fast as when she'd been a little girl. How she had wanted to be a fireman when she grew up.

Aside from the scenery, her trip to the store was uneventful. She carried the luncheon meat, quart of milk, and small jar of mayonnaise in a net shopping bag. The sun was slightly higher in the sky on the way back, and she was a little more tired than when she'd gone out. A cup of tea, a little rest and she'd be fine when Nan came.

But she still felt depleted after her brief rest and absentmindedly made the lunch, cutting crusts off the white bread, tossing scraps of meat to Mackie as he purred and rubbed against her legs. The last luncheon she'd prepared, a couple of weeks back, had been on a Saturday when Jean and Karen visited. She'd made them a cheese and fruit plate. Like so many of these young girls, they wouldn't eat animal flesh, wouldn't smoke or drink. These were things she'd never needed in abundance, but still, without drinking, without smoking, without eating in restaurants, what social life could they have? No wonder they got into emotional messes with each other. Their world was so small, filled only by themselves, friends just like them, and an old lady they seemed to think had drifted in from the moon.

Their fascination at meeting a lesbian in her eighties still lingered. *How do you handle this? How did you do that? Did you have a lot of lovers? All at once? Were you ever committed to just one woman?* Questions, questions, questions. As if their lives hadn't been so similar that transplanted to her time, they probably would have lived very much as she had.

There, she said, setting the pink glass plates with their sandwiches on a shelf in the refrigerator. She'd covered them with her clean kitchen shower caps. She had to economize in small ways or her money vanished before the end of the month, so no plastic wraps for her. She was clumsy with the metal ice cube trays, sending half the cubes into the sink, missing the tea pitcher. Replacing the trays invariably meant mopping spills; she kept a frayed towel handy, tossed it on the spills and moved it around with her foot.

Finally, she set the table with cloth napkins and tall glasses.

Out back of the house, on a tiny strip of land fenced off from the tracks, were a smattering of wildflowers. She went to pick some for the table, but stooping, got dizzy and walked unsteadily, with darkened sight, back toward the door, wildflowers drooping from her left hand, while with her right she felt her way along the warm stones of the house.

"Augusta," cried Nan on her way from next door. "Are you all right?" She hurried from her back door in that broad-shouldered, long-legged, yet timid way she had.

"Will be in a minute," Gussie growled. "Here, take the blasted flowers. They were to pretty up the table, but I see now I wasn't meant to pick that particular bunch."

"How many times have I told you about bending down? You're just like my husband. He would not listen to me till his dying day and exerted himself in every way he could find until he killed himself doing it."

Gussie had never been able to decide if Nan blamed herself or Mr. Heimer for his death while he was mowing his tiny patch of lawn under a hot sun, or even whether she really minded having her home to herself.

Nan was taller than most women of her time and bent over like a tree under a constant wind of anticipated disapproval. Above her body was a plain face, so unmarked by age Gussie initially wondered if there was any personality behind it. In time, she realized it was this very plainness, coupled with her height, that led Nan to a life where she could avoid the pains and rejections that line faces.

Given money and circumstances, Nan might have been raised a lady, but she became, instead, a girl forced to find her own protections. She found them in a husband who kept her home, though childless. She reemerged during the war, working until there were callouses on her hands and a certain courage that forbade a full retreat to her home. Still, the world's early imprint stayed in that stoop and in her hesitancy to meet the eyes of strangers. But her smile, when it came, was broad and unafraid, as if laughter was something she could easily share. Her hair was still brown, in feathery, fluffed up short curls. She wore thick glasses after cataract surgery gone wrong.

No wonder she didn't rent to a boarder, Gussie had realized: her shy safe home was sacred to her. "But what will I do if I go blind?" Gussie wouldn't answer her, not wishing to be presumptuous. Someday, she thought, Nan would figure it out, though Gussie would miss her own water wing of a home. Meanwhile, she got a kick out of seeing that strangely young face soften in her presence.

They walked slowly inside, and Gussie sat in her chair. Nan went to the kitchen for a glass of water. Mackie, sensing something wrong, rubbed against Nan. "Scat," she said, preoccupied. He ran and leaped heavily into Gussie's lap, startling her. The poor old boy acted so concerned she couldn't be angry. They nuzzled each other.

"Like a couple of old lovebirds, you are," said Nan, handing Gussie her water.

"He's worried."

"How can you tell?"

"By the look in his eyes."

"Hmph," said Nan. Was there a hint of jealousy there? "Are you better?"

"Yes. Much better. I'll sit a moment before I get lunch out."

"Why don't you let me? Is it ready?"

"But—"

"Well, why not? We've done this enough. I know your routine."

"You're my guest."

"And you've been mine. I already know how good a hostess you are. It strikes me," Nan said, leaning close to Gussie and looking her in the eye for a change, "that it's about time we treated each other like friends, not like old ladies come visiting."

Gussie felt the lines on her face deepen as she smiled and blushed.

Nan reddened, too, and peered quickly at the floor, as if someone else entirely had been speaking too frankly.

"Well, then," challenged Gussie, to relieve them both of their embarrassment, "why don't you move yourself on out to the kitchen and bring our lunch?"

"Yes, ma'am," Nan said, with a mock salute.

Gussie knew that war work had suited Nan. The military atmosphere had replaced many of the normal social conventions, which made her feel so shy. Not to mention that she worked almost exclusively with women. Gussie herself had been called *Sarge* then. As accountant, she'd taken over men's administrative tasks while they fought. This new authority, combined with her younger walk—like a tightly muscled drill sergeant—earned her the nickname. Now she and Nan fell into their wartime personas easily.

They ate in the cool parlor, Gussie with her feet up, Mackie pleading with his eyes and an occasional flick of his tail for more scraps, and Nan at her most relaxed, listening to Gussie's stories of the morning.

"Gussie," Nan said as they finished lunch, "you could make a story of anything, even a walk across the street to the store."

The two friends, meal done, chatted. An occasional annoying car sped up the street to one side of them, while silence hung over the railroad tracks. The sound of the present was, for the moment, louder than that of the past. Gussie dwelt on Nan's description of the stage of their friendship. It made her a little nervous to have grown this close to anyone at this late stage because she knew where it usually led in the past. She'd assumed she was beyond new love and hadn't expected this.

But before they could get any further in their friendship, she wanted to reveal her past to Nan, and she didn't know how Nan felt about lesbians. Nan sat quietly despite the energy Gussie sensed in that bent body. She wondered if Nan had ever questioned her own life and how she'd lived it. She wondered if she would question Gussie's life.

Despite her concern, there remained a pervading air of peace and comfort in the parlor. She was reminded of two old men who'd lived in her town when she was young. Their habit had been to sit together outside the fire station evenings, just inside if it rained. They'd been friends since childhood, and though you seldom saw them exchange a word, you knew that the act of sitting together, smoking cigars, was one of great intimacy, respect, and comfort. She imagined the air filled with the foul-smelling smoke, could smell it across the years. She must mention this to Karen and Jean—how when she thought of friendship between old people, she thought of two men.

The little two p.m. passenger train went quickly north past her windows. Five minutes later the train to the city slowed toward the station half a mile down the road. Mackie slept on the windowsill, his legs hanging over the edge. She began to talk again.

"I've been thinking of trains a lot lately, Nan. Every time I hear one, I remember something from my past. Trains meant a lot more then. They were a way of life for the families of railroad workers, and as for the rest of us, we became terribly excited when they ran through town on their way to big cities, to the coasts, to anywhere that wasn't familiar. As kids we played along the tracks and got out of the way at the first whit of vibration in the ground. We watched the enormous engines approach, then jumped up and down, waving as if without our signal the train would never reach its destination.

"In my travels around the country from job to job I liked to settle near a railroad." She laughed. "But you know that about me."

Nan looked quickly and darkly up, as if afraid of something in Gussie's still strong voice. A little too much intimacy, perhaps?

Gussie explained. "There was always a Railroad Avenue with rentals, and that's where I stayed, even when I could afford better. New London, Connecticut, was no different. As a matter of fact, I lived closer to the tracks than ever. When I first arrived and knew no one, I'd walk across the street on a Sunday to the big old station and sit on a bench watching, maybe talking to somebody waiting for a train." She paused to see Nan's reaction, but Nan was rapt.

"Can I offer you a beer?" Gussie asked. "Seems to me two old ladies might as well live it up this hot afternoon."

"Should you? After—"

"Of course I should. I had a little faintness from bending over, that's all. Go ahead and get it. I hope you don't mind a quart bottle of ale. The railroad tracks reminded me of it," she said, content for her words not to reach Nan in the kitchen. "I bought it the other day, thinking about and New London and Violet."

"Violets?" Nan asked as she arrived with a tray.

Gussie smiled to see the bottle. "That's one thing that hasn't changed much over the years."

Nan's eyebrows were raised in puzzlement.

"I remember sitting in a tavern in New London, near the station, drinking ale from a similar bottle with Violet."

She took a deep breath as Nan poured the amber liquid. "When I think of New London, it's Violet I remember. The job was different from other places I worked because Violet's father owned the factory. He'd built the first plant in his hometown, Providence, Rhode Island, then built the New London plant. As he got older it became more challenging for him to travel. Violet was his only child and not planning to be a retiring housewife. She wanted to take over the business. To prove her worth to her father, she took the train down to New London to troubleshoot, on top of doing the job he'd given her in Providence.

"That's how I met her. She was waiting for the train back to Providence. The rain was pouring down, but I'd made it inside the station before it started and sat there dry as a bone watching people come in bedraggled. Violet sat next to me, dripping, and placed the wet newspaper she'd held over her head between us. She sneezed. When she took out her ticket, I saw it was for Providence. The schedule board said her train would be two hours late, and I waited for her to notice it. Meanwhile I noticed her.

"She was tall, like you, thin and elegant, in a competent kind of way, if you know what I mean. Well-dressed in the latest fashions, but no frills about her, as if she dressed that way because it was the thing to do and she was going to do it well. Now, of course, she could use a change of clothes.

"I pretended not to hear a very unladylike curse under her breath. She'd seen the schedule board. I kind of smiled in sympathy toward her, and she shrugged and set off for the phones, leaving her suitcase behind. She stopped and pointed to her suitcase, and I nodded. Whoever she called, she felt better afterward. Perhaps a young husband? I had no way of knowing at the time she was not married. To a man.

"Some time after she returned, I realized it had stopped raining and I rose to go. On impulse, perhaps because she had asked me to watch the suitcase, I turned to her and explained that I lived nearby and was now headed home. Would she like to change into something dry at my apartment?

"At that moment we saw the stationmaster walk casually toward the schedule board. We both tensed watching him. He erased *Two hours late* and chalked in *Three hours late*. Violet rose and walked home with me.

"I began to make tea, but she admitted she'd like something stronger. Then as now, I kept ale at home, and that pleased her. I readied glasses while she changed. There was a fresh moist smell of deluged pavement coming in through my windows, and I felt moved—sexually, if you don't mind my saying so. The smell of summer rains has that effect on me. Too, there was something very sensual about Violet."

She watched to see how Nan was reacting to these words. Nan sat unmoving, legs stretched before her, ale in hand, a sleepy faraway look on her face as she gazed out the window. Gussie was not within her view.

"Violet came into the kitchen, all smiles. That she was a truly attractive woman I could see even more now in her dry clothing. *Might I*, she asked, *leave my wet things here with you and pick them up on my next trip?*

"Of course, I offered to send them, but she explained how often she was in New London, her position, where she stayed, and I agreed to keep them. We drank ale and talked in a way I hadn't been able to since moving there. I enjoyed her immensely, and she apparently enjoyed my company. I made her a sandwich before she left, and we had a jolly little picnic. When she learned I worked for her father's company, she was pleased. I never thought to say I'd bring her clothes to work with me, so we left it, when I walked her to the station, that she'd stop at my office and tell me when she was next in town.

"She returned sooner than she'd anticipated—the very next week. I had thought of her a lot in the meanwhile. Why not? I was lonely, and she'd been so pleasing to me, somehow, like slipping into a warm bath when you ache and luxuriating in its smoothness on your skin."

Nan turned to her then. Gussie thought, in for a penny, in for a pound.

"Violet agreed to come for supper, and I put on quite a spread. My pleasure in her company was almost incidental to the way I would have treated her anyway. She was, after all, the boss's daughter. And you see, I thought I knew why she was all smiles when she emerged from my bedroom that first visit. Never expecting company, I'd left certain books, certain photographs lying about the room as I usually did. One photograph in particular may have intrigued her." Gussie fidgeted in her chair a bit, thinking how these things never got any easier with age. She took a long draught of ale. "It was of myself and another woman. We were embracing. Kissing. A friend had taken it because she was so enamored of the way we looked together and wanted to show us why."

Nan said nothing, didn't move. Didn't even breathe differently.

She went on. She had come this far, what else could she do? "So, you see, I thought her smile might mean an acceptance of me. Or more. Perhaps a kinship with me. I hoped to find out which that night.

"Dinner went nicely. We went for a delightful walk. When it was time for her to go, I wanted with all my heart to tell her to stay. But then, she'd given no indication she'd be interested—and she was still the boss's daughter. I wanted so much to touch those long arms, to feel those long legs next to mine. She was, absolutely the sexiest woman I'd ever met. *I need to go back to my room*, she said, *to place a call home. I call Denise every night I'm away.*

"I knew this was my signal. Our kinship was real. *Oh, there's no need to go back there*, I said in my most nonchalant voice. *My landlady has a phone. It's very private.*

"She must have known I was offering more than a telephone because she hesitated, frowning at a crack in the sidewalk a long minute before saying yes.

"And this is another reason I've been remembering New London lately. Her pain. You've seen my friends Karen and Jean." Nan nodded very slightly. "Well, half the time they arrive crying about what they're going through. This one wants to be lovers with that one without letting the other go, and the other is tired of being lovers with others and just wants to stay with her own, and then this one is in pain because that one is in love. And on and on about how they must go through this in order not to stifle one another, to grow and change and I don't know what all. They ask me what to do, but I know they don't want to hear my answer, so I just listen to them thrash about in their pain and confusion, knowing no one can answer these questions for you.

"Once in a while I'll tell them a bit of my own experience, and they listen, oh yes, they listen, as if to some quaint fairy tale that has absolutely nothing to do with them. As if loving in my time was so very different, as if Violet did not hurt as much as they would by deciding yes, she would wrap her lovely long legs around me that night and a great many more nights while her lover off in Providence longed for her. As if I, wanting Violet so badly, being immediately seduced by her elegance, her sexiness, and lost, lost in the most intense desire I have ever felt for anyone, as if I could deny this to myself or listen to reason over the sound of what that had grown suddenly and spontaneously in my heart."

Gussie raised her voice as another freight train rolled by, unendingly. "Each time I hear a train I'm reminded of the joy of her arrivals, the sheer bliss to know she was walking down those wet steamy streets toward me, bringing the smell of travel, of railroad cars, of another city, another woman to me, bringing that long smooth body and those hands that did such magic in the night. And, too, I am reminded of the pain of her departures. I knew she would never be mine. I knew her love for Denise was deeper, stronger, longer than her love for me and that ours could only be a brief, intense love. But the sound of her train pulling out, the withdrawal of those hands from me, the exquisite sadness of it all—I cannot describe.

"And to see these girls belabor it, think they are different with their reasons for loving who they do. In time, in time, they will decide which is for them. As Violet decided it was the long slow comfort of what she had with Denise. The rich shared time and the common belongings, memories, friends. The familiar body in the bed. The warmth and comfort of a home.

"As I decided to pursue my heights, keep riding the trains, satisfy my thirst for experience. Violet was hungry for substance. We both knew and accepted this, though we never talked about it. Whether she told Denise I never knew. That was their business. Sometimes I suspect these girls are too young to accept that there are consequences to their decisions. They want the heights and comforts without having the pain, without having to choose, to lose anything along the way. They must talk it to death, beat one another over the head with their conflicts. What makes them act like that?"

"Cars," said Nan simply.

They sat quietly, Gussie trying to grasp what Nan meant. It had to do with the new ways, the fast pace, the mobility that cars brought. The young people were used to getting what they wanted and where they wanted fast. Aren't young people convinced they were the first and they knew how to do it, whatever it was, better?

Nan rose and filled Gussie's glass. She went into the bathroom. When she returned Gussie took a turn, rising with difficulty after sitting so long. She studied herself in the bathroom mirror. Her round reddened cheeks. Her shaggy white hair and its cowlick. The lines that traveled like tracks to her eyes, her still-full lips, her sensitive ears. She felt numbed by the ale, but good, warm and buzzing, as if her body was a hive of busy little bees cooking up something she couldn't quite cook up for herself. She smiled at her lively face.

"I hope my story hasn't upset you," she told Nan when she returned to the parlor. No train passed into their silence. Mackie had abandoned the window. "I needed to talk with someone my own age about what I see the girls are doing. I don't know how to help them. Probably, they have to live through it as I did, but in their own way. Was it so wrong of Violet to find her own answers through a hidden affair?"

Nan smiled slightly.

"Then again," continued Gussie, "perhaps this is hogwash. Just an excuse to tell you about myself." They were both silent for a moment, and the sunlight faded from the window. The sky darkened quickly, and huge drops of rain fell in sizzling splashes as they hit the hot street. A smell of wet asphalt came up, a smell of wet earth, the steamy smell of a quick summer shower. It slowed as quickly as it started, quieter and quieter. The sun found its way to the window again and made Nan glow.

Gussie knew she should rise and clear the dishes. Instead, she said, "You know, Nan, I think you're lovely."

Originally published in *Old Dyke Tales* (Naiad Press, 1984)

THE MIRROR

The only sound on the placid lake was the murmur of the tiny motor.

Careful not to startle her pensive lover, Connie whispered, "Trudy?"

Trudy jumped anyway but gave Connie a gentle smile. "Aye, aye, captain, you called?" She lifted a hand to her short gray hair in salute.

"Want to go for ice cream now or stay on the water longer?"

Trudy searched Connie's eyes behind their horn-rimmed glasses to get a sense of her preference. She loved the way the dark eyeglass frames set off Connie's nearly white curls. Connie was only fifty-three, three years younger than herself, but she'd gone straight from blond to white. Trudy leaned forward to muss the curls. "What do you think?"

"Trude!" Connie pulled away, making the boat swerve as she leaned too hard against the motor.

"Watch it," Trudy warned.

"Well, don't be scaring me like that in public."

Trudy slumped apologetically. "Nobody can see us out here," she explained. "Besides, all I did was touch your hair."

Connie was back on course. "You're right. I'm jumpy tonight. We've had such a beautiful, peaceful vacation so far, I suppose I'm afraid something will happen to spoil the second week."

Trudy rearranged her skirt where it had bunched under her on the boat cushion. "It's always peaceful up here, Con. I don't know why you worry. No one even suspects what we are to each other."

"Shh," Connie warned. "Every sound carries across the lake on a night like this. I think we'd better head in before the mosquitoes swarm us." She smiled lovingly at Trudy. "How I wish sometimes that we didn't have to go even back to the cabin, but could sleep on one of these islands, with no one else around, in a world of our own."

Teasing, as Connie turned the boat toward the ice cream stand's small dock, Trudy said, "And what would we do all night?"

Connie colored up. "Oh, I don't know, my strudel," she whispered.

Trudy leaned forward and caressed Connie's breasts under a large windbreaker with her eyes. Connie had always been embarrassed when Trudy looked at her body, but after admiring her for the eighteen years they'd been together, Trudy was fairly sure her lover enjoyed it as much as she did.

"You are awful tonight," Connie said.

"Must be Saturday night. You know how I get on square-dance night."

"I wish we could go, too. If we could only dance with each other, instead of the men."

They were silent as they docked in the twilight. Trudy lifted her heavy body out of the boat and tied up, then held the boat steady while Connie joined her. Their footsteps were muffled on the dock. The noise and light of the ice cream stand, a pastel vision that appeared from behind a row of pines, startled them. They did not look at each other as they joined the lines at the windows. Around them were teenagers and families, some from their own campground, and they greeted them like neighbors. Most, like themselves, had been coming to the lake for years.

They paid separately for their ice cream and started back to the boat. "What did you get?" Trudy asked.

"Chocolate chip. How about you?"

They sat at the end of the dock, their feet dangling over the water. "Peppermint stick."

"You order that every night."

"I love the crunchy bits of peppermint," Trudy said, licking around the pink ice cream, nipping a hard piece with her teeth. "Want some?" she offered.

Connie watched her lover catch melted pink rivulets with her tongue. Sticky-lipped, Trudy grinned. The lapping lake, the sheltering pines, the darkness draping itself around them, this was their happiness.

❖

The next morning, they woke to the sound of a small car crunching the pine needles outside their window.

"Uh-oh," Trudy said, abruptly wide awake and peering out the tiny window over their bed. "New neighbors."

"Get down, they'll see you," Connie whispered to her.

"They don't know we're both in this bed. Wait, it's two girls."

"It is? Maybe their husbands are following them."

"Not from the looks of that pup tent, Con."

"They're in the tent site out back?"

"Yes, and they're so excited. They look like us our first trip up."

"Do you think they are like us?"

"Maybe. You look and tell me."

"They can't see in?"

"They're too busy to look this way."

"Aren't they cute? Look at the one with the sailor hat."

"I remember wearing one of those when I was a kid."

Connie's face wrinkled in consternation. "If they turn out to be like us? I hope they're not obvious."

"Why? What have they to do with you and me? I don't think we'll be inviting them over for whist every night."

"No, but they're right behind us. If people see them and remember us being here, don't you think they'll put two and two together?"

"You've got a point. But we don't even know if they are yet, so let's have breakfast and worry about that later."

"We slept so late—we may never make it to church."

"You didn't want to go to sleep, honey." Trudy rolled over and reached beneath Connie's nightgown.

Connie slipped a hand under Trudy's pajama top. "Mmm. I wish there was more time."

"We'll take the Dodge down to church instead of walking." Trudy's finger skimmed Connie's soft breast. She was facing the window. "Oh dear," she said, her voice small.

"What's wrong?" Connie asked.

"I can see right in the side window of their tent, and they're doing what we're doing."

Connie looked over Trudy's shoulder. "How could they? Can't they see our window? You don't suppose the owner told them they were in back of a couple of queers and not to worry?"

"Of course not. I'd guess they're brand new and couldn't wait."

"We'd best get to church." Connie was already out of bed and moving toward the bathroom. "You start breakfast, and I'll take over as soon as I'm dressed."

As they ate, they watched their new neighbors through the kitchen window.

"At least they didn't do it outside," said Connie.

"Count our blessings. I love their dog."

"What is it?"

"A mix of something. They certainly love her. Don't I wish we had one."

"It would bark and make messes," said Connie. "And would you want people saying, *There go those two doddering ladies and their dog. They're always together, like man and wife*?"

"I don't know about you, but I'm not about to dodder anytime soon. Look how much fun they're having. And being affectionate with the dog makes it seem natural for them to be affectionate with each other."

"Maybe to you. What will the families think?"

"Those girls don't care. The big one's name is Sue."

"She called the short one Ally. And the dog is Mutt."

Trudy laughed. "What a cute name."

"It's unseemly. I'd at least want a pedigreed name."

"Fifi L'Amour?" Trudy suggested, laughing.

"Tommy and Yasir would pitch a fit if we stole their poodle's name. Poodles are for male homosexuals."

"And retired ladies."

"As you pointed out, we're not there quite yet." Connie went to wash the dishes.

"They certainly are full of energy out there. Maybe I should feel old."

"Oh no."

"Well, I do."

"I'm *oh-no*ing them. They don't care who knows. They hugged. Right out there with the dog barking at their shins."

Trudy joined Connie at the window and smiled. "I wish they wouldn't do it here, but it is nice to see. You know, I've never seen intimacy between two women other than us. Except those movies, *Sister George* and *The Fox*, but not in real life."

"Those horrid films," said Connie. "We'll never be able to relax here again, the way those girls carry on." Trudy nodded in frustration and disappointment.

❖

That Wednesday, they rode down to the town hospital fair. They looked forward to its white elephant and book sale every year.

"How do you like my Lake Winnipesaukee sweatshirt?" Trudy asked, modeling it for Connie as they left the hospital foundation booth.

"It looks comfy, Strudel, not masculine after all. Look at the number of books this year. I know you'll have a good time."

"They always have more white elephants for you than books for me, hon. Be fair."

"And I'm off to find them. Shall I meet you back here in an hour?"

"How about over at the refreshment stand?" Trudy whispered, "I'll buy lunch for my best girl."

The sun crept to its noon height while the fair became crowded. Children screamed on the few rides; other middle-aged women jostled Connie at the white elephant tent. She looked up from under her straw sun hat to see Sue and Ally. They smiled and moved away. Connie pretended not to notice and showed a tiny poodle figurine to a volunteer cashier.

"It's for friends with a poodle," she explained, willing herself not to look at the girls.

The cashier smiled pleasantly. "That will be one whole dollar. Thank you for supporting our hospital."

Flustered, Connie searched her purse. She didn't know if she was more frightened or excited that the girls had shown up.

"I have my money here somewhere." She gave the volunteer an extra donation for the dog, catching sight of the girls' Mutt at the end of its leash. Her heart thudded; the women both wore the same sweatshirts as Trudy's. She checked her watch; twelve more minutes to kill in this interminable hour. She might never find Trudy in the crowd if she went to look for her.

Sweating, Connie carefully put the poodle in her pocketbook and looked for a table she had not yet pored over. She was halfway through a display of crocheted potholders before realizing she'd examined them before. Worried Sue and Ally had noticed, she moved on, her agitation growing.

She was testing the swing frame on a plain heritage wooden shaving mirror when a woman right next to her said, "What good shape that mirror's in."

"Isn't it," Connie answered, expecting to see a volunteer next to her. It was Ally.

"Are you buying it?"

Connie could think of nothing but her urge to get away from this girl. She broke into an immediate hot flash.

Ally said, "I thought you might be a collector, too."

"This was for a friend. Here." She brusquely pushed the mirror at Ally.

Ally said, "Thanks, but we spent our limit on souvenirs when we bought our sweatshirts." The girl let a wide smile cover her face. "You're staying next door to us, aren't you? With your friend?"

Again, Connie fussed in her pocketbook for money, in her mind for a way to discourage Ally. "Where are you staying?"

"At Pine Vista, along the lake a few miles."

"We may be neighbors, then. Excuse me," she said and went to pay for the mirror.

She made her way out of the back of the tent and headed to use the portable restroom. Inside, she patted sweat from her forehead.

Why had the girl sought her out? Or had she—was it truly the mirror that interested her? She'd bought it in a blind panic and paid an unheard-of price for a thrift sale. It was uncanny that the girl Sue should collect mirrors. Restoring them was a passion of Trudy's, though very tricky, and this one would be a challenge. She stared at her dim self in the de-silvered mirror soldered to the door. Are we honestly so visible?

She could no longer stand the odor. As she slipped out the door, mirror under one arm, purse under the other, she saw Sue going into the unit one over. The girl smiled at her. Were they following her? Did they sense she was like them?

All these years they had slipped unnoticed, invisible, in and out of New Hampshire. What had changed? She set the mirror on a picnic table where, in the bright light, it caught her face clearly. Her eyes were pained. She said, aloud, "So what? So what if people know about us?" The face in the mirror relaxed. "So what?" she repeated and watched the face in the mirror smile.

Trudy appeared with a large paper sack of books.

"Maybe we should put your books in the car and eat in town," Connie suggested. It was a habit, escaping from women like themselves.

"No, it's our tradition to have hot dogs here."

Connie took a deep breath, then another, to relieve her fear. "You're right." She smiled and grew bold. "We'll sit in the open and have a good time."

"Is that for me?" Trudy was looking at the mirror, yearning in her eyes. "It's a beaut and in great condition. You must have spent a fortune."

"You only live once." She now noticed many people wearing Trudy's sweatshirt. "I bought something for Yasir and Tommy." She fished the china dog from her pocketbook.

"That's bone china, hon," Trudy said. "The boys will be thrilled. Here, your present is on the top of this bag."

Connie pulled out a copy of Gale Wilhelm's *Torchlight to Valhalla*, its jacket lightly frayed. "I can't believe you found a copy." She quickly stuffed it in her purse but didn't let herself look around to see if she had been observed. "I can't wait to read it."

"You can bring it to the beach this afternoon. Without its jacket, no one will know what it is."

Connie thought *What if someone asks?* but kept the thought to herself. "Maybe I will," she said with a smile.

❖

The next night was stormy with whitecaps on the lake. Connie and Trudy stayed inside playing whist. As the night wore on, Connie could no longer bear to keep her thoughts inside. "Do you think we're missing out on something?"

"What?" Trudy was entirely focused on the hand she was dealing.

"Something those kids have that we don't have. They seem perfectly happy and no one bothers them, yet they don't hide what they are."

Trudy stopped dealing. "They may be living more fully this moment, but what about later? Won't their flagrancy catch up with them when they try for decent jobs? Or they might be attacked."

"Maybe they'll suffer later if it comes to that, instead of suffering their entire lives."

The fireplace seemed jolly with its red and yellow flames. The whitewashed rough walls and unpainted beams made for a cozy shelter. Only the scraping of boughs on the roof and occasional distant thunder reminded them of danger. "I think we've lived the way we had to for us, and for our time."

Connie rose to stand in front of the fire. "I don't think I'll ever forget the sight of Sue and Ally frolicking under the pines with their dog or the longing they inspire in me to live like they do."

Trudy joined her. Their eyes looked across the firelight. Very gently and tenderly, they held each other on the hearth. "I'm afraid, Trudy."

"Of what?"

Connie laid her head on Trudy's shoulder. "The storm makes me afraid. But it makes me feel safe, too, here with you." She turned to look at Trudy fully. "What is it? What makes me so uneasy? What am I trying to say?" Connie turned from her lover's arms and went out on the porch. "I want to rip off my clothes and run out there onto the beach. I want to hide nothing."

Lightning, the lightning Connie had always feared, flashed across her face, and Trudy marveled at the woman who looked out from her eyes. Her face was changed. Its lines were deeper, but more delicate in the light of the storm; they were rugged, but filled with the stuff that had been her life thus far; Trudy could see pain and joy in them, instead of age and time. She looked as naked as she wanted to be, open, revealed. Trudy's heart expanded within her until she felt powerful, knew something was changing her, too.

The storm threw rain at the porch screens. Its cold mist stirred them to move inside where they warmed themselves, arms around each other, by the fire.

❖

On the morning after the storm, the lake, the trees, the other cottages were clearer than they had ever seen them before. It was their last full day of vacation, and they took their boat to their favorite island for a picnic.

"I hate to leave."

Trudy laughed. "You say that every year."

"I mean it more this year." Connie helped spread the blanket.

"Why?"

"I'm not sure. I'm connected to this place. It's touched me more deeply. Maybe it's middle age."

"Not yet, Con."

"Is it just me?"

"No, I feel it, too," Trudy admitted. "Let's take a walk. I need to work off that big breakfast you fed me."

"I did overdo it, but we'll be trekking all the way back to the campground after we return the boat."

Trudy parted the branches in front of them, and they found a path. The island was so tiny they reached its other side in a few minutes. "We're Robinson Crusoe and Friday," Trudy said.

"Uncharted lands. But it's much too rocky over here. Let's go back to our side."

"It must have been mind-boggling to live here before the explorers came," Trudy mused.

"Do you think there were women here like us?"

Trudy laughed. "Nothing but." Their blanket was in sight through the woods. "Want to pretend we're Amazons?"

Connie giggled, guessing what Trudy was suggesting. "You mean right here in the open? They at least had tents like Sue and Ally."

They kissed and hugged and touched one another for a long while, rolling around on their blanket, and Connie, though she kept watch for intruders, enjoyed herself thoroughly.

Their appetites whetted for lunch, they rearranged their clothing and ate ravenously, without words, grinning at each other. When they left, they didn't use their motor until halfway across the lake, but paddled canoe style, feeling, they told each other later, as if they were vibrating to every sound and sight and feeling of the lake. It was a shock when they reached land and had to talk to the woman who rented their boat to them. As she paid, Connie felt Trudy tug on her sleeve. "What?" she asked sadly, missing their silence.

But Trudy didn't say anything, only pointed to a hand-lettered sign which read simply, *Free Puppies*.

They looked at each other. "Can we see the puppies?" Connie asked.

"You surely can, ladies," said the proprietor. She spryly flipped open the well-worn wooden counter and led them into a back storage room. "Got two girls left, and ain't they beauties. The liveliest of the litter. They're grown enough to eat dog food and they go outdoors, don't have house accidents."

She thrust first one, then the other, at Connie and Trudy, who took them gingerly in their arms. "I know you girls are from town and need well-behaved dogs, so what you need to do is not even think of separating them, and they'll behave, because they have each other, like you two. You know life's a lot better in twos, no matter what you have to bear."

She rushed on as Connie and Trudy exchanged an uncertain

glance. "Now you go to the general store and tell Mrs. Daniels these are my pups. She'll give you a break on the collars and leashes."

She stood back and looked approvingly at her work, wiping her hands on her apron. The women shrugged in embarrassed, pleased resignation. "I have business to tend to, so I'll wish you ladies luck. What are you going to name them?" she asked as she led them out the front door.

Trudy looked at the puppy she held and said, "Sue."

"Ally LaMutt," said Connie.

They laughed as they carried Ally and Sue over to the general store, their puppies full of life in their arms.

Originally published in *Old Dyke Tales* (Naiad Press, 1984)

COOKIE AND TONI

My real name's Carmelina, but all my friends call me Cookie. You can, too.

They're supposed to be here, my friends, but they're late. Seems like no matter how long I take to put on makeup, to pick the right clothes—hey, you like this, the pink boatneck with the black ski pants?—I'm always the first one here.

So, I'm waiting here, and this lady with the tape recorder asks me to tell you a story. About my life now, in 1962, and about being femme. She says she'll put the tape away and play it in twenty years. How am I supposed to know what you want to hear twenty years from now? I can't guess what gay girls will be like in twenty years. Will you look like us? Will you tease your hair like I do? I know you butches will have short hair—that'll never change in a million years. And I bet you're cute. And freer. You'll hold hands going down the street and tell your moms you turned gay. You won't stick around when your dads slap you for going out with girls—you'll take off. Right? Or is that my wishful thinking?

I guess I can do this as good as anyone—only where should I start? What do you want to hear? A sad story about what it's like? Boy, I could tell you a few that would get you going. An adventure story? How about some *swa-vay* butch carries me off to a desert island? Never happen. Would you believe Fire Island? Or a love story. Are you changed that much you won't want to hear a love story? Want to hear about Toni and me? Yeah, I like that one. Besides, it's true. You mind if I chew gum? Oh, not into the mic. Okay, I'll have a ciggy.

Like I said, I'm femme. I was butch, too, before this, but I think I'll stay femme from now on. Something in the way I love women makes me want to be femme. The ways I like to take care of them. Homey stuff, you know? I can make a meatball and spaghetti dinner would melt any butch's heart. Maybe one of you wants to try my meatballs and spaghetti?

But Toni, she was from my town, Hicksville. Don't laugh. People really live there. Me and my family thought it was the greatest place going. We moved out from the city, from East New York. It was heaven. I was about eight. We had a backyard, and my school had a girls' gym—boy could I tell you girls' gym stories. Everybody had cars. It was the greatest. Someday, I'm going to find a woman with money, and we'll buy a place on the Island together. Do you kids have more money than us?

Say now, you're a girl with money. How'd you know I'd like a Tom Collins? Mixed drinks are too steep for me. What a treat, I even get an orange slice.

My Toni didn't have money. We lived the both of us in tract houses with muddy backyards. We had dads whose stomachs were out to here, who drank beer and thought our mothers should worship them. The difference was, though, Toni didn't see how it was, how her dad was a phony slob.

Toni graduated high school the year before and dreamed of moving to the city. I'd been out of school a couple of years, had my fill of city life, and moved home. My mother loved having me there. She didn't really care if I was gay. Oh, she'd moan and groan now and then about how she wished I'd get married, the house next door was for sale and me and my husband could move in—like being gay was a temporary thing—but she wasn't real pushy about it, you know? I stayed out of Dad's way. He'd been growling at me for years. I'd come out of the bathroom to go to work in the morning and he'd growl at me. Really. Can you imagine this hairy, foul-breathed pregnant-looking man waking you up like that? What a jerk.

Anyways, it was that last time I lived in Hicksville I met Toni. Her folks were on the other side of Bethpage Road from me, and I couldn't believe I never saw her before. She was gorgeous. We met the only place I know of on the Island, the Hayloft. A nothing special bar except it was closer than the bars in the city. I drove Dad's car down to the Loft one night and walked in all by my lonesome.

I sat at the bar. I didn't like it much, being alone, but I'd been out long enough to be able to do it when I had to. So, I'm sitting there, like this, making the beer last cause I don't make much at this aircraft place where I work putting together tiny pieces of planes. And in walks Toni who's butch as they come. She looked like this—here, let me stand up—real tough with her legs bent almost bowlegged, thumbs hooked in her jeans, cigarette in her mouth, her collar up, and an expression on her face that would scare a marine.

In this low sexy voice she asks, "Hi, doll, what're you drinking?"

Holy shit, I think. I mean it's early, I'm the only one in the place and I'm no dog, but nobody ever came on to me that strong and fast before. I guess my mouth dropped open or something. She gets shy explaining, "I know you. I mean, we practically grew up together. If I'd known you were gay, I'd've been over to your place long ago."

I felt really dumb and didn't know what to say. Here's this perfect-looking butch standing there in these pegged black pants, a white shirt, jean jacket, and boots, coming on to me when I was still in shock that she was gay. You know how it is with butches—half the time they're too shy to do anything but stand at the bar talking to other butches and you have to practically throw yourself at them to get them to dance with you.

Not Toni. I'd be sorry about that come-on style of hers later, but that night she swept me off my feet. No questions asked.

"We went to the same school together," she says, leaning against the bar. "Only you were always two grades in front of me. Hope you don't hold my age against me." She winked. I'm not kidding you.

So, we talked till I had to get the car home. She walks me to it and wants to know when we're going out. We make a date for the next night—you expected me to resist? And then she kisses me. I went rubbery. It was one of those long hot kisses that seeps into your heart. Not a soul kiss, but a real light long kiss without touching me with her hands. I was done for. She made herself easy to love.

And I did. I loved her for three months. All that time we lived with our parents. She'd pick me up in her dad's car, and we'd go to the Loft or the movies or parking. Mostly parking. Did I ever wish I had my place back in the city. But then I never would have met her.

Her parents had no idea she was queer. We used to make out down in their rec room while we pretended to watch *Route 66* or something. We sure loved that couch. I don't know how her parents never guessed about her, the way she dressed. Maybe it was her beauty that saved her. Those dreamy green eyes in a face that even without makeup could've won a contest. Her hair was long, real unusual for such a butch chick, but she wore it at the back of her head—I was surprised it was there the first time I noticed it. And a perfect body, though I never saw it under her clothes. She was stone butch. I wanted badly to touch her, but she wouldn't let me.

Yeah, this is a love story, but it's a sad story, too. Maybe I don't know any happy ones. Maybe nobody does.

This time it was Toni's dad who ruined things. She always wanted to be like him. Used to tell me how strong he was, how smart and handsome. Because he was a mechanic, she fooled around with cars since she was a kid. He played baseball on a local team, so she was always throwing a ball around. She wished she was a son, not a daughter. That's why she was gay, she said, because she wanted to love women like her dad did. And that's why she was different from most of the butches I went with—she used her dad's style of meeting women.

Then one day her dad didn't come home. Turned out he'd been cozying up with this real tramp over in Mineola where he worked. Her mom's brother tracked him down and beat him up pretty bad. Toni's dad went down to Florida with the chick.

This happened at the end of the third month we went together. We saw each other for a while more, but Toni was flattened, her style went up in smoke. Like, the collar on her jacket wilted, the way a plant will without water. She didn't kiss the same. She wasn't strong, in charge anymore. She'd be making out with me and start crying. And you know butches—they do not cry. Pretty soon she wouldn't see me. Her pride, you know? She couldn't keep up the butch pride, which, let's face it, they can't live without.

I eventually got it, that loving me reminded Toni of her faithless father loving Miss Mineola. She didn't want to be like him anymore. It never was her strength I saw, but Toni pretending she had his all along. And when she didn't have that, she lost who she thought she was.

So I'm home alone night after night, knowing I'd loved a real dummy, a fake with nothing of her own inside. I didn't go out with anyone for a long time because I started to wonder if every butch was like that, empty inside, fake men, you know? There used to be magic for me in that swagger they had, the tough poses. And then I started thinking: If Toni was such a fake, and if the butches were fake, then what about me? Who was I really? I'm sitting in these bars looking sexy, my face painted, waiting for the butches to light my cigarettes for me, but what was I really like? Was I a copy of my mother? Was I trying to be like some movie star? It started to drive me crazy, too, like I think it did Toni.

Little by little, though, I got back on my feet. Started to be interested in love again. Went back to the Loft.

And when I got back, it was with a vengeance. I was so starved for the gay life I couldn't stop dancing, being with queer women and men and enjoying the hell out of them. My dad got fed up and made the car off limits. He growled at me every time I asked. Screw him, I decided. I moved back to the city. Got a job operating a machine that glazed ceramic tile and really started doing the town. Butches had their magic back for me.

But it was different. There was more to it. Wait—I'll explain.

All this time I hadn't seen Toni at all. Then one night at the Swingalong on MacDougal Street I saw her walk in. She was talking and laughing, with a new kind of confidence. It wasn't empty swagger anymore. We said hello and danced a couple of times, but because she was going with somebody, I didn't push it. Besides, we'd been through so much since we were together, we were almost new people. But I didn't forget about her, and I thought a lot about her. And the magic of the gay life. I don't know if I can explain it exactly. You have to try and feel it with me.

See, I don't think we copy the straights. Some of our ways come from them—what else do we know?—some of the ways we dress and act, but that's only because they suit us. What I mean is, we choose our ways.

So when I say I like to make spaghetti and meatballs for my lovers, that comes from way inside me. It's me. Not because I want to act like a woman's mother, or it's the way I think a wife should act. It's cause I love to see a satisfied woman's eyes light up. Like Toni's were at the Swingalong that night. I love to be the one who turns that light on in a woman's eyes. And probably it's the same for butches. When a woman opens the door for you or makes love to you, I don't think she's doing it because she's supposed to. I think she's looking for that light, to show a woman she's loved and special.

And that was the difference in Toni. She wasn't doing it to be like her dad anymore. She learned that being him wasn't right for her, but there was stuff from him she could use to be Toni.

Though that didn't happen to me, but to Toni, I learned from it.

I know what I want now, and I have certain ways of my own to get it. And someday I'm going to find the one woman I please the most and who pleases me the most, and we're going to be pleased as hell together.

I'll be sitting here for a while, you know. Maybe in twenty years when she plays this tape to you, I'll be sitting here.

I hope not, but I wouldn't want to miss you if I am.

Come on and buy me a drink. Let me tell you another story. If we like each other, maybe you'll come over.

I'll make—you guessed it—spaghetti and meatballs for you.

Originally published in *Old Dyke Tales* (Naiad Press, 1984)

FRENCHY GOES TO VEGAS

There was no dark sky, there were no birds, no sight of moon or desert hills. There was only the water, cascading endlessly into pools under palms planted so regularly they looked unreal. And the fire. Flames that shot up with a roar, then down the falls and into the water, coming closer and closer.

"*EEEEEEE!*" screamed a preschool girl, turning away from the rail. Her father lifted her and pressed her to his shoulder. She sobbed in terror, hiding her eyes. He laughed.

"Hey, that's something else," Frenchy said, not admitting to the twinge of uneasiness she felt, too.

Gloria squeezed her hand under the cover of her cape. "I knew you'd like it, honey," she said.

"It's like being in an epic movie like *Ben-Hur* or, or—"

"It's exactly like being right where you are. Las Vegas. This whole shebang is one big show."

The fire receded to the original soaring flame and then that too disappeared. The excited babbling of the throng replaced the roar. Frenchy checked and saw the preschooler had dared to look. She pulled her father's hand. "Come on, Daddy, before it comes back."

"You don't have kids, do you, Gloria?"

"I have done a heap of dumb things in my life, Frenchy, but that is not one of them. Why, are you afraid I'm going to spring a surprise like that on you?"

"Hey, I spent less than a week in New York with you, and I just got off the plane here this afternoon. You might have a bunch of secrets."

"I don't, though, not from you. I showed you all my secrets again after dinner, didn't I?"

Frenchy, gratified that her lovemaking had roused Gloria to such heights, pulled her close. "You sure—"

"This isn't New York City, Frenchy," protested Gloria. "We have to be careful in Vegas."

"What, there are no gay people here?"

"Look at this horde."

She turned her back on the Mirage Hotel and its course of waterways magically constructed in the desert. Hundreds of women paired with men thronged the sidewalks, some of the younger ones pushing strollers. "You're right. Straight and narrow. Where are the queers?"

"We have our own bars and casinos. We can visit Paradise Road if you want, but I had other things in mind for us." She led Frenchy farther along the Strip.

"I don't know if I can go a week without gay people." At home in the Village, she was either at work or visiting people with AIDS or meeting with the neighborhood preservation group or hanging out at the bar on the corner. "Maybe not everyone in my life is gay, but a good fifty percent are."

"Aren't I gay enough?"

Frenchy grinned, remembering Gloria, pins out of her thick dark hair, breasts like globes waiting to be traveled, a white sheet covering up to her hips, more inviting than sheer nakedness. She'd left the sheet there, sat on the bed, touching and touching, kissing and kissing everything above the sheet until, with a high-pitched yip, Gloria dislodged it herself and pulled her down.

"Yeah, I'd say you're gay enough."

"Well then."

"It's hard to imagine, that's all. I never knew anybody like you. I mean, whoever thought Frenchy Tonneau, the original New York dyke, would get flown all the way out here by a woman fourteen years younger than her and richer than Jeff Bezos."

"Are you really fifty, Frenchy?"

"I turned fifty last month."

"You look, maybe, thirty-nine."

"I inherited young hair."

"Black as night."

Frenchy shaded her eyes with a hand against the blinking, rolling, rotating, glaring lights. "I'm surprised you Westerners know what night is."

"East Texas isn't like this, honey. Texas is real. Too real, some-times," she said with a sigh. "That's why this woman's got to leave it now and then if she wants to have a love life."

Frenchy stopped as a mob of raucous teenagers carrying drinks swarmed and passed them. "You mean I'm not the first woman you're meeting in Las Vegas?"

Gloria, about two inches taller, leaned to meet her eyes. Frenchy could see her cleavage where the cape parted above a gold-colored cocktail dress, which shimmered in the blinking neon. "Honey," said Gloria, "practice makes perfect."

Though she'd strutted through her own string of girls when she was younger, before the nine years with Mercedes, she'd sworn off that kind of life. Gloria was the first woman she'd been slightly interested in for a long time, and she'd accepted her persistent offer, half hoping to lure her back to the city. She'd pictured herself strolling the Village streets with this rich, beautiful, drawling woman on her arm.

Instead, she felt like an exciting new toy Gloria could wind up and watch as she played tour guide.

Then again, Gloria hadn't exactly promised a trip to one of the neon-lit marriage chapels. With distractions like that dress shimmering before her, maybe she'd relax and enjoy being a toy for a few days.

Frenchy raised an eyebrow and nodded in agreement. "I've had a load of practice myself."

"I noticed," said Gloria. Her teasing flirtiness unbalanced Frenchy, as if she was left out of the joke.

They stepped onto a covered, moving ramp. It carried them past reconstructions of scenes from ancient Rome. Through a window she saw real costumed couples strolling the paths of Caesars Palace between columns lit in white. The enormous building was covered with thousands of red and yellow lights, which gave the impression of gold. It occurred to her that Gloria had chosen her gold dress to match Caesars Palace. What a woman.

No one else was in the passageway with them. Gloria took her hand. "That suit enhances your appeal."

Frenchy stretched to her full four-eleven, filled her chest with air, and thrust her chin up. One of her friends was a costume maker. When she'd mentioned this trip, Amaretto beamed with delight for her and asked, "What will you wear?" It had cost her, but Amaretto deserved every penny for designing and sewing two perfect tuxedos, one black with lavender trim, one white with violet. "It was like making doll clothes," Amaretto said when she presented them to Frenchy. They had a fashion show right at the bar, with her changing in the bathroom and parading out for everyone to cheer. She knew she looked good.

She shrugged at Gloria's praise as if she was used to wearing such finery but dropped her hand as they approached the mouth of the casino. They were disgorged into the most amazing space she'd ever seen. "Is this for real?" She coughed. She'd been in plenty of smoke-filled bars, but this fake palace must pump in cigarette smoke.

Gloria laughed. "That's a matter of opinion."

Frenchy understood now what it was like to be a tourist back in New York. She made an effort not to gape. There was so much going on. The famous band of her teen years on a small stage in the middle of everything. The chandeliers and long mirrored bars. The green felt tables. The arcade-like signs reporting sports scores. The banks of TVs. The lavishly designed betting parlors. The slot machines—everywhere slot machines. The only thing there was more of was people.

"It's like Times Square, only this crowd has money," she said. Women in evening gowns played two slot machines, three, at a time, dropping coins in, cranking the arms of one, the next, and the next. Now and then a machine burped back winnings.

"Wild enough for you, Frenchy?"

Wild, loud, confusing. She must have looked like a lost kid, not at all confident and smooth.

Gloria didn't blink at Frenchy's disorientation. "Come with me, honeybuns. I'll treat you to a cup of nickels, and we'll have some fun."

She didn't notice the time until after two a.m. when the pace at Caesars Palace seemed to slacken. The merrymakers had departed; the diehard gamblers carried on. By the time she cashed out at the window, Frenchy won seven hundred and fifty dollars, the cost of Amaretto's tuxes plus. Gloria made nineteen hundred at some table she wandered off to. They took a cab to a small hotel on a quiet street off the Strip. For once, Gloria let Frenchy pay.

Gloria unhooked Frenchy's bow tie and made coffee. From their top floor window, they saw the lights blazing on a hotel that was a replica of a riverboat and, beyond that, the glow of the neon inferno. She remembered the child hiding her face from the volcano.

"It's hard to believe this is desert here. I mean, like 20 Mule Team Borax, real live mirages, and all that."

"Mirages are never real," teased Gloria.

"That volcano was tonight."

"It was fire and water, but not a genuine volcano."

"So even the real stuff is a bluff."

"People who spend too long in Las Vegas can lose their minds. They don't know night from day. They can't make rational decisions about money. This is an upside-down town where sin is in, money is the end-all and be-all, and everyone is forever young."

"How long is too long?"

"One night for some folks, honey."

"You're no crazy mirage."

"You'd better believe it." Gloria leaned over her on the couch and pressed Frenchy's head against that delicious cleavage.

They visited a different casino the next night, and the next.

"Don't you get tired of these things, Gloria?" she asked as they were led to a table in an ornate restaurant. Who wanted to watch half-naked women precision-kick to show music during dinner? She ignored them, thinking about how Gloria helped her increase her winnings to $2,200 which she'd converted to Travelers Cheques and stashed in the room safe. That was four months' mortgage. Soon she'd own her apartment outright.

"I'll bet you think I'm a chronic party girl," Gloria challenged.

"Well…"

"I can't blame you. You've only seen me traveling. And when I'm away from home, I like to play a whole lot."

"I noticed."

"I need these vacations. Like I told you, sweet thing, it gets all too real back in Texas."

"What does?"

"Having Daddy's money. Making it grow so it won't go away. Giving it to the right causes without letting on that I'm helping to support that ol' militant homosexual agenda. You may think it's nice work if you can get it, but…it makes it hard to be me."

Gloria held out her cigarette to be lit. Frenchy had unearthed her shiny Zippo lighter for the trip and flourished it.

"That's why I go to strange cities to meet women," Gloria explained. "There must be someone who wants me for me, not for my bank account. Money is a weight around my neck, something I can't escape. I do not have the knack of living lightly. Look at you. I say dress casual, and you wear a nice open-necked shirt and jeans. Me? A three-hundred-dollar jumpsuit in white that'll have to be thrown out if I get a drop of this sauce on it. I don't want to need these possessions.

I don't want to have this power to change lives with Daddy's money. I hate my life, I hate me sometimes, and I don't know how to escape me either."

The woman's seductive brown eyes were after more than a good time. Feverish, like the desert sun, did they melt or burn her lovers? She'd had enough experience to handle someone like Gloria, though. She polished the lighter on her thigh.

"I've been searching the whole world for the perfect woman, Frenchy. She's got a permanent vacation lined up for her. We can travel and lounge, jump out of planes, and dive under the sea. I can give her anything, and I'll only attach one string: she's got to love me. I wouldn't think that'd be so hard."

Was Gloria trying to tell her something? The waiter came with the dessert cart. She sensed her waist gradually thickening as creamy chocolate melted on her tongue. When they stood to go, she pulled her stomach in and looked at herself in one of the dozens of available mirrors, proof she was no menopausal has-been.

The next day Gloria drove far too fast to Death Valley. Frenchy was damned proud of how hard she worked and how important she was to her company. This once, though, she let herself dream, in the air-conditioned, spanking new Mustang, of a life of leisure, with this pretty brown-eyed lady entertaining her, giving her gifts, offering that greedy body up for more. She remembered her younger days, going along for the ride in another red convertible, on her first grown-up vacation to Provincetown. The young Frenchy had yearned for such a life then. Was it really within her grasp?

The roads out here were straight, the vista up to the mountain ridges unbroken. It was a bleak, hot, lifeless-looking landscape.

"I'll take the view from the World Trade Center over this any day," she pronounced.

"We'll go up into some of the passes, honey. Then you'll see splendor New York couldn't give you if the mayor hired an army of muralists."

Gloria pulled into Dante's View, over five thousand feet up. Though pretty boring, what with no buildings or parks or people, she agreed the sight was majestic. The sign said they were looking a mile down into the valley and twenty-one miles across to the next peak.

"I'll bet it was prettier when it was a lake."

"That was twelve thousand years ago, Frenchy. I can't impress you with anything, can I? Come on, let's have lunch."

The deli where they'd stopped on the way packed them pastrami and Swiss sandwiches on rye, with kosher dills and, the guy said, a special mustard imported from his uncle's shop in Hoboken.

"It's pretty strange sitting up here eating my usual lunch," commented Frenchy. "But it's not a bad sandwich for Nevada." She liked to say the Western place names—they felt so foreign to her tongue. She liked to think of herself in an exotic setting with a beautiful woman on her arm.

The brown eyes pleaded with her. "Do you think you could ever live anywhere except New York?"

Was Gloria sounding her out? She was careful in her answer. "Not here."

They took a couple more day trips and had a marathon slot night when they both took $200 of their winnings and played quarter machines until they were tired.

"Jeez Louise," said Frenchy at the end of it. "This must be play money, not the stuff I grub so hard for every week. I lost it all, and I'm laughing."

Gloria laughed, too, her face flushed. "It's a good thing for you we agreed to split our winnings." She handed Frenchy $73.50. "Do you get tired of it? The grubbing?"

"Does rain get tired of falling? You just do it. I'm going to make manager at the company before I retire. They don't like lady managers, but I'll do it."

"That's so demeaning, having men tell you what you can or can't do."

"Where would you be except for your daddy?"

Without a pause, brown eyes glowing, Gloria whispered, "Keeping house for a woman like you."

Frenchy narrowed her eyes and wished she'd never stopped smoking; there were moments in life when cool was all-important. "Want to?"

"Leave Texas?"

"We could find a bigger apartment maybe. But mine will be paid off in sixteen years, and it's near the store."

Gloria pulled her into a bar and found a table for two. The bare-legged waitress stopped for their order before they took their seats.

"A bottle of your best champagne," Gloria ordered. She lowered her eyes at Frenchy's surprised look.

"It's our last night and we're going to celebrate."

"Celebrate what?"

"I think I've found her."

Frenchy's heart pounded. Was Gloria really going to ask? Did she really want to wine her and dine her for the pleasure of her badass butch company? Maybe she'd cash in her pension and buy the red convertible she'd always dreamed of driving if she had a license, one of those small noisy sporty jobs. Hell, they could keep a pad in New York. She wouldn't be leaving forever.

The waitress served their champagne.

"Remember," Gloria asked, "when I talked about looking for the woman I could take home with me?"

"Kind of," Frenchy mumbled.

"I'm not all that fussy, Frenchy. I've actually tried a few women. I've learned one week of shacking up in Sin City doesn't predict forever."

Her ego plunged. How many gold-diggers had Gloria been with?

"But you. I want to celebrate being with you because you are the woman I never thought I'd find. It's in your every gesture, in everything you say. Usually, I don't have to wait till the last night to find an opening, but you are so self-sufficient, so proud, you're the right stuff. I truly admire you, Frenchy Tonneau."

"For what?" she asked, continuing to feign innocence. Was there anything besides fire in Gloria's eyes? Affection? Regret?

"You're the only woman I've met who'd say no to me. I won't insult you with the question. You're devoted to your career, your friends, your city. You're precisely the woman I'd want, but I won't ruin you by stealing you away from your life. I'm going to save you for special occasions." Gloria raised her glass. "To the woman who would refuse me."

Frenchy flushed. "Yeah," she said, feeling foolish, feeling like she'd been caught with her hand in the cookie jar, feeling unmasked to herself.

Probably, she thought, probably, I would have said no.

She could see that brief make-believe dream life burn and disappear with a hiss, drowned in a pool of real life. Did the woman use this line on all her rejects? She didn't want to look at Gloria, but there was nowhere to hide from the mirage of those volcanic eyes.

Originally published in *Cactus Love* (Naiad Press, 1994)

DUTCH AND SYBIL

I: Eleanor Roosevelt's Garden

Dutch Kurzawski and Sybil Trask passed in the high-rise hallways of Point 'O Woods Senior Living many times before they ever really noticed each other. The first time they met, after beginning dance lessons in the same class, they stopped to talk.

For a sixty-eight-year-old woman, Sybil was terribly shy. She was shortish, but not spread out, and her hair was a gray-streaked brown. Her glasses reflected the electric light of the hallway as she looked up toward Dutch. "My husband hated to dance," she was saying.

"So did mine." Dutch was tall and gangly. Her body was quite youthful looking, but her face showed its sixty-seven years in lines and saggings. Her short crisp hair was a fading reddish-brown that would go white practically all at once whether it happened this year or in twenty years.

Sybil went on, "I decided I wouldn't look a bit more foolish than any other granny in the class."

Dutch leaned forward to catch Sybil's soft words. "You're the youngest-looking granny I know," she said, throwing her arms out wide.

It seemed impossible to Sybil that she hadn't paid attention to Dutch before, the way she bounded down the hall. Except for the plastic flowered shopping bag, from the back she might have been a teenaged boy.

In the elevator Dutch was smiling, pleased to be getting to know Sybil.

Both women moved in only a few months earlier, after the deaths of their husbands. And neither had been ready to make friends until recently. Now Dutch was determined to have lots of friends and was planning how to throw herself into the project, in the same way she threw herself into everything.

They danced again later in the week, or tried to. Most of the ladies seemed to believe age had already robbed them of agility, rhythm, energy. Except for Dutch, who really worked up a sweat until she danced the basic four-step to her satisfaction. Then she set out to teach it to Sybil. At the end of the hour, they were the stars of the class, and everyone applauded their skill.

"Let's go to Doggie's to celebrate," Dutch suggested.

Once a year Sybil dutifully went out to dinner—on Mother's Day, with her overbearing, well-meaning children. But this invitation excited her. Out on her own with a friend, she was a woman of the world at last.

That Saturday night in Doggie's cocktail lounge they drank old-fashioneds. Dutch was overexcited from their triumph in dance class. She asked endless questions about everything—including her new friend. "Tell me about yourself," she said. "Where are you from?"

"Right here." Sybil's eyes were sparkling.

"All your life? Me, too. I grew up on Poplar Street and settled with George over on Glade, in his family's house."

"Poplar?" Now Sybil was excited, too. "I was born and bred two streets over."

It seemed they had lived parallel lives within the same town all those years.

"Come to think of it," Dutch said when the second drinks came, "you look like someone I should know."

"We could have been friends if I hadn't gone to parochial school."

Suddenly there was too much to tell each other. All through the salads, the fried seafood platters, the key lime pie, they reminisced about their adjacent lives. Even in the hallway outside their apartments it was hard to part. But Sybil said no to a nightcap. The food and excitement made her lightheaded. She needed to lie down.

Through the rest of the winter, they kept up their lessons, getting the steps down better than anyone else in the class. Now and then, at exhibitions held for all the classes, they would have to take turns dancing with one of the senior men; but it was always disappointing, pushing a clumsy, well-meaning soul around the floor while pretending to follow him, when they danced so well together that they really put on a show.

One night they sat in the third-floor lounge watching the last snowfall of winter settle deeper and deeper over the beach. Tomorrow they planned to bundle up and push through it with their high boots till they got to the water's edge. They'd watch the sea take chunks of the cold white stuff away.

But tonight, it was nice, sitting like they were. Though Sybil admired her friend's energy, the way she high-stepped through dance classes and her life, she wore her out. Dutch appreciated Sybil most at these times, too, when her friend's hands flew at her needlework and she talked long after the others went to bed, sharing more of herself with Dutch.

"You know what I've always wondered about you?" asked Sybil.

"What, little dear?" Dutch now called her friend *little dear*.

"How in the world you got your nickname."

"That's easy. When we were kids, George and I were awful poor. By the time we started seeing each other, we both worked. I couldn't let him pay my way everywhere—it went against all my common sense. When he finally gave in and agreed to share costs, he teased me about being his Dutch treat. After a while it became Dutch. And I liked it much better than Annabelle."

"Oh, goodness, yes."

"They named me for both of my grandmothers."

In front of the big snow-filled window, they smiled at each other.

"I'm getting tired of Dutch treats," Sybil said.

Dutch's hand went quickly to her heart.

"What's wrong?" asked Sybil, her face a portrait of concern. Living where they did, it was impossible not to worry about heart attacks.

"Nothing." But Dutch's face didn't look like nothing. She finally asked, "Do you mean you're tired of me?"

"Oh no." Sybil laughed. "Not at all. Why I've never been so not-tired of anybody before in my life." She blushed and dropped her eyes to her needlework.

Dutch exhaled in relief.

"All I meant was that I'd like to cook you dinner sometime. We always go out, and I like that, but as long as my snug hole-in-the-wall is home, I'd like to have you as a guest in it."

Dutch hesitated. "I could never ask you back because I'm such an awful cook. George hit me once with a smoking saucepan I'd left on the stove too long. I'd burnt up the canned peas." She pulled her sleeve back to reveal a burn scar.

Sybil looked torn between laughing and crying. She leaned forward. "Tell me. Aren't you sometimes a teensy bit glad"—and she lowered her voice to a whisper—"to be free?"

Dutch's eyes cleared, and the life in them spilled over onto everything. Sybil reached for Dutch's trembling hands and held them atop the complex afghan she was making for an imminent grandchild.

Then they pulled themselves back. Sybil took up her needles.

Dutch said, "I'd be delighted."

It was so late when they went off to bed that not even the insomniacs were creeping around the halls. They kissed each other's cheeks and parted, faintly puzzled over all they felt.

Spring came and their friendship grew deeper, their dancing feet fleeter.

"Oh, the smell of the flowers is exquisite. I don't think they were ever so sweet before," said Sybil. While the others on the senior bus tour to Hyde Park explored the Roosevelt mansion, Sybil and Dutch stayed in Eleanor's garden.

"Do you suppose she and Lorena worked on it together?" asked Dutch.

"Lorena?"

"That woman reporter Eleanor was so close to."

"Close?"

"How they were together." Dutch seemed to search for words. "You know."

"More than a special friendship?"

Dutch nodded. Sitting very close on a stone bench, they looked away from each other. Soon they got up to walk above the river and chatted of their grandchildren, about whom they seldom spoke. Yet all the way home on the bus Sybil's head lay on Dutch's shoulder, and each pretended to the other she was asleep.

Dance classes were over, but summer band concerts were held Friday nights on the town green. Dutch and Sybil both confessed to having longed to go for years. With their husbands uninterested, then ill, neither had. Now summer rushed toward them and with it the excitement of dancing out of doors. So far, they'd watched a few elder Romeos dance with willing ladies.

They continued practicing late in the evenings after the recreation room emptied, enjoying the time to dance alone together. One day, as they rested, they agreed to indulge themselves and dance together in public. Maybe other women would follow their lead.

"To heck with them if they don't," said Sybil.

"Why shouldn't we? Too bad if the men feel left out. I gave years to worrying what men feel. At our age, we can quit worrying about shocking people. Next thing you know we'll be dead and there'll be no dancing."

Sybil shuddered and watched as Dutch paced away her anger.

"Besides," Dutch declared, tucking her hands in her underarms and flapping her arms like wings. "We're still spring chickens."

Sybil laughed as heartily as she ever had and put aside the sweater—disguised as a gift for her daughter-in-law—that she was sewing for Dutch.

They went off to the center of town to buy ballgowns. Or so they called them. In reality they chose pastel-colored pantsuits. Sybil bought powder pink with an orchid jersey. Dutch bought the exact same style, but in white—"Like *Saturday Night Fever*," she said—and a lavender jersey.

The Friday night before the band concert, Sybil and Dutch were both restless. They decided to walk on the beach till dark—at least they'd get out of their apartments. It was a warm night, muggy, and an earlier rain made for easier walking on the sand.

"There goes Bella," said Dutch, pointing to a figure swimming laps between the breakwaters.

"Do you think we'll be in that good shape when we're eighty-two?" asked Sybil. As was her habit, she took Dutch's arm.

"If we keep our spirits in as good shape as hers."

"What a scrapper she is."

"She forced them to install that handicap ramp in the recreation hall."

"And started the Walking Club."

Dutch stopped. "We'll follow her lead, little dear. I want to live a long time now."

Sybil's eyes held that tender look again. "Do you think we'll still be friends at eighty-two?"

"Oh yes," Dutch said quickly. She looked as if she might take Sybil in her arms but instead turned toward the horizon. "How beautiful the setting sun is."

Sybil sighed. "All those colors. Like Eleanor Roosevelt's garden. I wonder—was she happy with her friend?" They hadn't mentioned her since the senior tour.

"They say so," Dutch replied quietly.

It was so natural, later, for Dutch to stay the night.

"We'll have peach brandy by the fire," Sybil giggled.

Dutch was watching her friend's preparations. "The fire?" she asked.

"My poor worn-out television set. Why don't you look in the guide? Maybe we'll find a favorite rerun on the late show."

The convertible love seat was all made up for Dutch to sleep on. It looked so cozy they climbed in together to watch *Dracula* and drink their peach brandy.

The set flung light at them; the room was filled with flashing shades of gray. As the mournful background music rose and fell, the ladies snuggled closer and closer, holding hands, looking at each other, their eyes wide with fright, their lips wide with smiles. Now and then, one watched the other's face a while, as the TV light hid, revealed, softened aging skin.

One such time Dutch lifted a finger and ran it across a line on her friend's face. Sybil didn't stir, but her chest rose as she breathed her response. It grew warmer and warmer in the room, but they wouldn't kick the covers off, afraid to break the intimate spell.

The horror show ended, and Sybil rose, reluctantly it seemed, to turn it off. She paused before the TV. It was time to go to her bed.

"Come lie with me awhile," said Dutch.

"Oh," Sybil said in a tiny voice.

For a moment all the two women could hear in the dark room was each other's breathing. A plane passed overhead then, and as if to move under cover of its sound, Sybil scurried to the bed and thrust herself against Dutch's waiting body.

This time they both breathed "Oh," as they pressed against one another and let their lips touch once, twice, then for a long, long time.

❖

For an hour before the first concert, people could be seen downtown walking slowly toward the green, or loading lawn chairs into back seats of cars. Dutch and Sybil hitched a ride with Bella in her much-traveled van.

"Got your partners lined up for dancing yet, girls?" joked Bella.

Smiling shyly at Sybil, Dutch answered, "No problem there."

As she parked, Bella surveyed them with a keen eye. She smiled and said, "Save one for me, won't you?"

Twilight was a way off, but the sunlight was softer than it had been all day. It lit up the greens of the grass and leaves while the breeze set them dancing. People were settling around the bandstand; the band was setting up. The flurry of activity matched the flurries of excitement inside Dutch and Sybil.

Of course, the mayor puffed himself up and made a speech, but as soon as he shut up, the bandleader whipped out his baton and began a lively Dixieland number. Dutch and Sybil blended right in with the applauding crowd, their graying heads nodding, their feet tapping with the rest.

It wasn't until the third number, when the bandleader paused to urge the audience onto a wooden platform, that the dancing began. Tiny Bella was up there first, her fused hip making her dance look elfin as she limped and swayed and clapped her hands and shouted to the others to join her.

Then it was Dutch and Sybil who drew the eyes of the crowd. Around the platform, dance after dance, the lady in powder pink followed perfectly the lady in white. When everyone danced in a line, as at dancing class, it was high-stepping Dutch who found the rhythm, who smiled and laughed and drew even more dancers up. Sybil was right beside her, now and then helping the less adept.

How elastic Dutch's and Sybil's bodies seemed, how filled with life their eyes and smiles. Their faces were flushed with a youthfulness not found in the faces of the teenage boys who lurked in shadows, jeering at the ancients on stage. Dutch was handsome, agile, debonaire. Sybil was lovely, graceful, gracious. Their high spirits, their obvious happiness spread like lingering sunshine way after dusk set in.

The park lights went on. A few dancers tarried in a foxtrot, then a good night waltz. There was a summertime of dancing on the green ahead of them.

Bella, tired for once, had gone and taken the lawn chairs with her. Dutch and Sybil strolled toward home. Their jubilance peaked long ago, and they were tired, too. But Sybil never expected to see tears falling onto Dutch's new white suit, brilliant under the streetlamps. "What is it?" she asked.

Dutch couldn't talk yet, could only walk, and cry. But finally, they reached a lightless spot where hedges hid them from view of the houses, and no cars passed.

Dutch stopped. "All those years," she was saying.

It was Sybil's turn to strain to hear her now.

"All those years with…" And Dutch's voice broke. She pulled herself together. "I suppose it was worth it to bring the children into the world at least."

Sybil watched her lover in the dark, filled with pain to see her pain, filled with pain herself as she anticipated what Dutch was about to say.

"All those years you and I could have been together."

The street was utterly silent. The horror of Dutch's realization was too heavy for them. They swayed there beside the hedges, facing each other, hands linked.

Dutch's disappointed voice came again. "All that wasted time."

Originally published in *Common Lives/Lesbian Lives* 10 (Winter 1983)

II: Beachfront Hotel

"Why not?" asked Dutch.

They were sitting on the lawn outside the Point 'O Woods Senior Living high-rise complex. It was only early summer, but the heat was overwhelming.

"I'd as soon sit right here under a tree and catch the breezes off the water," Sybil answered. "Why get into a stew packing and rushing off someplace no better?"

Dutch fanned herself with the travel brochure. "For the adventure of it. We're not even seventy yet. Look how many years we have left—why spend them all under this grizzled tree?"

"I love you, dear Dutch," Sybil said softly, "but you're not always very wise. I'm perfectly agreeable to a winter trip somewhere warm."

"So am I. But why can't we have two trips?"

Sybil looked very small, very frail as she turned her hands helplessly palm side up and shrugged. "The expense," she said.

"Damn the expense," Dutch said with vehemence, then looked around her. "Pardon my French, but there isn't enough to make a difference in our children's lives when we pass the money on. They seem to eat the stuff whole. Let's use it now. Do you realize it's been a year for us? This would be our anniversary trip."

They smiled fondly at one another, then shook their heads as if in wonder that they should, at their age, after their years of marriage to men, have become lovers at all. Sybil often told Dutch how inappropriate their passion must seem.

Sybil rummaged through her end table and handed a flyer to Dutch.

After studying it, Dutch said, "My precious little dear, how can I resist you? Point 'O Woods provides transportation, accommodation, and stops at historic sites. The hotel itself is historic."

A week later they were packed for their anniversary trip.

In their new apartment they drank a peach brandy toast. "Life has never been this wonderful," said Dutch, who talked nonstop about their luck in finding each other as long as Sybil would listen. "Our own private apartment together without anyone to peer at us every time we touch. And you have such marvelous taste."

Dutch's studio had been a clashing hodgepodge of favorite things. In this larger place, even with all of their belongings, Sybil had managed to arrange everything so that it was either stored or displayed in harmony with Dutch's possessions. What didn't fit—so long as it didn't deprive either woman of a past pleasure—was discarded. Both had found, with their new love, that they needed to keep a lot less of their pasts around.

"Have I told you how much I adore you recently?"

Sybil set down her crocheting. "Not since before dinner," she said, smiling.

Dutch moved next to her on the couch. "This will be our honeymoon trip as well." She encircled Sybil's shoulders, bending to kiss her neck. "Ouch," she said.

Sybil turned quickly. "You mustn't bend that way!"

"Damned arthritis won't even let me kiss my girlfriend."

"Yes, it will. You have to let me help and not do everything yourself." She fit herself into Dutch's arms.

"I'd rather make your life easier," Dutch crooned into Sybil's gray-streaked brown hair, her fingers tracing a wrinkle on her neck.

"You're impossible. Do you think you're a twenty-year-old boy?"

"Only if that would please you." She'd managed to slip Sybil's robe and nightgown from one shoulder.

"Heavens, no. I married one of those." Sybil leaned back while Dutch caressed a breast. "Besides, you do it much better than he could have imagined."

❖

The ride up to northern New England was long, the bus noisy, and the air-conditioning inadequate. Stella from the apartment next door insisted on talking across the aisle to them. She'd tried to sit with one of them, complaining that Dutch and Sybil were too much together.

"Look how lovely," said Dutch as they drove past the beach.

Sybil nodded tiredly. She needed to rest, to enjoy the view tomorrow.

"Do look," Dutch insisted.

Sybil craned to see out the window, then laid her head back. It ached, and Stella's chattering didn't help.

"Happy honeymoon," whispered Dutch as romantically as she could, with Stella trying to listen.

Sybil's wan smile worried her. When the bus finally pulled up to the hotel's entrance, Dutch hovered over her and helped her down the steps. "Breathe some of this cool ocean air," she ordered, "and lean on me."

"You'd think you two were man and wife," Stella commented crisply behind them, "the way you take care of each other." One or two of the other ladies tittered.

"Need help with the young lady?" asked a blustery man who, it was rumored, went on every trip because no one could stand him back home.

Dutch straightened. She'd had enough. "No. We're fine," she snapped.

The hotel was striking. Set on a hill overlooking the water, it was an old-fashioned, all-white structure with a porch running its full length. White chairs and tables lined it. In the purple twilight it glowed with a certain majesty, as if it was meant for royalty.

Sybil stopped a moment. "This is the sort of place you dream about."

"Good dreams, I hope," Dutch replied. "Because you're going straight to bed. I'll bring up food."

"No. I want to see the dining room, to enjoy every minute as long as we're here."

"Take a peek, but Doctor Dutch's orders, Miss Sybil. To bed with you."

Sybil frowned but was too tired, really, to insist.

Later, when there was a knock at the door, Sybil was already in her nightie. "Oh," she said in alarm, reaching for a robe.

"It's only room service, little dear."

A uniformed waiter wheeled in a cart of silver-topped dishes. "Only?"

Dutch rubbed her hands together in excitement. "Smells heavenly, every bit of it. And the wine is nicely chilled." She tipped the man and looked toward Sybil. "What do you think? Can you eat a snack?"

There was color in Sybil's cheeks now, and she smiled as she scolded. "You're a terrible spendthrift, Dutch Kurzawski."

"And you deserve a fine feast for your anniversary dinner in your honeymoon suite, Sybil Trask." Dutch ceremoniously removed covers to reveal shrimp cocktail, a steaming lobster bisque, melon and cheese for dessert.

The next morning, they could manage only a light breakfast. Sybil felt fit as a fiddle, she told Dutch, who nevertheless hovered and led her.

They left the hotel behind them, blazing white, austere, and walked into a brilliant sunlight, the sky cloudless. Along the water's edge they met Stella, Bella, and several other ladies, their shoes and stockings on the sand, their feet in weak waves.

"Come on in," squealed Stella. "It's delightful."

Bella was the only one in a bathing suit. "Delightful, my foot," she growled. "It's too cold to do anything but wade! Back home I can swim into the fall."

Sybil and Dutch walked on. The town sparkled as white as the hotel. Arcades stood next to hot dog stands, souvenir shops next to long, cool-looking soda fountains.

"I suppose we should have stayed on the beach with the ladies," said Sybil.

"Why?"

"I can almost hear them talking about us."

"If they have nothing better to do, I wouldn't worry about it."

"But what if they finally understand what's going on?"

One shop featured jewelry. "We're careful," Dutch answered as she led Sybil inside. They examined a case of rings set with Maine tourmalines. "These look innocent enough for us to wear as matching rings."

"I wouldn't dare."

"We could wear them when we're away from everyone else."

"If we had rings, I'd rather we use them. I'd love to see you on my finger."

"In more ways than one."

"Dutch!"

A saleslady appeared. "Not right now," Dutch told her. "Maybe before we go back home."

As they wandered on, the town gave way to an amusement park.

"A haunted house," Dutch said. "I used to love those."

"And a miniature-golf course. Let's play before we leave."

In the park, the salt breezes rippled fully leafed wide trees, tempering the sun's heat and drowning the sound of the ocean's waves. Dutch and Sybil buttoned their cardigans. They crossed the parking lot to a small zoo.

Dutch commiserated with a reindeer in a stall littered with leafy hay. "You need a high fiber diet like we do."

There was an artificial lagoon; boat rides were free. They chose a canopied pedal boat.

"Careful, careful," warned Dutch as they entered their bright green boat.

Sybil replied testily. "I can still walk."

At first Dutch ignored her mood. "How romantic," she said as they moved slowly past the animals and under the trees. She took Sybil's hand surreptitiously.

Sybil stopped pedaling; they slowed to a stop.

"What's wrong?"

"Can't we stay out here forever?"

Sounds were muffled on the small pod. They might be alone in the world if not for an osprey high in its nest, darting dragonflies, and a sprinkling of ducks.

They stayed in the stillness. The ocean was never silent. Dutch shooed a mosquito from Sybil's wide-brimmed straw sun hat and saw she was smiling, eyes closed.

The clunk of pedals made them stir. It was the blustery man, headed their way. They looked at each other and, as one, set their boat in motion.

"Lord, there's Stella and the whole crowd. Wave, Dutch, to keep the peace."

"I'd rather they kept our peace."

"It's a public park."

"Are they heading for the boats? Those doddering—"

"Stella's no older than we are."

"She acts at least one hundred and two."

"They're bound to break the peace—we might as well go in. We'll stop for fried clams and iced tea."

"Yoo-hoo," called Stella, fanning herself. Beside her, a widower from Point 'O Woods was doing all the pedaling.

"We're heading in," Dutch called back as sweetly as she could manage.

They came across Bella in the amusement park, swinging her fused hip as she walked, peering at the different rides.

"Been out canoeing, girls?" she inquired.

"Pedal-boating." Dutch laughed. "I'm well past my canoeing years."

"I can, can-oe?" Bella chuckled at her own joke. Her lined face was tanned from swimming, right up to the line the bathing cap left. "That's nonsense anyway. I canoed with my husband two years ago. It's very relaxing."

"You think we can do anything at all," Sybil said.

"You bet your bottom dollar. The day I stop believing that is the day I go swimming and don't come back."

"Don't even think it."

"Someday, girls. Rather than be cooped up with a bunch of old hens I can't get away from."

"Isn't that exactly what they are?" Dutch was glad of an ally.

"Say, the three of us ought to take a trip in my camper someday. I'd get to see the country like I did with my husband, and"—she winked—"I know enough to leave you two in peace."

Dutch and Sybil both flushed, but Bella said, "Let's plan something. It'll be fun." She swung off between two rides, calling, "Come back later, we'll ride the carousel together!"

They looked at each other, both grateful that Bella understood and liked them anyway.

❖

It was how they'd fallen in love, dancing. Defying convention by dancing together, defying age by dancing at all. This was their first dance in a real ballroom, and they did not intend to miss it.

While the band took a break, they went out on the long, elegant porch to rest in the cool twilight. Roomy wicker chairs with flowered cushions welcomed them. A waiter brought liqueurs.

"You're a heavenly dancer, dear one," sighed Sybil. "I'm transformed to a young girl and a cherished woman in your arms."

"And I'm the self I never could be before you. Imagine, had we met sooner, been brave enough, what a life we would have led."

"First, Paris, where there were women like us."

"Paris, New York—we could have seen them all." With a mixture of gallantry and caution, Dutch leaned over Sybil's hand to kiss it.

"Hi!"

Dutch stiffened, pretending to examine Sybil's nail polish in the fading light.

It was Stella, alone. She settled into another deep wicker chair and fidgeted. "I saw you two enjoying yourselves, as usual," Stella said, as if in criticism.

"We love to dance." Sybil's airy tone fell like lead into the space between her chair and Stella's.

Dutch frowned into the twilight. Along the curving shore, lights began to shine, although the porch remained in shadow.

Stella continued to fidget. "I need to talk to you both," she said in an uncomfortable, yet excited voice.

"Is there something wrong?" Sybil asked in her soft voice.

Stella said, "I wouldn't bother mentioning this if the other ladies hadn't begun to talk."

"Say it," challenged Dutch, her body gone cold with fear and resistance.

At Dutch's words, Stella's manner turned harsh; she straightened. "There's talk. About the two of you."

"What sort of talk?" growled Dutch.

Sybil's hand fluttered nervously at her throat, straightening her beads.

"They suspect your friendship is veering into dangerous waters. I'm sure you know the dangers I mean. None of us want you to come to any harm."

Dutch, her voice like a dagger, asked, "How can a friendship be dangerous?"

Stella stumbled on her words. "You always want to be together," she managed. "And then, all this dancing. It's not dignified at our age. It's not normal."

There was silence on the nearly dark porch, except for crickets and waves cleansing the sand. Dutch and Sybil reached across the space between their chairs to clasp hands. Without warning, the porch lights came on.

So it was in the kind, yet revealing, glow of the electric sconces above them that their hands announced what they'd feared to say.

Dutch asked Stella, "Are you afraid that we'll become lovers?"

"Not exactly," lied Stella.

They could hear Bella stump across the porch toward them. Dutch waited for her.

"Bella," Dutch said, "I'm glad you're here. I was about to reassure Stella about Sybil and me. She says the ladies were afraid we'd become lovers."

"Oh no," said Bella, with exaggerated horror. She slapped a knee with one hand, scratched her head with the other, and said, winking, "Whatever shall we do?"

Dutch laughed softly, squeezing Sybil's hand. "You can relax, Stella—we already are."

Stella's hand flew to her mouth. "You couldn't—"

"I could and do love Sybil dearly and wish we'd been together all our lives."

Sybil said in a voice weak with fear, "Dutch is my soul mate."

"Good for you," Bella said casually. "Come on, Stella, let's go dance."

Stella's eyes widened and her jaw dropped. "What should I tell the others?" She didn't look at Sybil or Dutch.

Dutch answered anyway. "Tell them what we said, of course. It's not as if they don't know about such things."

With Stella out of earshot, Dutch laughed.

But Sybil said, "Why did you say that?"

"What can they do to us? Now we can buy our rings before we go, and stop hiding."

"You had no right. We have to live with those people, as you well know."

Dutch's posture wilted. "But I—" They looked away from each other, staring toward the ocean.

Dutch asked once more, "Does this mean you don't want to be with me anymore?"

For an interminable time, there was no answer. Finally, Sybil said, "No. It doesn't mean that at all."

Dutch let out a long breath.

"You were right to say it, right to tell them. We haven't got enough time left to spend it all in hiding. No, that's not what's wrong at all. It's those ladies, and you."

"What do you mean?"

"I mean that I love you more than anything on earth, but sometimes, sometimes, you get a tad too bossy with me, like my husband was—"

"I'm so sorry. I didn't realize—"

"Let me say it all, while it's clear in my mind. You decided we should make this trip and flaunt ourselves. You made up your mind to tell them about us, and the heck with what I thought or felt."

"Sybil, no."

"I almost, almost, let myself walk right off this porch, but it wasn't you angering me. I was tied up in knots over the others following us, watching us, condemning us." Sybil took both of Dutch's hands in her own. "I love you, dearest one. Do you think you can be less bossy? The way we can be ourselves together is what I relish as much as anything."

Dutch pulled away to wring her hands. She cried. "I'm so sorry. I will change. I had to be like that with him. I didn't realize I was still doing it, and to you of all people. One reason I love you is your willingness to overcome your fears."

"And the ladies, the web they were spinning around us with their suspicions, their fear of what we are—"

"It should go away now. They can accept us or stay away from us."

"To think I was ready to give up on us because of their interference."

"And my pushy ways."

"But I love how you know what you want, Dutch, and how you get it. I'd like to be more like you."

"I won't step on your toes anymore, little dear."

"Not even when we dance?"

Laughing, they realized the band had started up again.

"Are we going to disappoint those seniors in there? They're daring us to dance." Sybil stood and bowed. "Shall we go in?"

They walked arm in arm to the ballroom. Everyone from their bus was there, waiting. Sybil smiled nervously.

They danced. Graceful waltzes led to foxtrots and polkas. Some of the women wouldn't look their way. Others smiled after a while, timidly, tentatively. The blustery man gaped, but his feet tapped out of control until he finally asked Bella for a dance.

The four of them, then two more women, then another lady and man, danced until the band played "Goodnight, Irene."

Originally published in *Home in Your Hands* (Naiad Press, 1986)

THE LoPRESTO TRAVELING MAGIC SHOW

The summer heat faded behind the train as the city landscape shrank to trees and lawns and long, flat beaches. The train ride—that train ride every summer to Aunt Terry's—let me shrug the heat off my body, shake my brothers and sisters like itchy drops of sweat from my hair, until I could whirl in my head in the new free space I found away from home.

Not that Aunt Terry's trailer was palatial. With her and me and Molly bumping around in the twelve- by thirty-two-foot tin box, as they called it, there was probably less room than home. But it was different. Maybe because I didn't have to weave through living room furniture. Or because Terry and Molly didn't have a TV to bump into or fancy ceramic figures dancing on unsteady tables. Nothing was breakable there or so sacred you couldn't knock it over, even the beer. The synthetic area rug in the kitchen was soaked in it so regularly they called it their beer rug.

It felt bigger at Aunt Terry's when I woke in the morning and squeezed my way in and out of the bathroom, walked the few steps to the front door of the trailer and stepped down, barefoot, to the damp, brown ground. There were no elevators or long flights of stairs to the earth there. Only a small child jumping down two wooden steps and many of those years I was so small I held two-handed to the metal edge of the doorway. Aunt Terry let me play outside in my pajamas even when I was very young, because she and Molly needed to sleep off the night before in the only closed room there, and they knew I valued my visits with them too much to wander out of earshot.

I'd sit for a long while on an upside-down crate watching the strange neighborhood wake up and start its day. The trailer across from Aunt Terry's was a mirror reflection of hers except for the slapped-together entryway the neighbors built to keep in the heat during cold months. It was filled with such a jumble of brooms and tools and boots and slickers that I was glad I didn't have to find my way through it quietly in the mornings. But inside, where I had been once, the walls were covered with imitation wood paneling, and the furniture fit like pieces in a jigsaw puzzle. The retired couple who lived there were as handy as Aunt Terry and Molly, and you could tell they spent almost no time at Gaffney's, the restaurant and bar next door to the trailer park, which so many residents treated like an extension of their tiny living rooms.

The park's trailers were an absolute circus of colors, shapes, sizes, decorations, and additions. The contrast with the symmetrical concrete and brick city where I lived enchanted me. I walked through the park trying to find a pattern of the trailer placements. At home, apartment buildings lined the blocks side by side, up the street and down the street. At Aunt Terry's some trailers were side by side, some end to end, some jammed between others so that only an end stuck in or peeked out, and a few stood in the middle of an invisible circle which could almost be called a yard and was certainly used as one.

When I got older, Janis Joplin's voice would always bring back to me that early morning scene of ragged community living as she sang about freedom meaning having nothing left to lose. Not because Aunt Terry's trailer park was as desolate a place as it looked. Simply because there were no frills, there was no money thrown about, no airs or unnecessary clutter. The ground bred no grass because it was too well used, the homes carried spots of rust and faded paint because fixing things up wasn't as important as stocking the refrigerator. There were no patios or gardens because leisure was either nonexistent or spent in the easier comfort of Gaffney's. Yet it was the most comfortable and unthreatening place I have ever been, and I wish now as I did then that Twelve Elms Trailer Park could have been my home more than two weeks a year.

Eventually Molly would come to the trailer door and call me in. Sometimes I'd be visiting with one of the many cats or dogs of the park—sometimes I'd get all the way over to the miniature-golf course and driving range out back that was run by the park's owner. On a weekend morning her call might find me halfway out the driving range, gingerly barefoot on that huge expanse of grass, my pajamas wet from rolling in the dew.

Once back at the trailer, Aunt Molly served breakfast for the three of us no matter how much they drank the night before. Before eating breakfast, Aunt Terry would cut a lemon in quarters and bite into its pulp, eyes tearing, shaking her head with the rind against her lips like a sunny, yellow smile. "If you're ever silly enough to get hungover, Princess"—as she called me—"don't forget Aunt Terry's cure. If you survive the shock, you're ready for a new day." Then she'd lift her juice mug and silently toast Molly.

Aunt Terry was quite a woman. I sensed it then and I know it now. Those breakfast feasts were a statement—whatever happened to her the night before, she was always very alive come daylight. Of course, I never shared the nightlife they led until that trip. I knew they went over to Gaffney's where Molly was the night cook. I knew they drank every night as much as my parents drank in a year. I knew my father would not approve of their friends.

Aunt Terry described to my parents a life of respectability and security. She lived, according to her, in a stable, tidy mobile home park, rooming with an in-demand chef, herself a clerk at the high school.

In reality, my aunt couldn't keep a job partly because she wanted at least one month off every summer. And she took it. "Two weeks for my Princess," she'd say, "and two for my Mol." It seemed like a good system to me because I had exclusive rights to Aunt Terry most of the day and did not have to feel bad about Molly, because her two weeks were coming. Besides, though Molly worked long hours at Gaffney's, she worked them when Aunt Terry was there with their friends.

My parents believed Aunt Terry. They believed that the same way the whole family had believed anything about Aunt Terry since she'd left home. I knew that Nonno LoPresto, my father and Aunt Terry's father, had kicked her out for some reason, but no one ever talked about it. When Aunt Terry, on a Christmas visit, first asked if they'd like to send one of the kids, me for instance, up to see her that summer, my parents jumped at the idea. To get one kid out of that apartment for almost nothing, they would have forgotten anything they'd ever heard about Aunt Terry. Especially since they refused to believe there was anything wrong with someone in their family.

I was seven the first year and twelve the year it all happened; I knew, or thought I knew, everything and everyone at the trailer park pretty well. My aunt Terry LoPresto was a short, feisty, skinny Italian daughter who the family said should have been a son. We used to compare our biceps at the breakfast table while Molly laughed and called us Bronx juvenile delinquents. Both Aunt Terry, because she acted so young, and I took that as a compliment. "Never took any responsibility," my mother said about her at Nonno LoPresto's funeral, and maybe she was right, or maybe Aunt Terry took the responsibilities she was able to fulfill.

In either case her forty-three years had left her looking a lot more than ten years younger than her brother, my poor, pale, shrunken father who, if he had a muscle, sure never let us see it. It was his choice in life, I know, to get married and strap himself down to supporting six kids on a clerk's salary. It must have shrunken his soul, too, because that was nothing like Aunt Terry's either.

She had an exuberance about her that made her leap around like she was my age. Her tight wavy hair was as short as she could get it, and her clothes, dungarees or chinos with flannel shirts or sweatshirts, required as little care as her hair. She worked hard every year, most of the year, at whatever job would take her. One of my favorite years she'd worked for a lumber store and got scrap wood free. She waited until I arrived to build the lean-to next to the trailer. We spent most of the two weeks on it. I was one proud nine-year-old. Aunt Terry called it my room and said she was going to build a special bed in it so they could rent it out to me when I grew up. I knew it wasn't big enough, but it was my dream house all the next year back in the city.

Molly was what people call the motherly type. She was short like Terry and had short gray hair, but hers was straight and cut longer so it looked soft when the wind mussed it up. She always wore pants, too, but they were elastic-waisted ladies' pants in black and navy blue—to hide cooking stains better, she said. She let Aunt Terry take the initiative in things, but hers was the restraining hand when Aunt Terry started to get into fights, and the comforting hand when one of us was sick. It was Molly who initiated my visits. She was the one who believed in keeping up family ties and saw that Aunt Terry had something to give my father's children no one else in the family could offer.

Over the years I met their small, odd circle of friends. Big, slow Bozo told stories of his several years in traveling circuses, but he was a sad person, resigned to the decreased demand for clowns who "wasn't the best," he said. Bozo's best friend was Ed, his next-door neighbor. Ed had been waiting for his wife to come back since I met him. He introduced new visitors to a gold-colored framed picture of a teased-haired, bleached blonde in a white angora sweater, as if she was his wife in person. Bozo and Ed were both lucky enough to work year-round on the town's sanitation crew and could only complain that they had to get up too early in the morning. They bragged of making the town fit to live in.

Minnie and Lester were a retired couple who were "full of fun," as Molly described them. He was the practical joker of the group, and big Minnie was the flirt. They always had cracks to make about everything and kept the others laughing. The whole group generally gathered, with a few drifters, at Gaffney's every night to down pitchers of beer.

Another of my favorite memories is from what must have been the first year I was up there, because I remember Aunt Terry piggybacking me into the restaurant in my pajamas, so I could quickly peck the cheeks of the whole gang before she converted the trailer's dinette booth to a bed and put me to sleep. And I remember falling asleep, alone in the dark as I was, warm and secure as I pictured them in my mind. They were all in a booth, squeezed together, smiling and laughing, spilling and shouting and smoking, and pleased as they could be that this child was theirs to tease and joke and play with for two weeks. I can still picture the wooden booth, dark and carved with initials, the table between them overflowing with ashtrays and glasses and empty pitchers. They were against an inside wall where the brightest light came from a dingy lamp hung under a dim shade, the shade decorated with horses jumping over hedges and red-suited men riding the horses. It gave my seven-year-old mind a sense of the adventure and excitement, specialness and danger of a fairy tale.

Each summer I left the Bronx with trepidation and anticipation squeezed together in my stomach. This particular summer was worse because as I stepped on the train, I realized my period had arrived for the third time in my life. I found my seat and sat frozen until the train moved out of the station. Then I hurried to the bathroom and, going through Harlem, threw up the sum of that past horrible year of puberty. I raised my head and, through the raised window, saw the ghetto's long narrow streets, demolished buildings, gated storefronts, packs of young men, and was sick again.

All that year I had felt prey to the terrors of the city. Vulnerable to men now, I feared them. Unable to compete with the girls on my block who had aptitudes for dressing, walking, and talking correctly, I feared their remarks and my inadequacy and did not understand why I should be like them. When my period came, I was ashamed.

My closest companion that year was the linden tree outside my window, which, surrounded by trash cans in our alleyway, managed to grow high enough for me to reach its jumbo leaves from the fire escape and smell its yellow blossoms in June. By July, the smell of garbage returned to our sixth-floor windows, and I felt badly for the tree. On trash mornings, between five thirty and six, I woke to the crash of metal garbage cans, the thunder of diesel motors, and the bellowing of sanitation workers who mercilessly threw cans back at the tree.

The second girl after three boys, I struck myself as the garbage tree of my family. My femaleness was not special as it had been for my older sister and had become familiar enough for my brothers to taunt me about it. That older sister, one of the popular girls, scorned my embarrassment and wore her femininity like a flag. For me, the last three months had been colored by hot, painful cramps, and shame. Now here I was, the only one on the train having to face this ordeal, alone and with no preparation.

Like my garbage tree, though, I adapted, made what repairs I could, and skulked back to my window seat awaiting release, after fifty weeks, back to the wilds of Aunt Terry's world. I was pleased as punch to see bowlegged Lester at the station, beaming up at me through a window. He had few teeth and his shrunken cheeks were covered with short white bristles. The day was city-hot, but he wore the navy-blue watch cap I'd never seen him without, and Minnie had pressed his black chinos until they were shiny. His bony wrists were a welcome support as they emerged from his sweatshirt, and his hands swung me, suitcase and all, off the steps almost before the train could stop.

Lester drove a cab to supplement his Social Security. I sat importantly in the front seat, gaining confidence as he sped me to Twelve Elms. He tried to give me the year's news in the ten-minute ride along the blessedly familiar Post Road, and by the time we arrived, I didn't let myself cry when I confessed to Molly what my needs were.

She hugged me and sent me into their bedroom to change while she rustled through a cabinet to find the right supplies. Then we sat at the pull-down kitchen table and Molly told me what she had gone through at my age. When Aunt Terry arrived after shopping, I was laughing and telling Molly about my garbage tree and wishing I could transplant it to Twelve Elms to live better.

Aunt Terry gave me a loving punch on the arm in welcome. Molly got up to fix lunch while Aunt Terry and I walked around the park, Aunt Terry showing me the small changes since last year, the new important people, the new drifters. We got to the edge of Twelve Elms and Aunt Terry pointed to activity at the far end of the driving range.

"Carnival coming in," she told me.

"Here?"

"That's why we changed your weeks, to surprise you. The owner makes peanuts off this golf thing—he's renting it out to the church people for a fundraiser. Going to be a big one, too, by the looks of it. Bozo's plant is on summer shutdown—he'll be a clown all weekend."

I was too excited say anything, but Aunt Terry looked at me, then gave me a rare hug. She, too, was excited about this carnival in her own backyard.

When the trucks arrived sporadically that night, I heard them as I writhed on my dinette bed. Molly told me the cramps would ease if I relaxed, but how did someone in so much discomfort relax? Images of the city came to me in my sleep, but I woke and was comforted in the knowledge that the trucks brought carnival people, not garbagemen. I imagined people pitching tents, setting up what Bozo called the carny camp, rolling the rides into place.

I learned better the next morning when I ran barefoot to the driving range and saw not dozens, but five unadorned tractor trailers motionless on the field. I was disappointed until I saw workmen pull signs, lower sides, and while this scene might not have the magic of my fantasy, there was a transformation in the works.

By Thursday morning, the driving range was transformed. Where days ago the grass shone a dewy bright green, it was trampled down or covered with carnival equipment. The tractor trailers had been driven into a wagon-train circle, and their cabs driven off to rest on another part of the range. The circle was open on one end, and an admission booth stood half assembled.

Cautiously, myths of kidnappings in mind, I walked between two tractors and stood inside the circle. Overnight, a merry-go-round and other rides appeared in the center of the circle. In the early stillness the carnival rides revealed themselves. I saw the machinery that ran the Ferris wheel, the Scrambler, the Kiddie Teacup ride, saw the grease and stains, dents and repairs, patched paint. The vehicles that delighted me were naked, out of costume, without the motion which gave them their magic. Unassembled cotton candy and lemonade huts, a Big Six wheel and a ring toss game were propped against them, waiting for hawkers to bring them alive and entice the crowds to their treats and prizes.

When I turned back to the trailer park, it looked like another sleeping carnival. Crazily, it now was shoddy, used-looking, cheerless and disappointing. A smidgeon of sun broke through the clouds and lit up two pots of red tulips outside a trailer; would the carnival be canceled if it rained? What did it matter anyway, I thought as I walked to Aunt Terry's, very alone and sad to have lost something I couldn't name.

You'll have growing pains, one of my teachers warned our class. What good did putting a name to it do? I wanted my summer world to be exciting again. I might as well be back in the Bronx with my tree, dreaming. I wished there were red tulips everywhere. I'd read about kids running away to travel with carnivals. The laughing workers on their way back from breakfast at Gaffney's made carny life look fun. But, no, that would get Aunt Terry in big trouble.

As I approached Aunt Terry's trailer, she stepped down from the door, pulling a long black robe around her shoulders. She saw me, and with a grinning awkward pride I hadn't seen in her before, she said, "I got picked."

"For what?"

"To be the vampire," she answered, swinging the robe across her face and leaping at me.

I couldn't help but laugh. "What vampire?"

"I'm only kidding, Princess. They want a magician, the people who are planning this. And theirs disappeared. I don't blame him. Sometimes I wish I knew how."

"But you can't be a magician," I protested, remembering the few basic gimmicks Aunt Terry amused me with on rainy days. "You can't do any real tricks."

"That's what I said, Princess. But no. Your Aunt Terry is the sucker."

We sat on upended milkcrates gazing toward the carnival site. It didn't look as stark from that distance, with the Ferris wheel now poking over the trucks, the pointy top of a red and white tent staggering into stability, and another ride's rockets poised to take off.

"Besides," Aunt Terry explained, "somewhere along the line it came to me that it's not what you do so much as how you do it. Look."

She pulled a deck of cards out of her shirt pocket as she explained how she'd been railroaded into the job, and how she'd improved on tricks she learned a long time ago—before Molly—when she'd traveled around the country. As she talked, I realized, first, that I knew nothing of Aunt Terry's life before Molly except childhood family stories, and second, that she had performed two card tricks in front of me before I noticed.

"That's really magic!"

She shuffled the deck and winked at me.

"I mean, I know it's supposed to be, but you really did it."

"This is really the only thing I ever learned to do well enough to be proud of it. Not that I can make much money at it, but I can do it."

"I bet you could make money. You can do anything."

"Maybe, but the only way they let ladies practice magic is in a long-sleeved gown with gobs of makeup. That's what Mahala was like—my friend who taught me what I know. But she played second to a man magician, and that's as far as she could go. Not for me, Princess."

I'd never thought of magic or any other profession as realistically as Aunt Terry had, so I accepted what she said without too much thought. I tried to picture the romantic figure of Mahala and wished I knew how Aunt Terry ever met someone like that. Aunt Terry wanted to get right to work polishing her tricks and would do so off and on until Saturday with hardly a beer in between. My downhearted disillusionment was gone; I was eager for the carnival.

When I think back to that Saturday, it's a whirl of activities I can hardly separate. Molly and Ed and Lester and myself had made a platform for Aunt Terry with a draped table and a sign that read *The LoPresto Traveling Magic Show*, which we thought was very clever. Aunt Terry was nervous, crumpling empty pack after pack of those short Pall Malls she loved, until Molly made her have a drink over Aunt Terry's protests that it would ruin her reflexes. There was an excited spirit of cooperation. Once Aunt Terry started her shows, the two days became a blur of images: her black-robed figure surrounded by children, Bozo cavorting through the crowds, swirling reds and yellows and blues—a big, striped tornado.

We'd all been to the carnival as customers Thursday and Friday nights when Aunt Terry and Bozo were not performing, so we'd had our fill of cotton candy and rides. Molly and I were free Saturday and Sunday to run back and forth between Aunt Terry and the wandering clowns—Ed and Lester finally signed on to clown with Bozo—and our trailer. We carried cold drinks and Band-Aids and supplies for Minnie to repair makeup when the heat of the day rolled it off the men's faces.

Aunt Terry played magician to crowd after crowd of kids and parents. She simply stood there in her cape, her black jeans, a shiny red shirt we'd found at Goodwill and, of course, a high black hat that fit perfectly over her short hair. She'd become unexpectedly tall and imposing, composed and graceful on her stage. To our surprise, the show she did Saturday night was a big success, despite the older, rougher crowd. There was something about her—her own magic—that fascinated them. One particularly obnoxious man demanded a rabbit out of a hat. Aunt Terry pulled it off when Lester snuck her a stuffed rabbit he'd won for Minnie at the water-gun booth. The crowd roared, and Aunt Terry, for those two days and forever after in my mind, was a real magician.

When it ended Sunday night, the bar was already closed. Everyone piled into Aunt Terry and Molly's trailer. They were so exhausted one beer was all most of them could down to celebrate the show, and they spent the next day resting, slowly falling from the weekend high of activity. But we got restless toward the end of the day, and Aunt Terry took Molly and me to the movies to thank us for our help.

She borrowed Ed's deteriorating Bonneville to go to the drive-in where a Katharine Hepburn show was playing. Aunt Terry was so infatuated with Katharine Hepburn that she hadn't paid any attention to the movie's subject matter. It was *Suddenly Last Summer*, my first Tennessee Williams film. I was transfixed by the power of the story and the acting and the more painful scenes. I looked away when the sand came alive with baby turtles, and hungry birds, otherwise so innocent and beautiful, attacked. Molly and Aunt Terry gave each other frequent looks over my head, but they needn't have worried. I didn't understand a lot of the movie.

As we drove out of the drive-in to take Molly to work at Gaffney's, I climbed into the back seat. I was unsettled, as if I was about to get my period again. I didn't feel like crying, but I couldn't talk either. I was teetering on the edge of something, as if Tennessee Williams had been speaking to me, as if he'd wanted to tell me something that had to do with all the puzzling I was doing. Cramps, the garbagemen hurting my helpless tree, growing pains, the carnival's secret machinery; excitement, the handsome magician; fear, the handsome man in the film—so many images hurtled around the small space of my mind.

"That was a pretty weird movie, huh, Princess?" Aunt Terry finally asked over the front seat.

I must have mumbled something; I saw Aunt Terry glance again at Molly. "I don't understand," was what I wanted to yell as I worked hard to figure it out.

I knew the turtle scene was upsetting me, but it was more than that. It had something to do with the handsome man, sometimes not like a man—at least, not like Bozo or my father. I remember the sensuality of the film, the sexuality emanating from the handsome, magical figure. Something he was doing was wrong. More wrong than the murderous young boys and birds. But he was beautiful. The boys wanted part of that beauty. No, they hated it, wanted to destroy it. I didn't hate it. I never wanted him hurt. I wished I could erase those destructive scenes. What if the children had turned on Aunt Terry, I thought as, drowsy, I drifted into fantasy in the back seat. I shuddered as the cool of the night blew through the open windows. I comforted myself with the thought of Molly rocking me while I cried.

"Listen, after that, Princess, I think maybe you don't want to be alone. What do you think, Mol? Want to take the kid to work?"

I came back to the world quickly and sat up straight, hoping Molly approved. "Sure," she answered.

"If a cop chances by, you scoot into the kitchen and hang around Mol. Okay by you?"

"Best idea ever," I said.

"But don't you tell your father, or that will be the end of your summer camp."

"I don't tell him anything," I answered. "Truth."

"I don't blame you. Truth."

I will carry the scene forever, like the night I was carried over there in my pajamas. Minnie and Lester were at the table with Bozo and Ed. They'd made a ring of the night's long-necked bottles and pitchers which Aunt Terry and Molly surveyed with a look of mock awe. Ed ducked his head and smoothed his flat, unwashed brown hair in embarrassment as he slid farther into the booth to make room. It didn't help much; Ed was as short as Aunt Terry and Molly and as stout as both of them together. Next to Ed was Minnie, whose eyes, in her shiny round face, misted up at the sight of me, her "adopted daughter."

"In her cups," Lester explained, as he moved from his side of the booth to sit next to Minnie. Minnie smiled and squeezed toward Ed, her pink beads pulling over one of the bottles on the way. "Oh no," she cried as the beer fell into her lap. She sat very still, staring at the small puddle that formed in the slack of her skirt where it hung between her heavy legs. When Lester jumped to avoid the spill, Aunt Terry hauled Minnie out of the booth like she was used to doing so and led her off toward the bathroom, Molly in tow. "Take care of Princess, guys," Molly called. "We'll be out in a jiff."

Bozo, playing the gentleman, rose and guided me into the booth, sliding in after me. As huge and red-faced and sour-smelling as he was, he continued to be the wonderful carnival clown, and I beamed at him.

"It's the little Princess, is it?" He smiled across at Ed, leaning his heavy arm across my shoulders. "Well, what do you think, Ed? Ain't she turning out grand? Who'd of thought Terry'd have a good looker in the family?"

Ed looked embarrassed again, smoothed down his hair till it stuck out straight over both ears, and took a long gulp of beer.

"What do you mean?" challenged Molly as she passed the table on her way to the kitchen. "Nothing wrong with Terry you could complain about."

"Only kiddin'," he said, lowering his cheek to the top of my head and squeezing me to him. "It's that..." He turned to look at me, his warm breath smelling garbagy, with overtones of garlic and beer. "Well, a guy like me don't spend too much time around pretty young girls, you know, Princess?"

"Hey, Boze." Ed cracked all his knuckles. "Leave the kid alone—you're strangling her there."

"Sorry, Princess," Bozo said, and I thought he meant it, the poor guy not knowing how to play anything but rough. He slid his hand, which I remember thinking was as big as a beer pitcher, across my shoulders and onto the edge of the table, keeping me smack up against him. I shuddered again like I had, thinking about the movie, but Bozo was one of the good guys.

Minnie was back, Aunt Terry behind her with two folding chairs, sealing off the booth altogether. The motion of the turtles writhing in the sand under the shadow of approaching birds flashed across my mind. I was overwhelmed by Bozo's big, dumb, helpless bulk leaning over me. He wasn't a clown tonight; he was a grown man. All at once, I wanted to be stepping out of the trailer in my pajamas onto the cool, damp dirt in the early morning.

He put his hand on my thigh, and I jumped and looked up, and there, like magic, was Aunt Terry glaring at Bozo, asking what he was doing.

"Nothing, Terry. Keeping the kid in good hands till you got back."

"The hands are the problem. Move it on out," Aunt Terry ordered, motioning with her head for him to get up.

"Sit back down, Terry. Let me stay with the Princess a while longer," he whined.

I stared at Aunt Terry, scared I'd done something wrong, letting him touch me like this. He was hammered, like my dad said, and overfriendly in the crowded booth. Aunt Terry looked angry, but I couldn't wiggle away from Bozo and was scared to say that.

I had no idea why, but I knew it would be bad for Aunt Terry if I took her side and got free of Bozo.

"Get your hands off her, Bozo," Aunt Terry said quietly.

And flashing through my mind were the young boys who attacked the pretty man. I knew with perfect clarity, Bozo was jealous that Aunt Terry was the magician and he was only a clown.

I have to stop here, I always have to stop here and picture the terrified, panicked kid I was, unable to name the source of my terror. I was perched on a precipice, trying not to fall, every sense open to the revelation I sought and didn't want to find. Bozo's big paw violated me on one side, while a magician summoned me from the other, and I only sensed what she offered to or refused for me.

Bozo drew out his words. "Why, Terry, do you want her for yourself? Do you want her to be queer like you?"

The friends were paralyzed. Innocence had turned into malevolence. Comradery, into jealousy. Stupidity into meanness. Aunt Terry was a baby turtle, good-natured Bozo on the attack. Molly wasn't there to defuse the situation. Both Ed and Lester looked back and forth between Aunt Terry and Bozo, horror on their faces.

Then I sprang, it seems in retrospect, straight up, walked as hard as I could over Bozo's two huge legs, and leaped out beside Aunt Terry.

Minnie reached over, smiling drunkenly, and patted Bozo's arm, saying, "Always clowning, ain't you, Bozo? Can't leave a night alone without some clowning, can he?"

Ed's face relaxed, "Hey, Boze, you drink enough yet? Barkeep," he called, "another round." His voice made us all aware that the rumble from the other tables went on, that our moment of wrath and not quite truth had lasted no longer than a jest, was no more significant than a simple magic trick.

"Taking the Princess home, Ter?" Minnie asked. "God, we could get arrested for letting her breathe the same air as us, we're so polluted."

An edge to her voice, Aunt Terry said, "Don't you think it's time? If I don't come back, tell Mol I'll see her at the trailer."

Aunt Terry took my hand as if I was her baby niece still and turned me toward the door—then abruptly dropped my hand. "Let's go, kid," she said, pushing my shoulder roughly toward the side door.

She waited for me on the blacktop outside, looking along the empty road. I pushed the door shut behind me and stepped into the cool, smokeless night air. I had a huge relieved smile waiting in the taut muscles of my face.

Aunt Terry turned away from the road and waited for me. I put my hand in hers as we left the puddle of lamplight. She looked at me with a great pained question pulling her features out of whack.

I let my big ready smile take over, and I watched it spread beyond me all over my Aunt Terry's fine queer face.

Originally published in *Sinister Wisdom* 12 (Winter 1980)

MARIE-CHRISTINE

I: Valentine's Day

The sun, reddish from smog, set later and later in these waning days of winter, like a blazing heart reluctant to rest. It was Valentine's Day, and Marie-Christine longed more and more poignantly for the last moments to pass before she could lock The Pleasure Shop for Women and step into daylight. She longed too for someone with whom she could share the night.

She'd broken up with her most recent lover and hadn't the heart, yet, for a new full-fledged relationship. But Valentine's Day was meant to be shared, and the frequency of her erotic dreams was getting out of hand.

She finished the display cases and straightened, pushing back her loosely curled hair. "Merde. I will not spend Valentine's Day alone," she vowed in her French-Swiss accent. Tonight, somewhere, somehow, she would find a woman warm enough, appreciative enough, romantic enough—and free enough—to celebrate with.

The shop door opened. Annoyed, Marie-Christine set the duster on its shelf. But she was smiling when she turned. She was, after all, a businessperson, and she'd have to wait until after-hours to begin her hunt. Smoothing her soft mauve sweater over loose clinging palazzo pants, she took a closer look at her customer.

"May I help you?" she asked, her voice melodious, reassuring in this shop whose wares frightened many of its first-time customers.

The woman, in white uniform shirt and pants under an open black trench coat, was shorter than herself; her hair, also short, was wavy, black mixed with iron gray. Laugh lines sprang into the corners of her eyes as she looked up. Then she sniffed the air audibly, nostrils flaring. "Tabu?" she asked, her lips half smiling, teasing.

"My favorite scent," replied Marie-Christine. Instinctively she emphasized her accent. Was she beginning her hunt this soon?

"Mine, too." The woman's hoarse laugh shook her lean frame. "Never wear the stuff," she added.

Midforties, thought Marie-Christine. She liked her lightly lined face, the soft wide lips, her humor. A rush of excitement overtook her, from her cheeks to her chest, to her fingertips, to her thighs. "Our newest model..." she said, indicating a vibrator on the glass case between them.

"So that's what they look like." Gingerly, the woman took the vibrator from Marie-Christine and examined it as if it might bite her. She looked up, the laughter in her eyes a cover now for embarrassment. "You think I'm pretty naive, for a grown woman. You're right as rain."

"Not at all. Most of my customers are even more terrified than you."

Again, the hoarse, body-shaking laugh, but hollow, Marie-Christine noted, as if an automatic reflex. "It shows, does it?"

Marie-Christine smiled, keeping eye contact till the woman looked away. A pleasant chill swept down her back.

"Would you believe"—she was a native New Yorker from her accent—"my doc sent me?"

"Dr. Sterne?"

"Wouldn't you know it. Not the first referral she's made?"

"She's an, ah, old friend."

The teasing half smile returned along with a nod of understanding. The woman spoke quickly, nervously, as if energy ran loose through her body and into her words.

"Bursitis," she said. "I'm a baker. Heavy trays, bowls, mixers. When you're twenty-five your shoulders don't notice. After forty-five..." She shrugged, then winced and massaged her right shoulder.

Marie-Christine found herself, against all her own business-hour rules, wanting to touch that salt-and-pepper hair. She laughed to herself. It would be just like Sara Sterne to assume a patient was having trouble making love—either to a lover or to herself—because of shoulder pain and prescribe the vibrator for the shoulder, knowing very well that the patient would find it useful in other ways, too. But then, perhaps Marie-Christine herself could help. She had a quick vision of the baker in bed—all that experience. Marie-Christine was twenty-nine.

"You can try it back here." She pushed aside a heavy blue curtain to reveal two doors beyond.

"What's this?" asked the woman, laughing that empty laugh, vibrator in one hand. Then her tense face loosened promisingly. "If I choose the left-hand door, I get the girl? The right—I'm stuck with a boy?"

She smiled, looking her up and down slowly to let her know she was gay, too. She wondered if the baker was warm enough, appreciative enough, romantic enough; then decided that with this one she'd settle for available enough.

The baker still hesitated. "Seriously," she said, edging inside the left-hand room, the vibrator held before her, a skeptical look on her face. "Is this the one you'd recommend?"

"It's got every optional attachment imaginable."

"Yeah, but do I need them all?"

Marie-Christine returned to the showcase, slipped another out. "This is my personal favorite," she said, running a hand along it, as if her gentle touch could turn it on. "But then," she said, looking at the machine, "I don't use it for bursitis."

"Oh?" asked the baker. "Pray tell what do you use it—" She stopped herself.

Marie-Christine looked up, caught the baker blushing.

The woman laughed again. "That's okay, that's okay. Sorry I asked." She put down the first vibrator and reached for the second.

"It's quite wonderful," offered Marie-Christine.

"I'm sure." The baker didn't meet her eyes and pulled the door shut behind her.

Back on the sales floor, Marie-Christine listened for the low buzzing sound. Her heart was fluttering. Out the windows the city's lights beckoned against a charcoal sky, one cluster after another, promising and promising.

The left-hand door opened. "Uhh—" said the baker before laughing that tight embarrassed laugh. She'd slipped her slightly soiled white uniform shirt off her shoulder. "You rub with it?"

Really, thought Marie-Christine, it was perfectly simple, unless you *wanted* help. Was this a good sign? She grabbed a bottle of massage oil, and in a moment set the vibrator buzzing and massaging the woman's shoulder.

"Way to go," the baker said.

"Good?" To relax her further, Marie-Christine asked, "What else have you tried?"

There was a silence, as if the baker was considering what she might mean. "Shots. Heat. Not using my arm," she finally answered.

Marie-Christine worked on.

"But how could I stay out of work? I've got a co-op, three cats, a mother to support."

"You live with your mother?" She wasn't interested in that type.

"No. I give her money." She twisted her head to see Marie-Christine. "My parents founded the bakery, and I grew up in it. Mom wanted to sell it when Dad died, but I put the kibosh on that."

Marie-Christine thought of her own mother, wife of a diplomat, presiding over banquets—and over any scandals Marie-Christine might precipitate. They sent her money to stay in America.

She took the baker's left hand and guided it to the injured shoulder and did the opposite with the right hand. "Feel how much warmer with relaxed muscles."

A smell of hot bread came from the baker's body. She placed the vibrator in her hand and silently taught her to use it, her plum nail polish bright against the baker's hand—so pale it looked as if the years of white flour had bleached it. She stood behind her, massaging the base of her neck hard, gently, hard again, struggling with herself toward and away from this attraction, so unlike anything she'd allowed herself in the shop before. She never went into a back room with a customer. But she smelled the bread smell in the baker's hair, felt the warmth of her fill the tiny room. Her own nipples belied her better judgment and rose, as if reaching for the warmth beneath this well-worn white shirt.

She was startled when the baker declared, "This is miraculous. I'll take it."

Marie-Christine moved away, relieved the spell was broken. The baker turned to look at her. One brow was arched; the wide mouth smiled a crooked smile.

"And how," asked Marie-Christine, as professionally as she could, given the huskiness her voice had taken on, "would you prefer to pay for it?"

They were facing each other.

"That depends."

It was Marie-Christine's turn to arch a brow.

"On whether I'll need cash to take you to dinner tonight."

Marie-Christine took the vibrator. "MasterCard? American Express? Visa?"

❖

"I'd rather call you Baker," she said at dinner, running one stockinged foot up Baker's leg under her slacks. Baker had turned out to be charming, the owner of one of the best bakeries in the city and full of funny stories about fussy customers.

"As you wish." Baker escorted her to a bar next. Marie-Christine could tell by the way Baker held her elbow as they crossed the streets what kind of dancer she was. On the dance floor, there was a certain way Baker led—Marie-Christine's body felt heard.

As they spun their brief romance under a twirling light, Marie-Christine celebrated her find. Baker had this night off but worked six others, her schedule opposite from Marie-Christine's—a relationship was impossible. She pressed against Baker's soft shirt, wishing it was summer when she'd be wearing less and could feel Baker's hands against bare skin. They danced more and more closely; Marie-Christine developed an affection for Baker's thigh and the sensations it produced.

It hadn't been an easy thing, getting Baker to come home from the bar with her. The closer they got to Marie-Christine's apartment, the more Baker lost the warmth that had flowed between them all evening.

Now they sat together on Marie-Christine's soft black crushed-velvet Salvation Army couch. Marie-Christine asked Baker to light every candle in the room, excusing herself to change into her peach-colored chiffon halter dress.

When Marie-Christine returned, Baker was staring into a candle flame.

"I'm not sure I should be here, you know," Baker said. "I mean, I want to be with you, you're a breath of fresh air in my life, but maybe I don't want to be with you for the purpose you might expect." Her laughter was nervous now.

Marie-Christine sighed deeply, breathed again, took another sip of brandy and savored its rich flavor. Perhaps Baker was too good a Valentine's wish to be true. The nervousness, the worrying. She'd applied fresh Tabu and sat on the couch, attentive. She imagined Baker's uniform shirt open, her breasts unconfined.

Baker spoke again. "I fell in love with a woman for the first time at nineteen. We were together eighteen years. She took her life." Baker paused, her brow creased. The brandy glass went round and round in her hands. After a moment she looked at Marie-Christine. "It was too painful. I haven't been with a lover since."

Incredulous, Marie-Christine asked, "You haven't had a lover for years?"

Baker shook her head, looking at the worn oriental rug as if ashamed of herself.

"And you don't own a vibrator?"

Baker took a breath and let it all out in her hoarse full laugh.

Marie-Christine opened her arms. Baker went to her. "Did I say something wrong?" Marie-Christine said, teasing, holding Baker close.

In answer, Baker squirmed closer.

Marie-Christine set her glass down, liquid tilting side to side. She took Baker's glass and placed it beside her own. "My heart is bruised, too," she said, her sure slight fingers unbuttoning Baker's white shirt, "and will be gentle with yours." Baker's skin was silky under her fingers, despite the tough work she did. She smelled richly of her famous bread. As the shirt fell open, though, a sweeter smell emerged, as if only a pinch of sugar, a pinch of cinnamon, had been used for flavoring, yet permeated everything.

Baker watched Marie-Christine, her forehead again creasing with wrinkles. "I don't know if it's worth it," she said, her voice breaking, a flush of desire on her face.

"This?" Marie-Christine asked. She finished with the buttons, drew the shirt out of Baker's pants, and slipped her fingers underneath.

"What if I fall in love with you?" Baker asked shakily.

"That would be wonderful."

Baker looked at her with worry—no, fear—in her eyes.

"Tonight. I'd love you to fall in love with me for tonight. Only tonight," she finished in a whisper, close to Baker's ear.

That she'd have her heart back intact after Valentine's Day was all the reassurance Baker seemed to need. The words had barely left Marie-Christine's mouth when Baker's hands reached up and firmly pulled her closer.

"Baker," she said, as if tasting the name. Her voice felt like butter. So did Baker's lips on Marie-Christine's throat, her cheeks, her lips. Her tongue tasted like the sweet rolls served with dinner. Her hands were smooth and dry as if, indeed, she had dipped them in flour first before pushing Marie-Christine's brief dress up to her thighs.

God, she wanted this woman. What incredible hands, square,

quick, short-nailed, and everywhere on her now that she'd let them loose.

"Let's go to bed," she said as Baker began to lift the dress toward her hips. It was all she could do to keep her thighs together when they felt as if they were melting apart.

Baker opened her eyes; they filled with panic. At the sight of Marie-Christine she whispered, "I'm not sure I'm ready for this." She replaced the gown over Marie-Christine's legs as if to spare her modesty.

Marie-Christine sat straighter. "Baker, my Valentine, you've been ready since long before you stepped into my shop."

Baker nodded. "I know, I know. But I never want to feel that bad again."

She slid a gentle hand along the outside of Baker's loose white slacks, from knee to crotch. "Let's bake up the sweetest memory we can imagine tonight. Decorate it with fancy hearts and bunches of flowers. If it's sweet enough, it'll eclipse your bad memory. You must be very, very tired of it, *non*?"

Baker, in another of her sudden turnarounds, laughed with real gusto. "You," she said, following as Marie-Christine rose. "You make it sound possible."

Very slowly and deliberately Marie-Christine blew out all the candles but one and carried that one as she led Baker by the hand toward the bedroom.

At the bed she touched more intimately than before the coarse waved hair. She removed Baker's shirt entirely. Her breasts were soft dough. She kneaded them. Baker's nipples had hardened; she shivered as if cold. Marie-Christine feared she was losing her again, but Baker's laugh was completely heartfelt this time. Her breasts moved with it.

"My heart," said Baker, holding out a hand curved as if around some small precious object. "I trust it to you tonight."

"Thank you," she whispered, looking into Baker's eyes as she unbuttoned the white pants. She closed her own eyes then, lifting the gown over her head. When she opened them, Baker was pulling her own white panties off. "Gingerbread girl," she whispered to Baker. "Under white frosting. Oh, how sweet," Marie-Christine said, licking and kissing.

When their naked bodies met under the covers it was shock that did, this time, melt her thighs apart, that let the quick pale fingers find her drenched labia. Baker kept up a steady stream of sweet words.

She relished Baker's total concentration on her, feeling admired, adored. No wonder Baker had been devastated. Eighteen years of devoting herself like this to one woman? She pulled Baker to her, made her stop as she held her tight. Ran her hands down her strong, elastic back.

Baker shuddered. "It's been so long," she said and began to move again. She lay back, wonder in her eyes as Marie-Christine caressed her body with those fingers tipped in plum, or with her mouth, her full breasts.

And this was the recipe that worked, finally, this moving, resting, giving, taking, till they both came, separately, with all the urgency that had brought them together.

The red hearts of Valentine's Day, laced in white, danced in Marie-Christine's head. Each heart birthed another, and another, a swarm of them loosed and coursing through her veins, down her limbs.

Nearly breathless, she said, "Happy Valentine's Day," as Baker's hand began to stir her once again.

Originally published in *On Our Backs* (Fall 1985)

III: A Butch Named Dinah

At one time in her life, Marie-Christine was outrageous enough to say that she collected butches. She had less taste now for that kind of excitement, but her relationship with Annie Heaphy allowed an occasional impulsive addition to her years of accumulation. The sight of those low green San Francisco hills after her recent slushy trek to New York's Kennedy International stirred the acquisitive flame in her seductress heart. She ran her fingers through her curly blond hair and smoothed her soft white sweater. Her makeup would have to wait until she found a stable mirror.

She hadn't been this excited about a trip since her first visit to America at age ten. Fifteen years later, when her father abandoned his efforts to cure her of her penchant for good-looking women and excitement at any cost, he funded her New York boutique as a stabilizing agent in her life. This year, business was the best yet, plane fares ridiculously low, and Marie-Christine decided that it was time to see the gay capital of the world.

Now her first problem surfaced. It took so much time, was so exhausting to persuade and then train the embarrassed Annie to operate the vibrator and feminine products shop, that she'd completed no preparations for her trip beyond buying tickets. She needed guidance to at least get herself into the city, and none of the complications that came with asking a man.

When the passengers scrambled to rush from the plane, Marie-Christine spotted her solution. Was it her amazingly erect posture that made the woman stand out so? Or the thick pure-white short hair, swept back in an old-fashioned wave? She was a big woman of perhaps sixty, who wore her good looks with assurance, even dignity. A gentleman butch if Marie-Christine ever saw one. She began to hope for complications.

She came abreast of the woman in the corridor to the terminal. "Excuse me," she said in her purposefully musical French-Swiss accent.

The woman, almost her own height, smiled pleasantly but gave no sign of recognition, no look by which to acknowledge that she noted and appreciated Marie-Christine's gayness.

Of course, thought Marie-Christine, femmes are harder to identify. "This is my first trip to San Francisco," she said. "I'm afraid I need some help with directions."

"Welcome, then, to my hometown."

She looked directly into the woman's eyes, challenging her to recognize that she was a lesbian.

"You have choices in San Francisco, dear."

Subtle, thought Marie-Christine. One certainly did have choices in this city, if anywhere. Was this the signal? But *dear*? Not very butch. She studied her face.

"You can read some of these information machines that have replaced people," the woman said and then added, smiling, "or you can follow me."

They got their luggage and sat together on a city-bound shuttle bus. The woman had lifted both their bags to the overhead rack.

"Even the airport is different than back East—hills everywhere."

"Only your first treat," the woman assured her. "Wait until you taste the tang in the air. See the fog come in—it's our daily miracle. Look from any hillside window onto a scene that should only be allowed on postcards. It'll make your heart stop."

Marie-Christine turned to the woman and admired her face, patterned with very touchable-looking lines. Could she have any idea how close that face came to stopping her heart? She spoke of the scenery to calm the thrill. "The homes, they're like suburban tracts with a twist."

"My twisted city," said the woman proudly. "Maybe that's why I've always loved it."

Twisted city? Another signal?

"By the way," said the woman.

Marie-Christine turned eagerly toward her, ready to say yes to any invitation. Oh, that gracious smile.

The woman held out her hand and said, "My name is Dinah."

Dinah? As she reached for Dinah's hand, she heard a list of names in her head: Terry, Kip, Toni, Dee, Gabby, Scottie, Rickie, Nickie, Jo—but a butch named *Dinah*? The name didn't match her gorgeous guide.

Monday, Marie-Christine rushed into the Japanese restaurant where she'd agreed to meet Dinah for lunch. All morning she'd been thinking of this butch with the femmey name, imagining how it would be to tour the city—among other things—with her. She'd walked long, wide Valencia Street in search of its famed lesbian haunts, and visited with a sister adult novelties shop nearby. This was half the reason she'd chosen San Francisco for her vacation, to spend some time with another purveyor of pleasure whose clientele was intentionally female.

As she walked the area earlier, she'd breakfasted on California fruit, savoring its intense tastes. She couldn't get enough of it. Were native San Franciscans as much of a delight? At each corner she stopped to look up and down the roller-coaster hills lined with their colorful, intricately designed buildings.

Dinah wore a black tailored pantsuit and white blouse with a military-looking black crossover tie. She was seated at the gleaming wooden sushi bar, waving, her smile welcoming.

"How can you bear to live in this incredible town?" Marie-Christine asked, unable to temper her excitement.

Dinah laughed low. Her eyes roamed the length of Marie-Christine's salmon-colored one-piece jumpsuit, tightly fitted at the waist, the neckline moderately plunging. "You like it then, dear?"

"I adore it, but please call me Marie-Christine." She took the stool beside Dinah. "*Dear* makes you sound thoroughly vintage. And I have a feeling you're not."

"But I am vintage, dear," teased Dinah. "I've been visiting my newest grandchild out in St. Louis."

Marie-Christine studied the menu, but her appetite faltered. There were lesbian mothers galore, she reassured herself. And where there were lesbian mothers, of course there would be lesbian grandmothers. On none of her jaunts so far did she see one woman with anywhere near Dinah's style. If she was a sculptor, she could ask for no better subject than such a strong heavy-browed face. Dinah's would be the archetypical face that launched ten thousand lesbians.

"Are all your children grown?" she asked, swiveling toward Dinah, who only then finished ordering in a knowledgeable and authoritative voice.

"Yes, all," said Dinah. "For some years now."

"That must be freeing," she hinted.

"To say the least."

Their plates arrived with small mounds of pickled ginger, green horseradish, and shredded turnip, the sushi banked alongside. Marie-Christine tasted each, nodding her approval at Dinah.

"You live alone now?" she asked.

Dinah, a bit of succulent red tuna on her chopsticks, looked up, snowy eyebrows raised. "No, I live with Jeannie."

"Merde," whispered Marie-Christine into her tiny teacup. A lover. "Jeannie?"

"My daughter."

She sighed in relief but was tiring of this game. She dipped a dainty makizushi in the ginger and eyed it in exasperation. It might be her spiciest treat this trip.

But Dinah was fun, with her bell-like laughter that rolled from her like a cable car down a San Francisco hill. She took Marie-Christine to the Noe Valley where she lived. They window-shopped together, tasted goodies from this shop and that, and finally rested on someone's front steps.

"I am sixty-three, you know," said Dinah wearily.

"No, you act my age."

"My lifestyle keeps me young. As well as my city."

"Your lifestyle?" Marie-Christine hinted, one last time.

"Leisure to do what I want. To run off on trips, attend concerts, read, squire a companionable woman like you around." Dinah paused as if to consider all this. "Speaking of lifestyle, would you like to do the Castro tomorrow evening?"

So Dinah thought she was squiring her? Maybe there was hope yet. Before she accepted a tour of the fashionable gay male ghetto, she had to know. "Dinah," she boldly asked, "are you gay?"

Dinah's eyebrows rose. She seemed to grow to the height of the highest city hill and her laughter to ring down, bouncing into this narrow, shaded street. "No, no, my dear," said Dinah. "A grandma who loved her children and home too much to go risking it all for such frivolity as romance. One didn't, you know," she said, leaning confidentially toward Marie-Christine, "not in my day. And by the time my husband left, I was beyond chasing anyone, of any sex. And so," Dinah added with a huff, "was he."

Strangely, Marie-Christine wasn't disappointed. She felt her heart thump as she asked, "You know that I am?"

The sun made her squint with its radiance. There on the bright blue-painted steps, her white hair radiant, Dinah took Marie-Christine's measure, with stimulating effect. "I thought it likely."

"And you don't mind?" she asked, her mind racing to the challenge of this lesbian virgin who thought herself too old, and therefore safe from the likes of Marie-Christine.

"Mind?" Dinah laughed again, but quietly. "If I were your age, I believe I would welcome the knowledge."

❖

She didn't plan to rush Dinah, but time was growing short. By late afternoon Wednesday she was home from gift-hunting and had bathed. She polished her nails a pearlescent pink to go with light but beguiling makeup and a dress that would show her soft shoulders when she removed her shawl to dance, if Dinah would dance. Her energy might be more profitably spent by focusing on a surer goal, but what fun would that be?

It would have been as easy to meet Dinah at the restaurant, a vegetarian spot decorated with hanging plants and natural wood, but she wanted to make Dinah's role clear, at least by implication, and asked to be picked up where she was staying, not far from Dinah's house.

She took Dinah's arm at every street corner on their way to the restaurant. At dinner she admired the crisp man-tailored pantsuit this unlikely grandmother wore. She longed to escort her to a shop where she could buy an ascot to match.

By the time they finished dinner, she'd stroked Dinah's hand enough, talked enough of the joys of lesbian love, flattered her more butchy traits enough, let her shawl slip from her shoulders enough to know that Dinah's eyes glittered from more than the bottle of red wine they'd shared.

When Dinah proposed a walk, it was easy enough to croon, "This once I'd love to go dancing in San Francisco." She lowered her eyes and voice and asked almost shyly, "Would you mind coming with me?"

Dinah lit a cigarette. Laid a charge card over the bill. Looked at Marie-Christine and laughed once more—it sounded self-conscious.

"You know, my charming friend, in all the years I've lived in this town, I have never been to a woman's bar."

Marie-Christine said nothing.

"I don't know why. Some of my husband's friends would go any-where, do anything. I went home early more than once to avoid sight-seeing in gay bars." She paused and shrugged her square shoulders. "It felt wrong, the way he gawked."

Still Marie-Christine kept her silence. But she did take Dinah's cigarette from her lips, slowly, for one drag, leaving lipstick marks on the filter.

"And maybe I was afraid. Maybe I didn't want to see what I knew perfectly well inside. The gay life was an alternative for me. I could have been happy with a woman like you." She reddened. "Perhaps even happier than I was." She looked steadily across the table into Marie-Christine's eyes. "So yes. Yes, my dear. I'd like very much to go dancing with you."

"Thank you. I've been gawked at more than once for dancing with a woman. And," she continued in a seductive rush of words, "I guarantee you will enjoy yourself tonight."

"Maybe," replied Dinah, as they rose, "that's what I'm afraid of."

❖

Marie-Christine awoke before noon the next day, stretching. The phone rang, and she exulted at the sound of Dinah's voice.

"What a dancer you are," she exclaimed. They teased each other for closing the bar. Dinah proposed picking her up again that night.

Marie-Christine leaped from her bed and dressed in a rush. She called a cab to take her to a huge secondhand shop she'd noticed. She'd only packed one on-the-town outfit.

The streets of the Mission District were more populated than the well-to-do parts of town. People stood in the doorways of older two- and three-story buildings, or sat on benches and stoops. The day was overcast, but still the light glowed, as if blessing a tribe that dared to build wooden homes on a fault line. Marie-Christine stepped from the cab with a sense of belonging to that tribe, of being among the zany, the determined, who valued magic light and heart-stopping hills above secure foundations. She entered the Purple Heart Thrift Store, certain this wouldn't be her last visit to San Francisco.

Dinner at a small neighborhood seafood restaurant was intimate. They drank white wine sparingly, as if in silent agreement that they wanted more than last night's euphoria.

It was later, while dancing at a bar, that Marie-Christine became certain she'd won her butch. She watched their reflection in a mirrored wall, Dinah slightly shorter, broad and erect, holding the slender, black-sheathed Marie-Christine. The lightness of their hair, blond and silvery white, the way her shoulders glowed against Dinah's charcoal. The way Dinah's white hand spread over her bare back, pressing her more and more tightly.

"Could this be happening to me?" whispered Dinah between dances, her hot breath tickling Marie-Christine's ear.

Marie-Christine slipped a hand under Dinah's jacket, dug into her back. "I certainly hope it's you. Because I want it to be you. Very badly."

"There's never even been anyone other than my husband."

"Then," she said, speaking almost against Dinah's lips, "it's about time."

She felt Dinah sway toward her, stop herself, lean again. Felt the first light touch of the tense lips, ran the tip of her tongue over those lips till they returned, full force and soft against hers, over and over.

Against them Marie-Christine said, "I have a lovely room of my own."

Dinah pulled back, obviously dazzled.

"Would you like to share it with me tonight?"

That had been Thursday. They'd slept long into Friday morning and made love again, shades wide open, that bleached light everywhere in the room, especially on their bodies, locked together again and again. This week's wanting for Marie-Christine, and sixty-three years of wanting for Dinah, kept them in that white room above the city all day long.

By Saturday, Dinah invited her home. Marie-Christine checked out of her hotel, thinking it strange that Dinah would want to bring her to her daughter's home for their last night. But Dinah was squiring and Marie-Christine would follow her lead. She was, she reminded herself, collecting butches.

Dinah picked her up and drove through the Presidio, up to the Golden Gate Bridge, then to the shore for Marie-Christine's first walk along the Pacific Ocean. They visited the Japanese Tea Garden, resting in the contrast of its stillness. Dinah had become Goddess of the Gay City as she claimed her own place in it.

"My city," said Dinah, as they left the Tea Garden. "I've loved it my whole life, but do you know, you've magnified its enchantment?"

Marie-Christine laid her head on Dinah's shoulder.

"Is it you, or is there really something magical about being gay?"

Small-scale waterfalls spilled from pool to pool. The sky shed light stripped of every tone but whites. "I only know that to be gay is to be specially blessed."

"When you told me how wonderful it is to be lesbian, I listened with a grain of salt. But you were right. It may have to do with accepting one's whole self: wife, mom, businesswoman, traveler, aging woman."

"You are a wise guide," whispered Marie-Christine, rubbing her head against Dinah.

"You and your cuddling," Dinah said, squeezing her close. "If I never kissed you again, if we never made love again, I'd settle for your cuddling."

She laughed. "You don't have to worry about getting me into bed again." Then she remembered where they were spending the night. "If you have privacy at home."

"My daughter likes her privacy as much as I do mine," Dinah assured her, but frowned. "It'll be fine. Come. Let's get some dessert to bring home. Something special. This is a big night."

With twilight, the evening began to have about it an air of mystery. Was it the mystical qualities with which she'd endowed Dinah? Her home was strange, too, not the kind of household she'd assumed; it was a large, well-lighted, newly decorated town house.

"This daughter, she has no grandchildren for you?"

Dinah plated the cream cake. "No, Jeannie's much too busy with her career."

"Hi, Mom!" Jeannie stood in the kitchen doorway, looking like a smaller-boned, dark-haired version of her mother. Her clothes were as well-cut as her mother's, but more feminine. "Charlie won't be home right on time for dinner but said we should go ahead."

Dinah made introductions. Jeannie looked from Marie-Christine to her mother and furrowed her brow. It must be difficult for a straight woman to even consider that her mother might be...

At the table Jeannie and her mother began a tentative banter. Jeannie had barely begun to question Marie-Christine about New York when the front door opened.

"That's Charlie." Jeannie jumped up and hurried from the room.

She tried to catch Dinah's eyes, but Dinah wouldn't look up.

Then Charlie walked into the room. "You must be the fabulous Marie-Christine. I hear you've been painting the town purple with my mom-in-law." Charlie offered her hand to Marie-Christine.

She heard the word purple, took one look at Charlie—stocky, with hair short in front, long in back—hand in hand with Jeannie, and threw open her arms. Dinah's head snapped up as she hugged Charlie, then Jeannie.

"How did you know?" asked Dinah.

Charlie's laugh was hearty. "Mom, we've been praying you'd see the light for years. And the few minutes you've been home this week all you could talk about was this new friend you'd met on the plane. Only we thought you were talking about a man."

Jeannie was hugging her mother.

"Why," asked Marie-Christine of Dinah, "why didn't you tell me about Jeannie and Charlie? And tell them about me?"

Dinah's face looked torn between pleasure and extreme discomfort. "I couldn't bring myself to," she said. "The girls—what would they think, at my age? And you. Would you be more interested in these kids than in me once you met them?"

"Dinah, no. Ten thousand times—*non*, non, non," she said, covering Dinah's face, her hair, her hands with kisses.

"To be truthful, these blessed days you've given me were not something I wanted to share. Not right away."

Charlie crossed the room. "We'd better sit down to dinner. If Marie-Christine's flying out tomorrow, you two will have a long night ahead of you."

The grin never left Jeannie's face. "So what do you think of my mom?" she asked.

What was it the cowboys did in those American Westerns? Put notches in their belts? With great affection, Marie-Christine imagined notching her belt to mark this addition to her collection. "I think," she told Jeannie, "that your mother is one of a kind—a butch named Dinah."

Originally published in *Home in Your Hands* (Naiad Press, 1986)

CACTUS LOVE

I: Windy Sands

Until that night, I'd have bet my bottom dollar I was a washout. It'd been ten years since I touched my last woman in love. Too much like walking barefoot into a sprawling snake cactus in the dark. I didn't have the energy for love.

Then Van came, with her youth and her brains. I hired her to run the retail end of my cactus ranch. That left me free to spend all my time on the growing, the watering, and…well, I ran out of things to do. I'd watch that young body run around, enjoying the heck out of life. Even after her breakup with Ivy she was back in the saddle before you could say Jack Rabbit.

That was October. I can see her standing in the bright sunlight outside my trailer, one foot on the metal step, saying, "I'm going down to the bar tonight. Want to bet I find a lover before Christmas?"

What did she do then? Went out and got one. I confess that girl's been an inspiration to me. I went out and got one, too.

Whoopee! I want to dance with my cactuses.

Billie is older than me by a couple of years, but she doesn't look like anybody's cute grandma. Van called her the Matriarch, from the way the young ones at the bar chewed her ear.

I watched Billie.

I liked looking at her, sitting straight as a ruler's edge at the bar. She's part Irish, part Zuni Indian, tall, very skinny. Her bones were broad, the flesh so meager the muscles stood out. You'd think she was some desert wild thing. Maybe that's what put me off at first. I'd always been one for your younger, femme types. But Billie, she's not interested in that. She's not butch, not femme. She's no garden-variety dyke at all. She's a monument. I could listen to her talk about her life all night.

But it wasn't listening I did that first night.

She had about as much stomach for that smoky, loud joint with its watered-down country jukebox as I did. She always left around eleven, before the gang went wild. I decided after the first few times I saw her that I wanted at least to talk to her, but I dithered and dithered. Before I knew it, it was eleven and she's leaving and I can't think of a blamed thing to say to her anywhere as good as, "Would you like to dance?" Which wasn't what I was after. Or so I thought.

I'd missed my chance. I let it go another week.

But you know, she started coming into my head a lot that week. In bed at night, I'd imagine her with that long, strong body next to me on the white sheets. I imagined the life story she'd tell. And I imagined her hands on me. I'd noticed them at the bar while ordering drinks next to each other. Some arthritis, some stiffness and knobbiness. I suspected that bit of bother would be as likely to stop her as spines stop a wren from nesting in a cactus. I imagined the seasoned fingers on my hip, on the other parts of me that were never this cushiony for my earlier girlfriends. I kind of ran her through my head, to see if I'd like it, or if I only wanted her because we were close in age. I became wiggly at the thought of Billie's touch. Not many women can seep into my head in the dark like she did.

The next Saturday night, that lulu of a night, for lack of a better way to connect, I did ask her to dance. She looked down at me and said nothing, nothing at all. But there was a hint of smile that puckered the corner of her mouth. And those brown eyes like polished jasper looked like they were laughing. Then she swept me out onto the dance floor. Swept me out there and danced me around those young couples like she'd put me on wheels. I'd never been this light on my feet. That darned woman took my breath away. I didn't want the dance to end.

I asked her back to our table. Van was sweet-talking her new girl, not paying us much attention. Luckily, it'd taken me till ten thirty to get up the nerve to buttonhole Billie. By this time, it was getting on toward eleven and noisy in there. I told her about my business, asked her if she'd ever seen a cactus ranch by moonlight.

"Well, no," she said, laughing. "I can't say that I have, or heard such a barefaced line."

It turned out she lived near the bar and didn't have a vehicle. I drove her out here in Pickup Nellie, my blue Chevy 3100. We parked behind one of the hothouses. Wonder of wonders, there was a moon shining down. Not quite full, but full enough. The moon looked like it was pounding up there in time to my heart. The night was pretty darned hot for November.

We walked out on the desert, without a flashlight. She was wordless, quiet-moving. I enjoyed the company, come what may. Big patches of waning yellow desert broom like earth-moons glowed at our feet. We didn't go far enough to disturb nocturnal critters.

On the way back, she took my hand. I thought I'd melt right there at her feet, like some teenaged person.

"You want to see my trailer house?" I asked.

"I didn't come all this way to turn around now," she replied, her teeth white against that sunburned skin. There was a dog tooth missing. I thought of her moist tongue seeking out the empty spot. Holy Toledo, I know I'm a goner when ideas like that creep up on me.

Billie squints while she talks, like she's measuring you.

"I've been noticing you at the bar," she said, over some iced coffee I whipped up. "You're not my type at all."

I had to grin. "You're not mine either."

She nodded. "If there's one thing I have learned in my life, it's that you have to take things as they come. It doesn't do to fight your spirit— it always gets its way. If it wants to go changing my tastes in women at the ripe age of seventy, well then, I'm ready."

"Same here," I said. "I never wanted another girlfriend. The heartache. But…" And I told her about Van coming, and about the blood that was stirred up in my veins. "I was able to live with the lonesomes," I told her. "Until I started wanting again."

"I hear you. I sit in my cinder block bungalow and tell myself I'll stay home with the cat, read a good book, watch the TV. I don't need that bar. It's not the liquor that calls me. Half the time I order milk, trying to put some flesh on these bones." She lifted her arm like I hadn't noticed the scrawniness poking down from her T-shirt sleeve. "Maybe I feel useful there. The kids come and pour their young hearts out to me. Sometimes they think they want to get me into bed, but to tell the truth, their energy drives me up a wall. I'd never get any peace."

She paused, setting down her glass. "I'm thinking, Windy Sands, maybe I could stand a change of pace."

I told you the lady was big. Those arms were long. She reached clear across my narrow tabletop. Now her eyes were like some wise desert creature's looking into mine for, I don't know what, for some kind of sign, I suppose. Then she kissed me, her hands kneading my shoulders. And I kissed her back, giving her everything I had to let her know it wasn't only the kids who wanted her.

I stood. Led her to the bedroom, her hands on my shoulders, like she didn't want to let go.

"I guess we both know what comes next," I said, laughing. "But I'll keep the light out if you don't mind."

"Why, because your body's aging?" she asked. "Hell, it's not even as lived-in as mine."

"Yeah, but you're slender as the needles on a pinion pine."

"I'm a poor specimen, you mean. And I have scars."

She switched the light on. I saw the scars. An artery taken out of her legs for heart trouble. Gut trouble where she'd been sliced open a couple of times. That took my mind off me. I was whole, even with this body round and pale as another earth-moon.

We lay full-out against each other, like we were hungry. Like we were on fire and by pressing ourselves together we could put it out.

We held like that. We held like that for a long time. It felt good, but it didn't put out my fire. The longer we held, the hotter I felt. I wondered if the same thing was happening to Billie but knew I wouldn't find out till I reached between her legs, and it was too soon for such a move if I wanted to be respectful.

After a while I started moving, pressed together. She kissed me again, and I tasted the iced coffee and felt her sweat and the heat of our bodies in the trailer's hot air. Her skin felt slick, and marked like the moon. We kissed and pressed into each other. Then, swift as a crafty rock dweller looking for shade, she wriggled her arm between us. Oh, she found out I was raring to go. I heard her inhale. I don't know for sure that she was excited before then, but hot-ziggety if that didn't do it for her.

She took her lips from mine and started kissing and licking my neck and my face, her tongue in my ear, in my mouth. I rode the heel of her hand like she was some fine horse taking me out across the desert under the blue, blue Arizona sky, taking me up a mountainside, green and lush like it gets over on the east end of Tucson. We rode fast. I heard the leaves stir from our passage until the sound of a rushing waterfall began to grow. She stopped so I could see, so I could feel, so I was that water falling from the mountain. Falling down and down and down.

Ten years of bottled-up pleasure. Everything spilled out of me.

What I said after that was, "I'm too darned exhausted to turn over. Can we talk for a while?"

"Sure thing, Windy, if you have the breath to talk. Was that too much for you?"

"Not enough," I panted, "not hardly enough, Billie."

It was the first time I heard that laugh of hers. The mysterious-sounding, low, back-of-the-throat laugh that reminds me of crooners in my younger days singing about come-hither looks.

She began then, telling me about the places she was raised in New Mexico. I tried to listen, but sleep came over me like a red-tailed hawk onto a tasty pocket gopher. All I recall is nights up there in the mountains were too cold for her. She migrated south in her truck and took factory work where she could. Now she lives on Social Security.

I was out long enough for the moon to find my bedroom trailer window. Billie was asleep, too.

Oh, the moonlight on that body. Billie was less than slender; she was as bony as an ancient saguaro turned brown and ribby. Hips, shoulders, rib cage made her like a cradle I fit into. My hand waltzed over the juts and hollows of her. I felt weak—from exertion? Lust? Maybe what I needed was a snack.

No, I couldn't leave the sight before me, the white moonlight on the deep-toned body. She was handsome as all get-out.

It didn't take long until one of my caresses woke her. She opened her eyes and her mouth and groaned for me. I plunged in then, wondering if she'd ever had babies, she was so big. Plunged one finger, then two, then a third. She made herself smaller around me. I was too short to reach up and kiss her. She was too hot to bend down to me. I rested my cheek on her breast, plunged harder, deeper, softer, slower, quicker. She brought her hands flat across my shoulders and drummed and drummed and drummed as she came.

"If I smoked," she said after a while, "I'd say that calls for a cigarette."

"Cigarette nothing, a ten-gun salute."

We settled for snacks.

She sat up grinning, a kid going to a party. We padded to the kitchen bare-assed, dragged every darn thing out of the icebox that appealed, and had ourselves a feast.

Billie didn't stop beaming the whole meal.

What am I talking about? Looking at the gap in her teeth, the mussed gray hair, at those brown eyes like mirrors full of desert roads and pickup trucks, honky-tonk gay bars and jukebox-dancing women, full of seventy years of love and disappointment and love again. Ah, jeez, I knew I'd found somebody who was going to make the mess and bother of love worthwhile, and I'm still grinning right back at her to this day.

Originally published in *Cactus Love* (Naiad Press, 1994)

II: Windy and Van

At five foot two, I swear I'm taller by a full inch since I retired early in 1968. The best move I ever made, though the Motor Vehicle Department wanted me to stay. I was good at my job, kept the drivers laughing, moved them out fast. Maybe I'm standing more upright, knowing they wanted me and I got away, knowing I'm free as a roadrunner.

When I look in the mirror, I see an Old Woman cactus. Very much like the white-haired torch cactus most folks call Old Man—I can pass for a gnomish grandfather. Too many years out here in the desert all by myself. The gang at Motor Vehicles ought to see me now in my straw hat that's ready for the trash heap, lording it over my empire of rusty trailers, shacks, and shanties—and the hothouses that make up my business, the Windy Sands Cactus Ranch.

You've heard it on Tucson radio: *"Stick with us—we'll grow on you!"* That's me. The retail end of this business is more trouble than a fishtail cactus that's got it in for you. Most of the small businessmen around here have their wives to help them. My life would be simpler if I had a wife, too. But I've learned my lesson in love: it's not worth it. So I've been trying for ages to get someone decent to manage the darned shop.

"What I want from you, honey," I told the next to last applicant I interviewed, who wore a teensy gold cross around her neck, "is the gumption to run this operation like your life depended on it, meaning working twelve hours a day like I do, getting in there and dirtying your fingernails, taking orders from me whether you agree with them or not, and never, never bothering me with details unless I ask for them."

I gave her my best coyote squint, saw her look at how the desert sun had turned my complexion red brown and wrinkly. Then I leaned forward on my squeaky wood swivel chair, fists on my knees to show her I meant business. "Do you think you can handle it?"

Her eyes looked terrified. "Oh yes," she answered, sweet as pie.

"Bullshit," I barked. She jumped like a startled toad. "You haven't got the backbone of a gecko. You might do for a flower stand, but not for a cactus ranch. Do us both a favor—go on back to town and get yourself a civilized job."

The woman got up like her chair was on fire. She smoothed her skirt over her legs, seemed like she was going to answer, but changed her mind and skedaddled. I heard her starter grind three times before she managed to get on the road. I kind of wished I had someone to laugh with about it.

But I don't. Never was able to hold a woman long. Don't know why I keep wishing. The dogs, two small poodles I took in when a friend of mine died, came and sat to either side of me, panting, looking like they adored me. I don't treat them like powder puffs, either. They're smart, good company, and devoted. What more can I ask?

I swiveled my chair around and rode it to my desk like a burro. There was one application left.

I gave my MVD cheer, like I'd done for a thousand lines of grumbling drivers at the MVD. "Van Bourne!"

She was quick. I liked that. She came striding through my office door with big round horned-rim glasses perched over a tiny sharp nose, and brows arched over them. Her face was all huge startled eyes, like an elf owl under a flashlight.

"Did I surprise you?"

"No, ma'am," answered Van Bourne, standing over me, wearing her thirty-odd years with authority. I wondered what her Achilles heel would turn out to be.

"Sit down, girl. Don't stand on ceremony with me."

That wide-eyed look stayed, but she was grinning ear to ear, like one look at me told her all she needed to know.

I rattled the girl's application for a while. You can't hire her on sight.

"You ever steal from an employer?"

"Hell no."

"Hide your mistakes?"

"No."

"Quit without notice?"

"No."

"Slack off on your job?"

"When I was a kid. At Pizza Hut."

"I would've, too. Do you learn quick?"

"Yes."

"How'd you end up a prison guard?" I jabbed, thinking this was good experience to keep the customers honest.

"I needed a job and thought I could do it better than some people, with my college training."

"Did you?"

"I hope so."

"Why'd you leave?"

"I kept feeling it could be me in there, if I hadn't had a few breaks in my life. Didn't feel like I had a right to be outside when those women were in."

"And the nursery you managed?"

"I thought I'd feel more comfortable telling plants what to do. Some of my friends worked there. We had a good time. The boss couldn't believe a bunch like us could bring his sales up so high and keep his store looking so good."

"A bunch like you?"

Without hesitation, Van answered, "Gays." She watched me through those big steady owl-eyes.

I couldn't help smiling. I leaned forward and offered my hand, calluses and all. "Glad to meet you. What brings you to Tucson?"

Van shook hands like she walked, quick, purposeful, without taking her eyes off mine.

"My grandmother. She raised me. I followed her down in case she needed me. She lives in that senior housing complex out by the air base."

"Bet she enjoys those bombers doing their trial runs all day."

"Says they make her feel secure." Van shrugged. "We don't agree on much, but she's my family now."

"Seems to me she's got a point about security."

Van just smiled.

"Tell me what you'd do to improve this place." I wanted to know what the ranch looked like to those young eyes.

Van looked around the office, as if she could see all of the operation from her seat.

"The whole thing takes up about four desert acres," I told her, hoping I was training her as I did. "Half an acre in young trees. The rest hothouses, full of tables covered with cactus plants and succulents.

The walls are half corrugated metal, half clear plastic, except where these original wooden buildings are standing. This started as a weekend hobby, but it grew like purple mat in early spring. I told the people at work what I was doing, and they flocked out here like tourists. Who'd have thought there'd be such a thirst for cactus in the desert?"

Van had an earnest look on her face. "I don't know enough about the business to suggest improvements yet. Maybe there don't need to be improvements. I'd want to take things slower than that."

"I need you to start right now, today. I open in an hour, and I fired the last manager two days ago. I'm backed up on my other work."

"No problem."

"Where do you live?"

"I'm in a fleabag motel off Stone."

"If you're interested, I have a trailer in pretty good shape I can let you live in for the upkeep. I wouldn't mind someone else on the property. Might keep an edge off the lonesomes on a Saturday night."

She gave me a sharp look, like she was wary that I was wanting an ear to bend on my time off. Well, maybe I was.

"I'd like to take a look at the trailer. After work," she answered slowly. I stopped myself from doing a jig.

This time, it was Van who offered her hand. I watched for the warm smile again, but the elf only nodded solemnly, like she feared to jinx her good luck. I wondered what made her so scared when I was sure she'd be a success.

That was in March. We had a lot of rain for that time of year, washing away what seemed like half the outskirts of Tucson. The usual reckless teenager had got swept into a washout in his pickup, the papers screamed about flooding, then the land dried up quicker than a jackrabbit dodging tourist cars, and May came, the month when the saguaros, the whole desert, and the last of the vacation invasion bloomed. There's nothing better than the return of that clean-smelling dry air.

I was bushed from supplying Van with plants. She sold them faster than my nursery crew could get them in pots. Pincushions, necklace vines, angel wings, ruby balls, and painted ladies: I saw them in my dreams. Maybe she noticed how tired I was, maybe she was proud of her trailer and eager to show it off. It was right after the Memorial Day weekend that she invited me to dinner for the first time.

The trailer revealed the same care as her shop did. The inside and outside were scrubbed, patched, and stripped of its fixtures. The interior was one big room now. A few comfortable pieces of secondhand furniture made it homey, but not crowded. She built a slender sleeping loft over a space that held a TV and stereo, books and a chest of drawers.

All around and over the trailer she'd put up a ramada. I sat under the thin slats of light and shade, feet up on a milk crate, and swilled some kind of red-colored iced tea that tasted like water. Van was working in the camp kitchen she built by setting a stove and refrigerator outside the trailer. I could remember being as energetic when Dad died, leaving me the four acres and his sagging shack.

"My empire," I said as Van served beans and rice. "This whole place began as nothing more than falling-down wooden buildings."

"Then what happened?" asked Van. She wore a modified cowboy hat with a flashy red band around the crown.

"Then I bought this trailer. Then a bigger trailer. When I needed a building for the cactuses, I put in plumbing, had the electric run out here, got my trailer how I wanted it. I do prefer a trailer house. I like to know I can get up and go any old time."

"But you've always lived in Tucson."

"I like to think I could leave it all behind. I will someday."

Van looked up.

"Everybody has to kick the bucket sooner or later, though I'm not sure I believed that at your age. I won't be fussing about where I live then."

We were quiet for a while, eating. A car whooshed over on Mile Wide Road. The cactus wrens, shouting *chug, chug, chug, chug, chug,* sounded like they were having their Saturday evening baths. A warbler flicked its tail feathers at us, rummaging like an early bird at a garage sale. The land smelled hot, and spicy from dinner.

Van dabbed at the sheen of sweat under her glasses. She looked so innocent with those big round eyes. And she held her head like the elf owls, tilted to one side. She'd brought her grandma over a couple of times, and darned if the woman wasn't a miniature version of Van, only ladylike.

Tonight, though, as the sun started to dip like a yellow bucket after water, I noticed something new about Van's eyes. In the shop Van was always busy; zooming around to inspect soil and containers and moisture levels. Tonight, I saw shadows under her eyes as dark as noontime shade.

"Did you ever think of another kind of life?" Van asked, like she knew where my thoughts were.

"I had another life," I told her. "Lived in town, worked for the state, went to the club every Saturday night."

"Alone, though?" she asked. "Always alone?" Those eyes were aging by the second.

"I suppose Cupid could've been kinder to me," I admitted, setting down my fork. I leaned back in the easy chair that Van had pushed me into. "No," I decided on reflection, "Cupid didn't do a darned thing wrong. There were plenty of willing women." The warbler chitted some, like she was encouraging me to bare my soul. I looked back out to the desert. This wasn't the youngster's business, not a bit of it, but I could still see those hungry eyes in front of me. Where had I gone for answers at her age? "I couldn't hang on to a one of them, that's all."

I heard Van put down her fork. When I glanced her way, she was all eyes and ears.

"I always thought I was a giver," I explained. "I'd buy them things, move them in with me, cook, clean, do the lovemaking—all of it. After a while I'd get sick of it and start to stew. Then, next thing I knew, I'd be fooling around with someone new, head over heels in love." The first cool breeze of evening drifted by, in no hurry, and rattled the leaves of a palo verde that shaded the outhouse. "If I had as many friends in this town as ex-lovers, I'd never be lonesome."

Van looked like she didn't believe my burst of laughter. She was right. The day had been long, my face was gritty from dust, my eyes stung from sunlight. I'd skipped my usual nap, ironing my yellow Western shirt to wear to dinner. I felt flat and empty admitting my failure at love. "So I married a cactus ranch. The varmints may be prickly as women, but they don't make me stew."

Van took off her hat and swept back her sweaty hair. She fanned herself with the hat. "They'd blossom for you," she said.

I was tickled that she thought so.

We picked at the last of dinner, listening to the birds. Then Van asked, "Are there turtles out here?"

"They're called desert tortoises."

"That's what I feel like. Pulling my house over my back and settling in."

"You left some lady behind, too?"

"She was paroled last month," Van said in a small voice.

So here's the chink in your armor, I thought. I knew the story without another word. She told it anyway.

"I never touched her. She was a prisoner, I was a guard. I would've lost my job, she would've lost her chance at parole. It was the looking that did it, those hot looks, and a word here and there that left me out of breath. I slipped her my address before I left, and I've dreamt of her every night since then. But I was told jailhouse love is like growing cacti," Van said with a sigh. "Your success rate goes down with transplanting. She wants to come here."

"And you?"

"I'm not sure I want anyone under my shell with me, especially not with her history."

I didn't want to know about it. I'd found love hard enough with the simplest and most commonplace of women. "It sounds to me as if you are headed in exactly the right direction, partner," I told Van. "Out."

She looked around my spread. "Don't you ever wish you had someone to share this with?"

My answer was quicker than a roadrunner crossing the Speedway. "No. I'm through with love."

It was another month before Ivy showed up. I saw the attraction right away. Ivy was pretty, in her early twenties, with thick strawberry-blond hair, maybe not her true color, and a real feminine way about her. I couldn't imagine what she'd been locked up for and never did ask. There was that one meeting, and a glimpse of her now and then in the early morning, after she'd stayed with Van.

I imagined what went on in that trailer of mine, but Van had installed an air conditioner, so I couldn't hear a thing. All I knew was that Van didn't stop smiling from dawn to dusk for the length of the summer. She seemed to smile her biggest when that Ivy waltzed around in her skimpy bare-shouldered tops and short shorts that made my underpants look like coveralls. After jail uniforms, I decided, the woman needed some freedom. I wondered, though, exactly how much freedom she was taking, and with whom, while Van sweated in the hothouse shop.

"I don't own her," Van insisted one time when I made a remark about the unreliable nature of women in general.

"You mean you wouldn't mind if she went with someone else, too?"

"Mind? Yes, I'd mind. But what could I do? Half of me is still scared she's even here." Her glasses glinted in the sun when she laughed. "The other half wants to tie her down and marry her."

Van took a customer then, and I went back to my office, where I fought with columns of numbers till I couldn't see straight. Why was I having such a problem with the books today?

A few days later, at closing time, I heard my nursery workers slam their car doors, the usual tires on sandy gravel. Then unexpected footsteps crossed to my office. I wondered if Van had come back early from the Tanque Verde Greenhouses, where I'd sent her to work a trade on the items we can't seem to move and they can't keep on the tables.

But Van wouldn't knock at the door like this. I was on the phone with a supplier and yelled for the knocker to come on in. It was Ivy. She looked like a thunderstorm and stood tapping her foot, letting every flying insect in Southern Arizona inside while she propped the screen door open. I finished my business pretty quick.

"Y'all know where Van got herself to?"

The woman's hair was frazzled, her eyes wild, but she stood perfectly still now, as if her life depended on my answer.

I swiveled my chair to check the calendar. "Let's see," I said, purposely slow and dumb. "It's a Tuesday, isn't it?"

"Yes," came the answer through her teeth, like a snake impatient to make its strike.

"Then she's over on the other side of town at the greenhouses."

She was out the door before I'd finished and I was immediately sorry I'd spilled the beans. Damn. What if this youngster went over to Tanque Verde and raised some kind of ruckus? That was when I thought to look at the time. Six o'clock—Van would be long gone from there, probably stopped somewhere on the Speedway for groceries.

The tiny pang of guilt I felt for telling Ivy wrong propelled me from my chair. The car was pulling out as I yelled. No one heard me. It was a convertible, sporty and yellow. The driver looked like a long-haired pimp. They drove hell-bent for leather toward Mile Wide Road, raising more grit than a dust devil. What kind of townspeople had Ivy taken up with?

Though I searched Van's eyes the next day, I read nothing except business there. The yellow car did not return. Saturday night, as usual, Van went to town and brought Ivy back with her, late.

This was none of my business, and I didn't think too much about it. I was gladder than a rancher with his first barbed-wire fences that whatever dramas were stampeding through Van's life, I was long past them. Still, I missed Van's cheek-busting smile from the first month Ivy was in town, those eyes that looked like they'd discovered paradise, the loosened walk of a well-loved woman. I knew something wasn't right. I asked her to dinner at my place this time.

I barbecued up some beef for us, with nice hot refried beans. I was bound not to pry.

"How's your love life?" my windy mouth asked before I could stop it.

"Gee," she answers, elf owl in the flesh.

Then she takes a huge bite of the beans and lets out a howl. By the time I'd poured a gallon of water down her throat she'd had the chance to get us on a new subject and didn't stop talking all night. I'd never known Van to be shifty before; my cooking wasn't any spicier than hers. I started to worry for real.

Ivy didn't come home with her the next weekend, nor the next. I didn't have a minute to observe Van, though, because one of my exes, who'd been through cancer more times than I'd thought a body could stand it, was in her final illness. I was spending every other night with her, and some weekend days, to spell her lover. In my time off I was trying to keep up with the ranch and my life, but it wasn't possible, not at my age. I left a lot of the business in Van's hands those three weeks, and she did such a fine job I stayed on when my ex passed away to help make the arrangements and go through her affairs.

I came back with my truck piled high, full of a bunch of junk her lover and I didn't want. I thought Van might like some of the furniture and Arizona knickknacks.

Spending all that time with my ex had brought back a flood of memories, not every one of them bad. She was a fine-looking woman, even at the end. We'd danced till midnight and beyond many a Saturday when there was no TV, no money for anything else. We whirled around and around a barroom floor, glad to have a place out of sight of the kind of folks who'd do us in first chance they got, grateful if the bar wasn't raided that weekend. Emma was her name. Emma, my golden girl, I'd called her.

I hadn't asked if I could drop by Van's to talk about the bounty. But I was feeling so low that I meandered over after supper with the dogs.

There was shouting coming from the trailer. I stopped at the corner of the last hothouse.

I recognized Emma's voice. Emma? Couldn't be. It was Ivy. I

heard something crash against a window. My head filled with the unforgotten horror of love transforming to such rage.

"Out!" bellowed Van. I peered around the side of the hothouse and saw that she was trying to push Ivy through the door. "I told you I didn't want you like this."

Ivy staggered out, her laugh like an angry jay's screech. "You're so straight you might as well still be wearing your uniform, screw," Ivy taunted.

"I won't even give you the courtesy of a ride home if you can't shut your mouth, Ivy," Van yelled as she pulled the door shut behind her.

I watched her hustle the woman into her pickup and run around to her side. The whole scene had taken less than three minutes, and they were gone. My stomach churned. How many times had I lived through the selfsame short, fiery hell? Even with Emma.

I heard her brakes squeal at the stop sign up the road. The dust was settling outside her trailer. The land became serene again, the warblers and wrens beginning to sing their twilight songs. I wondered if this really would be the end of Ivy for Van, if she would pull her house over her back and stay inside, like I'd done when I wasn't much older than her.

Look at the damage love brings to otherwise happy women. Loneliness wasn't much of a price to pay for peace, was it?

I headed back to my trailer with the dogs. A coyote yipped off toward the hills. I loved this place, I loved my life, I hated the fuss and bother of women, but I couldn't get Van's cheek-busting smile out of my mind. When was the last time I'd smiled like that?

Harvest time came on this year all of a sudden, swooping down like the Great Revenuer from the sky. The asters, the fleabane, are dying out. Great bunches of yellow desert broom would soon be the only things around to please the eye.

It only took till now, November, for me and Van to settle into our routine: I make supper for her every Saturday night that she isn't making supper for me. Sometimes she'll go into town afterward.

Sometimes now, I go with her.

I'm not looking for somebody. Van and Ivy's last fight makes me think twice before I ask anyone to dance.

On the other hand, it's one thing to be pleased that you raised a beautiful cactus, a whole other thing for a smile to take up residence on your face. Even for a little while.

Ivy ended up in prison again. She got picked up for possession and sent back to Arkansas—she'd broken parole by coming to Arizona. So I suppose you could say she's gone to jail for love, for wanting to be with Van.

Who is once more on the lookout.

Sometimes I think we keep repeating our crimes over and over. Some of us go to jail. Some of us lock ourselves in for self-protection.

Windy Sands is coming up for parole herself. I'm on my best behavior.

Originally published in *Cactus Love* (Naiad Press, 1994)

BABE AND EVIE: THANKSGIVING

It was Thanksgiving Eve Day, but the Christmas cactuses bloomed blithely in the hothouse, each new color like an early gift.

"What are we going to do with you?" scolded Evie in a gruff but loving voice. She leaned over them, at fifty-five her big-boned body looking soft even through the green city park uniform.

"Has this jungle got you talking to yourself, or did you and Babe finally put some money in the bank?" asked Freddy, her best groundskeeper. He stood at the open back door in a green uniform identical to hers, and looked like an aging muscular altar boy, bearing a shovel instead of a chalice. Cold air stirred the moist heat of the hothouse in the Botanical Gardens.

She ran a hand in aggravation through her grizzled gray hair. Every year the Parks Department held a Christmas flower display, and the cactuses were a highlight. "This early blooming business is enough to make me retire this minute." She looked down at them and mumbled. "And I would if I didn't think giving in to my dream would make Babe miserable."

"Aren't they gorgeous," said Freddy, closing the door and coming in closer to peer at them. He was too vain to wear his glasses.

Evie made shooing motions. "Every time you come in here wearing that tool belt you knock one of these poor babies over." She picked up her clippers and began to snap at begonia stems.

Freddy scuttled back to the doorway. "Babe doesn't want you to retire?" he asked, as if to take the attention away from himself.

She thought for a moment. "You know Babe. Mum's the word. But I know she wants to travel. And if I retire now, we won't be able to afford to. Babe's always said I should wait right up to sixty-five to get my full benefits. But if I don't retire, who knows if I'll even be here in ten years to finally open my repair shop up on the Avenue?"

"When's your notice due to the city?"

"If I want to get out at twenty-five years, they'll need it Friday."

Freddy shook his head in wonder. "Wow. Two days from handing in your retirement. When I'm fifty-five, I'll only have…He concentrated, and ticked off years on his fingers. "If I started here when I was thirty-one, and I'm forty-six—"

"Fifteen years," Evie calculated for him.

"Okay, fifteen. So I'll have to work till I'm…" He paused again, but this time waited.

"Fifty-six."

"Ten years more."

Evie laughed. "Why don't you get Theodore to support you?" she joked.

He sighed. "Theodore says he's so much older than me, he'll die first. And, since we can't be married, I'm not likely to get widow's benefits." His face showed dejection as he stared at a huge chrysanthemum.

She went to him and poked at his waist to tickle him. "Look chipper, boy, your turn will come."

He squirmed away, laughing helplessly. "Beast!" Then, catching his breath, he said, "It's not only retirement I'm worried about."

"Are the dachshunds sick again?" she asked, backing him around a table of plants, fingers at the ready.

Freddy shook his head and, up against a sink, said in a small voice, "You didn't want me to tell you the next time."

"Oh no," she said, throwing up her arms and stalking to the end of the table. "Theodore's gone again, isn't he?"

Nodding, Freddy perched on a stool. He smelled like lime aftershave. His eyes, sad again, seemed even bluer, and younger, more innocent and trusting. "What'll I do if he's not home by Thanksgiving?"

She slammed her clippers on the wooden table, not caring that Freddy jumped. "I don't know why you put up with that man. You'd think he was a goddamned movie star, not some white-haired beanpole of a city employee."

"He's a good man," Freddy said in quiet defense. "A fine man. He's bold in his dreams."

"And you're a fine good man who deserves his boyfriend's respect."

"Shh," Freddy said quickly, finger to his lips.

Evie grumbled, "Serve him right to have to support you for getting fired over being upset about him."

"If only I knew for sure whether this latest dream is a new poem, or a pretty twink. I haven't gotten any younger these past twenty-one years." He patted his round belly.

Evie was spading soil into pots with a vengeance. "Why does he have to disappear for days on end to write a poem?"

"Epics," Freddy explained with a sigh, as if he'd been over this before. "He writes epics. Like Homer. You remember studying *The Odyssey* with Mrs. Schneider at the high school. They take a long time to write."

She glowered at a newly rooted plant as she readied its soil, remembering the first time she'd watched this happen, not long after she and Freddy, having worked together several years, met at a party and discovered their common sexuality. She had never suspected her impishly handsome young Irish Catholic coworker of being gay. In fact, she'd imagined him to be one of those youngest Irish sons, not bright enough for the priesthood—one brother already a soldier, the next oldest already a cop—who lived with his mother and prayed away impure thoughts. They'd been great friends ever since their revelations, occasionally double-dating, each couple careful to include the other at mixed parties.

"If he gave some young fella half a chance," said Freddy, "the kid would be crazy not to grab Theodore."

Evie liked Theodore, but her loyalty was to Freddy. "Personally, I don't think you have to worry for a minute. Theodore's sixty, for chrissake," she said, making room for the newly potted plant on the edge of a shelf of its elders.

His eyes and voice soft, Freddy said, "A distinguished looking older man."

She stopped herself, resisting further criticism of Theodore. After all, Freddy probably couldn't imagine what she saw in her curly, white-haired Babe, nor what Babe saw in her. "Here you go, Junior," she said, passing a fallen, slightly wilted flower to him. "Wear it in your lapel. Maybe someone will notice you and be your consolation."

"Yuk," said Freddy, a look of comic disdain on his face as he rose to return to his digging. "You know I can't stand other men. There's not another in this town who'd dance to Johnny Mathis with me."

It was so seldom Freddie acted camp that Evie had to smile.

"Do you think," he asked, delicately fingering the flower with his work-roughened hands, "we'll ever have one of our dance evenings again, the four of us and Johnny Mathis?"

"Get your lazy tail out of here," she scolded good-humoredly. "Of course we will. Johnny and Elvis and Mantovani's whole damn orchestra. You know Theodore will be back. And to stay this time, if I have to retire to keep my eye on him. You can go traveling with Babe."

"It's a deal," said Freddy, swinging his shovel to his shoulder. It struck the newly potted plant and pushed it crashing to the floor. He looked guiltily toward Evie, then ran for the door as she menaced him with her clippers.

At holidays, Evie's family had always massed in one another's homes, Evie's *roommate* Babe included. But then her parents, aunts, uncles, older cousins, had one by one died, and her sisters and brothers were celebrating Thanksgiving at the homes of their children spread across the state and country. For the past several years it had been Babe, the boys, her and the cats: Boots and Leonardo da Kitty, the latter named by Theodore. Evie savored their holiday rituals as much as the cats savored their special holiday treats.

"Hey, Babe," she hollered up the steep outside stairs to their third-floor flat.

Babe, a smiling, sprightly figure, opened the back door and held the cats at bay while Evie struggled in with a bag of groceries and the turkey. Neither woman used the front entrance, or the front stairs. Something about all that oily-smelling polished wood intimidated them, with their arms always full of laundry, or electrical supplies for Evie's tiny workshop under an eave, or Babe's sewing materials. Babe made or repaired much of their clothing.

"Such a big turkey," Babe said, laughing as she waited for Evie's annual joke.

"I'm no turkey," Evie said in that gruff affectionate voice. She set her purchases on the yellow Formica tabletop and turned to envelop Babe in a long hug punctuated by loud kisses. "Smells good in here already," she said after one last squeeze.

"Leftover casserole for supper. But I see I don't have to worry about menus for a while. You're planning on turkey soup, turkey casserole, turkey pot pie—turkey ice cream, maybe?"

Evie laughed in the center of their orange and yellow kitchen. The cats had left their dinners and circled for affection. Evie picked both up at once and hugged them, too. They leaped to the floor, indignant and disgruntled. She grew serious. "Theodore's taken off again. Freddy will come for Thanksgiving anyway."

"Stuffed or with an apple in his mouth?" Babe asked, winking. Then she, too, grew serious. "The poor guy. He'd better come to dinner. Tell him to be here by two. I won't have him ordering the blue plate special over at the diner all by himself because Theodore's put on his genius cap again."

Evie held her close, loving her for her warmth, her caring, her immediate reply.

Babe handed Evie a clean tablecloth and gave her a gentle push. "Set the table. This is ready to eat." She pulled the casserole from the oven.

The cooking smells were everywhere. Babe was preparing stuffing and homemade cranberry sauce. Evie could hear her singing along with a radio station that played Peggy Lee, Glenn Miller, Julie London, and imagined her sipping sweet Manischewitz wine and waltzing with the celery, with bags of cranberries, throughout the evening.

She went to her narrow workbench to finish rewiring her second-cousin Gertie's heirloom lamp, an ornate heavy thing the woman doted on. "When I'm retired," she told it, "I'll fix monsters like you full-time." She looked askance at it, trying to remember if she'd ever repaired an uglier lamp. Even if no one came into her shop because she was a woman doing the repairs, she'd have her pension to fall back on. On the other hand, how could she lose? Mr. Guadino was about to close up his repair business and move to Florida. She'd grown up in the neighborhood so people knew her, and he said he'd recommend her.

She'd miss working at the park—best job ever. But no more kids assaulting the souvenir booth she ran summers at the zoo, no more catching colds in winter going from the hothouse into the snow, no more dumb city politics. She'd look out a neat storefront with a big window. She'd watch everything that went on in the neighborhood, and wave to everyone. She'd be her own boss, and Babe said she'd be happy to do the books. Grateful customers would pour in, arms filled with lamps and radios and vacuum cleaners and fans.

She'd miss Freddy. As far as she knew, she'd never worked with another gay person. He made up for all the guilt-filled years she spent lying to bosses and coworkers, always worried about exposure and angry that she needed to be. Yet she'd miss the routine, the ease of familiar tasks. Miss being part of something big, belonging to a group.

Smiling, she pushed wire through the monster's base and remembered her pride when they began to let her repair rowboats with Freddy, even though she was a woman. The next year she wired the souvenir stand for a popcorn popper and hot dog machine. It was the proudest moment of her career when the City electrician checked it out and found no faults.

She stripped the end of a wire, thinking of Babe, of her yearning to travel. When they first talked of retiring, they started setting aside the difference between their wages and the amount of their anticipated pensions, and saved it up to use for travel. They'd both accumulated months of vacation time. California, Nova Scotia, the Grand Canyon. Evie was the only one in her family who'd never been out of state, but she was more eager to open Evie's Electric than to travel. Seeing the world remained Babe's dream.

In bed long before Babe finished her holiday preparations in the kitchen, she dreamed of dining on a cruise ship off some tropical coast and taking delight when they served Babe's luscious cranberry sauce and turkey stuffing.

At two a.m., she woke to the sound of Babe, wineglass in hand, passing through to the bathroom. She heard her brush her teeth, then saw her slip into the light blue silken nightgown she saved for special occasions. A pleasurable shudder moved down Evie's body as she watched Babe hurry to bed. This was her favorite part of their holiday eve tradition, begun way back when Babe cooked their first Thanksgiving dinner.

She gave a low wolf-whistle at Babe in the glow of the dim nightlight and lifted the covers to welcome her into the warm bed. The startled cats fled. She felt Babe's cool hands slip immediately under the waistband of her pajamas, felt her gentle fingers dig into the flesh around her waist.

What faraway place would Babe conjure tonight for their lovemaking? A few nights ago, it had been Spain, hot and brilliant white at siesta time. The week before, the ice palace they'd seen in *Dr. Zhivago*. Evie's favorite was the Vermont trip in late spring, either a daytime interlude naked among the wildflowers, or the image of a heavy quilt and a brick-warmed bed in the cool nights. Travel was Babe's passion in more ways than one; if they couldn't yet indulge in the real thing, they didn't do without. She pulled Babe to her and squeezed her bottom with both hands.

"You smell like Manischewitz," she whispered as she slid the blue nightgown up. "And stuffin'."

She felt Babe push her warm body against her, silently, eagerly, as if she didn't want to play tonight. Babe took Evie's hand and pressed it against herself. "That's right," she said.

❖

They rose late on Thanksgiving Day, stretching and cuddling under the blue and white quilt Evie had gotten in a trade with a sister-in-law for assembling some Tiffany-style lamp kits. Once up, Babe immediately started cooking, and Evie tuned in the parade on TV. She stood in the middle of the living room, laughing at the cartoon character floats in her flannel pajamas and long velour robe, then she marched into the bathroom to the music of an Oklahoma high school band.

By early afternoon everything that could be done was done, and Babe urged Evie to sit on the back porch with her.

The air felt light and cool after their warm kitchen. The porch was a narrow wooden planking that connected the stairs to their door, and they'd strung three chairs along it facing out over the rail. Their view was of a vacant lot, in spring filled with chicory and dandelions, but covered now with brown leaves that scraped as the November breeze disturbed them.

They looked knowingly at each other as Theodore's red Chevette pulled up to the curb. Theodore was driving.

"Who invited him?" asked Evie.

"One very happy boyfriend," Babe answered.

Freddy ran up the steps, bringing a rush of his lime scent. "Hi, girls," he said in his bashful way. "I hope you don't mind one more. Theodore's home."

They watched as Theodore slowly mounted the steps. He was very tall, very thin, and sported a white goatee, mustache, and slightly long white hair.

"I don't know how anyone can climb these steps with your dignity," said Babe in welcome. She rose to hug the men.

Freddy settled nimbly on the porch rail while Theodore slowly lowered himself to the third chair.

"Rough epic?" asked Evie. Babe frowned at her sarcasm and passed a bowl of walnuts, salt, and a nutcracker.

"Not an epic, but yes, very rough. My best poem ever." He had an air of heavy sincerity somewhat similar to Freddy's, but his was worldly-wise, not innocent. He wore a tweed jacket, gray wool slacks, a red sweater vest, smoked a pipe, and looked, Evie thought, a tinch too much like a poet was supposed to look. Still, he was back, and back in time to share the holiday with Freddy. In his favor, he took his poetry as seriously as she took her electrical work. And he was president of the poetry group that met in the big church basement downtown and held readings she and Babe dutifully attended.

"For me," added Freddy, his voice reverent. "The new poem is about me." He cracked a walnut and passed the meat to his lover.

Theodore nodded, accepting the offering, then filled his pipe. "About Fred and myself, our life together." He nodded again, this time toward Babe and Evie as he lit the pipe. "And about you and you, together."

"A love poem," Freddy bragged. "But not all dressed up with big words this time. And not about the olden days or long trips or foreign places." A quiet wonder came into his voice. "About growing old together and loving each other, whoever we are."

November clouds covered the sun, and the sound of the rustling leaves left on the trees made the wind seem colder. As Freddy slid off the rail, Evie goosed him. He squealed and ran past Theodore who stood aside, a gentleman always, as the others filed inside.

They gathered at the table, the fragrant feast before them. Theodore made much of each steaming dish, of the bright white tablecloth, the highly polished silverware, the design Babe had embroidered on the linen napkins. Babe told them to sit while she made still more preparations. "Are the pies in the oven to heat?" called Evie. Freddy concentrated on eating. He must have existed on canned chili while Theodore was away.

"But why do you have to go away to write your poetry?" Evie asked.

"It won't come at home. I've tried. I've taken days off, staying home when Fred's at work, but end up doing this kind of thing." He indicated the food. "Cooking great banquets for two. Or cleaning. Or rearranging the living room."

Freddy heaped mashed potatoes on his plate. The scent of heating pies began to vie with the smells of the meal.

"And it's not as if I travel to the Riviera," Theodore continued. His weary somberness began to fade, as if he'd wrapped himself in it to protect himself from their disfavor. "I find the tackiest motel around," he went on, "and live in the midst of other people's squalor and drunkenness. I sleep—if I sleep—on overwashed sheets and lumpy mattresses, feed myself out of grocery bags and an electric pot I carry in my car. I'm like the traveling salesman in the next room, a man required by his work to displace himself, to move through worlds not his own in order to accomplish what he's meant to do."

Sometimes Evie thought Theodore talked because he liked to listen to himself.

Then he winked. "Except, of course, for the company those salesmen keep. Any rough trade will do for them."

"But," Evie said, ignoring his attempt at levity and lifting the cider jug as each glass was passed to her for filling, "don't you know how miserable Freddy is?"

Freddy looked up, a startled expression replacing his passionate chewing. He'd put on a white shirt and tie for the occasion, and his cheeks were red, as if from shaving extra close. He gazed at Theodore and explained, "I'm only miserable that he might not come home, not that he goes away."

Babe had finally stopped running back and forth between the kitchen and the holiday table. She undid her apron and bowed her head over the plate Evie had filled for her.

"Listen, Ev," Freddy said, wiping his mouth. "You know those sparrows we have in the park?"

Evie nodded, closing her mouth on sweet buttered squash.

"How I feel about Theodore going away is like one of those sparrows." He held his large hand over the table, palm up. "It hops on, see?" The three others watched. "And as long as I keep my hand open, like this"—he held it flat—"it stays. That's love, that sparrow on my palm. But if I do this"—he closed his fingers around the imaginary bird and made as if to squeeze it—"if I hold it too tight, it'll die." Freddy looked across the table at his formal, fastidious lover. "After all these years I know I can't make you come back or tell you what to do when you go. I can only keep this hand open and be thankful when the bird returns."

Evie watched Babe close her eyes at the taste of her homemade cranberry relish and slowly realized that her retirement dilemma might not be that different from Theodore's need for a separate place.

Like Christmas cactuses, everyone bloomed better in her or his own hothouse. Who could say when she'd best blossom?

Babe wanted to travel—but was it the wrong season for Evie? And Babe somehow had known that if she pushed her desire on Evie, whose own personal hothouse was her planned electrical shop, she might well squeeze the life from her.

By running off on his odysseys, by playing poet in grungy motels, by doing what he, not Freddy, wanted, was Theodore being selfish? She herself wasn't a selfish woman—was she?

She watched Theodore pat his mustache with a napkin, elegant even as he ate, and she looked at Freddy, who, twenty minutes into the meal, still devoured potatoes like a starving adolescent. She rose to pour cider all around again, silent as Theodore told traveling salesman stories.

No, she decided. How could it be selfish for Theodore to be himself, to act like the man Freddy loved? He always did come back, didn't he? He always did run off with a poem, not a twink. That fear was Freddy's, and it didn't look as if it had ever had anything to do with Theodore at all. Asking Theodore not to write poems at Thanksgiving, or any other time, was like asking Christmas cactuses to bloom by name, not by nature.

Unexpected tears came to her eyes. She tasted the cider, wondering if it had hardened after a week on the porch. But then she realized her tears were of gratitude, for a lover who, like Freddy, cherished their love too much to try to change her. Who'd never pointed out that Evie's insistence on her dream clashed with her own. Who was willing to read about faraway places she might never see. If choosing to retire and therefore lose her part of their travel savings was selfish…

She ate, talked, joked, and all the while thought through her dilemma. Could she tempt Mr. Guadino to stay with the repair business a few more years? Having made her decision to retire, immediate retirement seemed less pressing. What about those compromises Babe had suggested? Leaving work at fifty-eight. Or at sixty. She'd have a bigger pension, too, in case those customers trickled, rather than poured, in.

At last, Freddy sat back, patting his stomach. They rose and, in playful procession, cleared the table. The cats were in the kitchen, helping themselves to everything on the counter. Freddy groaned and held his stomach as he beheld the steaming pies.

Evie folded her arms and looked sternly at him. "You don't have to eat our mince pie, Freddy. Or my fresh apple pie with cheddar cheese melted on top," she said.

A look of shock came to Freddy's face. "Are you kidding? What kind of Thanksgiving would that be, showing no gratitude to friends who can make a dessert smell like paradise? And to one who can keep a city park running single-handed if she has to."

He looked down at the oversized slab of pie she handed him. "You're not going to retire and leave me there alone for fifteen years, are you?"

"Ten," she reminded him. Then, without another thought, she said, "No."

She looked at Babe, who had paused, fork in midair. "No, I want it all. There'll be time to open my shop if we start seeing the world right away, on long vacations." She'd always refused to take much time off, afraid things would get out of hand if she wasn't around. "Why wait? Freddy knows my job well enough to cover. I don't want to sit up here looking out at the seasons going by, wondering what they'd look like in the Petrified Forest, or Ireland. I want more than dreams," she said. "I want memories."

Babe's mouth across the table wavered so much that Evie didn't know if she would laugh or cry. Like last night, in the dark, Babe said, "That's right."

Thanksgiving Day. She looked at Babe, Freddy, Theodore, and out the window at the transformed leaves, each readying for its flight.

"Thank you," Evie said in a whisper, to no one, to everyone, the word blooming, like the park's Christmas cactuses, in any season.

Originally published in *Home in Your Hands* (Naiad Press, 1986)

BABE AND EVIE: SUNSHINE

Sun shone through the slats of the venetian blinds. Babe crossed the living room and ran her hands down their smooth surfaces, trying to shut the sun out more. But the lines of light only shifted slightly on the orange rug. There was no keeping the heat out this summer. Any more than there was any keeping Evie in.

Babe sighed. There wasn't much she could do. After their years together, if Evie had something to go through, and she suspected a post-retirement depression, she'd wait it out. And keep her mind occupied as best she could. At least Evie hadn't moved out. As much as Babe loved this third-floor flat at the top of a steep staircase out back, two dark and polished dress-up flights through the front of the house, she couldn't live there without Evie. Even though Evie acted as if she was only staying because she had nowhere else to go. Even if Evie had taken to sleeping on the couch.

She touched her newly permed and rinsed hair. She'd known Evie wouldn't notice and had done it for herself, partly from habit, partly from certainty she would feel better. She did.

And she was circling, she knew that, circling and circling. Fifty-eight years old. Another Saturday night coming on fast. All dressed up with no place to go and no one to go with. Evie, recently retired from thirty years on her city job, had virtually disappeared from her life when she should have had even more time for Babe. What did they used to tell one another, misty-eyed with happiness at the kitchen table on a hot summer's afternoon like this, droplets of moisture running down the red and yellow flower decals on their pretty glass pitcher—we ain't got much, but we got plenty.

She could circle no longer. She crossed the room and this time ran her fingers lovingly over the digital piano's keyboard. It had been sitting there since Christmas. She'd longed for one for years and years.

She walked to their flowered couch and sat gracelessly, as if her legs had lost the will to hold her up, as if she'd finally let go of the will she'd tightly clung to these two hard, hard months. At the office, she'd asked for extra work to keep herself typing at the other keyboard in her life. At the grocery store, she agonized over quantities of Evie's favorite foods, because she didn't know if she'd come home for dinner. In bed at night, she'd turn to slip an arm across the absent Evie, burrowing closer and closer to no one.

The upright piano, sedate, solid, stared back at her. She'd sold her piano when she left her parents' home to live with Evie. Before Evie got the city job that eventually paid decently, they'd needed to buy furniture—like this couch they'd reupholstered twice since, each time in the bright flowered patterns they agreed on, but Evie only wanted to please her.

Christmas Day she'd played the piano gingerly, reverently, afraid to smite the air with her neglected chords. It was too real, this making of music. She hadn't dared play as she longed to, really play from the heart, play loud and lovely like the lovemaking she'd shared with Evie. Even at Christmas time, a month before Evie's retirement, she'd felt as if she had to walk on eggs. Evie flared at the slightest thing. Went silent for hours at a time.

After Evie left her job, Babe played only when she was certain to be alone, and then as quietly, tentatively as she could—the way she felt. In the house Evie was moody and puttered whole days in the spare room she'd converted to an electrical workshop years ago. It was a disappointment that she didn't putter seriously, like she'd planned. Evie had been going to rent a storefront up on the Avenue cheap, from her brother's boss's friend. But she hadn't done any of it. Who knew when Evie would be home now, darn her. Who knew what she'd do now, Babe thought a little desperately, but at the same time rising, going to the piano, switching it on.

She played a chord and felt its vibration like a delightful shiver down her back in this small hot room, glowing with indomitable sunlight and color. She played the same chord, louder, then louder still, and as she began to play melodies it was the colors she sought, even in the simplest strains of classic songs—"Side by Side," "You Are My Sunshine," "On the Sunny Side of the Street."

How they'd sung, over the years, rowing up at the lake on

Fourth of July picnics with Evie's family. Riding with a busload of city employees and their families to a boat tour around Manhattan. Or walking, just walking the neighborhood at twilight and quietly singing together, letting their love rise on sweet melodies into the air, into the world that wouldn't accept or acknowledge that love, but let lovers sing.

She paused for a moment, heard a step, then another, on those funny steep back stairs so typical of their flat, so typically, oddly like them, different yet exactly right for what and for who they were. Of course, it was Evie, come home to idly putter, to stare at the TV, to ignore her. Well darn it, she'd got her hair fixed for herself, and she was going to play for herself, the heck with sourpuss Evie.

And she played. Some of the familiar songs, some new ones in the song book that came with the piano, by the Beatles and by Elton John. In her mind she had them stomping, had the world dancing and clapping to her beat, swaying to this rhythm of love, of feeling, of daring to enjoy no matter what her fears.

A breeze pushed the venetian blind in. She could see a corner of that long iron handrail and realized Evie had stayed outside the door. She craned to see. There she was, sitting out there all this time, listening. Was she waiting till Babe was done, till everything was over so she could steal inside and hide?

She played on, choosing a favorite sad song called "Melancholy Baby." Then she stopped. She'd had her hour. The sun had shifted, and the room darkened.

Into the silence came the sound of applause, strong and loud on those back stairs. Evie opened the door and stood there grinning shyly in a way Babe hadn't seen in so long, and clapping up a storm.

"I didn't know you were still that good," Evie said.

Babe tried not to smile too hard but knew her face had gone bright with flowers of pleasure and embarrassment.

Evie stepped into the dimness, her hands still. She looked at Babe, then slipped her hands into her pockets, and shuffled off to the kitchen.

Babe held her breath. She rose, her back to the piano, eyes fastened to the flowers on the couch, hoping without words. Just hoping.

"Hey, Babe," she heard Evie call from the kitchen. She heard, too, the sound of ice cubes swirling in circles against glass, that summer sound of happy afternoons. And she heard whistling. Evie was whistling "You Are My Sunshine," slowly, as if pulling it back into the light of day was painful.

By the time she reached the kitchen she knew what she'd see, and there Evie stood, stirring ice into fresh-made frozen lemonade, in the glass pitcher with red and yellow flowers.

"I was thinking about going out for a pizza pie tonight," Evie was saying. "It's kind of hot to cook. You want to go out for a pie with me?" She motioned Babe to the table. "Have some lemonade," she said, sitting in her chair.

Slowly, Babe walked to her own chair. It was the kitchen the sun had shifted to, and the sun lit its colors till they glowed bright as the living room.

"I don't know," Evie said. "Maybe I retired too early. Maybe I should go back part-time."

"Thank you," she said as Evie handed her a glass of lemonade, ice cubes cracking in the heat. She'd guessed right: Evie missed her job.

She was trying to respond to Evie without letting her voice sound as teary as her eyes. But all she could see was a picture in her mind of the two of them, glowing like their kitchen, singing their way down their funny back stairs, going out to dinner. She couldn't wait.

Originally published in *Home in Your Hands* (Naiad Press, 1986)

TRUCK STOP WOMAN

For Jodi Stutz, Writer, 1958–1987

Jody'd been driving trailer trucks most of her life. Ever since she was a kid starting out, she thought of herself as the Lone Ranger and called her trucks Silver. Her hot cab smelled of grease and rubber and the nutty home-cooked banana bread MayElla would send with her. The hours got long on the macadam range, so she recited old English ballads over the vibrations and shifting gears. Right now, at home, a favorite ballad rang through her head.

> *Thus in my sumptuous man's array*
> *I bravely rode along the way...*

The songs kept her company on the road, and MayElla had kept her company at home. She'd never minded the lonesomeness of trucking before.

She was tickled that the men on the road never bothered her, despite a certain cavalier style of hers and her striking violet eyes. For all her chattering and balladeering at home with MayElla, she hadn't much to say in the rough independent world of the truckers. Besides, she'd been around forever, and a person who's around forever, even if she originally stuck out like a sore thumb, becomes invisible. If men were her only choice, she'd stay lonesome.

That's how she believed she came across at the truck stops: invisible. She'd walk along a baking hot parking lot, ignoring the men, and enter the noisy restaurant. The cold of the air-conditioning was almost skin-searing. Once the waitresses figured out she was female, they frosted over, too. She knew it was because she scared them, in her GMC cap and her work clothes, but it hurt anyway. It shouldn't have mattered: she had no desire to talk to women who acted like they enjoyed the ogling, the pinches, the bawdy jokes of the truckers. Over the years she often left the turnpikes for meals, though it meant more distance and less pay. MayElla didn't mind. She said she would do the same thing.

MayElla was attractive to men with her curvy top and her curvy sides, her spring-flower perfume, and the way she put one hand on a hip and kind of threw back her hair, then looked you straight in the eye. Jody could hear her flat nasal Nebraska vowels, saying if it was her, she would have had her fill of being stared at and propositioned without going to some lowlife place it was bound to happen, like a truck stop.

So when Jody decided she couldn't keep her eyes open any longer, she headed for the secondary roads and found greasy spoons. Seldom the same one twice, though. And she never stayed in a motel. If someone with evil on his mind saw a truck by the side of the road, he was likely to believe there was another man inside. If he saw it was a lady driver registered for a room out in the middle of nowhere, with nobody around but a lot of screechy crickets, well, Jody didn't believe in asking for trouble. Let them go to the truck-stop girls who earned their living that way. They were more lowlife than the waitresses.

For twenty-five years, so far, she earned her living hauling freight for Standard Wheeling and was proud of it. MayElla cooked her a special dinner to celebrate that anniversary. It was only a week ago, that turkey dinner. Before they knew about MayElla's heart problem. And now MayElla was dead and buried. Dead and buried, Jody repeated to herself, trying to make it real.

Jody never thought about this happening. They were only fifty-four and were together since they were kids living across the hall from each other right here in Omaha. They liked being together from the day Jody moved in. Both of their families had slipped down from their comfortable livings before the Depression to wartime factory work. Despite that, their parents, Jody, and MayElla had no use for the slummy kids who were their neighbors, or for the games they played: King of the Mountain, which MayElla found too rough, or Hide and Seek, which Jody hated because she was terrified no one would ever find her. MayElla was good at thinking up other games anyway.

Library was one. MayElla loved to be the librarian. There was a dark back hall, which they agreed was lit like the public library and smelled like it, too, a mite dusty, a mite mildewy, a mite mysterious. The stairs back there, which no one used, were the shelves. MayElla would set the books up. Jody contributed her stash of comics, which MayElla called an Illustrated Encyclopedia and her father's newspapers, which she refreshed weekly. A few children's books lined the next shelf down, then came the *Reader's Digest* and *Good Housekeeping* magazines that people threw out. On the very bottom shelf were four books belonging to MayElla's parents, a Bible and three volumes about World War I.

That wasn't everything on the bottom shelf. Each year MayElla won the poetry recital contest in school, and her prize was a book. One time it was Emily Dickinson, another Longfellow. Jody occasionally checked one of these out, mostly because MayElla was so proud of them.

The year MayElla won the book of English ballads, though, Jody renewed it every week. Those ballads caught her and pulled her in. She read them time after time and memorized some, so she always had them with her. It felt like they matched her own inside rhythm and she found herself walking to school with their beat in her head.

> *O waly, waly, up the bank,*
> *And waly, waly, doun the brae,*
> *And waly, waly, yon burn-side,*
> *Where I and my love wont to gae!*

There were other games, games none of the shouting, shoving children played. Like the Roosevelts—Jody was Teddy; MayElla, Eleanor—who traveled the world together, leaving the boring task of government to Franklin D. It was as if in childhood the two of them were marked to prepare differently for the different life they would live; were given dreams they would share with no one but each other. They were careful, even then, not to reveal their world to anyone who would sully it.

MayElla prepared well for the life she wanted. She went to library school, supporting herself as a gal Friday. Though she hated working with the common girls at Standard Wheeling, the trucking company she worked at before graduation, she made the most of it.

None of the choices schooling offered suited Jody, and she refused to spend her life cornhusking. She took a job after high school delivering messages on a three-wheeled motorbike, but wished she could see some of the country. MayElla bragged to her boss at Standard

Wheeling about Jody's perfect driving record and convinced him to take a chance on her. She'd been on the road ever since.

One of those small gray birds that MayElla fed was on the window sill, up like her at the crack of dawn. Jody rose, a stiffness in her back from the years of driving. She'd planned to take a couple of minced ham sandwiches on the road, but the potato yeast buns in the bread box went moldy, so she broke them up for the birds. What in heck would they do with her away on the road and no MayElla to overfeed them? Never mind the birds, what in heck was she going to do without the games, without the poems. How could those birds sing now? How could she?

> *And then my love built me a bower,*
> *Bedeck'd with many a fragrant flower;*
> *A braver bower you ne'er did see*
> *Than my true love did build for me.*

Well, there was a load to pick up. The freezer still held five of MayElla's runzas and she wrapped two in aluminum foil. She locked the door, and for the first time in a week went out to the tractor, zipping up her company jacket. She pulled herself into the seat of the cab, glad for something to do. Glad Silver hadn't changed.

But he had. He still smelled of rubber and grease, but the fresh-baked banana bread? For a minute she couldn't see through the mist of tears across her eyes. Everything really was the same, except for what MayElla touched. And MayElla touched everything.

She started the truck without thinking. Its vibrations, its low roar, were comforting. They reminded her that she was a driver. That hadn't changed. She heaved a sigh. She hadn't cried yet, and she wasn't about to cry now. In the first place, it was hard to drive if your eyes burned with salty tears. In the second place, what if somebody along the way saw her, a truck driver, crying. Third, if she let loose once, everything would change. Like MayElla being away was just part of how different things would be. She was afraid she might let Silver run off the road, aimed for a bank of trees or a concrete wall or a cliff. Anything so she could be with MayElla again.

She squared her shoulders, put the truck in gear, and went over to Standard Wheeling. She hitched up her trailer, full of something, it didn't matter what, so she could buy bread for MayElla's birds. Sooner or later, she needed to start eating again, too. They gave her papers, and she saw she was going to Oklahoma with pallets of dog food. Dog food, of all things, to keep her going through life. Well, it paid the bills.

She hit the highway, window rolled up to keep out the early morning chill. The miles of Interstate 29, then 35, felt as familiar as home. Sometimes she thought half the reason she took to the road was to return home. To crawl under the covers and listen to MayElla in the dark, or to recite ballads till MayElla, still excited that Jody had come to love words, too, reached for her and quieted her with warm lips that told poems silently to Jody's mouth.

O waly, waly, gin love be bonie
A little time while it is new!

Jody passed through the suburbs of Omaha, trying not to think about home. They liked the city okay, but they'd bought the Ford to allow themselves more freedom. MayElla was born with a yen for greenery, so when the Homestead Garden Apartments were built on farmland outside of town, they rented a one bedroom brand new, and that's where MayElla died eighteen years later.

MayElla loved to plant flowers outside their place on a spring weekend. She'd ask Jody to go out and turn the soil before the baseball games started on TV. The baseball games that bored MayElla. But it worked out fine, especially in the summers. MayElla, letting the back screen door make that summer *thwomp* sound behind her, took her books to read in the scent of new-mowed lawn. She admired the flowers she'd planted, passed the time of day with the neighbors, stared out at the horizon, making up poems in her head.

It was the same with the neighbors as it was at the truck stops. They didn't see Jody. Oh, the men might tip their hats, eyes to the ground, the women nod with automatic smiles, but no one stopped to talk as they did with MayElla. She was pretty sure they, like the waitresses, didn't want to see her. It didn't matter, the times the waitresses acted snippy and walked away, but she knew it hurt MayElla that the neighbors worked at pretending she wasn't there—that one living with pretty Miss Bowen.

She passed out of Nebraska and into Kansas. The steering wheel was a comfort—warm and solid in her hands, the sound of the shifting gears like friends greeting her. The sun grew brighter and brighter; in fall it stayed strong. She wasn't looking forward to spring this year, with MayElla's perennials shooting up like elegies in color.

It wasn't that everything went smoothly the whole time. There were spats. One or the other might grump around the house for hours, sure she was in the right. Now and then they faced away from each other in bed at night, unable to untangle some mess they talked themselves into. It didn't take a whole lot to get unsnarled, though. Jody would bring home a batch of flowers. MayElla would apologize by lying beside her in the dark, telling a new poem. It always melted Jody's heart.

What was she going to do now? Who would hold her, listen to her, help her through this? They never wanted, needed anyone but each other. Their families thought that they were nothing more than best friends. It would make it easier if she could show how bad she felt, but show her straitlaced mother, her deacon father?

O mother, mother, make my bed,
O make it soft and narrow;
Since my love died for me today,
I'll die for him tomorrow.

The rhythm soothed her most of the way to Oklahoma City.

The dispatcher gave her a choice: either turn around in Oklahoma or go out to California. There were loads either way. "It's warm in California," the dispatcher said. Jody could tell none of the other drivers wanted to go as far as the West Coast. She joked with him, letting him know she heard what he was up to, making him think she was doing him a favor. She was sure before he asked that she didn't want to come back to Nebraska for a while. Couldn't. Not till she ended this inside churning she was going through, not till she found a way of not hurting so badly without a break.

Another old-time driver nodded hello to her at the depot in Oklahoma City. He was headed home. Home to a wife probably. Not many people lost a mate this young.

It was as if she and MayElla were married, and married people had their wakes and everyone's sympathy and the head car in the procession. Jody was—well, at least she was seated in the second row at the church, but MayElla's family acted as if she was supposed to give them consolation, not the other way around. She waited till the funeral was over before she went to the cemetery.

Then she stared through the rain down at the coffin, into that damned hole in the earth, not feeling one bit connected to what was inside. She stared and waited for something to happen. All that happened was the machine came to cover the coffin, and she walked carefully away on the muddy grass, in her family occasion dress-up shoes, back to the Ford, Ford number three.

Ever since, she was twisted up inside and couldn't unknot herself, like she used to feel during a spat. No one was claiming to be right or wrong this time, though. No one was coming to bed that night with a poem to make it better. And the flowers she made sure were at the funeral wouldn't make a bit of difference sitting up on top of a mound of earth. She would at least have liked to turn over the soil, like she did so many times for MayElla's plants.

And then my love built me a bower
Bedeck'd with many a fragrant flower...

She started driving out of Oklahoma with dark coming on, grateful the company was anxious to move this new load to California because she was full again in no time. She drove straight into the middle of the night, to Texas, before her eyes wanted to close. She'd been hallucinating figures out on the road for an hour.

She was reluctant to leave the straight line of the highway tonight; it was the only thing in her life that wasn't strange. At an enormous truck stop she pulled in next to a line of rigs. There was a motel, a restaurant, a truck store, showers, a Laundromat. The neon signs, the red and gold lights outlining some of the idling trucks, the fluorescent bars of light flooding the pump area, gave the flat cement world a partying look, like a carnival was setting up smack dab in the middle of the Panhandle.

Here and there she saw a truck stop girl accost a driver. Why didn't these women do something clean and useful, like drive a truck or work in a library? Sometimes the momentary couple would disappear into a room, sometimes into a truck.

The quick and the dead, Jody thought, remembering the phrase from some poem MayElla recited. She wondered what life was like for these truck stop girls. At least they were quick, not dead, she thought with a bitter anger.

She stretched and yawned, but that small pleasure only unleashed her pain. She leaned her head against the hard narrow steering wheel.

How could she feel good now that there MayElla was, in that box, as if she was playing one last game. She hit the steering wheel with a fist. MayElla had promised never to leave her out.

Jody swung open the door of the truck and stepped down with a groan, her back aching from the drive, her anger tying the knot inside tighter. She gulped the cold night air, relishing the familiar smells of fuel and oil and a lone cigarette somewhere on the lot. Though food was a waste, the runzas were long gone, and she knew she'd never make the rest of the trip without something. She strode toward the restaurant.

"Nice evening, mister," she heard a voice coo from the shadow of another truck. A lady's voice.

She scowled toward the voice and said, "Howdy," as gruffly as she could. It was one of the truck stop girls.

"Whoops," said the girl. "I thought you were a guy."

It had happened before.

"Sorry," the girl called to her back.

Jody crunched along the gravel toward the restaurant. She wondered what it was like for the men, these anonymous contacts in flat parking lots. Was it for the sex alone? It was disgusting, she thought, but maybe some of them were widowers, or never found someone to come home to. Maybe sometimes they only needed to be held.

The girls, though, why did they do this? She pictured the slummy neighbor kids of forty-five years ago. Did some of those girls later lurk alongside trucks or in Omaha doorways, selling themselves? For the first time Jody felt a kind of link with the girls she and MayElla refused to play with. They were in their fifties, too. What happened to them? Were their lives over like hers? What did it matter in the end if you wrote poetry or whispered *Hey, mister* at strangers?

Inside the restaurant there were enough diners to keep two waitresses busy. The air-conditioning was on unduly high. The cigarette smoke smelled stale. She moved a dirty ashtray aside and stared at the jukebox on the counter, as if she hadn't seen one in years. She liked to play a song or two while she ate, to hear the poetry, or to take a rhythm with her on the road. Dinner was her usual mashed potatoes, stringy pot roast, peas and carrots with a wilted salad in a small heavy side dish. The dinner roll was cold, but the coffee was scalding hot and helped her wash it down. Only one thing was different. The waitress was friendly.

"Where you from, sister?" asked the sharp-faced woman with a weary warm smile.

Jody was afraid that she would break down then and there.

"Long ways from home, aren't you?" commented the waitress a while later, warming her coffee. She looked, under the cosmetics, to be about Jody's age.

Jody tried to mumble an answer to this, too, but the only words that wanted to come out were *I love you*, and at her silence the waitress shrugged and turned away. Now, why would she want to say that to the waitress, to anybody, with MayElla dead? Her eyes filled with tears. She stood but was dizzy. Maybe she was the one who was different.

"You okay, kiddo?" asked that same waitress.

What must she look like to the woman: stooped, gray-haired, staggering like a drunk?

"Tired is all," answered Jody, straightening. She didn't need the concern of some all-night waitress with makeup plastered on her face.

The chilled fresh air was so clear it kissed her awake. The wide-open spaces of the Panhandle touched directly in her soul. She felt small and mean for thinking poorly of the waitress. On the highway, trucks roared by, restless, pushing west or east. She stood off to the side of the restaurant watching the stars blink. Could MayElla be something like a star now, up there, gazing down and loving her, wishing her well?

How could she be well, Jody asked the stars, feeling a new flash of anger. Could she play games by herself? How about, *Pretend Someone's Home, Waiting*. There was nothing back there. MayElla's family took everything away with them, including the poetry MayElla so carefully wrote out by hand. That poetry wasn't for them. It wouldn't keep them alive. "Tell me what to do now," she whispered faintly through her trapped tears, to the prettiest star.

> *Marti'mas wind, when wilt thou blaw,*
> *And shake the green leaves aff the tree?*
> *O gentle death, when wilt thou come?*
> *For of my life I am wearie.*

The anger drove her back toward her rig. Maybe dinner hadn't been a good idea. Maybe she ought to drive on now and let Silver take her over a cliff.

"Hey, mister—oh, it's you again."

Jody stopped and took in the woman this time. She was on the tall side, sturdily built, stuffed into tight fashion jeans, ruffled Western blouse, and wine-colored short vinyl jacket. In the shadow of the trucks, she saw how the woman's tiredness had worn lines in her face, as if she lived her troubles, too.

"What're you looking at? Didn't you ever see a lady of the night before?"

Jody felt herself flush. "It's because—" How could she say it, what she felt inside? The air out here, the way she felt touched by something as big as, bigger than these western spaces. She began to tremble. Here was a woman, flesh and blood like her. For rent, maybe, but warm and alive. She shivered, pulled her Standard Wheeling jacket closed and zipped it up. That pretty star caught her eye.

What if she did play a game tonight. This once. What if she pretended that star was MayElla, and this woman the friend MayElla thought she ought to have to listen to her, to give her the sympathy MayElla's folks, the neighbors, no one else gave her. Maybe to hold her? No, she thought.

When cockle-shells turn silver bells,
And mussells grow on every tree,
When frost and snow turns fire to burn,
Then I'll sit down and dine wi' thee.

Well, maybe the cockle shells were turning to silver bells, thought Jody, taking a deep breath. And maybe it was about time.

"Listen," she said to the woman. Awkwardly she grabbed her trucker's wallet on the chain she wore clipped to a belt loop. With some bills in her shaking hand she said, "My name is Jody. My lady passed on last week. Can you…" She offered the bill, seeing the woman wavery through the tears that would not wait another minute. "Can you spend a short while with me? Not to…" The woman looked startled. Jody thought she was going to back off. Could she gun the truck out of here in time to outrun the cops? To outrun her humiliation?

But the woman was saying, "You poor thing. Haven't you got anybody else in the whole world?"

Jody's ears roared with tears which sounded like the trucks going by. "No," she admitted hoarsely.

The woman took the money. "Come on with me, Jody. I have a room over in the motel. I want you to tell me all about it. My name's Michelle."

Michelle's words were as simple as a ballad. Her eyes, when a truck rolled in behind Jody, shone like a star's. As she let the tears fall,

Jody thought there might even be a smidgeon of MayElla in those eyes. MayElla in a truck stop woman. Who would have guessed?

The dry Panhandle wind sang across the parking lot like an early English rhyme. She followed Michelle.

Originally published in *Cactus Love* (Naiad Press, 1994)

INEZ

When Inez walked down from the hills through town at night, it was as if the streets rumbled under her feet. Big-boned, hefty, and solid, she felt wholly alive, hardy and powerful. If she could hold a tune, she'd bellow out a song with all twenty-eight years of life in her.

The fog had been thin in the hills, but close to the river it filled the streets. There were no lampposts in this part of town, only occasional warehouse side door floodlights. She rumbled on, sucking the damp night air into her lungs as if it nourished her.

When she opened the door of the bar, the blast of heat and music were almost enough to knock her backward onto the street. The bouncer, a man even taller than she was, irritably motioned for her to pull the door shut. She exhaled all that night air, all that confidence, and dug in her pocket for the two dollar cover. He wrapped her money around a roll of bills. Saturday night at the River's Edge Tavern they packed them in.

Inez looked for a seat. There was one table empty, jutting onto the dance floor. She took it and, feeling more and more like a swollen sore thumb, sat for twenty-five minutes before the waitress brought her a Coke. That was a relief, to have something to do with her hands and with her eyes. She didn't smoke, and she was embarrassed to stare at the dancers, or at the sitters who were staring at the dancers and at one another.

Once inside the Edge, every week, she wanted nothing more than to get out, to be back on the streets, filling up to her full size, yet invisible in the night. She'd tried leaving and then returning, but the bouncer charged her every time. She didn't have money to waste—she was an assistant cook at the mental hospital. Whenever a cook quit, she thought she'd get the promotion, but they always hired a man over her.

She watched the bubbles in her soda. She sipped. The crowd played the Chiffons, the Chantels, the Capris, and some of the mushy hits she loved. When "Moon River" came on she longed to dance in some woman's arms, but when "Lollipops and Roses" played, she wanted to cry.

It was this big body of hers that was the problem. She'd always liked her strong arms and legs. The shadow of a mustache that had been getting more obvious since her late teens ran in her family. She was an inch short of six feet, and her mom and dad bragged of her strength and robustness. But who'd bring the likes of her lollipops and roses?

She peeked at the dancers. Now that one gave her the shivers. They called her Kookie after the TV character because she was always combing her hair exactly as he did. She drifted into a daydream: Kookie asks her to dance to "Moon River." Kookie suddenly grows almost a foot as she leads the way to the floor. Inez lays her cheek on Kookie's shoulder. "You're so easy to lead," Kookie tells her after hours of dancing. Outside, Kookie opens the door to her midnight-blue Mercury Monterey and protectively closes Inez in. Like magic, they're in Kookie's wide soft bed, and Inez is being undressed. She lies back, an adored, trusting kitten, while Kookie caresses her everywhere.

"Hey," Kookie shouted at her over the din of the bar. "We're going to do a stroll line here. You want to move this table back?"

"Okey-doke," Inez said, lifting the table with its heavy metal stand and moving it one-handed.

"She's strong," said Kookie's girl.

"She's a moose," said Kookie, too loudly.

Inez scuttled behind her table, trying to hide the red of her face. I've got to get out of here, she thought, but felt too conspicuous to leave. If she left, where else could she hope to meet a woman to love?

"You should've punched her out," said a small voice from the table newly beside her.

She whipped around and glared toward the voice.

"Don't look at me that way. I didn't call you any names."

Inez lowered her eyes. "Sorry," she said, her throat clogged with tears.

"I mean it. Why don't you go put her lights out?"

"Yeah," said a stunningly handsome gay man beside the woman. "I'd do it for you, but I might ruin my nylon."

She looked down at his crossed legs and saw that under his khakis he really was in stockings. He twisted his calf to show her the black seam.

She grinned despite herself. "I wish I could wear those," she said, hearing how incongruous such a desire sounded in her bass voice.

"Do it, sweetie. It's a gas."

"They'd look goofy on me," she told him. The spunky woman was viciously stripping the label from her beer bottle, frowning. She was pretty, Inez thought, with tiny bones and baby-fine hair almost to her shoulders, dimples, and freckles.

The stroll line was long, each couple self-consciously taking a moment in the spotlight. Some giggled, some were intensely cool. Kookie combed her hair all the way down the line. Her girl, in tight black skirt and spit curls, watched Kookie dotingly.

"How come you two aren't dancing?" she asked the pretty woman and the handsome man, to make conversation. The woman's scowl came up like a cop's nightstick in a raid. She used her head to gesture behind the boy. Inez winced when she saw that he was sitting in a wheelchair. The table hid its arms. "Sorry," she said. "I'm so used to them at work I never even noticed. Did you have polio or what?"

He picked up his left pant leg and showed her the brace. "That's why I dress the other one up. Cinderella and her ugly stepsister. My name's Walter. This is Cherensky. She hates her first name."

"Don't you dare," warned Cherensky in her high-pitched voice.

"I think it's you, Daisy. I don't know why you hate it so."

The stroll ended and a fast song came on. "I won't mind if you two dance," Walter said.

Cherensky used her severely clipped fingernails to scrape the bottle bare. Inez sighed. Another matchmaker, pairing her with a woman she was supposed to squire around. She wanted to bolt to the street but couldn't be that rude. The waitress came by. Daisy Cherensky bought them all a round of drinks. They talked over the music. Walter was a secretary in a state office.

"I work in a nursery," Cherensky said quickly, as if afraid Walter would talk for her again.

"I love babies," Inez shared. "Did you have to go to school for that?"

Cherensky screwed up her long-lashed blue eyes in a look of disgust. "Not babies. Trees, shrubs, birdbaths. That stuff."

"But that's heavy work," Inez protested. "I did it all through high school."

Cherensky shrugged off her jacket and stuck out a skinny arm. She clenched her fist and said, "Feel that."

"The girl's got muscles on her toenails," confirmed Walter.

Inez laughed as she squeezed the bit of bicep brawn. "I never would have guessed. How'd you get so strong?"

"Wheeling him around, for one."

"We've been best friends since high school," Walter explained. "She had to build herself up if she wanted to go anywhere with me." He leaned forward and whispered, "But I didn't know I was creating a monster."

Daisy Cherensky slugged him in the arm.

"Ow—I'm ruined for life," said Walter. "Would you believe Cherensky thinks she's butch? That's why I bring her down here, to learn to act like a lady."

Inez expected the woman to hit Walter again but saw her go red around her freckles.

"Drag her around the floor a few times, Inez, so she knows what she's missing."

"I'm not much of a dancer," Inez said. What good would it do to admit that she followed beautifully—they'd told her so back in gym class.

"I can ask for myself if I want to, Walter," Cherensky snapped.

There was another silence at the table. Inez wished some nice boy would approach Walter. He was so good-looking and funny, why would anyone mind his chair? Dancers packed the floor and the noise was raging.

"What?" she asked when she realized that Cherensky was talking to her.

"DO YOU WANT TO DANCE?" screamed Cherensky.

She tried not to stare in shock at this slight woman. Out of politeness she stopped herself from refusing.

"The Twist" was playing. Cherensky jostled a path for them onto the floor. Inez had learned the dance over at her parents' house from her brother's six-year-old kid. She did feel like a moose doing the twist above Cherensky, but the woman had a good sense of rhythm and didn't pay any attention to what Inez was doing. Inez caught Walter lifting his hands over his head like a champion athlete.

When the music ended, Inez grinned at Cherensky and turned to go to the table. Cherensky grabbed her hand and yanked her back. "Wait," she shouted at Inez. "Maybe the next one'll be good, too."

Inez waited, but when "Moon River" came on, she decided she'd plain refuse to lead Daisy Cherensky around the floor. She shrugged. Cherensky boldly stepped up to her, put one hand behind her back and closed the other over Inez's hand. Was the woman nuts? Her head didn't even come to Inez's chin, for crying out loud. But before she knew it, they were out on the dance floor, close, Cherensky leading her every bit as well as Kookie did.

Amazed, Inez closed her eyes. Cherensky's gentle pressures led her into a romantic darkness where Inez filled to the brim of her full strong size. Inside, she bellowed along with the song. Under them, the floor seemed to rumble.

Originally published in *Cactus Love* (Naiad Press, 1994)

About the Author

Lee Lynch (http://www.leelynchwriter.com/) wrote the classic novels *The Swashbuckler* and *Toothpick House*. Her most recent novels are *Accidental Desperados* and *Rainbow Gap*, two of a planned quartet of books featuring a lifelong lesbian couple and the diverse additions to their ever-expanding family. She is the namesake and first recipient of the Lee Lynch Classic Award from the Golden Crown Literary Society, the recipient of the James Duggins Mid-Career Prize, the Alice B. Reader Award, an inductee to the Saints and Sinners Hall of Fame, a two-time Lambda Literary award finalist, and additional Goldies from GCLS.

Lee's first short stories appeared in *The Ladder*, *Sinister Wisdom*, and *Common Lives/Lesbian Lives*. She retired her column of thirty-six years in 2022.

Born in N.Y.C., she's settled on the Pacific Northwest Coast with her beloved wife, Lainie Lynch, and their rescues: King the cat, and Betty the dog.

Books Available From Bold Strokes Books

A Good Chance by Ali Vali. Harry, Desi, and Desi's sister Rachel are so close to getting everything they've ever wanted, but Desi's ex-husband is coming back to get his revenge and rip apart their chance at happiness. (978-1-63679-023-7)

A Perfect Fifth by Jaycie Morrison. Streetwise pianist Zara Keller and Lady Jillian Stansfield couldn't be more different, yet their connection brings a new awareness of who they are and what they truly want in their lives—including each other. (978-1-63679-132-6)

Catching Feelings by Ana Hartnett Reichardt. Andrea Foster expected to catch a lot of pitches from the Alder Lions' star pitcher, Maya, but she didn't expect to catch feelings. (978-1-63679-227-9)

Defiant Hearts by Lee Lynch. In these stories, you'll find your lovers, friends, and lesbians you wish you knew—maybe even yourself. (978-1-63679-237-8)

Love and Duty by Catherine Young. All Princess Roseli wants is to marry her three lovers, but with war looming, she must instead marry Princess Lucia to establish a military alliance between their planets. (978-1-63679-256-9)

Serendipity by Kris Bryant. Serendipity brings jingle writer Annie Foster and celebrity pop star Bristol Baines together, and their undeniable attraction keeps them close, but will their different paths drive them apart? (978-1-63679-224-8)

The Haunted Heart by Jane Kolven. A ghost, a ring, and a quest to find a missing psychic—it's a spell for love. (978-1-63679-245-3)

The Rules of Forever by Nan Campbell. After reconnecting at their high school reunion, Cara and Lauren agree to embark on a textbook definition friends-with-benefits relationship, but trying to keep it uncomplicated is harder than it seems. (978-1-63679-248-4)

Vision of Virtue by Brey Willows. When virtue and desire come together, be prepared for sparks in this next installment of the Memory's Muses series. (978-1-63679-118-0)

The Artist by Sheri Lewis Wohl. Detective Casey Wilson and reclusive artist Tula Crane are drawn together in a web of passion, intrigue, and art that might just hold the key to stopping a killer. (978-1-63679-150-0)

Cherry on Top by Georgia Beers. A chance meeting leaves Cherry and Ellis longing for a different life, but when Ellis's search for truth crashes into Cherry's insta-filter world, do they have any hope at all of a happily ever after? (978-1-63679-158-6)

Love and Other Rare Birds by Angie Williams. Ornithologist Dr. Jamie Martin and park ranger Rowan Fleming are searching the Alaskan wilderness for a bird thought to be extinct, and they're about to discover opposites really do attract. (978-1-63679-108-1)

Parallel Paradise by Mayapee Chowdhury. When their love affair is put to the test by the homophobia of their family, community, and culture, Bindi and Rimli will need to fight for a chance at love. (978-1-63679-203-3)

Perfectly Matched by Toni Logan. A beautiful Cupid named Hannah, a runaway arrow, and just seventy-two hours to fix a mishap that could be the best mistake she has ever made. (978-1-63679-120-3)

Slow Burn by Missouri Vaun. A wounded wildland firefighter from California and a struggling artist find solace and love in a small southern town. (978-1-63679-098-5)

The Inconvenient Heiress by Jane Walsh. An unlikely heiress and a spinster evade the Marriage Mart only to discover true love together. (978-1-63679-173-9)

The Value of Sylver and Gold by Michelle Larkin. When word gets out that former Boston Homicide Detective Reid Sylver can talk to the dead, the FBI solicits her help on a serial murder case, prompting Reid to assemble forces once again with Detective London Gold. (978-1-63679-093-0)

Wildflower by Cathleen Collins. When a plane crash leaves seven-year-old Lily Andrews stranded in the vast wilderness of Arkansas, will she be able to overcome the odds and make it back to civilization and the one person who holds the key to her future? (978-1-63679-244-6)